OF THE ABYSS

Young Adult Novels by Amelia Atwater-Rhodes

Den of Shadows

In the Forests of the Night

Demon in My View

Shattered Mirror

Midnight Predator

Persistence of Memory

Token of Darkness

All Just Glass

Poison Tree

Promises to Keep

The Kiesha'ra

Hawksong

Snakecharm

Falcondance

Wolfcry

Wyvernhail

The Maeve'ra

Bloodwitch

Bloodkin

Bloodtraitor

OF THE ABYSS

Mancer: Book One

AMELIA ATWATER-RHODES

An Imprint of HarperCollins*Publishers*

This is a work of fiction. Names, characters, places, and incidents are products of the author's imagination or are used fictitiously and are not to be construed as real. Any resemblance to actual events, locales, organizations, or persons, living or dead, is entirely coincidental.

EPub Edition SEPTEMBER 2016 ISBN: 9780062562135

Print Edition ISBN: 9780062562142

10 9 8 7 6 5 4 3 2

Of the Abyss *is dedicated to Ria and Zim, whose challenge to try NaNoWriMo sparked this entire crazy trilogy; to Mason, who tolerated (or perhaps encouraged) my obsession; and to my mother, who introduced me to Freudian theory and has been one of my best beta-readers this round.*

I also tip my hat to UMass Boston's QSC and Classics Club, two organizations that provided invaluable resources, inspiration, and encouragement as I first created this world, and to Remy and the rest of my writing group, who have helped me bring it together in final form.

OF THE ABYSS

PROLOGUE

The surface of the Abyss was covered with an immense desert that had once been a fathomless ocean. It was a place of glistening black sand, venomous beasts, creeping vermin, and of course the Abyssi—those perfect, beautiful predators who ruled the infernal realm by fang and claw.

One such creature looked past the gray, smoky sky above him to a realm where the ocean was cold and tasted of salt, where verdant green cascaded across rich earth, and where the mortal creatures lived.

Soon, *thought the Abyssi.*

It was a powerful thought, for one of his kind. Most Abyssi had no concept of soon; *they could only consider* now, *and whether what stood before them could be devoured or enjoyed in other ways. They certainly did not have the patience to create a mancer, an effort that took many careful years siphoning power into one of the frail creatures of the mortal realm. A mancer who would—soon—be able to break the barrier that separated this world from the one before it.*

In the mortal world, the creatures who considered themselves strongest had nearly no fur. Their teeth were dull as if for grinding grass, and their nails were short and rounded, useless for shredding flesh. In the mortal world, the Abyssi would play.

PART 1

AUTUMN
YEAR 3988 IN THE AGE OF THE REALMS

CHAPTER 1

The mingled smells of brine, fish, and sweat from the docks failed to bury the cloying, meaty odor that greeted Lieutenant Hansa Viridian as he shouldered open the back door of a small warehouse that had seen better days. As the stench rose, he swallowed repeatedly in an effort to keep the bile from fleeing his stomach, along with everything he had eaten that day.

When Captain Feldgrau had given him and his second lieutenant, Jenkins Upsdell, the assignment less than an hour before Hansa was supposed to be off duty, he had assured them it was probably a false alarm. The landlord was fed up with a tenant who refused to respond to complaints about vermin, and instead of filing a complaint with the harbormaster or the minister of health, he had cried sorcery and summoned soldiers.

A brief survey of the warehouse made Hansa doubt

this was a quick job. He drew his sword and visually swept the room, looking for threats.

The interior was dimly lit; the windows had been boarded up long ago, so the only light left came from candles burning on every raised surface. Most had melted completely but a few still flickered feebly, illuminating the carnage of small animals—mostly rats, though some were bigger. Some had simply been cut apart. Others had been disemboweled, skinned, and set around the room in ritualistic form, primarily on top of a leather altar Hansa *hoped* was made from a cow.

Something moved in the shadows of the back wall and Hansa raised his weapon, stepping out of the way so Jenkins could join him. They made their way across the room, trying to ignore things that squished and popped under their boots, increasing the rank odor that already rose from the decaying sludge that slicked the floor.

Movement caught Hansa's eye—pale fingers twitching in the far corner. Splashes of blood and darker fluids had camouflaged the man who lay sprawled in the back of the room.

"Jenkins?" Hansa asked before moving closer. Jenkins had the sight, which meant he could see the magic sorcerers used, though he couldn't control it himself. He might be able to tell if the man was a threat.

"I can't tell," Jenkins replied. "There's too much power all over this place."

That left finding out the hard way. "Watch my back," Hansa said as he sheathed his sword and knelt to establish if this man was a victim or a villain. In any other situation, it would be difficult to imagine a naked, unarmed man could be a threat, but a mancer wasn't only dangerous if he was dressed and armed. Abyssumancers were more powerful in the presence of blood, and they had an unsettling ability to hide weapons in plain sight.

"Sir?" he said. "If you can hear my voice, please let me know."

The body didn't move again. The man's skin was so ashen Hansa began to wonder if he had really seen him move in the first place. He reached forward to check for a pulse and Jenkins whispered, "Left hand, Hansa."

His eyes flickered down, and he saw the small dagger within inches of the injured man's left hand. Hansa knocked it aside with a boot, then once again leaned over and this time set two fingers to the man's throat, looking for any evidence of life.

He jumped back when the man's chest rose in a hitching, pained breath that soon became a rattling, wet cough.

"Help me," the man whispered. He lifted one languid arm.

"Do you need a doctor?"

"Need . . . to get out of this place," the man answered. "The . . . Abyssumancer . . . could come back. *Please.*"

"Can you walk?" Hansa asked the injured man.

"Not . . . on my own."

"How did you get here?" Jenkins asked. Meanwhile,

Hansa tried to ascertain the extent of the injuries and whether it would be safe to lift the man—for him, and for them, if he turned out to be dangerous.

"Don't know. I—" He coughed again.

A slash across the man's rib cage revealed the white glint of bone, and three parallel slices like claw marks savaged his thigh. Many of the injuries should have caused death within moments, but this man wasn't dead. Though blood was smeared across much of his skin, it wasn't concentrated around the wounds, which meant it wasn't his. That meant he wasn't as helpless and innocent as he pretended.

Hansa tried to suppress his instinctive frown, but the man must have seen something that said his ploy of being pathetic wasn't working. He struck; Hansa cried out as a blade swiped across his withdrawing hand, drawing blood and sending pain like fire up his arm.

The pain wasn't just the wound—it was magic. When it reached Hansa's heart, it wrapped around that vulnerable organ, and suddenly the air was smothering, dark, and hot as ash. Hansa's knees hit the ground, and then his palms, and then—

The air cleared and he coughed as he drew desperate, cool breaths. He struggled to draw his sword before he realized it wasn't necessary.

Jenkins had buried a small dagger in the Abyssumancer's back, just under his shoulder blade. It wasn't enough to kill, but it had been treated with a fast-acting poison that would put the sorcerer into a deep, powerless delirium for several hours. While he was out, they could search him more thoroughly and get him back to the cells beneath the Quinacridone Compound.

"Are you all right?" Jenkins asked as he helped Hansa to his feet.

Hansa nodded, sheathed his sword again, and instinctively checked his left pocket, which held a gold ring wrapped in white silk. The ring was set with a star ruby and two small diamonds.

"Do you ever plan to actually propose?" Jenkins asked as he trussed their prisoner's wrists. In addition to being second lieutenant of Hansa's company, Jenkins had been his best friend since before they could walk. Despite how long they had known each other, Hansa was still a little unsettled by Jenkins's ability to tease him about something like proposal nerves while they were surrounded by the gory remnants of magical malfeasance.

"I meant to tonight, but then this came up."

"Rubbish. You've 'meant' to every night for weeks now. A girl like Ruby isn't going to wait forever." His tone mellowed some as he hauled the mancer to his feet, and removed his own travel cloak to wrap around the naked man. "And in the meantime, do me a favor and don't make my sister a widow before you make her a wife. How's the hand?"

"It's not deep," Hansa said. Now that there was no magic backing it up, the wound itself was barely a scratch. "Let's get this gentleman back to the cells and see if he can tell us anything useful."

He spoke optimistically, but they both knew interrogating a mancer was normally futile. Men who made deals with demons were not easily caught in petty verbal traps, and anyone who would willingly walk the Abyss wasn't intimidated by a human soldier.

They left the warehouse with their prisoner slung over Jenkins's shoulder and entered the raucous bustle of the Mars docks.

The capital city of Kavet changed from one world to another the moment they crossed Harbor Road. The neat lanes and well-maintained stone and brick buildings of the upper city gave way to a haphazard, ramshackle wooden maze of flophouses, warehouses, shops, taverns, and inns that only those who lived there knew how to navigate. The jangle of merchants hawking their wares blended with a half-dozen languages spoken in drunken volumes, the ringing of instruments played by street performers, and the screaming of sea birds.

Immediately around Hansa and Jenkins, those noises quieted. Sailors out of Silmat and Tamar wouldn't know what a mancer was—they had their own forms of magic, but nothing as dangerous as sorcery—but they still responded to two men in official uniform carrying a bound, bloody man. They drew back, taking their games and drinking back to their own ships, or otherwise further away from authority.

The whores and thieves—or, as they called themselves, *disciples* of A'hknet, a religious order that, as far as Hansa could tell, believed in nothing—followed their clients or disappeared into the night, few wanting to be noticed by members of the 126.

"We're always so popular here," Jenkins murmured, the words just loud enough to reach Hansa's ears. Raising his voice, he shouted at two men half-hidden in the shadows, "You two, break it up."

The taller man was wearing the uniform of a Tamari sailor; he turned to Jenkins with a glare before the other half of his illicit embrace realized what was going on and jerked back. The sailor tried to catch his arm, but got an elbow in the ribs in return. Whatever the prostitute had hoped to earn by engaging this particular fare, it must not balance out with a charge of perversion and public display.

"Like we have time to chase after them tonight," Jenkins said, keeping an eye on the sailor long enough to establish he wasn't going to pick a fight after losing his intended roll in the hay. "As it is, we can't carry this fellow all the way back to the city square."

The Quinacridone Compound at the heart of the upper city had been a palace before the revolution, and was now the center of Kavet's government. Most citizens just knew it for the great hall where debate and voting took place, but underneath the pale, honey-colored stone was a dungeon where mancer powers were suppressed by centuries-old magics built into the foundations. That was where they needed to bring their prisoner, preferably before he woke up and attacked them again.

"Ma'am," Hansa said to an older merchant woman

who was watching them without fear, "may we borrow your cart?"

The elderly woman swept him with an expression that should have been as deadly as the mancer's power, and asked, "Can I *stop* you?"

"Not really," Jenkins admitted, "but you'll be compensated, and we will make sure it is returned—"

The woman took a step back and spat at their feet. "Quinacridone brats. Just so you know, I voted *against* Initiative One-Twenty-Six."

Hansa sighed, as Jenkins shifted the mancer's weight. "I'm sure you did," he said.

Citizen's Initiative 126 had created the small, elite band of soldiers to which Hansa and Jenkins both belonged. Occasionally they were called in when lesser authorities could not deal with a civil problem, but mostly they had the dubious glory of walking into dens where sorcerers wielded power enough to breach the veil to the realm beyond. Some mancers could manipulate the thoughts of those around them, or even outright possess them. Some caused sickness. Some just killed, bloody and violent, in ever-escalating patterns. This one started with rats, but he would have moved on to his neighbors soon enough, if he hadn't already.

Yet women like this protested the authority that gave Hansa and Jenkins the power to walk into such places and risk their lives to protect the citizens of Kavet.

Jenkins nodded to Hansa, who pulled the cart forward. The woman wore the symbol of A'hknet on a pin at her throat. If she had any trouble with her belongings because of the missing cart, other members of that order would assist her. They had scattered at the appearance of soldiers, but would return quickly to get all the gossip once Hansa, Jenkins, and the mancer were gone.

"Numen-crossed Quin. You call us thieves, and here you are in the night taking what's mine."

Hansa winced. Was she *trying* to get arrested, giving them a hard time when their nostrils were still filled with the odor of rotting rat viscera and Hansa's head pounded from whatever the mancer had done to him?

"Ma'am," Hansa said tiredly, struggling to be polite, "if you give us your name, we will have the cart returned. If you prefer to remain anonymous, you may come to the compound to pick it up tomorrow. Your only other choice is causing a scene right now and spending the night in lockup for interfering."

He had no interest in arresting this old woman. He just wanted to get this over with and get home.

"Let's go," Jenkins said, lifting the cart and ignoring its owner, who continued to glare but stopped arguing. "It's going to be a long night."

Hansa suspected "long night" was a gross understatement.

CHAPTER 2

You won't hurt her, will you? Xaz thought. She tried not to let the distrustful words form clearly enough in her mind for the Numini to hear them, but knew she had failed when she sensed the chill of their disapproval and saw the rime of frost appear on her nails.

Speaking with the Others of the divine realm was always a delicate, apologetic dance. She had been learning the steps since her power first manifested when she was a little girl, but still hadn't mastered it.

Why would we harm a child?

Their voices were musical, but if the beauty of them had ever moved her, she didn't remember it. The Numini claimed mortals craved the divine instinctively, the way plants bowed toward sunlight, but Xaz never had. The only reason she knew for why people wanted to go to the Numen when they died was that the alternative—the Abyss—was so much worse.

Why *would* they harm a child? She didn't know. She also didn't know why they wanted a child. The Numini didn't explain their demands, and a smart mortal didn't question them. There was a young girl named Pearl who lived in the city. The Numini wanted Xaz to bring her to them, and they wouldn't tolerate reservations, excuses, or hesitation.

"As you will," she whispered. She ran her hands once more over the embroidered white silk altar-cloth, then pushed to her feet.

The altar had once been a hand-carved cherry footstool, purchased from a tree-farmer near her childhood home. It was one of the few things she had brought with her when she cut ties with her family, leaving her parents with the memory of their youngest daughter's swift death falling from an apple tree instead of the true memory of catching her conversing with the Numini. She had only been fifteen, but it wouldn't have mattered to the soldiers who would have come next.

Her parents, hours away in Kavet's highlands, had five other children. Losing one was probably a blessing.

She took a small, silver disc from the altar and tucked the rest under a spindly nightstand draped with a decorative woven blanket to hide the damning evidence. Most likely, no one would have seen it even if she had left it out. The bed blocked the view from the hall and no one but her had reason to come into this room. The few friends she had made in the city were almost all married now, but it didn't seem likely for her.

By Kavet's standards she was *almost* eminently marriageable. She was educated, unafraid of hard work, healthy, and at least passably attractive. Twenty-six was older than many women married out in the country, but in the city, it wasn't unusual. The only thing getting in the way of a long and happy life of domestic bliss was the automatic death sentence on her head, should her husband discover a Numenmancer's tools in her possession.

She liked her privacy, anyway.

She ran a brush indifferently through her cinnamon-auburn hair before tying it back with a faded blue ribbon, then pulled a heavy wool outdoor dress over her shift. Thick stockings under scuffed boots, tan leather gloves, and a gray hooded cloak completed her outfit. The disc went in a small pocket concealed in the cloak's lining, hidden from sight or pickpockets but available if she needed it during her mission. She wished she could curl up in front of the hearth fire until the chill left from talking to the Numini had dissipated a little, but that wasn't an option. Worse, she could sense shards of ice in the brewing storm clouds; there would be snow soon.

When she paused on the front step, gathering her nerve, the door of the home across the street from hers opened. Xaz groaned inwardly, but outwardly smiled, because people smile when a neighborhood friend appears. Normal people, who aren't dreading running an errand for the divine.

Had Ruby's beau finally found the courage to give

her the ring everyone knew he had been carrying around in his pocket for the last week?

"Oh!" Ruby said, her face brightening in an answering smile as she crossed the street. "I was on my way to see if you were up for dinner. I was expecting Hansa, but they just sent word he won't make it, so I have more food than I need." A frown tried to overshadow the smile when Ruby mentioned Hansa's delay; Xaz saw her struggle a moment, then hide it. Disappointment that the expected proposal had been delayed another night, or fear for her soldier boyfriend?

Xaz could have pried further, but she had enough of her own worries without trying to divine Ruby's. She kept her expression carefully neutral as she wondered whom the 126 had caught that night, and whether it was someone she knew—or who knew her. There were many reasons most mancers didn't keep ties to others. Quin interrogation was the first.

"I'm sorry, I'm on my way out," Xaz said. "I have some errands to run before the markets close."

Pearl, the child Xaz was supposed to fetch, liked to come out in the evenings to bring cider to the guards coming off duty at the Quin compound. Since she otherwise lived in the Cobalt Hall, which might as well have been a fortress against Xaz's kind, that would be the best time to grab her.

"Are you still not feeling well?" Ruby asked. "Did the tisane help at all?"

It took Xaz a second to connect Ruby's words to the way she was looking at Xaz's cloak with concern. Ruby was wearing a lemon-yellow bodice over a simple, ankle-length day dress—prettier than the smocks and pants she normally wore at the herbaria where she worked, and far lighter than what Xaz had on.

Ruby didn't wait for Xaz to answer. She put a hand on Xaz's cheek and said, "You're still chilled. You should lie down. I can run to the market for you if you need."

How much of Xaz's life was dedicated to avoiding suspicion? She had declined an invitation to have dinner with Ruby and her boyfriend the previous night by claiming to be under the weather. Feigning illness to a senior journeyman at the herbaria had resulted in Ruby solicitously preparing and delivering a mixture of herbs designed to clear up the symptoms Xaz had made up on the spot.

Xaz hadn't been sick; she just hadn't been in the mood to feign friendship with Hansa Viridian. Ruby's boyfriend wasn't as paranoid or power-hungry as many of his cohorts in the 126, but he *was* still a soldier and a devout Follower of the Quinacridone. His only ambitions in life were to marry his childhood sweetheart, raise a perfect Quin family, and protect them all from those dastardly mancers. It didn't help that Ruby occasionally invited her brother Jenkins along with the hope of setting him up with Xaz. Keeping her power hidden from a man with the sight all evening was exhausting.

Ruby wasn't easy to keep at arm's length, and Xaz couldn't afford to alienate her. Her best protection at the moment was the fact that Ruby and her high-ranked soldier boyfriend liked Xaz. They trusted her, so no one else gave her much mind.

It was an adequate situation.

A sensation like the trill of harp strings, vibrating across her skin and not quite resonating in her ears, reminded her that she had work to do.

"I'm going," she whispered.

"Excuse me?" Ruby asked, taken aback by the irritated tone.

Xaz hated using magic on someone she lived so close to, but she didn't have time for this social dance. She put a hand on Ruby's shoulder and said, "I'm sure Hansa will be home soon. You should go wait for him."

Her power drove the words into Ruby's mind. A brief objection rose in Ruby's thoughts—she wasn't the kind of woman who waited passively at home—but Xaz's magic squashed it.

Without saying goodbye, Ruby walked away with languid, dazed steps. She would snap out of her trance in a few minutes and think going home had been her idea. Hopefully she wouldn't run into anyone else before then.

Before any other well-meaning neighbors could appear, Xaz returned to the house long enough to drop off the cloak and transfer the silver disc to the inner pocket in her dress along with her spending money. It was late autumn, but the last few days had been unseasonably warm. For most people, it was not yet cold enough for winter-wear, even if the chill in her bones seemed to justify it.

Dressed less warmly than she wished to be, she started out on foot toward the market square at the center of the city, a little under two miles away. It was one of the last places she ever went willingly, but defying the Numini was a worse idea.

Those who dared to speak of such things said the Numen was where good souls went in the afterlife, but anyone who thought its denizens the Numini were all peace and joy and love had never met one. They were not as bloodthirsty as the Abyssi, but they were still Others. They didn't think like humans, and their displeasure was distinctly unpleasant.

Few people did speak of the Others. The Followers of the Quinacridone believed focusing on the realms beyond drew value away from the current day and world, and the Order of the Napthol warned overfascination with them could begin one on the road toward sorcery. Of course, what they taught was irrelevant, since it was illegal for anyone to write or speak about them anyway, with the exception of a select few highly placed individuals in the Cobalt Hall.

Those laws were enforced by the soldiers of the 126. The black-and-tan livery of that group had always reminded Xaz of rattlesnakes, even back when she had been an innocent little girl with nothing to fear from them.

Like Pearl.

Xaz spotted the girl talking with a spice merchant selling nutmeg, cinnamon, and other goods imported from Kavet's trading partners. Business was apparently slow enough the man tending the stall didn't mind Pearl's chatter.

According to Xaz's father, the city square had once been packed with foreign traders selling every luxury imaginable. She could almost see it. The ground was cobbled in blocks of irregularly-sized stone from around the world; she recognized marble in a dozen colors, sandstone, limestone, granite, and slate among others she couldn't name. Like the ornate well in the center and the towering buildings to the north and south, it suggested a time when Kavet was a prosperous trading power, not a large but unimpressive backwater.

The grand marble and limestone four-story building that towered over the north side of the square had once been the palace. Now it was the Quinacridone Compound. The old ballroom had been filled with benches and turned into a meeting hall, and the long halls of bedrooms that had once belonged to the royal family and visiting dignitaries now housed President Winsor Indathrone in one wing—along with offices for government use—and Quin monks in training in the other.

She had only gone there once, when shortly after moving to the city she had gathered the nerve to attend a debate about a trade ordinance she wanted to vote on. She had lasted less than an hour before the effort of hiding her power from sighted guards and her general anxiety at being in the belly of the beast had chased her out.

Stop stalling.

Forcing her steps to be calm and casual, she approached the spice merchant. All she needed to do was put a hand on the girl's arm and whisper a few words and she would be able to sneak off with her. It had to be done now, before Pearl went back into the Cobalt Hall.

Pearl lived with the novices and initiates of the Napthol Order, who had taken her in when the girl's mother had abandoned her on their front step. Once she returned home to the Cobalt Hall, she would be out of Xaz's reach. Supposedly many areas of the Hall were public, since the Napthol Order offered spiritual counseling and the best medical care in Kavet, but mancers weren't able to enter the building.

Xaz suspected the only reason Kavet hadn't passed a law ordering every citizen to prove their innocence by crossing that threshold was that no one understood *why* it worked.

I don't want to do this, Xaz thought, as much a prayer and a plea as a private contemplation.

A cool, shimmering sensation responded; the Numini reminding her of their presence without bothering to answer in words.

Xaz had almost reached the spice merchant when soldiers approached from the west, the direction of the docks. She recognized Hansa and Jenkins. Out of the corner of her eye, she could see a miasma of lingering dark power on Hansa, but it looked like he had won the fight in the end. Jenkins was pushing a cart that held a bound, unconscious man.

If it had been Numen power that marked Hansa, Xaz could have read it clearly, but this came from a hotter, darker plane, which meant the unconscious man was an Abyssumancer, not one of her own kind.

Xaz wasn't the only one who stared, but she was certainly the only one who felt her stomach drop as she saw one of the soldiers on the door whisper to the other, who went inside, probably to fetch more guards. A man in the violet robes of the Napthol Order saw the commotion and started striding protectively toward Pearl.

The Numini had to understand, Xaz couldn't afford to act now. She would end up in the cart next to the Abyssumancer, and then in a cell, and then in the next world. She started backing away, careful to avoid drawing attention.

She couldn't decide if she believed the Numini might accept such an excuse before the Abyssumancer stirred with a groan—then moved with impossible speed, rolling out of the cart and cutting the bonds on his wrists and ankles with a black blade as long as his forearm, which Hansa and Jenkins surely would have taken from him if the mancer hadn't hidden it magically.

The soldiers of the 126 surrounded him, and he met them with a bared blade . . . and then his eyes went past them, to Xaz, and she could see on his face the same expression she must have worn earlier when the Numini had asked her to get Pearl: utter terror, and resignation.

He threw the knife with a smooth, fluid motion.

She didn't see how the Quin responded, because the knife had not been aimed at any of them.

She looked down, and discovered two things:

She was numb.

She had a hilt jutting out of her stomach, marking the spot where several inches of blade had pierced her body.

The Quin started to turn toward her.

If they saw her, they would try to bring her into the Cobalt Hall so their healers could tend to her. The Hall would reject her, and they would know what she was.

She stumbled back as the pain hit her. Leaning against a building, she slid to the ground with one hand on her stomach bracing the hilt of the knife, and the other fumbling in her pocket for something she needed.

Desperately, she tried to conceal herself and to use her power to control the bleeding as she started to pull the knife out of her guts.

The blade moved maybe an inch before the pain became intolerable, and her stomach heaved, wanting to throw up and in the process shredding itself more.

Help, she prayed, as her hand closed around an etched silver tablet. The Numini did not like bloodshed, but this wasn't her fault. They had to help her.

I did what I can, was the only message she received, as her mind drifted at the edge of unconsciousness. *You do the rest.*

CHAPTER 3

Cadmia jumped as the door to the temple squeaked behind her. Her first thought was a guilty one—she had been failing to meditate, and had a feeling she had actually dozed off—followed by, *I need to have someone wax those hinges,* and only then by the question, *What is a soldier doing in the Cobalt Hall?* The Cobalt Hall was part hospital and part holy sanctuary, and was the home and workplace for initiates in the Napthol Order.

The man who entered the room, escorted by one of the Order's youngest initiates, was dressed in the black-and-tan livery of a soldier of the 126, including a sword at his belt. He was probably in his midtwenties, tall and broad-shouldered like most professional soldiers, with dark hair worn short and brown eyes set in a face that seemed undecided as to whether it should be pretty or rugged. He was pale and looked exhausted, adding to the latter impression, but he lacked the agonized twist of doubt and despair that marked many people who entered this place. Instead, his expression was tired but gentle.

The softness was probably directed at Pearl, his guide. The seven-year-old had been taken in by the Order of the Napthol after her mother abandoned her on their front step four years ago. She had few official duties at her age, but delighted in taking snacks and warm drinks to the soldiers assigned to guard the marketplace and the doors of the Quin Compound.

Pearl's face was set in a determinedly solemn expression, as if she wanted to smile at the man with her but knew her responsibilities were serious.

"Sister Paynes," Pearl said formally, "Lieutenant Hansa Viridian of the One-Twenty-Six has come to request your counsel."

Cadmia rose, smoothing down the violet robes of her office and schooling her face to patience. Anyone had a right to come to the hall for healing or spiritual guidance, but if Hansa had come for that reason, he should have come as himself, not as a soldier.

"I would be happy to meet with Hansa Viridian," she said firmly, "if he returns in civilian clothes, unarmed." Cadmia didn't normally work with soldiers, but knew Sister Marigold, who specialized in granting them counsel, refused to let them into her office while they were in uniform.

"I haven't come for myself," Hansa explained. "A prisoner has asked to see you."

She raised a brow, intrigued. Normally a courier

from the justice department brought news her services were needed.

Cadmia's cohorts generally thought it odd that, out of all the more illustrious opportunities her years of study and hard work could have earned her, she had decided to specialize in offering guidance to the dredges of Kavet society. Even the older ones, who knew what a checkered history had preceded her vows, didn't really understand. Thankfully, she now had a high enough rank that she didn't need them to understand or approve.

She almost asked why a man in such an elite position was in charge of delivering this news before the obvious answer came to her.

"Is this the mancer who was arrested last night?" She had not witnessed the scene in the marketplace, but she had heard about it from Pearl and the other novices who had been minding her.

"It is," Hansa answered. She couldn't think of him as *Lieutenant Viridian.* They might have been the same age, and he must have been good in his field to have achieved the rank he had, but guards in the 126 always seemed young to her. It was the idealism, she supposed. "If you wish to refuse, I understand."

She shook her head. "If he has asked for counsel, he has the right to it." She meant the words, even though the concept of trying to provide guidance and solace to a sorcerer chilled her.

"Hansa will keep you safe," Pearl chimed in, her tone nervous and her mismatched blue and green eyes trained on Hansa as she added firmly, "Right?"

Hansa ruffled the girl's hair and gave her a tired smile, saying, "That's my job." To Cadmia, he added, "He has been disarmed and branded. I cannot guarantee he is *harmless*, but he is powerless."

Without his magic, he should be no more dangerous than many men she had counseled. Drunkards, abusers, murderers, thieves; Kavet's laws gave them the right to be heard.

"Lead the way, Lieutenant," she said. "Pearl, thank you for bringing Lieutenant Viridian to me." The novices and other initiates all knew to funnel requests from criminals and other disreputable sorts to her, but Cadmia was impressed that Pearl had been astute enough to bring Hansa to her and not to Marigold.

Pearl nodded, ducking her head shyly.

Without delay, Cadmia followed Hansa across the street and into the Quinacridone Compound, wondering why a mancer had asked for a representative from the Napthol. Maybe he was just trying to stall his execution by a few minutes, but maybe he genuinely wanted forgiveness. Maybe he wanted to tell them something.

Though she had been to the sections of the Compound that served as Kavet's main government building many times, she had never taken the rough stone staircase that led downward to a row of cells, evidence of the building's darker past.

"Why keep such a dangerous prisoner so close to the President?" she asked. Winsor Indathrone's living quarters were upstairs in this building.

"The cells are warded," Hansa explained. His voice dropped, as if he knew from experience that the stone walls would make his words echo unpleasantly. "They dampen a mancer's power. The forge we use to create the brands is built into the wall down here, too. It can't be moved."

"How does the warding work?"

Hansa glanced back and gave her a puzzled look, as if wondering why she asked. "We don't know," he said. "We think the royal house must have had some connection to sorcery before the revolution—some say they were in charge of controlling it, but others say they were overthrown partly because they were enabling it. Either way, the tools they left behind are the only ones we have."

Cadmia shook her head, making a mental note to see if she could find more information. She was highly enough ranked in the Order that it seemed like she should have heard of these indispensable tools before now; that she hadn't might just mean the information wasn't widely shared, but she feared it could mean there was no more knowledge to be had.

Quin in general weren't encouraged to ask questions, and soldiers in the 126 were given only the information they needed to do their jobs and warned that too much curiosity into the nature of magic could put them in danger of becoming the sorcerers they hunted. If they ever had trouble with the indispensable tools they needed for that hunt—these cells, the brands, and the poison used to apprehend mancers—they would come to the Order of the Napthol for help. If at that time no one had the answers, it could spell disaster.

At the base of the stairs, the hall was lined in dark stone, and bone dry despite its proximity to the coast and elevation below sea level. The air, which was neither hot nor cold but seemed flatly odorless, left a chalky sensation on Cadmia's skin and a bitter taste in her mouth.

As they neared the first cell, she caught a brief whiff of . . . something, like frying meat.

Hansa must have smelled it at the same time. He paused and drew his sword, and approached the cell cautiously.

Cadmia followed closely. The mancer had been left a candle for light, and he was sitting at the table with one of his palms just above the flame. He held his hand in place, not flinching, despite his own skin cooking, charring.

"Stop that!" Hansa barked, obviously unnerved.

The mancer looked up, but his pain-darkened eyes did not focus on Hansa. He moved his hand away from the candle flame with dreamlike slowness. As he did so he shivered, and Cadmia noticed every bare inch of skin was covered in goose bumps.

"Let me in," she ordered. Mancer or not, the man before her was in agony—not from the burn, but worse, so bad the burn itself had been *nothing* but a way to pass the time.

"Are you sure—"

"Open it."

Technically, she was speaking to one of the few individuals in the entire country of Kavet who could unilaterally overrule her. Citizen's Initiative 126 gave these guards the authority to make any decisions they deemed necessary to protect the populace from mancers, but they were trained to defer to the expertise of the Cobalt Hall, so Cadmia didn't expect Hansa to argue.

Hansa asked, "Do you want me to bind his hands first?"

She shook her head, and he unlocked the cell.

"I'll stay near," he said, and in those words she heard a firmness that said he *would* object if she tried to insist the meeting be private. In truth, she was relieved.

The mancer did not look threatening as she approached, but then again, they didn't have to be physically menacing. Their magic did the damage.

"Cadmia," he said. "I hoped it would be you." His voice was dry, hoarse, but the water pitcher he had been left was still full and the mug next to it unused, so if he felt thirst he had not chosen to alleviate it. "Do you remember me?"

She did not allow the familiar greeting to unsettle her, but tried to search his face. "I'm sorry," she said. "Have we met?"

"Fifteen . . . twenty years ago?" he said. "My—" A compulsive shiver took him, severe enough that Cadmia feared he was having a seizure, but when she moved forward he waved her back. "My father used to visit with your mother."

The list of men who used to visit Scarlet Paynes, initiate of A'hknet, was very, *very* long. The list of boys who had come with those men was much shorter.

"Baryte?" she asked. Did she recognize somewhere deep in this sorcerer's eyes a child she had played with while her mother worked?

The mancer sighed, and nodded. He reached toward the candle flame again, then jerked back, clenching his hand into a fist.

"Does that hurt?" she asked.

Baryte frowned, as if he had no idea what she was asking. When he followed her gaze to his hand, he opened his fist and turned upward a blackened, blistered palm. Cadmia swallowed to keep from gagging.

"No," he said, "it doesn't hurt."

He reached up with fingers that trembled a little, and began to undo buttons on his shirt. Cadmia waited quietly, ready to protest if he went further than his shirt. If there was something he needed to show her, it was her job to see.

Beneath the shirt were bandages covering most of his ribs and much of his arms. The brand was visible on his left forearm, a coin-sized burn from which black lines like blood poisoning seeped.

"What are you doing?" she asked, concerned, as he started unwrapping one of the bandages on his arms.

"Worried I'll bleed to death, or get an infection?" he asked, his voice now sharply derisive. "Thank you for the concern, but it's rather irrelevant. I'm a convicted mancer, with sorcery and murder to my credit. They will execute me as soon as you have been dismissed."

"Murder?" she asked, almost hoping he would deny it.

He looked up at her with a gaze gone flat and ugly, with no hint inside it of the boy she had once known. "The power gets hungry," he said, utterly unapologetic, as he removed the last of the bandage he had been unwinding.

The wounds beneath were a set of parallel cuts that could have been made by a blade—but Cadmia suspected not, given who and what the victim was. They were claw marks.

The cuts had been stitched closed, though blood still crusted the surface.

"I wouldn't be here, but it got in my head and wouldn't let me defend myself," he said.

"Who?" she asked.

"The black Abyssi," he said. "Talking to him did this to me. Cut me open. I had to . . . the things I had to do to crawl back up from that . . ." He shuddered, and closed his eyes.

"Are you saying you were forced to do what you did?" Cadmia asked.

The condemned often tried to explain why they were not at fault, but even if this man had once been an innocent child, he had admitted he was a murderer.

"I'm *saying*," he snapped, "that he wanted me to get caught. Even in the market, once he woke me up, I could have escaped. I was armed. I could have slit the throats of the two guards next to me and disappeared before anyone else could touch me. But he made me throw the knife away."

I could have . . . Again, his voice and face held no guilt about having contemplated two additional murders. Mostly, he sounded angry.

"You asked for my counsel," Cadmia said, somewhat sharply, as she began to wonder whether the mancer might have had no goal but to unsettle her. "Most people who call for me want the Napthol's blessing, but you—"

Unsurprisingly, the Abyssumancer started to laugh. "Don't waste your blessings on me, Sister," he said. "We all know the Numini will never let me into their realm. I asked for you because the Quin will ignore me, but it is your duty to listen, and to meditate on a man's last words.

"Abyssi are creatures of heat, lust, impulse, and hunger. As a rule, they do not *plan*. But the black Abyssi is planning something important enough that he was willing to—"

He stopped abruptly, and his burned hand went to his throat. He coughed wetly, and droplets of blood and blackish bile spattered from his lips.

"Hansa!" Cadmia called. She didn't know what to do as the mancer continued to cough, falling out of his chair, shaking and desperately trying to draw air.

Soldiers streamed into the room, with Hansa at the forefront, but what could they do? The fit might be a trick or might be magically induced. Either way, none of them dared touch him as it ran its course. A few minutes later the mancer lay on the stone floor, still and silent.

Baryte, she told herself. She had distanced herself mentally from a man who had chosen a life of sorcery and violence, but now she forced herself to think of him by name because the man had once been a boy and perhaps that boy had been innocent. Cadmia had been taught that mancers started on their path to sorcery through an unhealthy fascination with the Other planes combined with a selfish obsession with power . . . but she had never been able to find a definitive source to prove it. No one seemed to know for certain how a child grew up to be a monster.

One of the soldiers nudged Baryte onto his back, and his head lolled to the side, eyes staring sightlessly at the ceiling. Cadmia tried not to imagine what his spirit gazed upon as his mortal eyes clouded. Even for a Sister of the Napthol, that was a contemplation best avoided.

CHAPTER 4

When Xaz woke, she was certain it was not for the first time.

She was bathed in sweat, and felt flushed and feverish. Turning her head to the side to try to see where she was made the world swirl, so it was difficult to make out any details of the rough room in which she found herself. All she knew for sure was that she was not in a cell. Curtains covered most of the nearby window, but they weren't thick enough to completely block what seemed to be midmorning sunshine.

She was wearing a man's shirt, a sleeveless, shapeless piece with eyelets at the throat empty of lacing. It fit her loosely, but she was more concerned with who had stripped her than she was with her modesty.

As she tried to recall anything of how she had come to this place, her hand went instinctively to her stomach. Tugging up the hem of the shirt, she discovered bandages wrapped around her torso.

She was alive—how? And where? And almost as important, *why*?

Xaz struggled to her feet, conscious of the twinge of pain in her guts but not knowing what to do about it. She couldn't stay here, no matter where *here* was.

She barely managed to stand before blackness encroached on her vision and she needed to catch herself on the bedside table, sending several items that had been on it to the floor with a tremendous clatter. A small hand-mirror shattered as it hit the ground.

The door opened from the outside before Xaz tested whether or not she could take a step.

An ancient-looking woman wearing a loose nightdress stepped inside. Her gaze fell to the mess on the floor, and she shook her head. "Sit down before you hurt yourself."

Xaz had little choice but to agree, since she did not have the energy necessary to remain standing. The old woman wasn't overtly threatening, except that Xaz was so exhausted it was an effort to sense her own power, making her feel helpless and jumpy.

The woman put a hand on Xaz's forehead. "You're still feverish," she said.

"How did I get here?"

The woman shrugged. "I found you hurt."

Animamancer? Xaz wondered. There were four kinds of mancer—five, if you were willing to believe myths and whispers. Abyssumancers and Numenmancers gained their power from the Other realms. Necromancers were rumored to disturb the dead for power to extend their own lives and achieve control over other mortals. Animamancers were healers.

According to the Quin, the seemingly benign ability had a dark price. They claimed animamancers healed by siphoning healthy energy from the living into their patients.

It might even be true; to her knowledge, Xaz had never met one of the healers before. If they were anything like Numenmancers, the power still needed, *demanded* to be used. Maybe one of them had stumbled across Xaz, and nature—if there was anything natural about a mancer's power—had taken over.

"You should eat while you're awake. Is there anything particular I can get you?"

Again, though the woman said nothing specifically indicating she was a sorcerer, or asking if Xaz was, the question was telling. The different kinds of mancer each had their own tools, their own sources of power, and their own needs. In her discreet way, the old woman was trying to ask what Xaz was.

"I don't think I could eat anything right now," Xaz answered. Her stomach was churning, perhaps from the wound or the fever, but perhaps from pure terror. She had never been identified before, much less captured. The fact that this woman did not seem to be about to turn Xaz over to the Quin did not mean her intentions were benign.

"I'll let you rest, then," the woman said. "If you need anything, you can ring, or if you're strong enough to walk, you can come out to the parlor." She leaned down, bracing herself on the bed, to retrieve the bell that had previously been on the table. No wonder it had all made so much noise, falling.

"I'm sorry," Xaz said.

The words covered much. *I am sorry I broke your mirror, and made you bend down to care for me. I am sorry I cannot trust you enough to answer the questions I see in your eyes. I am sorry I need to do this. . .*

She reached up, and with what little power she could muster, she pushed at the woman's mind.

"Thank you for helping me while I was ill." She sent an image of sickness, but not injury. There was nothing suspicious about a fever in the fall. In return, she felt the edge of a secret; this woman had told someone else the same lie. Hopefully she'd also had the sense to hide Xaz's bloody clothing. "I will repay you in any way I can."

The old woman's eyes unfocused for a moment, then she nodded. A chill swept over Xaz briefly, a break in the fever accompanied by new droplets of sweat that appeared on her brow, before the sensation of heat returned.

"It's my way," the old woman said. "You sleep now. Ring if you need anything, and Cinnabar or I will be right in."

As she turned away, Xaz saw the shoulder of the woman's nightgown had slipped a little, revealing a scar that could only be one thing—the brand. How had she escaped execution? Had there been a time in this woman's long life when a branded sorcerer had been allowed to leave the detention cells alive?

Xaz's eyes were not sharp enough, but her power could see where the edge was marred. This branding had been done in haste, and it had been imperfect.

It wasn't much of a crack, but it might have been enough to allow the Numini to whisper in her ear and send her after one of their mancers. Their ability to manipulate her, however, did not mean she would be sympathetic to Xaz's plight; having escaped execution once did not mean she would be willing to risk herself now for a stranger. Thankfully, she would now give no more thought to odd injuries, or to how swiftly her guest healed.

The moment Xaz was alone, she put both hands over the wound, shut her eyes, and went into deep trance. She was no animamancer, but she could encourage her own flesh to return to its proper form.

Her power responded sluggishly, alarmingly so, and as she tried to work around the wound pain shot through her.

Poisoned. The knife the Abyssumancer had hit her with had been steeped in power that was the antitheses of hers. Unfortunately, the ritual needed to purify her magic would be more complicated than she could afford to do here. She forced the healing enough to function, but then she stopped, obeying her body's warning signs.

Using so much power while she was already weakened left her starving.

Still a little unsteady, she managed to walk to the door. She had intended to keep walking and find something more solid to wear along the way home, but the rush of warmth, the aroma of cooking food, and the sight of a handsome man with a violin locked her in place. The man plucked at each violin string in turn, eyes half-closed as he listened to the note brought forth and occasionally adjusted a tuning pin.

The man was lounging against several of the mass of pillows that filled almost the entire floor save for a sensible distance around a large, cast iron wood-burning stove. He was wearing loose-fitting slacks and nothing else, comfortable in his own home. His skin still held onto summer's tan and his muscles remembered a season of hard labor, possibly aboard a ship. Yet those chapped, hard-worn fingers started to pull a haunting tune from the violin. He was still picking at the strings instead of using the bow, but it was clear he had finished tuning the instrument and was now testing it with a deliberate melody.

Watching his hands, Xaz noticed the ring on his smallest finger, which boasted the symbol of A'hknet. That might explain why he hadn't asked too many questions when the woman had brought Xaz home. Members of the Order of A'hknet followed a philosophy of, "Do what you wish, and accept the consequences." They were as likely to help a stranger as rob her . . . which reminded Xaz she had no idea where her clothes or possessions were.

The musician looked up with an amused half smile, and remarked, "Normally, when a woman stares that long, her next question is 'how much do you cost?' "

Xaz jumped and felt her face flush as she realized how long she had been standing there, watching him. "I'm sorry," she said, hoping the blush would be mistaken for a product of the fever. Yes, he was an attractive man, but it wasn't like her to be captivated by a pretty form. "I didn't mean . . ." She wasn't sure how to finish the sentence.

The man unfolded gracefully, leaving the instrument propped against the wall as he said, "Sit down. You're shaking like a leaf. Mother made me prepare some tonic for you, and leave some hot and put some out to cool. Given how flushed you are, I imagine you would rather have something cold."

She nodded, grateful he had forgiven her rudeness and decided to change the subject.

"My name is Cinnabar," he said, when he returned. "I think I've seen you working near the main docks' marketplace. Am I right?"

"That's right." The work she did there—whatever needed doing, really—should be inoffensive to the Order of A'hknet, unless this particular member objected purely because it was legal.

She sipped the tonic he had provided, welcoming the cold the way she normally did heat when she had worked too much magic.

"Mother brought you in during the middle of last night," Cinnabar said. "What were you doing out alone in this kind of condition?"

"I didn't realize how sick I was," Xaz lied, effortlessly. She had been providing excuses for her behavior for as long as she could remember. "I went to the market to buy tea." Halfway through the explanation, she remembered she hadn't had any money on her, a fact most followers of A'hknet were unlikely to miss. "I must have been delirious. I don't think I even brought my purse. Did I faint? Where did your mother find me?"

"Not *my* mother; that's just what we all call her," Cinnabar replied. "She takes long walks sometimes, when nightmares trouble her. She found you near the upper market."

Nightmares. Probably the Numini whispering to her. They must also have hidden Xaz from searching Quin guards, since otherwise they would have discovered her when they tried to find the knife the Abyssumancer threw.

"She gave you her bed, which means she's in mine," Cinnabar added, with a raised brow, "so I can't invite you back there even if you *are* feeling well enough."

Apparently he *hadn't* decided to ignore her earlier stare. The only safe answer seemed to be, "Pity," before she took another large sip of the tonic. He and Mother had taken her in, saving her life in the process, so there was no need to tell him she would sooner swim in the frozen Mars harbor than engage the services of a prostitute.

That the Numini objected to such practices was only part of her hesitation. The other part was pure resentment: despite Quin disapproval, prostitution remained legal.

The Order of A'hknet was a small, foreign sect that stood in the face of almost everything the Quin believed, but it was a powerful force in Tamar, one of Kavet's major trade partners. Without Tamar, there was no rice, tea, or coffee, not to mention a variety of luxury goods. There were no mancers in Tamar, or Silmat, or even the Wild Islands or anywhere Xaz had heard of.

Therefore, the freedom of the Order of A'hknet had been carefully safeguarded, while the laws that made a mancer's life ever more difficult—such as restrictions on the use, possession, or trade of key spell components—were constantly refined and expanded. Occasionally Xaz daydreamed about hopping on a Tamari or Silmari ship and traveling to one of those other countries, but passenger rooms were exorbitantly expensive and few hired foreigners.

"I need to get ready to head out," Cinnabar said, glancing to the clock ticking on the mantel. "You are welcome to stay a while longer, if you need the rest."

"I think I can make it home now."

Cinnabar looked skeptical, but it wasn't the Order's way to interfere if someone wanted to be stupid. He was right that Xaz would not be able to walk far in her condition, but she needed to get out of this house and away from these strange, prying eyes, and thought she could manage as long as she took it slow.

"You'll want your belongings, then. Let me go see where Mother put them."

He disappeared into the next room, and emerged again several minutes later with a clean set of clothes in about Xaz's size. There was no sign of the knife. She fervently hoped it had slipped from sight, as Abyssumancers' tools tended to do until called back by their owners.

CHAPTER 5

Captain Feldgrau of the 126 listened diligently as Cadmia reported word-for-word what the mancer had said to her before his black magic caught up to him.

"What is your opinion?" he asked, before voicing any thoughts of his own.

She took a deep breath, passing the mancer's statement through her mind again. As Baryte had said, it was her duty to remember and meditate upon a man's last words, which meant her training had prepared her to recall and reproduce those words exactly.

"Baryte was angry," she said. "He felt the Abyssi he was working with had betrayed him, and he wanted to thwart whatever plan he believed it was trying to enact. The fact that they silenced him implies they did not want him speaking." With a mental shudder, she added, "That they *could* silence him, even though he was branded and in a warded area, is a little frightening. They shouldn't have been able to do that."

Feldgrau nodded, slowly.

"He mentioned having a knife, which the Abyssi made him throw away. Has anyone found it?"

"The guards who arrested him say the mancer produced another knife when he woke," Feldgrau confirmed, "but they did not see what happened to it, and we have been unable to locate the item." Unsettling. Anyone could have picked the knife up, in which case what might it be doing to them? "Do you believe the Abyssi could be planning something?"

Cadmia shook her head. "I was taught Abyssi *can't* plan. My guess is that Baryte assigned human motivations to creatures incapable of such forethought, but I'm not comfortable dismissing his words entirely."

Feldgrau nodded again. "I'll confer with the other captains about what precautions they think we should take. Thank you for your counsel."

"Of course."

She wished she had not been the one called. All her study supported what she had told the captain; Abyssi were not creatures of rational thought. They were powerful, bloodthirsty monsters, but they lacked the ability to scheme. So why were her instincts still telling her something was deeply awry?

She had barely stepped out of the Quinacridone Compound when she was confronted by another individual from the Order of A'hknet. This one was not a run-down mancer but an exhausted monger, as that order called its members who engaged in the trade of questionable goods and services. He was dressed in the loose, casual pants, shirt, and vividly colored vest he favored. His fashionably-long hair, which Cadmia knew was naturally a weathered straw color before an application of henna turned it rich, chocolate brown, looked like it had been hastily tied back without the benefit of a mirror. For Cinnabar of A'hknet, who took pains with his appearance as a professional asset, that was positively unkempt.

Cadmia smiled in greeting while instinctively putting a hand on her small purse. "Were you looking for me?" she asked. There was no other reason for Cinnabar to loiter outside the Quinacridone Compound, within sight of four members of the 126.

Noticing her distrustful gesture, Cinnabar said, "I wouldn't steal from family."

"We are *not* family," she pointed out.

"Not by blood, thank Numen," he replied with a flirtatious smile that was as engrained a habit for him as breathing—and which still made her blush. "You look good, Caddy."

Cadmia stifled the impulse to check her own hair and clothes self-consciously, even though she was confident the wavy, strawberry-blond hair Cinnabar had once admitted to envying was held primly back with wooden hair combs and the plum-violet robes of her order were neat and modest.

If he had been a stranger or a distant acquaintance it would have been easier to meet his eye and respond as a Sister of the Napthol should, but she was keenly aware the nearby guards were watching her. It didn't matter that they didn't know her history with him. *She* knew.

"What do you need with the Order of the Napthol, Cinnabar?" *If he teases, I'll just turn my back and walk away. That's all.*

"I need to show you something," he said, all flirtation leaving his face and tone. "Can we go inside?"

She led the way into the Cobalt Hall. Only once over its threshold did Cinnabar begin to relax.

"I lifted this from a guest we had recently," he said. "I took it because it looked like silver. I didn't examine it until she was gone." He flipped the disk onto the table between them, using the end of his sleeve to keep his hands from touching it directly.

The round disc was about the size of Cadmia's palm around, but thin as a coin. The upward-facing surface was marked with elaborate geometric designs that shifted and made Cadmia's eyes water as she tried to make sense of them.

When she picked it up, cold flashed up her arm as far as her shoulder. It spun twice before falling to the floor with a bell-like ring.

That kind of cold could only come from the Numen. The divine realm was supposed to be the destination for good souls when they died, but Numenmancers were not content to wait. They manipulated the Numen and disturbed the peaceful dead to command the Numini and achieve more power in mortal life.

Though not as physically brutal as Abyssumancers, Numenmancers were in some ways more dangerous, as they altered the nature of divinity and so could endanger not just this life, but the next.

"I came to you because I know you'll trust me it isn't mine," Cinnabar said, his voice soft and desperate. "Mother got up last night after one of her nightmares, and brought back a woman who looked half-dead. I figured it was ship-fever, something like that, until I saw this. She was *in my house*, Caddy. She was alone with Mother."

Mother Avignon was one of the oldest and most respected members of the Order of A'hknet. She had lived through the revolution, or so people said, though she never spoke on those days. Cadmia had left that order and joined the Napthol when she was seventeen, but she still shared Cinnabar's instinctive outrage that a mancer had come so close to Mother.

"I know Mother probably will not wish to, but both you and she are welcome to stay here until the mancer is identified and captured," Cadmia said. No one knew why mancers could not enter the Hall, but Cadmia had seen one faint trying. She did not question the blessing, but appreciated that there was one safe place in the city. "Can you give me a description of the woman?"

"Description, name, workplace," Cinnabar answered. "I've seen her around before—*not* professionally," he was quick to add. "She's moderately attractive, a bit on the thin side, average height, brownish-auburn hair, brown eyes. Well-spoken when called to be, but she keeps her head down. She calls herself Dioxazine—Xaz—and she works down at the docks market almost every morning. I don't know where she lives, but I'm sure someone there can tell you. I can't believe I—" He broke off. "Just *find* her, please."

"Would you be willing to come with me to make this report directly to the One-Twenty-Six?" Cadmia asked, because she was expected to, though she was certain the fear that had driven Cinnabar here would never get him across the threshold of the Quinacridone Compound. She didn't bother to ask if he wanted guards posted near Mother's home.

Cinnabar shook his head and said, "I trust you to do what needs to be done."

So it was that Cadmia crossed to the compound for the second time in one day, and found Captain Feldgrau conferring with one of the guards that Cadmia recognized as one of Pearl's favorites. Bole had a daughter near Pearl's age, and so had a soft spot for the orphan girl who lived at the Cobalt Hall.

Tiredly, she said to Captain Feldgrau, "I think I have another one for you." She handed over the disc, now carefully wrapped, and said, "A monger just brought this to me. He stole it from a houseguest, then realized that it is obviously a Numenmancer's tool. He said the woman's name is Dioxazine, and that she works down at the docks."

"Did he say what she looks like?" The soldier who interrupted them appeared alarmed. "Pardon me, Captain."

Captain Feldgrau indicated for Cadmia to continue, so she repeated Cinnabar's description, and watched the soldier go pale.

"Do you know her, Bole?"

The soldier nodded. "I know her. She moved in to the river way in the south district about a year ago."

"Near Lieutenant Viridian?" the captain asked.

"Right next door to his childhood sweetheart." Bole grimaced. "With your leave, I'd like to go warn him immediately."

Feldgrau shook his head. "We don't know if she might be watching him. Sister Paynes, thank you for the information. We will handle this from here."

Cadmia returned to the market square feeling unsettled. It seemed like mancer activity had been steadily increasing in the last few years, despite every effort to control the threat. Of course, the 126's efforts were sabotaged by the fact that every paranoid farmer and fishwife cried sorcery whenever anything went wrong, so the few soldiers with the sight were constantly running around trying to determine if slaughtered chickens were the result of mancers or foxes.

That wasn't to say mancers weren't far more dangerous than foxes. They had the ability to stop a person's breath with a touch. The power was addictive, and just like a man who had fallen to Tamari crystal elation or even something as mundane as alcohol, those who meddled with sorcery seemed to need more and to become more irrational about how they supported that magic.

The power gets hungry, Baryte had said, to explain why he had committed murder.

The soldiers will deal with it, she told herself. *That is what they are for.*

She spotted Cinnabar again in the market, this time with one hand on an empty wooden pull-cart as he spoke with a honey merchant, his famous smile no doubt getting him a deep discount. If he was still worried about the mancer, it didn't show—but then again, a man in his profession had to be good at hiding his thoughts while appearing to be an open book.

He glanced up and noticed Cadmia watching him, and raised a hand in a half wave, half salute.

This time she managed to school her face. As a Sister of the Napthol, especially with her specialty counseling individuals who had fallen on the wrong side of the law, it was expected that she knew all types of people—even an Order of A'hknet prostitute. Others who observed them had no way to know Cinnabar was also the man to whom she had lost her virginity long before Kavet's legal age of consent.

"The Quin stole Mother's cart," he explained as she approached, patting the worn wooden handle. "It took a while to get them to give it back to me. Did you . . . get everything sorted out?"

She appreciated that he kept the question intentionally vague to avoid being overheard and causing a disturbance. She nodded, and told him the only part he would care about. "It will be dealt with. I didn't need to use your name."

"Thanks." He smiled again, and this time she thought it was genuine. "Do you want to walk down with me? You haven't come to visit us in ages."

"I used to come to visit Mother—*my* mother," Cadmia reminded him. Scarlet Paynes had died two years prior, caught in the middle of a fight for her affection between two men who would have forgotten her within the day. Cadmia had never known her father, so Scarlet's death had meant the last of her blood family was gone, and with it the last of her responsibility to visit with those who followed A'hknet.

"She isn't the only one who looked forward to your visits," Cinnabar said, softly.

"Have a good day, Cinnabar," Cadmia said, trying to disengage from the conversation.

"If I asked for your counsel—"

"If you put in a request for counsel, I will be sure to send one of the Brothers." It was more common for men interested in religious study to dedicate themselves to the Quinacridone and become monks, but there were a few among the Napthol as well.

Cinnabar quirked a brow, reminding her wordlessly that his flirting wasn't limited to women. Despite Kavet laws and Quin norms that made same-sex relations strictly illegal, Cinnabar willingly worked both sides—he was just a little more careful not to get caught when his clients were male.

Her scowl made him say, "You used to be fun."

He turned away, and Cadmia found herself relieved and disappointed to see him go—and fighting the urge to *watch* him go. Cinnabar had been awkwardly cute when they were younger. Now that he had grown into his broad shoulders and sharp, dramatic features it was clear how he was so successful in his chosen line of work.

It might have been easier to stoically toe the "no sex outside marriage" line both the Quin and the Order of Napthol held so dear if Cadmia had been as naïve as most initiates were when they took vows, but Scarlet Paynes's daughter had needed to start fighting off amorous intentions, often from sailors twice her age, when she was twelve or thirteen. Though only a couple years older, Cinnabar had taken it upon himself to become her protector, which included sleeping beside her with a dagger in his boot. They had become lovers when she was fourteen.

When she was seventeen, Tamari slavers had beaten Cinnabar senseless while attempting to claim him and Cadmia. She had put Cinnabar's dagger in the slaver's back, carried Cinnabar to the Cobalt Hall for healing, and dedicated herself to the Order of Napthol on the spot.

She only occasionally regretted the decision.

CHAPTER 6

Hansa had faced down murderers, sorcerers, would-be-slavers, and all manner of violent, dissolute men and women, but this was probably the most frightened he had ever been—at least since the *last* time he had tried to propose to Ruby, back when he was twenty-three and she was twenty.

She hadn't said "no" last time, but "later." She wanted to establish herself in her career before settling down. She was three years younger than he was; he had understood why she wanted to wait. Four years later, he prayed the answer would be different.

At least his nerves were keeping him awake. Between returning home late after overseeing the mancer's branding and getting up early to honor his request for counsel before his scheduled execution, Hansa had managed only a few hours' sleep. After the horror of the mancer's grisly death, he had almost put this off one more time—going home to sleep sounded very nice—but told himself no. Dealing with horrors was the nature of his work. It was time to stop using that as an excuse to put off the good parts of his life. As soon as Sister Paynes had finished her report, Hansa had reminded his commander that he had asked for the day off, then gone back home.

Now he tried to focus on cooking. Smell suggested the sweet bread was nearly ready, as it should be. He had fresh cider warming on the stove, and homemade maple butter ready on the table, which covered almost all of Ruby's favorite breakfast foods with the exception of fresh strawberries, which were unavailable this time of year. Trying to replace fresh strawberries with preserves was likely to end with the jar dumped over his head. At least the warm bread and hot cider would be appreciated, in the face of the cold wind that had started last night and brought winter in like a thief in the night.

Ruby started work very early in the morning, but was often able to come home for a few hours while an apprentice minded the distillery, so they frequently met at her home on days when Hansa was not scheduled. Hansa tended to breakfast more heavily when left to his own devices, but Ruby preferred to eat like a butterfly and snack all day, so they normally compromised when they met for brunch. But today was all about her.

When she walked in, her cheeks were pink from the cold outside and her gray eyes were bright. She pulled off her heavy overcloak and hung it on the peg next to the door before she greeted him with a kiss on the cheek and the words, "Do I smell sweet bread?"

She moved in a wreath of her own spicy-sweet scent, which lingered from her work at the herbarium. She spent much of the day distilling essential oils, which judging from the orange stains on her fingertips, today meant wild carrots. The seeds left behind after the lacy white flowers were gone had a variety of medicinal properties.

Hansa was just glad today hadn't been devoted to garlic, or skunk cabbage. It was hard to be romantic on skunk cabbage days, which had been all too frequent during Ruby's apprenticeship as an herbalist. She was now a senior journeyman and spent much of her spare time working toward her master work piece, an illustrated account of Tamari herbs and their cultural and medicinal uses.

"Oo, and maple butter, you darling!" Her delight abruptly shifted and she focused her gray eyes on him with suspicion as she asked, "What's wrong?"

"Wrong?" he repeated. Did she know about the mancer who had taken a swipe at him? She always berated him for choosing such a dangerous position . . . no, she was responding to the meal, which had her favorites and nothing he would have prepared for himself. "Nothing's wrong."

"Just tell me it's not another woman," she said, wide-eyed, with one hand to her breast, and her gray eyes sparkling in a way that unbalanced Hansa, unsure if he was supposed to be comforting her, defending himself, or laughing.

How had she always been able to do that? Even when she was just "Jenkins's kid sister" tagging along on their boyish adventures, her friendly teasing and sharp wit had been able to cut circles around his.

"You know there's never been anyone else," he replied, hoping to recover some of the nerve he had spent most of the last two weeks gathering.

"Oh, good." Moving to the oven, she peeked in and took the bread out, knowing he would have had it just ready. "You put in such an effort, I'm sorry to say I need to eat and run. I left the boy alone with a whole crop of bitterwort, and you know the Cobalt Hall will be on me if we let it scald. You'll forgive me, won't you?"

Forgive her? He might *strangle* her!

"Oh, darling," she said, moving close and putting a hand on his cheek. "Don't look at me so. I suppose I could stay a *few* minutes . . . but only if it is a very shiny ring."

"You evil woman!" Hansa declared as she danced back, the gleam in her eye now decidedly mischievous. She knew exactly why he had put this all together.

"*I'm* evil?" she asked. "Your mother has been asking me every day for the last week where this is." She held up her hand, and in it was the small silk bag that had been in his pocket a moment ago, before she had snuggled up close to him. Like many young ladies born to conservative Quin families, Ruby had spent some time fascinated with the Order of A'hknet when she was younger; in her case, the interest had caused a fall-out with her parents that persisted to this day despite Ruby's return to a more decorous lifestyle. Her nimble, sticky fingers still held the skills she had learned in her eight months with the mongers, though these days she mostly employed them to perform sleight-of-hand tricks for children.

Before Hansa could even begin to sputter a reply, much less a proposal, a knock on the door made them both frown and turn from their playful teasing. Hansa debated ignoring it, but the pounding was too insistent.

"Sorry," he said.

Ruby followed after him as he went to open the door.

"Jenkins!" she scolded upon seeing her older brother on the front step. "Hansa was just about to propose. Do you mind coming back in a few minutes?" She swatted Hansa on the arm to add, "For your information, *I* took the afternoon off for this."

So did I, Hansa thought. *Jenkins knew that, and knew why.*

"Keep smiling, Hansa," Jenkins said, his voice soft. "The captain only gave me permission to give you the heads-up because I swore up and down that none of your neighbors would question my coming here for a social visit while I'm off duty."

"But this isn't a social visit," Ruby said, voice flat.

"Unfortunately, no, and I'm very sorry it had to happen today of all days. Let's go inside."

"What's this about?" Hansa asked as Jenkins let himself in despite Ruby's glare.

In response, Jenkins handed him one of the small stilettos carried specifically for use on sorcerers. The poison on it was difficult to craft and broke down quickly, so only on-duty officers carried it.

"We just got a report from a reputable source naming Dioxazine of 16 River Street as a mancer. I know you're supposed to be off today, but I thought you might want to be involved in this one. Also, I understand that you're neighborly enough that she might not panic if you knock on the door."

"*Xaz?*" Ruby asked incredulously. "But she's so . . . so . . . and I . . ."

She trailed off, probably considering the exact same things Hansa was: *She's so quiet and reserved, shy, always polite.* Like someone who had something to hide? It was hard to imagine the woman Ruby had occasionally coerced into joining them for social calls as a mancer, but that seemed to be what people always said when someone was named.

"You're sure?" Hansa asked.

"If she isn't a mancer, she's at least a sympathizer," Jenkins said. "The report came from a Sister of the Napthol."

"No," Ruby said, wide-eyed. "Hansa, you are *off duty.* I'm not letting you—"

"You know I need to go. I need to know what she has been doing here."

Xaz had been living next to Ruby for *months.* Even

if a mancer did nothing directly nefarious, the power itself was dangerous and unpredictable. Ruby could have been hurt—and that was assuming Xaz had the best of intentions, and had not put herself near someone so important to a lieutenant of the 126 for her own purposes.

Ruby crossed her arms silently.

"Go or stay, Hansa," Jenkins said. "I told them I wasn't sure what you would choose to do. If the rest of the company doesn't see us soon, they'll break in."

"You've re-treated this since last night, I assume?" he asked Jenkins, as he took the stiletto and palmed it. The Abyssumancer should not have been able to wake as quickly as he had.

Jenkins nodded. "The paraphernalia found on her was clearly a Numenmancer's, so I was able to mix this pure for one of them. It should put her out fast and keep her down for a long time."

Hansa nodded. Like the brands, the poison was a remnant of an earlier age; it could only be distilled using equipment no one fully understood in the basement of the Quinacridone Compound, and it needed to be matched to the specific type of power the mancer wielded. If they knew going into an arrest what kind of sorcerer they were dealing with, they could use more effective poisons.

"You could both let them go without you," Ruby whispered, but the slump in her shoulders made it clear she knew they couldn't. "Why couldn't *one* of you have become a . . . a *florist* or something?"

"Sorry, sis," Jenkins said. "I wasn't cut out to be a monk." Jenkins had been born with the sight. There weren't a lot of options for him outside the Order of the Napthol and the monks who followed the Quinacridone. "Hansa, we have to go."

"We'll talk later," Hansa said to Ruby, knowing time was short. The last thing he wanted was for the others to move while both their lieutenant *and* second lieutenant were here. That would leave only Captain Feldgrau with the poison needed to bring the mancer down.

Ruby nodded sharply. He resisted the urge to keep arguing with her. She was afraid now; later, when they had all returned safely, she would understand why they had gone.

Trying to school his face to a friendly, open expression, Hansa stepped through the door. He couldn't see the other men from the street, but he trusted that they were nearby and would move quickly if Xaz tried to resist and Hansa could not subdue her immediately.

The shades on the Numenmancer's house were drawn tightly closed as Hansa approached.

He knocked politely, resisting the urge to pound on the door. If Xaz didn't answer, they would need to break in, which was risky. If she was out entirely, they could set an ambush, but that was still more dangerous than having her willingly come to the door.

Abyssumancers had the unsettling ability to be armed even after being searched and stripped naked, but Numenmancers could summon lightning or make the air turn so cold it could freeze a man's blood. Dangerous sorcery like that normally required a ritual, which gave men like Hansa an advantage if they moved quickly, but that potential delay was dwindling quickly if Xaz had realized what was going on and was at her altar preparing her defense.

Hansa reached for the doorknob, and then jumped as it turned and the door opened from the other side.

Xaz was normally a pretty enough woman, with auburn highlights in her brown hair and wide, expressive eyes, even though she constantly seemed on the side of too thin and too tired. At that moment, she looked feverish and exhausted, and she hung back from the door just enough that she would have room to jump back if he reached for her.

Hansa wasn't much of a natural liar, so he let neighborly instincts speak for him. "I'm sorry to bother you. I didn't realize you were sick. Did I wake you?"

She shook her head, and asked, "How did the proposal go?" Then she frowned and her eyes focused before she asked, "What are you doing here?"

Xaz had handed him an excuse, so he was about to say that Ruby had asked people to come over to celebrate—he would feel a little guilt later for using her that way, but it was better than tipping the mancer off—but before he could speak or even hesitate and fumble a lie, the Numenmancer must have guessed the truth.

She darted back and slammed the door behind her, but didn't have time to lock it before Hansa shouldered it back open and went after her, trusting the rest of his men to follow.

He found her in the living room, trapped and wide-eyed like a deer. Jenkins had taken some of the men around back; they had probably slipped in through the windows as soon as Dioxazine had come to the door, and now they had blocked her escape.

"Quin bastards," Xaz hissed, looking from Hansa to Jenkins with an expression of betrayal that eerily mirrored how Hansa felt. He had thought, before now, that Xaz was a friend.

She twisted to face Jenkins when he started to step forward, which left Hansa with a clear enough shot that he was able to bury the blade in the meat of her shoulder.

She hissed in pain and stumbled to her hands and knees—but stopped there.

The temperature in the room rose abruptly as she shoved herself back up and turned toward Hansa again, reaching out and seeming to realize only as she did so that there was a knife in her hand: a black-bladed bone knife that Hansa recognized instantly from the Abyssumancer Baryte. How did *she* have it?

This wasn't the time to ask; the poison seemed to disorient her, but it hadn't taken her down entirely because it was designed for a Numenmancer's power, and that clearly wasn't what she was using. Someone had made a disastrous mistake. They hadn't come here prepared to fight an Abyssumancer.

Bole must not have seen the knife before he attacked. His sword took a slice out of the mancer's arm before she dodged, but then she struck back and her blade found him between the ribs. It wasn't a heart-wound, but it was close enough, and with that kind of magic . . .

The air seemed to darken, becoming thick and hard to breathe.

Xaz shouted, "Just *help* me, damn you!" and then the world became red ruin as Bole's skin steamed and split.

Hansa couldn't see it, but he knew it was there by the bloody claw marks it left across the skin of the next soldier to reach it. *Abyssi.* It would only be put back by killing its master. Jenkins was closest . . . so it was Jenkins who, a moment later, was nothing but a crimson splash, a few shards of bone, and a slowly falling residue of ash. Meanwhile, Xaz fled through the back room.

Hansa couldn't see anything, beyond a fourth soldier flying across the room and hitting the wall near the door hard enough that he fell, dazed, and another kneeling on the floor with an upraised arm suddenly becoming a mass of clawed meat. Hansa swung at where the creature had to be, but hit nothing; his sword moved as if through air, even as whatever it was continued to claw at the other guard.

It wasn't possible for a man to fight a creature from the Abyss, but thankfully it was also impossible for a mancer to control one for long. This one would eventually turn on the Abyssumancer who had summoned it, and in the process it would send itself back to the Abyss.

Hansa just needed to survive that long.

While the Abyssi was focused on one of the others, taking its time now that no one was directly threatening the escaped mancer, Hansa slung an arm under the unconscious guard it had thrown across the room, lifted him, and then ran.

He had barely reached the street when he felt claws down his back. He fell hard, twisting to try to avoid slamming the head of the guard he had tried to rescue into the stone path.

And then he *could* see. Nothing solid, just a general shape, but that was enough because that shape was made of nothing from this world. It was darkness and pain incarnate, and as it went for the fallen guard, Hansa's nerve broke.

Hansa had always considered himself brave, or at the very least *loyal*, but in that moment he abandoned those illusions. He stood, and he ran. He fell because of the wounds down his back and crawled instead, dragging himself away from the horror of a mancer's wrath.

CHAPTER 7

Xaz collapsed, her limbs too heavy for her to even crawl any more. Her vision was blurred, her head was pounding, and the contents of her stomach seemed to have turned to lead. She didn't know where she was, or where the guards were, or exactly what had just happened.

She had barely made it home before collapsing into a deep, trancelike daze. When she finally recovered enough energy to try to speak to the Numini, she had discovered that the disc was missing, which made calling on the Numini for help nearly impossible unless they initiated the communication—which they didn't. She would need to get to the mancers' temple, a magical rift between the planes, in order to communicate with them.

Aching in every muscle of her body, she had tried to sleep, only to find herself unable to tune out the damn

Quin's obsessive anxiety about his intended proposal. She was normally able to keep others' thoughts from intruding on hers, but her power was so muddled she couldn't seem to form the mental walls that she had habitually maintained since childhood.

The inability had probably saved her life. When Hansa had knocked on the door, Xaz had assumed that he had come to deliver the good news in a jovial, neighborly way, but that hadn't been the focus of his thoughts when he looked at her.

Like every mancer, she craved the touch of her power's realm, but knew the dangers of succumbing to that desire. She had never dared try to summon the Numini into the mortal realm. However, the alternative at that moment seemed to be branding and execution, so she responded instantly when one of the Others reached to her and whispered, *I can help you. Pull me over.*

Then she had felt the poison. It had disoriented and weakened her even more than she already had been, turning fear into panic. The Abyssumancer's bone blade had appeared in her hand without her in any way intending to summon it, and then the blood of one of the guards had been on her skin and she had shouted for help and fled as soon as the circle broke.

"Come back," she said, trying to speak with power in addition to her voice. It was difficult. *"Please. I need your help."* The creature appeared before her in an instant, but looking at it just made her head hurt even more, so she shut her eyes as she pleaded, *"I need to be somewhere*

safe. I need to rest until the poison wears off, where they can't find me. Help."

As you wish. Its voice reverberated through her muscle and bone. She felt herself lifted before she fainted.

She had dreams of a little girl. Pearl, from the Cobalt Hall. The girl was shy, had always been shy. She had a long, dusky-gray feather in her hand, and was deep in prayer. But there was a wolf at the door, and it was hungry.

The black Abyssi watched, knowing. Once the girl was at the temple, he would be able to reach her.

Xaz woke, gasping, from a nightmare she couldn't quite recall. The last thing she *clearly* remembered was the command from the Numini to capture Pearl and bring her to the temple . . . what happened after that? She had been injured. She had woken up in the home of one of the members of the Order of A'hknet.

At that thought, she realized that she was curled up against what felt like a man's chest. It was too dark to see anything, so her sense of touch was all she had. Her first thought was, *Cinnabar*? She wouldn't have bedded him—

She tried to pull away, but there was a wall against her back and the ceiling was only inches above. Where *was* she?

Not with Cinnabar, she realized. She had left there. Gone home.

The soldiers.

She realized suddenly that the "man" lying in front of her had to be the creature she had pulled through the veil. She shouldn't have had enough power to do that without days of elaborate ritual, but she had been so scared . . . and the Other had helped, more than she would have expected. As a rule, Others did not like to tie themselves too tightly to mancers. It made them vulnerable.

She relaxed and curled closer, grateful for its warmth. Despite knowing what it was, knowing intellectually how much trouble she could be in, the Other's presence was comforting. The tie between them, the lie of power's voice, was what made this creature feel so safe; Xaz was aware of that. But in that moment, she was tired, and the creature was warm, and they were both wrapped in what felt like fur and silk.

The Other opened its eyes, which were deep indigo and shone like a cat's—except a cat's eyes just reflected present light. This creature's glowed from within, with an electric black luminescence.

Only once she noticed that did Xaz realize that part of the fur she was feeling was the creature itself. With her arm around its waist like a lover, it was hard to miss the feel of hard muscle beneath the fine, silky-soft pelt.

"You're Abyssi," she said in shock. Her voice seemed very loud.

"Yes?" It sounded amused.

"That's impossible." She tried to pull away, and remembered that she couldn't.

"You're mistaken." Despite its infernal origins, the creature had a beautiful voice, like water flowing over stone, or the warm crackle of fire. "It must be possible, for I *am* here, and I *am* Abyssi. You may call me Alizarin. And you are a Numenmancer."

"That's the *problem*," she said, fully aware of the amused lilt in the Abyss's tone. Now she remembered the blade, and the blood, and the screaming of soldiers after the Other appeared, but none of it made any sense. "I *cannot* have summoned you, much less pulled you through a rift into this plane. The human plane. Are we still there? Where have you brought us?"

"We're still on the human plane. We were both too weak to survive a passage through the rift, or to travel far. I found somewhere close."

"How far are we from the city?" she asked, trying to ignore metaphysic impossibilities for the moment and focus on what obviously had and was going on.

"We are in the city," Alizarin answered.

"*What?* They'll be searching for us. They'll find us. We need to go—"

"Hush, Mancer," he bid her, pressing a fingertip to her lips. She felt the barest hint of a claw tip against the sensitive skin above her upper lip. "They will not find us here. And you need to rest longer before we travel again."

Struck by a horrifying notion, Xaz pressed her hands to the "ceiling" again, feeling padded silk. Then the walls. A fourth wall on the other side of the Abyssi. A wall just above their heads, and a last one below their feet.

"Dear Numen, we're in a coffin." Since the passage of Citizen's Initiative 126, all bodies had been burned to keep them safe from necromancers and Abyssumancers, but there were still some old graveyards left.

"A *royal* coffin," Alizarin said. "A standard one would be far too small to fit us both. About a century ago, a prince was lost at sea. His body was never found, but the king and queen nevertheless buried a coffin, filled with furs and silks and jewels, in the family crypt. The jewels were looted from the coffin before it was even sealed, but the box remains. We are behind walls of stone, and then soil. The Quinacridone itself ordered the crypt filled in, after the royal family was disposed of."

"But, the *air*," Xaz protested. "There can't be enough air in here."

"While I am with you, I can sustain such a slight need," Alizarin explained. "The power it takes for me to do so is even less than that which it takes for you to fill and empty your lungs."

"Still, we should move on. We . . ." She trailed off. What could she possibly do next?

"You need to *rest*, Mancer. As do I," Alizarin insisted. "You are too weak. Without your own power to assist, I would probably lose my grip on you if I tried to bring you back to the surface now. Sleep a while. Sleep deeply, and I can leave enough power to keep you alive long enough for me to go to the surface and feed."

"Feed," Xaz repeated, concerned. "Feed on what?"

"No one you would care about." He licked her

cheek, making her flinch. "You still taste like their poison."

"I don't care," she snapped. "I want to get out of this grave. Bring us to the surface."

"Right now?" he asked, tone too innocent. "Right this instant? Into the freezing rain that is currently falling? And, around in which the Quin guards are wandering as they search for you? Give it time, Dioxazine, until some of this settles."

She sighed. What choice did she have? "Okay. We'll wait, just a little while longer."

Except that, waiting in the darkness, she couldn't help but think. Very softly, not wanting the answer but unable to resist the words, she asked, "How many of them did you kill?"

"Don't trouble yourself, Mancer," Alizarin replied.

"How many?" she repeated.

"I killed no one who would not have killed us first," he said this time. "And I will feed upon no blood that would not be willing to spill ours. Would you have me do differently?"

Her chest was tight, maybe from tears for those whose lives had been lost . . . and maybe from her own knowledge that no, she would not have had him do differently. She had fought for her survival.

She had done exactly what the Quin most feared, what they had passed CI–126 to try to prevent.

"I'm a Numenmancer," she asserted, feeling at the edge of outright hysteria.

"The Numini rejected you because you were bloodied trying to do their bidding. When you tried to call for help, they fled, fearful of being enslaved by a mancer who could control them. I alone chose to answer you, Mancer." He added, very significantly, "And it was a *choice*. It was a choice for me to come to your side when you called, as well, and it was a choice for me to bring you here. So do not trouble yourself over the bodies behind us. Not until we both know how much 'choice' I have left."

Dear Numen.

He was right. She had no innate power over the Abyss; she had successfully summoned a creature over whom she might have absolutely no control. He needed for her to survive, since without her he would be forced back into the Abyss, but if she could not find a way to rule him, it was possible that he could just lock her away somewhere secure and think about her only enough to allow her to sustain his tie to this plane.

"You and I, Mancer, are going to have an . . . interesting partnership," Alizarin speculated. "Now close your eyes."

CHAPTER 8

There was blood in Hansa's left eye. He blinked, and it seemed to take an impossible effort to open his eyes again after that.

He was on the street, in a residential area. Someone was kneeling next to him and weeping. Everyone else had run.

Almost everyone.

His vision was going dim, but nevertheless, he couldn't help but see that one person had stayed, and was kneeling next to the body of the soldier Hansa had carried out with him. He was a man, and then, for an instant . . . not a man. He looked up at Hansa, and his detached expression quickly changed to concern.

"Help me?" Hansa whispered.

The man flinched as if Hansa had struck him.

"I'm *trying.*" He recognized Ruby's hitching, fiercely-controlled voice. Had she seen the man? Was he even there? "You're—you're going to be okay. I've sent for a healer, and I'll do everything I can until someone arrives." She shifted, and he realized she had all her weight on the wounds on his back. Shouldn't that hurt more?

"Please," Hansa whispered.

The man snarled, his lip drawing back for an instant, and then he shook his head and walked toward Hansa, his movements a delicate glide, catlike. He put a hand on Ruby's shoulder and said, "Go."

She stood up, then paused, frowning down at Hansa as if confused. "I should—"

"Go," the stranger said again, his blue eyes seeming to flash.

"Okay," she mumbled, still frowning. She took several steps back, as if trying to remember what she had been doing, then turned to leave. Hansa almost called after her, but his voice broke.

Still standing above Hansa, the man said, "I can heal you, if you ask me."

Not human, Hansa thought. A mancer? Why would a mancer be offering to help him?

What else could he be?

"I could leave you to die if you prefer," the man said.

Hansa wasn't brave enough to accept that offer, no matter what the man might be. "Help. *Please.*"

"One boon," the man said, the words sounding very formal.

He knelt, and pressed a hand directly to the wound on Hansa's back, making Hansa whimper. He was too weak to scream any more.

The world went black. For a while, Hansa was sure he was dead, but then he opened his eyes. The pain was still present, though lessened, but the growing pool of blood was . . . gone. He managed to reach a hand back, and found his armored vest tattered, but his flesh whole.

The man stood and started walking away.

"Wait!" Hansa called, through a throat that was raw from trying to scream. The man hesitated, his frame going rigid. "What . . . who are you?"

He twisted, just far enough for electric blue eyes to meet Hansa's. "My name is Umber," he said. "And I only assisted you because, if you lived, the taint from the Abyssi might have made you dangerous. Do *not* call to me again."

With that, he stalked from the plaza.

Everything was blurry. The pain had gone away and the blood had disappeared, but Hansa still felt too tired to lift himself from the cobblestone plaza.

But he *had* to get up. The Abyssi could still be around. The others might need him.

He pushed himself to his knees, but was shaking by the time he got there, and his breath was coming so hard the muscles in his chest felt strained. He tried to go further, to stand, but ended up collapsing all the way back to the cold ground. Maybe he could just rest a little while . . .

"H*ansa!"*

"Uuh?" Couldn't he sleep a bit longer?

"Hansa, I can't carry you. You have to get up! Can you hear me?"

Ruby. That was Ruby's voice.

In what he considered to be a remarkable act of willpower and valor, he opened his eyes.

"That's it, baby," Ruby said. "Wake up. You hear me. You can't stay here."

"Ruby," he mumbled. "You . . . you have to run. It could come back."

"I had to see what happened," she said. "Thank the divine you're all right. But you have to get up. I don't think you're badly hurt, but you'll freeze if you stay here. Oh, here's the healer. Sister, here he is! Please help me."

One of the violet-robed Sisters of the Napthol ran to his side, and knelt down, telling Ruby, "Don't move him. If he's as hurt as . . ." She trailed off, and said, "Let me get some guards to help me carry the stretcher. Miss Upsdell, you should go back inside."

"I'm not leaving him," Ruby protested.

"Then at least go fetch some warmer clothes. You'll both freeze this way. Then you can come with us to the Cobalt Hall." She raised her voice as she continued, "Guards! Could you please help me?"

He was pretty sure he could sit up. He struggled to do so, while the healer from the Cobalt Hall conferred with the guards. He recognized them from his own company, which meant some had survived.

That was good.

But how many were dead?

He was half-upright when one of them said, "Here, let me help you," and offered a hand.

"Thanks."

He reached out for the hand. Took it. Was barely aware of the needle-like blade in the man's other hand, which caught him by surprise an instant before the darkness did.

Hansa woke cold, damp, and half-naked, and unfortunately he knew exactly where he was. The perpetual gloom of the Quinacridone cells was distinctive.

He was somewhat relieved to discover that he was in one of the first-floor cells, instead of the deeper ones, which were reserved only for irredeemably evil and violent offenders . . . but that was only slight relief, since it still left him in a cell in a prison only used for sorcerers and their sympathizers.

Also, he had a roommate, a middle-aged woman who was staring at him with curiosity and suspicion. Given this cell was generally only occupied by mancers, that normally would have terrified him, but he knew this woman; Rose had been a member of the Order of Napthol before joining the Order of A'hknet. He couldn't count the number of times she had been picked up due to her outspoken ways, only to be released as a favor to the Cobalt Hall.

"A mancer in the One-Twenty-Six," Rose said, each word bitten off sharply. "I'm not sure who I would accuse you of betraying worst."

"I'm not a mancer," Hansa protested. Across his

mind's eye, the images of all his fellows' bodies flashed. The memory of their screams. Could anyone really think he had something to do with that?

"That's what they say," his roommate said. "I heard them arguing after they tossed you in. Some of the guards don't want to believe it, but there are dozens of witnesses who say the demon killed the man with you, but let you live."

"I couldn't . . ." He had spoken to someone. Asked for help. He didn't understand exactly what had happened or how he was alive, but he knew he wasn't a mancer. "The mancer summoned it. Maybe she—"

"A Numenmancer couldn't summon an Abyssi," she scoffed, "and a Numini wouldn't have bloodied the soldiers that way."

Hansa had seen just enough of the Others—both divine and infernal—to know Rose was right. Numini could kill, but they did so softly and silently, without ever spilling a drop of blood.

"They identified her wrong," he whispered. "We were *told* she was a Numenmancer, but she must not have been. I . . ."

Ran away. His friends had been attacked, and he had run.

"I ran," he whispered. "They were dying. I couldn't see what was doing it, and I couldn't fight it, and they . . . everyone was dying. And I ran. And it came after me. I don't know why I'm not dead."

The woman clucked her tongue. "Well, neither do I. You're sure you're not a mancer?"

"I think I'd know," Hansa said sharply. "And even if I didn't, my second lieutenant has the sight. We've known each other since we were kids. He would—" He broke off as his throat closed up. Jenkins *had been* Hansa's second. Before . . .

Hansa raised a hand, wanting to rub blood from his face even though he knew it was already gone. If they even *suspected* he was involved in sorcery, they would have searched him and washed away the blood. Blood could be a tool for them.

Apparently deciding he was either honest or harmless, Rose said, "For your sake, I wish you would clear your name and get out of here, but you and I both know that is impossible. One-Twenty-Six gives them the right to hold you here as long as they like. With evidence against you from members of the Order of the Napthol, and multiple dead bodies to account for, they won't need to give you a trial."

"I know," Hansa said. "Damn it all, I know. Is this why it helped me? So it could then watch me rot?" he wondered aloud.

"'It?'" Rose asked. "So that part's true, about you being helped by one of them?"

He nodded, miserably. "I was dying, I think. There was someone—something, I guess—there, watching. I asked for help. He said . . ." He tried to remember exactly what the creature had said. "He said it was a boon, and he was only doing it because the taint from the Abyssi could make me dangerous if I lived."

Rose sat forward, her voice going soft and excited. "A boon, really?" she asked.

What did it matter? Hansa nodded, looking around the gray cell and wondering if this was to be the place where he would die.

He understood how damning the evidence against him was. He had come to much the same conclusion when he had realized that the man they found in the warehouse in the wharf was covered in claw marks that gaped without blood. He was grateful to be alive, but short of sorcery, it was hard to explain how he was.

"Did you ask its name?" Rose asked.

"Umber." He was amazed he even remembered.

"Hansa, you may have a way out of this yet," she whispered, keeping her voice pitched low. "That wasn't an Abyssi who helped you. I don't know what made the Abyssi leave you alone, but the person who helped you wasn't a demon, and he wasn't a mancer."

"Thank you; I now have the faith of a fellow prisoner. What are you in here for this time, anyway?" Hansa asked. "Must be terrible, for you to get stuck in a cell with a man who is accused of slaughtering his friends."

"Just be quiet and listen to me."

"Like you said, I don't get a trial," he said. "Even if he was just some foreign witch—not that that would be appreciated, but at least it's better than a mancer—it won't matter, because he'll never speak to—"

"Shut your self-indulgent mouth, you idiot!" Rose

interrupted. "For your information, I'm in here for collecting and studying every text I've ever been able to find on mancers and Others—and on the spawn."

Was she making any kind of sense? It was hard to tell, past the spinning sensation left by the crumbling of Hansa's entire world. "The what?"

"It takes a fool of a sorcerer to tear the veil and invite one of the Others into this realm," Rose explained. "It takes an incredible amount of power to control them, and Abyssi especially can be vicious if the summoner loses control. But as difficult and dangerous as it is, some mancers do it anyway. And some of them go further. Very, very rarely, the Others breed on this plane with mancers or other humans who run afoul of them. And that is how you get spawn."

She certainly sounded like a mancer. No wonder she was lucky enough to get thrown in a cell with someone accused of consorting with creatures of the Abyss. "Lucky me," he said, sarcastically. "I have a champion crossbreed."

"Shut *up*," Rose snapped. "The spawn walk in human form, but they are incredibly powerful. Whereas an Abyssi or Numini needs to bond to a mancer in order to remain on the mortal plane, the spawn have their own mortal blood to tie them here. However, the Other power continues to seek a bond, so they are susceptible to—"

Hansa waved a hand, cutting her off. "I believe that you're trying to be helpful, but keep in mind that, despite the accusation, I am the one of us who has *never* studied sorcery. I don't understand a word you're saying."

Rose drew a deep breath. "The spawn granted you a boon. The first boon has to be willingly given, but after that, a link is formed. If he gave you his name—and you're lucky you asked him, since otherwise he most certainly wouldn't have—then you can summon him, and he will be forced to grant another boon you demand. Spawn are incredibly powerful. Call him now, and he could make these charges disappear."

"You're actually suggesting that I should summon a half-demon creature in order to *clear* myself of practicing sorcery?" Hansa asked, incredulous. "That's *insane*. No. I just need to think clearly. Stop panicking. Mancers don't get trials, but they can have *counsel*. That's all I need."

They hadn't branded him while he was unconscious, or bound him physically, which meant *someone* out there believed he was innocent. He had been a soldier since he was eighteen; he had joined the 126 when he was twenty-three, had been promoted to lieutenant when he was twenty-five, and had spent a year in that position.

In the entirety of his life, the only time he had been in trouble was when Jenkins's poor timing and often off-color sense of humor had convinced some new soldier that they had some kind of disturbing sexual relationship. Officially, both Hansa and Jenkins had been suspected of illicit behavior and perversion, but in reality, their superiors had gone through the required motions without any belief that an investigation was warranted. Jenkins was chastised and warned to watch his words in the future, and it had ended there.

No one who knew Hansa could believe this nonsense about sorcery. He could ask to speak to one of the Sisters of Napthol, and tell them what the spawn had said about healing him only to keep him from becoming dangerous. The Sisters studied the Others; they probably knew about the spawn, and would be able to understand and explain why one of them would have helped him without his delving into black magic.

He had joined the 126 because he believed in the laws and the system that enforced them. He had to trust them now.

CHAPTER 9

Maybe I should move in, Cadmia thought, as she entered the Quinacridone Compound for the third time in two days.

She remembered the young guard who had come to fetch her to speak to Baryte, which meant she was simultaneously one of the strongest witnesses in his defense, and against him.

Hansa had arrested Baryte, and therefore had been closest when the bone knife that later showed up in the Numenmancer's home had disappeared. He had also been closest when Baryte had died, obviously destroyed by Abyssi even with the brand on his skin that should have blocked the Other's power.

Hansa had for some reason been on point when they made the Numenmancer's arrest, though witnesses who stayed behind said that before they left the compound, Captain Feldgrau had said Hansa should not be spoken to in case the mancer was watching him.

No one could ask Captain Feldgrau, because Hansa Viridian was the only survivor of the group that had gone to arrest Dioxazine.

On the other hand, Hansa had crossed the threshold of the Cobalt Hall, which supposedly no mancer could do. That was a strong point in his favor, but not a definitive one; no one understood how the Cobalt Hall protected itself, so it wasn't impossible that a mancer could find a way to bypass the magical defense, just as many of them learned to hide from guards with the sight. It was also possible that Hansa was a sympathizer, working with the mancers somehow but not one himself.

Finally, he might have been framed. Cadmia had spoken to several of his surviving peers; they loved him, and were horrified by his supposed betrayal, and terrified by the idea that a man in line for captainship in the 126 could have been a sorcerer all this time. What better way to unbalance that illustrious group, than turning them against each other?

"The black Abyssi," as Baryte had called it, had injured him enough that he was caught, had instructed him to throw away the knife, and had probably killed him.

If one of the Abyssi had gained the ability to plot directly against the 126, Kavet had far more frightening problems than one turncoat soldier.

She heard the shouting as she approached the cells—a woman's voice, raised high. "You bastard!" she shrieked. "How long have you known? How long have you and Xaz been playing with me? With Jenkins?"

"Ruby!"

Cadmia hurried her steps toward the sound of a scuffle, and found two guards watching a petite woman rail at the occupant of the visitation cell in front of her. One of the guards had a bloody lip, but had obviously decided he would rather stand back than manhandle the distressed woman.

"I saw it with my own eyes!" she shouted. "I saw wounds down your back that should have killed you. I was still covered in your blood when the healer arrived, but you *weren't* any more. I forgot at first what I had seen, but I couldn't understand where the blood came from so I asked one of the guards with the sight to tell me and—*it killed eleven people,* Hansa! It killed *Jenkins*! How could you—"

"Ma'am!" Another guard had rushed into the room, and shot a cold look at the two who seemed reluctant to touch her as he stepped forward, cutting between her and the bars.

Hansa's voice came from within. "Ruby, I swear to you, I—"

"I don't want to hear it," she whispered. "Take me out of here," she pleaded, of the last guard who had come in.

She leaned on him, and seemed oblivious to Cadmia's presence as they exited together.

"I'm sorry," one of the guards said, to Hansa. "When she asked to come in, she didn't seem . . . I didn't think she—"

"Soldiers are not permitted to speak with prisoners suspected of sorcery," Hansa interrupted, his voice cold and bitter. "Such prisoners are also not allowed personal visitors. Maybe for all our sakes you should consider enforcing those rules."

"Yes, sir," the soldier replied. As he saw Cadmia, he added, "Do you still want counsel from the Napthol?"

"Is she here?" He came forward to the bars, and then backed away and sat at the table at the far end of the room without being told. "Please, send her in."

Still an officer, even in here, Cadmia thought. Even with such a pile of evidence against him, the other soldiers were unwilling to completely turn against him. If he *was* a mancer, they were all in trouble.

"The prisoner has a right to privacy," she told the two guards after they locked her into the cell with Hansa. They obligingly moved down the hall, far enough that they would hear her only if she shouted.

She sat across from Hansa, who looked as pale and drawn as any man she had ever faced in such a position. Was he responsible for the deaths of nearly a dozen men, or was he an innocent victim? How many times had Cadmia sat at a table like this one and wondered that?

"You asked for me?" she asked.

He nodded. "I'm innocent," he said. "I might be a coward for running away, but I'm not a mancer."

"What happened?"

"I took point because we knew she would come to the door for me," Hansa explained, his voice calm and even, as if he had given these words much thought and knew perfectly well that this was the one chance he had to defend himself. "I think they must have been wrong about what kind of mancer she was. Jenkins had mixed the poison for a Numenmancer, but it didn't work. She stabbed Bole with that damn bone knife, and summoned what had to be an Abyssi."

"What did it look like?" Cadmia asked. Hansa Viridian did not have the sight, and the Other powers were invisible to anyone without it.

He paled, his skin going ashen gray at the memory. "I couldn't see it until it took a swipe at me, and then . . ." He trailed off, his gaze distant, lost in traumatic memory. "There was so much blood, and I didn't know what to do but run away. I tried to help one of the others, but I think the creature got him, too. Then it hit me."

"And you survived."

"The mancer must have called it back."

He must not have known that the evidence at Dioxazine's house made it very clear that she worked with the Numen powers. An altar hidden in the closet had been covered with white silk embroidered with gold and silver thread. Small silver vessels holding honey and what was probably rainwater had also been found. Those were not the tools of an Abyssumancer.

"You say the Abyssi hurt you before it disappeared?" she asked, returning to that point.

"Yes," Hansa said, tightly. "I know that's why I look so guilty." *That's the least of it,* Cadmia thought, but she let him continue. "I thought I was dying. There was someone there, and I think maybe whatever let me see the Abyssi let me realize he was different, too. He was looking at the bodies, and then he came up to me and told Ruby to leave. She just walked away. The man said that, if I survived, the taint from the Abyssi might make me dangerous, so he healed me. I guess he expected exactly what happened, that I would be arrested, and so assumed I would never be able to track him down later." He drew a deep breath, and added, "Rose, the woman who was in the cell with me when I woke up, says he was probably one of the . . . the spawn?" He said the last word as if he was not entirely certain of its meaning, but repeating something he had heard. "She says they are powerful enough to do that."

The spawn had been vaguely referenced in Cadmia's study, but never in detail. Most members of the Order of the Napthol believed they were a myth, something of a cautionary tale for mancers.

"Can you describe this man?"

"He had blue eyes," Hansa answered. "That's all I really remember. They seemed to glow. Have you ever heard of the spawn? Do you believe me?"

"Hansa . . ." She sighed. "Guards have searched Dioxazine's home, and the tools they found make it clear she is a Numenmancer. How could she get an Abyssumancer's blade, or for that matter, summon an Abyssi?"

"You are more qualified to answer that than I am." Hansa's expression closed off, becoming more withdrawn. "Surely there is *some* possible explanation?" She shook her head. "Sister, *please*. I'm not a sorcerer!"

He seemed so sincere, so desperate, but there was no rational explanation for events that did not involve his having power. He said the spawn healed him to keep him from becoming dangerous, but if that were the case, why hadn't it let Hansa die, or helped him along, to eliminate the threat in the simplest way?

"I will meditate on your words," she said, rising to go.

"Sister . . ." He trailed off, looking defeated. "This is impossible."

All she could offer was one last assurance. "They will brand you before they execute you. If you are innocent as you say, you can at least have the comfort of knowing your name will be cleared at that time."

"Small comfort," he replied. "Have you seen what the brand does to a man without power? I have."

She had never seen it, but she had heard of the case a few years before where a sorcerer woke and managed to turn the brand around on the guard who held it. One of the other guards who had been there had come to the Cobalt Hall afterward for counseling. His description of the event had been graphic.

"I'm sorry."

She was, really. Hansa seemed like a good man. Then again, so many of them did, once it was too late for it to make any difference.

After she made her report to the remaining captains and left the Quinacridone Compound, though, she stared at the Cobalt Hall and couldn't stomach returning to it. She went in only long enough to exchange her official violet robes for simpler dress, and walked down to the docks.

Unsurprisingly, she found Cinnabar first, leaning back against the outside wall of the King's Ransom. He had his arms crossed and was shaking his head to a sailor who was obviously trying to buy his time.

Normally, Cadmia would have walked by without bothering him, but Cinnabar noticed her and waved, extracting himself from his would-be-client with a smile.

Cadmia kept her face as politely blank as she could as Cinnabar hurried toward her, but he must have read something in her expression, because he took a look at her and laughed. "What have they done to you up there, Caddy?" he asked dramatically. "Such a scowl over a perfectly legitimate business transaction."

"Odd," she remarked, "it looked like an utterly illegal business transaction to me."

"Not if we go back to his ship," Cinnabar answered. "Tamari ships adhere to Tamari laws."

"You wouldn't—"

"I didn't, obviously," he pointed out, his tone softening in response to her alarm. "I'm not stupid enough to put myself on a Tamari ship. They turn slaver as often as the sun sets, and they know Kavet officials would never object to one less child of A'hknet. Speaking of, Rose is in jail again."

"I know," Cadmia sighed. Rose had traveled the opposite path as Cadmia had, becoming a full Sister of the Napthol before giving up that life and turning to A'hknet. She had refused to cease her studies, but she was well enough respected from her time in the

Cobalt Hall that the Quin tended to arrest her, keep her a few days, fine her, and then release her. Hansa had mentioned her, but Cadmia's focus had been on Hansa himself. "I'll check on her the next time I am up there." *And talk to her about giving ideas for excuses to suspected mancers.*

"In the meantime, what brings you down here disguised as a lowly monger?" Cinnabar asked, with a gesture toward her casual clothes.

Maybe the same thing that drives Rose to the Quin jails time and again, Cadmia thought. "I decided you were right—it's been too long since I visited."

Followers of the Quinacridone and the Napthol were not supposed to question much. They certainly were not supposed to hear enough evidence to convince anyone of guilt, and then look at a condemned prisoner and be gut-certain that he was innocent.

She couldn't start doubting her mind and logic and everything she knew now.

CHAPTER 10

After the guards took him back to his own cell from the meeting room where he had spoken to Cadmia, Hansa found himself for a long time unable to form words or do anything but stare at the cell door. The soldiers outside had moved a greater distance away, and had not tried to talk to him since his return.

Rose spoke his name at least twice before he turned toward her.

"She doesn't believe me." That much had been clear before Cadmia left. "They say the mancer we went to arrest was a Numenmancer. She couldn't have summoned an Abyssi, so they think I must have done it." Rose did not say, *I told you so,* but the words were visible on her face. "You know about these things!" he pleaded. "There must be some kind of explanation. I'm not a sorcerer."

"Then you'll die an innocent man," Rose said.

"At least you'll have the comfort of knowing that the Numen takes those who died righteously."

He shook his head, remembering the look Ruby had given him before she left. She also thought he was guilty. How would she feel when they told her he had died screaming, innocent, under the brand?

He tried to squash the instant of satisfaction he felt as he pictured those who had condemned him when they realized they had been wrong, so wrong.

"I don't think I'm a righteous man," he admitted. His parents, his friends, and Ruby would all be devastated when they realized what had happened. How could he even for a moment have felt . . .

"There may still be time to ask the spawn for help," Rose said, softly, with a glance toward the guards who were standing well away down the hall. They didn't want to be near him.

"Why would he be mad enough to come here so I could ask him anything?" Hansa asked. Was he really contemplating dealing with a demon, practicing black magic, in order to convince everyone he was innocent of dealing with demons and practicing black magic?

Could two wrongs make a right?

"You can summon him," she explained. "His power will force him to come to your call, as quickly as he can."

"How?"

His only other choice was to sit here and rot until his friends conquered their squeamishness and took him to the branding chamber. Until his friends, unaware until it was too late, murdered him.

"When Umber helped you, did you get any sense of feathers, or fur? A tail, scales, horns, wings, anything?"

Hansa closed his eyes, trying to remember. "All I can recall is how blue his eyes were. They seemed to glow."

"Half-Abyssi, then," Rose said, nodding sagely. "That's good."

"Good?" Hansa whispered. "Aren't the Abyssi the nasty vicious ones that tear people to pieces? Isn't an Abyssi what—"

"Yes, yes, what nearly killed you. But this is a crossbreed, and bonded to you now from the first boon. He can't hurt you."

He had no choice. He had decided to go for this mad plan, so he had to trust her now. "Okay, half-Abyssi. What does that mean?"

"It means, you shed blood, and you say his name, and he will appear."

Blood. Why did it have to be blood? He wiped at his face, unable to forget the sensation of Jenkins's blood raining down on him.

They would never have left a suspected Abyssumancer with any kind of cutting tool, but Hansa had gone in and out of this cell often enough to know there was a sharp burr on one of the metal bars. He had nicked himself on it accidentally more than once. Trying not to think too much, he slid his hand down the bar now, quickly, feeling the bite of the metal as it sliced across the meat of his thumb, deeply enough that the cut bled freely.

"Umber . . ." As the crimson drops fell to the ground, Hansa wondered what the guards outside would do, if one glanced in now and saw him. No, he didn't need to wonder; they would kill him on sight. "Umber, come to me now."

As soon as he uttered the words, Hansa had a sensation of force, pressure, pushing against him from all sides, as if he were deep under the ocean where only strange, eyeless fish dwelled. He struggled to draw breath, and felt Rose trying to help him back to his feet. He managed to make it back to his cot to sit, but the sensation did not abate.

"He feels it, too," Rose said. "He will come."

Hansa shut his eyes and focused on breathing, not thinking, not feeling, just breathing. Not passing out. Not wondering if the first person to come would be the half-demon, or the executioner.

He heard a conversation down the hall, but was unable to focus on it enough to know who it was. The impossible thickness in the air did not clear until the moment someone dragged him to his feet.

"I'm quite certain I told you *never* to call to me again," the spawn snarled. The cell door was open, and there was no sign of the guards down the hall, who otherwise would have come running in response to the ringing impact of Hansa's shoulders hitting the metal bars as Umber shoved him into them. "And yet suddenly I hear my name, and I feel the pull of blood. Do you have a death wish, Quin?"

"No," Hansa squeaked out. Healed of the Abyssi's

wounds, he could no longer see the demon inside this man, but he knew it was there—and even if Umber had been just a man, the fury in those eyes would have frightened him.

"He called you to demand a second boon," Rose said.

Umber hissed at her, a feral expression that no pure human could accurately mimic, and then looked back at Hansa. His face only inches away, he asked, "So the witch has been giving you ideas. Has she warned you of the consequences?"

"There are no consequences to a second boon," Rose insisted.

"Every time power is used, there is a price," Umber returned.

"For you," Rose said. "The first two boons only bind *you*." To Hansa, she added, "The second boon will force him to protect you, since harm to you will be harm to him."

"And vice versa, of course," Umber added. "It goes both ways."

"Not much can hurt one of the spawn," Rose pointed out.

As they argued, Hansa tried to pull away, only to have Umber shove him back against the wall and then take another step forward, so his body was flush against Hansa's, pinning him against the bars. The spawn's lips hovered just above Hansa's as he whispered his warnings.

"I granted the first boon because you had been so infected by the Abyss that your survival would have made you a mancer, and the last thing Kavet needs is for one of those bastards to have an elite position in the One-Twenty-Six. The first boon leaves a connection, but it dissolves quickly. The second boon binds two souls tighter, and longer." Umber continued, his breath warm, and his voice a gentle whisper. "And in case you find this to be a convenient way to correct your problems, you should know that the third boon creates a permanent bond, one that can take many shapes." He ran a hand up Hansa's chest, slowly sliding skin against skin. "The submissive party—and that would be *you*, pretty man, since you have no power of your own with which to make it otherwise—may find himself losing all he is, his every thought, every breath, devoted only to his master. It's called a soul-bond. Sometimes the bond takes a less intense form, a gentle ache when the master is away, one that can be ignored and lived with, but often it is an all-consuming passion.

"Know this, boy: I do not want you as my slave. But if you force me, I assure you, I *will* enjoy you."

At that, he kissed him.

A punch to the jaw might have been expected. He would have known how to respond to *that*. Strong fingers twining in his disheveled hair, holding his head in place, were not. Umber's body was almost fever-hot, hard against his, and his mouth was unapologetic, demanding, challenging.

Hansa hesitated, off-balance, unable at first to process the bewildering move so he could respond appropriately. For a wild moment, he could only think,

If Ruby kissed this way—He managed to jerk his head to the side only when Umber bit him, drawing blood from his lip, and then licking it away.

"Guh!" He shoved at Umber with all his strength. The move only pushed the spawn back a couple feet, but at least it was *something*. "Don't you *ever* do that again!" he shouted. "Ever!"

"He's trying to scare you," Rose said.

"It's working," Hansa grumbled. He scrubbed at his tingling lips with the back of his hand.

You're the one who called me here, pretty little soldier, Umber replied, his voice an invasive ripple in Hansa's mind. He stepped forward again, placing one hand on the bars to each side of Hansa's head. *Tell me to go, and I will leave you alone. Insist on this boon, on the other hand, and you will not be rid of me for years, until the bond fades. Harm to you will mean harm to me, and since your status in the guard makes you less than popular with Abyssi and mancers, you can be assured that I will be nearby. All the time.*

"You aren't asking for a third boon, Hansa," Rose said. "Just a second. And as far as I can tell, you don't have much of a choice, so whatever he is telling you . . . it can't mean much."

She was right, but having decided that this was the only way to save his own life did not mean he was willing to inflict this creature on his friends and family. He asked Rose, "If I do this, how do I keep him away from me after?"

Rose answered carefully. "When you speak your

demands for the second boon, you can and should be very specific."

Hansa drew a deep breath.

"Okay."

His voice cracked. He cleared his throat, trying to get his pounding heart out of it, and started again.

"Okay. This is what I want:

"First, I want to be cleared of all charges. Make a new, reliable witness, do whatever you have to do—don't hurt anyone," he added quickly, "but I want to walk out of here with a personal apology from Winsor Indathrone and an agreement that I can return to my job if I want, but that when I choose to leave it I will receive a continuing salary, for life, in order to make up for the false charges."

"That's easy enough," Umber sighed. "What else?"

Easy. Any release from this cell would have been sufficient; Hansa had aimed high because he had expected to be told it was impossible, and he wanted to know the limits of the creature's power. Now he realized he had no idea what an Abyss-spawn might be capable of. He asked, "Can you bring Jenkins back? My friend, who was killed by the Abyssi. Can you—"

Umber started shaking his head before Hansa finished. "I know how Abyssi kill. There probably wasn't enough left of that body for even a necromancer to revive, and that's before the Quin burned the remains."

He had to swallow twice to rid his throat of the lump that had suddenly developed there. So far, Jenkins's death seemed like an abstract thing, but he could feel the reality of that loss waiting for the moment when he was past his panic of this moment and stopped to breathe the first sigh of relief.

"Then . . . what I said before. I go free. And I want you to stay away after that. You aren't to go near Ruby, or anyone in my family. You don't talk to them, you don't make eye contact, you don't even stay in the same *room* with them."

This time, Umber did not just accede to the terms. "Two exceptions. You have enemies, and I have enemies that could use you to get to me. Therefore, I go where I must, to protect you, should I need to, regardless who else is there. And, should one of your kin approach me, walk into the market where I am shopping or into the hall where I am dancing, I'll avoid speaking to them but I won't get up and run away just because you wish it."

Hansa turned those words over in his mind, but they seemed reasonable. "All right." He glanced to Rose.

"Your freedom," she said.

"What?"

"A clause anyone who deals with the Others needs to know," she said simply. "You want to add the condition that he must do nothing to impinge upon your freedom, beyond what is absolutely necessary in order to ensure your reasonable safety. Otherwise, he could lock you in a room somewhere without violating the agreement or endangering himself."

Again, the thought, *What am I getting myself into?* flashed across Hansa's thoughts.

It isn't too late to change your mind, Umber suggested.

Yes, it was.

"Finally, you are to do nothing . . ." He tried to re-create Rose's exact wording. "Nothing that impinges upon my freedom, beyond what is absolutely necessary to ensure my reasonable safety." He glanced to Rose again, but this time she just nodded.

"You're sure of this?" Umber asked, though by now he no longer sounded as if he expected the answer to be anything but "Yes."

"I am."

"The boon must be sealed in blood."

Blood . . . of course it was blood. If this was a taste of what a mancer lived with, Hansa could understand why the Quin wanted so strongly to wipe them from the city.

"Okay," he said, nervously. "How—"

Umber lashed out with a small dagger, which Hansa hadn't even noticed sheathed at the creature's waist. Hansa recoiled, unsure at first if he had been cut. Then he noticed the beads of crimson, along a cut low on his stomach. It wasn't deep, but the blood welled immediately.

Umber hooked one hand over Hansa's belt, and then knelt, holding Hansa in place as he licked the blood away with leisurely laps of his tongue. Hansa looked desperately to Rose for guidance, but saw that she had blushed and averted her gaze.

Umber rose, and pulled Hansa close again, to whisper in his ear. "A taste for me—and a taste for you. Call to me again, demand of me anything else, and it will be more than a taste."

"I thought you couldn't hurt me," Hansa managed to choke out.

" 'Hurt' is a relative term." Umber pulled away with a grin whose joviality was disturbing in context. "I'm off to meddle with the legal system. Hansa, I'm sure your fiancée will come running up, eyes swimming with her apologies. Give her a kiss for me."

At that, he walked away, pausing only to close the cell door behind himself again with the words, "We wouldn't want anyone to be suspicious." How he had opened it in the first place was a mystery.

Hansa collapsed to the ground, cutting the back of his shoulder on the same burr he had used to slice open his thumb earlier. "Damn it," he cursed, pressing a hand to the new wound. The others, he realized only then, had both closed. The one on his thumb was gone completely, and the hand-long slice across his stomach had faded to a shiny scar.

CHAPTER 11

"Mancer?"

Xaz grumbled, and tried to turn about in her sleep.

"Wake up, Mancer."

"Five more minutes." Pulling the edge of her cloak more tightly around her, she rolled onto her stomach, burying her face in the fluffy silk and fur beneath.

Someone crawled onto her back. She was almost awake enough to protest when he nipped her on the fleshy bend between her neck and shoulder, hard enough that she yelped and jerked up—slamming Alizarin into the ceiling of the coffin. He hung on, so when she fell back to the coffin's floor, he collapsed on top of her.

"Awake now?" he asked.

"Yes, I—stop that." That last, as he started to lick the side of her neck, lapping away blood. The bite hadn't been hard, but an Abyssi's teeth were sharp like daggers, and cut through flesh easily. "Get off me."

Instead, he started to purr, the deep rumbling making Xaz's whole rib cage and spine vibrate.

"You taste uncomfortable, and a little angry," Alizarin pronounced. "But you also taste of power. A little dusty, cold like the Numini, but still power."

"Okay. I'm awake," she snapped. "What did you want?"

"I don't remember," he said.

She drew a deep breath, resisting the urge to cuss, before she asked, "Did it have to do, just *maybe*, with our leaving this Abyss-spawned *coffin*?"

"Maybe it did."

She waited patiently, but no more information was forthcoming. "Get off my back," she said, trying to sound more confident than she felt. "You're making me nervous."

"Am I?" He nuzzled at the back of her neck, and then leaned his cheek against hers. "You and I are going to have to deal with each other, Numenmancer. It would be best if we learned to get along. Or something like that."

"It would help if you would get off me," she answered, "and then promise not to bite me again."

He did roll to the side enough to let her shift onto hers, but he chuckled as he did so. "Mancer, Mancer, you forget who you're talking to. Letting a little blood occasionally shouldn't upset you."

"Well, it *does*." She raised a hand to where he had bitten her, now that she could. The wound was gone, though there was a warm wetness, almost like her own sweat, from his saliva. "And I have no desire to do it again."

"Pity." He wrapped his tail around her waist, holding her close. "Because I *do.* And you're going to have to deal with the fact that you are not dealing with one of the Numini. Hold on now."

"Hold—what?"

She clung tightly to his shoulders as she felt the world dissolve and spin. Suddenly she was upright, aboveground, standing—clinging to him—and *freezing,* wondering why she had wanted to come back up to the surface.

She pulled back, which made her immediately realize that she was still wearing nothing but her nightgown; she had lost her robe in her struggle with the guards, and the following flight. The cotton was thick and warm for its intended purpose, but it did not provide nearly enough protection for what seemed to be midafternoon in the city of Mars.

"Where are we?" she asked, through chattering teeth, though a moment later she recognized the salt tang in the air. "Are we at the waterfront?"

"Not far from it," Alizarin said, "but people do not go to this section much since the Abyssumancer was discovered here. They do not like to walk where demons have been called."

"I c-can't imagine," she drawled, through chattering teeth. "I need to g-get ins-side, and warm up. Need cl-clo-clothes," she added. She couldn't walk into any human establishment looking like this.

"This way," he said.

He put an arm around her waist, and despite her intellectual desire to pull away, she could feel his heat radiating through her nightgown and into her, and she was glad for it. As he had said, the Numini were cold creatures. They didn't produce warmth. Abyssi were creatures of fire.

"We can't let people see us," she protested, as he led them into an alleyway that would cut into one of the busier streets.

"It will be fine," he assured her. "No one in there has the sight, and I can hide us from anyone else."

Nevertheless, she cringed as he guided them both past a pair of men speaking in furtive tones at the alley's mouth. Xaz brushed against one of them accidentally, but he did nothing more than scratch at his arm after she passed.

Alizarin pushed open the door of one of the most popular taverns on the wharf, and she tentatively followed. If any of the sailors here *did* notice a scantily-clad woman walking into this kind of place, she was going to be in trouble. Or, they were going to be in trouble, since Alizarin was likely to kill them all.

No one even glanced their way.

The demon walked past the innkeeper, who didn't blink as Alizarin put a hand to the door to the back room and pulled it open. Neither did the matron tending the kitchen, as Alizarin and Xaz stepped inside, the Abyssi guiding his mancer to the fire.

"If you wait here, I can find you more suitable clothes," Alizarin said.

"Don't kill anyone?" she asked, knowing she was powerless to keep him from doing so, if he wanted.

"Then you'll have to wait a little longer. Warm up. Take food if you want it. No one will notice you. I will be back."

He turned and disappeared into the main tavern hall.

Xaz's willpower lasted perhaps a heartbeat, and that was only because she was still unconvinced that no one would notice her, especially now that Alizarin was gone. Her shivering body and empty stomach swiftly vanquished her fear of being caught, as well as any vestigial desire to obey the law, and she edged past the kitchen matron in order to serve herself a bowl full of the stew being kept warm on the back of the stove.

There was something fundamentally unnerving about being in a room with someone who was absolutely oblivious to her presence. On the other hand, it was far preferable to being in a room with Quin guards who *were* aware.

She snatched a piece of bread before retreating to the fire. She wondered what the matron *did* see. Surely she would have noticed floating food, or if the things Xaz took just disappeared.

Those thoughts didn't last long, as Xaz began to scarf down the food, burning her tongue on the thick venison stew, nearly choking on a piece of bread as she inhaled the nourishment she so desperately needed—as well as the blessed, blessed *heat*.

She had finished the bread, and was down to only

an inch left of soup, when a pile of clothing fell with a *fump* to her right. "I had to seduce a barmaid out of it," Alizarin drawled.

Xaz turned, prepared to say something witty in response, but her mind went blank as for the first time she actually *looked* at the Abyssi she had pulled through a rift and onto this plane. She hadn't been able to see him when they had been in the coffin, and she hadn't been aware of much of anything besides how *cold* she was when they first got to the surface.

She knew Abyssi had fur, fangs, claws, and tails. That was an intellectual kind of knowledge. What she had not known was that they looked like *this*.

He stood just over six feet, and was mostly shaped like a man. His chest had muscles as well-defined as a lifelong sailor's, which could be seen despite the soft pelt of fur that covered him everywhere she could see. The fur itself was shiny, mottled blue and green, like the plumage of exotic birds. It was thick and luxurious like a short-haired cat's fur along most of his body, but shortened until it was the texture of moleskin on his palms. She had actually stood and reached out a hand, drawn to touch it and learn if it was really as soft as it looked, before she realized what she was doing.

His face looked almost like a man's, though it was androgynous, slender, with high cheekbones and full lips. His almond-shaped eyes were surrounded by lashes that were actually white, making the iridescent orbs stand out that much more. Atop his head, the fur changed to hair, which was inky black with highlights the same colors as his fur; it tumbled to his shoulders in a waved mass.

His tail twitched, wrapping his body, drawing her attention downward, at which point she found herself grateful that he, too, had found at least *some* clothes. He was wearing oiled black suede breeches, of the style that was common among men who worked down on the docks, though he had slit the back a bit in order to accommodate his lashing tail. He had not chosen to add shoes to the outfit; his feet were also covered in only short, fine fur, and he stood balanced on the balls, catlike, apparently comfortable that way.

"Like what you see?" he asked.

It wasn't until then that she realized she had been standing, staring, one hand half lifted. She shook herself and took a step back, trying to resist the continued instinct to touch him, to lean against him and rub herself along that so-soft looking fur.

No, she chastised herself. This attraction was a lie crafted by Abyssal power. She didn't have to give in to it. Instead she turned away, picking up the clothing he had brought.

"You weren't joking about seducing a barmaid, were you?" she asked, looking at the clothes. They were not badly made, but they were rough, and Xaz was certain the bodice had been designed for a woman with more curves than she had, and more of a desire to show them off. On the other hand, they were clean, and included an outdoor underskirt, and a heavy gray woolen cloak with a border of black fur. Last in the bundle were a pair of soft leather boots, also lined in fur. "Thank you," she added. The dress was more risqué than she normally chose, but overall the clothing was practical, and fit better than she would have imagined. He must have made an effort to find someone the right size.

He seemed unconcerned about her gratitude. It was also quickly evident that he did not intend to look away to give her privacy to dress. She suspected that asking him to do so would only invite one of his dismissive remarks, so she turned her back on him instead and tried to pretend he wasn't present. After she dressed, she looked back to see that he had wandered over to the counter of food, and was looking at it skeptically. He picked up a cheese pastry, sniffed it, and then threw it at the cook. He hit her on the top of her head, making her start, and wave at the air beside her head as if to discourage an annoying fly.

Xaz couldn't help snickering, which made Alizarin smile. "There may be hope for you yet, Mancer." He brushed flaky bits of pastry from the tips of his fingers. "So. What now? Do you run and hide? Smite those who have wronged you? Clear your name? Or just stretch your metaphysical legs, and see what you can do with them? Because, in case you are not aware, you currently have access to more power than you have ever had in your life. There's no knowing yet exactly what you're capable of—a Numenmancer tied to the Abyss. But I, at least, look forward to finding out."

Having for the moment nowhere else to go, Xaz sat

in front of the fire, enjoying its warmth but not her own thoughts. Alizarin lounged next to her, his body bending in a way that suggested bones and joints not quite identical to a human's.

"I don't know," Xaz admitted. "I'm being hunted. I cannot return to my own home." For the moment, the demon was keeping her from being noticed, but his kind was not known for consistency. As soon as something distracted him, she would need to fend for herself. "We killed—I don't know how many guards we killed. They will not stop searching for me. I will have to find a way to change my appearance. Flee to the countryside. I—" She brushed his tail away as it wrapped around her, and tickled her nose. "Stop that."

"You're being dull," he remarked.

"I'm answering you."

"The soldiers have already found their prey," he reported. "The spawn saw to that. He fed them an Abyssumancer to appease their bloodlust."

"What?" Xaz had heard of spawn before, but had never met one, and certainly never earned one's friendship or loyalty. "Why would one of them help me?"

"Not you," the Abyssi answered, rolling onto his back and stretching like a dog who wants its belly rubbed. "The guard who led the hunt for you. The one who poisoned you. He summoned the spawn and had a second boon of him. The spawn's reply did not clear your name completely, but many believe the words against you and the Numenmancer's tools found in your home were an Abyssumancer's trick, to lure the guards close and make sure they prepared to face the wrong power."

"They believe that?" she asked, incredulous. How would an Abyssumancer have acquired such belongings as they would have found in her home?

"It is easier to believe in an Abyssumancer's plot," Alizarin replied, his grin revealing sharp teeth, "than to believe a Numenmancer breached the Abyss, and a loyal guard meddled with blood-magic. That would be unthinkable."

He sprang to his feet in a fluid movement that seemed to reveal shadow and flame beneath his otherwise beautiful, almost disarming, form. Xaz flinched back instinctively, and in the next moment he was gone. As she pushed herself up and looked around, it seemed that the cook turned at the sound; Xaz hurriedly sought the door, and as she pushed through it, she heard the cook call, "Hello?"

Likewise, back in the main room, she was once again visible. One man swatted her on the backside and called for a meal, mistaking her for a woman working in the tavern, but she kept moving until she was back outside.

Where did you go, you foul little blue beast? she wondered.

No matter what assurances he had given her, she knew she needed to get away from the docks. She was too well-known there, and if Cinnabar was the one who had reported her, then the gossip that she was a mancer had surely made it through the entire Order of A'hknet by now.

Her heart nearly stopped when she saw Cinnabar and Cadmia Paynes walking together; she ducked back into the shadows of an alley as they passed, and only remembered to breathe once they were well away. She kept her head down as if against the cold-blowing wind, and tried not to give anyone reason to look twice at her as she cut through the outskirts of the city. There was no firm plan in her mind except to flee those who would gladly turn her over to the soldiers again.

CHAPTER 12

It *had* been too long, Cadmia realized as she walked through the market with Cinnabar.

Unlike the central market, the one by the docks was loud, crowded, and rank. The brine of the ocean mingled with the smells of fresh and rotting fish, and the inescapable odor of sailors who had been too long without a proper bath.

A sealing ship was loading casks of salt in preparation for its journey north. The captain of a Tamari vessel heavy with rice, coffee, and assorted luxury goods was arguing loudly with a customs officer, while the mate of a Silmari vessel was soliciting crewmen for its next trip out.

The noise, smell, and general commotion was overwhelming now, though Cadmia knew that there had been a time in her life when this had been commonplace. Certainly Cinnabar had no problem with it.

They stopped at Mother's cart-based shop. Though she carried some useful items like herbal remedies—the ones for hangover were always the best sellers there—most of Mother's trade was in trinkets and gifts suitable for a sailor returning home to a sweetheart he hoped to find waiting.

She smiled warmly when she saw Cadmia.

"If it isn't Scarlet's girl," Mother greeted her. "It's been too long. Is life in the violet order not treating you well?"

"It treats me fine," Cadmia answered. "I had an impulse to come down here. I *have* missed you. I'm sorry I haven't visited more often."

"They say an impulse you can't explain is caused by the Others whispering in your ears," Mother remarked.

"Hm." There was no good way to reply to that. Cadmia's education with the Order of the Napthol had covered concepts like that, but she was not supposed to discuss them with anyone outside the order. "How has business been?" she asked instead, deliberately changing the subject.

"Better when the Quin aren't down here stealing from me," Mother griped. "Those boys think they own the city."

Not any more, they don't. The thought struck Cadmia like a kick in the guts, but again, her knowledge of the attack, the arrest, and Hansa's protestations of innocence weren't things she could talk about.

She was searching mentally for another subject when

Mother nodded to someone in the crowd, and said to Cinnabar, "Looks like someone's looking for you."

Cadmia and Cinnabar both looked up and caught sight of the man Mother had noticed. Handsome, well-groomed, and immaculately attired, the dark-haired gentleman stood out in the crowd of sailors and mongers. He was working his way deliberately through the crowd, his eyes on Cinnabar.

"Do you know him?" Cadmia asked, under her breath.

"Never seen him in my life," Cinnabar murmured. But he didn't look down. Instead, he boldly met the other man's gaze, and smiled.

Cadmia took a step back, uncomfortably recalling why she generally didn't come here, even for a brief visit. Even though it was barely a twenty-minute walk between the docks and the city proper, location of both the Quinacridone Compound and the Cobalt Hall, this place fostered a disregard for the laws of the land. Too many foreign sailors, unfamiliar with or flat-out disdainful of Kavet customs, turned the port into a morally gray place.

For example, Cadmia had no doubt that Cinnabar had already balanced his desire to be friendly with Cadmia and the risk of getting arrested against the likelihood that this stranger had as much coin in his pockets as his attire suggested. He hadn't exactly put his back to Cadmia, but he had shifted position so they didn't appear to be together.

"Are you Cinnabar of A'hknet?" the man asked,

once he was close enough not to need to shout over the crowd.

"That's me," Cinnabar answered. "What can I do for you?"

"So very many things," the man said, bright blue eyes raking down Cinnabar's body before returning to his face. "But right now, it's more about what I intend to do for you."

"I'm flexible."

"I've heard that." *Time to leave,* Cadmia thought, knowing her face was bright red at the verbal byplay. When she started to try to slide unobtrusively back into the crowd, however, the man unerringly caught her gaze and said, "You may wish to stay, Cadmia. Our conversation might interest a Sister of the Napthol."

Cinnabar tensed, obviously reevaluating his impression of this man, and his assumptions about what he wanted.

Mother broke in, asking, "Are you here to buy something, or to be a pest?"

The man quirked a brow, then reached into his pocket, and dropped a pair of silver coins on top of the shelf she had set up across the wagon handles. "The red silk shawl there."

Mother looked at the coins, then the shawl. She took the former while wrapping the latter in white paper, then handed the merchandise over without bickering about the price, which meant that her customer had just offered so much money that she didn't want to risk having him realize his mistake.

"A gift for a special lady?" Cinnabar asked.

"An engagement present for a friend's fiancée."

"Men who buy red silk for their friends' future brides usually aren't terribly interested in preserving the friendship," Cinnabar observed.

"That all depends on how you define friendship," the man said. "You and I, for example, could probably have a lovely one, assuming you don't rot in a Quinacridone jail, or have your guts torn out by an Abyssi."

"*Excuse me?*" All Cinnabar's practiced flirting disappeared in the face of the stranger's blunt words.

"Your testimony against Dioxazine led to the deaths of nearly a dozen Quin guards. They think you misled them deliberately, sent them into a trap against an Abyssumancer. The mancers, of course, just think you report to the Quin."

"Who *are* you?" Cadmia demanded.

"Someone who's willing to help out your friend . . . and yourself."

"They captured the mancer," Cadmia asserted, a little less certainly than she would have liked.

"They captured an innocent man and you know it. The Quin know it now, too, which puts the two of you in an awkward position. They wouldn't dare cause trouble for a Sister of the Napthol, but they wouldn't think much about using a monger as a scapegoat."

Cinnabar had gone pale, but that wasn't where Cadmia's gaze was locked. Instead, she was looking at blue eyes. Electric blue.

"I thought you deserved a warning," the man said

to Cinnabar, who nodded without a word. "I also happen to know of a Silmari trading vessel shipping out soon that's still looking for an extra hand or two."

"Why are you helping me?" Cinnabar asked, pulling himself together. "I don't even *know* you."

"I would hate to see a man punished for daring to do what he thought was the right thing," the blue-eyed man answered.

Or he's trying to remove a witness, Cadmia thought. Instinct, or paranoia? She remembered what Hansa had said about the creature who had helped him. All he saw was blue eyes. *They seemed to glow.* This man's eyes weren't exactly *glowing,* but they were brighter than she had ever seen.

"Can you tell me what exactly has happened?" she asked, trying to keep her tone calm and nonjudgmental. "I think I've missed something."

"Well . . ." The man paused, as if he needed to think about it. "Hansa Viridian has been released, but I suppose that's no surprise to you, as the Sister who interviewed him." Did he see her shock and ignore it? Or was he so certain of the truth of his statement that he was oblivious to her response? "The Quin discovered the real Abyssumancer, and in interrogation he admitted to planting a Numenmancer's tools on Dioxazine so the guards would walk into his trap unprepared."

"What about Viridian's wounds?" She wasn't thinking about Cinnabar any more. She was thinking about what she had seen, and heard . . . and *said.* Could she have spoken against an innocent man?

"What wounds?" the blue-eyed man responded, innocently. "The only person who claims to have seen them was Hansa's hysterical fiancée."

It was at that moment that Cadmia became stone-sure that there was more going on than this man was reporting.

Cinnabar, like any good child of A'hknet, shook his head and said, "Doesn't matter to me if he is or isn't guilty. What's the name of that ship?"

"The *Tally-ho*. I've already spoken to the captain on your behalf, but the sooner you report, the more he'll probably like you."

"I . . . thank you."

The blue-eyed man smiled once again, and said, "Maybe I'll look you up onboard later."

"Any time." Cinnabar's smile was a ghost of its usual stuff. "Caddy . . . I'll see you around." He kissed her cheek, barely a peck, said goodbye to Mother, and then hurried off as if Abyssi were chasing his heels.

Maybe they were.

The stranger started away from Mother's cart, and Cadmia followed.

Softly, she said, "I saw the tools they took from Dioxazine. No one but a Numenmancer would have had them. An Abyssumancer wouldn't even have been able to acquire them."

"Sister, you may be allowed to discuss the Others with impunity, but as a simple citizen of Kavet I do believe it would be illegal for me to speculate on the subject."

But his eyes were dancing with amusement.

She bit her tongue, because he was right . . . *damn it* . . . even if she was certain he was playing with her.

She was still trying to form another question for him when she saw Novice Sienna waving at her through the crowd, trying to get her attention. When she ran forward, Cadmia thought she would mention Hansa's release, but that wasn't the subject on her mind.

"Cadmia, do you have Pearl with you?" Sienna asked, breathless.

"Pearl? Why would she be with me?" Cadmia responded.

"I have no idea why, but I was hoping anyway. She's been missing for . . . I'm not sure for how long, actually, but no one remembers seeing her for *hours,* probably since she last went outside."

"Would she have run away?" the stranger asked.

Cadmia wanted to snap at him to stay out of this, but Sienna answered, wringing her hands. "She's always been happy at the Hall. And she *never* goes anywhere without permission. I think she's afraid if she wanders off, no one will be there when she comes back."

"That girl should not be alone in this city." In contrast to his cavalier or frankly manipulating tone earlier, the man now seemed genuinely concerned. To Sienna, he said, "You should go back to the Hall."

"No, we should alert the guards," Cadmia argued, trying to think of the best way to respond . . . only to realize that Sienna had already turned away, and was ignoring her as she followed the stranger's "suggestion."

"You don't want sighted guards looking for her," he said.

"You're not implying . . . Pearl is the sweetest little girl I've ever met!" Cadmia hissed. "Every guard in the One-Twenty-Six already knows and adores her. She likes to bring them cookies and cider and talk to them while they're on duty. And how would you know anything, unless—"

As her mind caught up to her mouth, Cadmia realized her suspicions had not only crystallized into certainty, but that the stranger knew it. Cadmia took a step back, eyes searching for the nearest guard as she drew breath to call out.

"I have no intention of harming you," the man said, his tone still casual, as if he were discussing the weather, "and in fact, I may be able to help you find Pearl, but if you raise your voice at this moment I *can* kill you, without anyone in this plaza noticing, much less raising a hand to help you."

"Do you know where she is?" Cadmia asked, in a soft, trembling voice.

"I may be able to make some inquiries," he responded, "*if* you agree not to cause trouble for Mars's newest Quin hero."

"You monster," Cadmia hissed. "You would really hold the safety of a nine-year-old child hostage, just for my silence?"

"Your voice is getting loud," he warned, prompting her to snap her mouth shut again. "And yes, I would. I don't do *favors*, but I will make *deals*. You stay out of our way, and I will do my best to return Pearl to you, or, if she is already safe and wishes to stay where she is, to let you know as much."

For all she knew, he was the one who had taken Pearl—just as she was now quite sure that he had healed Hansa, and probably manipulated events to secure that guard's freedom.

The Others cannot lie, she thought, *and if he is spawn, like Hansa believed, they also cannot back out of an agreement once they have given their word.* If she was right about what he was, then he would *need* to help Pearl, as long as she kept her mouth shut about Hansa.

She had felt Hansa's innocence when she went to him. If this creature had healed him for its own reasons, then every word Hansa had spoken in his own defense had probably been true. He wasn't a mancer; he had been caught in a trap involving magic and creatures beyond his training or understanding. In that case, did she even *want* to cause more trouble for him?

Or was she just justifying her own actions, when she said, "If you will do everything in your power to ensure Pearl's safe return to the Cobalt Hall, then I will refrain from mentioning my . . . concerns . . . to anyone."

"If I discover Pearl had a good reason to leave the Hall of her own free will, I will not force her to return. But I will see to her safety."

Cadmia nodded. "Do I say thank you?" she asked.

"We shake hands," he said, "and then you don't see me again until I intend for you to."

They did, and then he was gone in the crowd, as if he had never been there.

CHAPTER 13

After a meeting with Winsor Indathrone, in which Hansa was informed that he had acted valiantly when he had confronted the demon and slain the responsible Abyssumancer, Hansa returned to his apartment with the intention of curling up in bed and not thinking about the fact that he had obviously done no such thing.

In the morning, he would visit Ruby and beg her forgiveness.

How would he approach her? Should he apologize outright? Should he wait for *her* to apologize?

Would he ever be able to tell her what really happened?

Self-consciously, he touched fingertips to the front of his new shirt—compliments of the Quinacridone—over his new scar.

Insist on this boon, on the other hand, and you will not be rid of me. . .

He shuddered as he pushed open the front door of his apartment. Exhausted and heartsick, he pulled off his winter outerwear and kicked off his boots. He would have liked a hot bath, to help take away the chill of the Quin dungeons, but didn't have the energy required to haul and heat water.

He was halfway across the living room when the assault came. All he could do was brace himself. The door slammed as he fell back against it, his wits slow to catch up to the fact that the slender shape that had launched itself at him was *Ruby.*

"I was waiting for you . . . I had to talk to you . . . I'm sorry," she whispered, her arms still wrapped around his neck, and her soft body leaning against his tense one. "I'm so sorry. I don't know how I believed that horrible story. I'm sorry!"

I saw the blood with my own eyes, she had said. Had Umber come up with an alternate explanation for how Hansa had been injured one minute and healed the next, or had he erased the memory of the brutal wounds from Ruby's mind? "Ruby, there's something I have to tell you—"

"Not tonight," she said. She raised onto her toes and kissed him with trembling lips. "I can't talk tonight. I need you to just hold me and tell me you're okay and that you forgive me."

"Of course I forgive you." How could he *not*? He was the one who should have been begging *her* to forgive *him*.

"Jenkins is dead, Hansa," Ruby whispered. "Did they tell you that?"

"I saw it. I'm so sorry. It was too fast. There was nothing I could do."

She let out a whimpering cry and buried her face in his shoulder. Her body trembled against his, soft and rounded but alarmingly chilled.

I do believe my little sister has a crush on you, Hansa. Be nice. Jenkins's teasing warning from years before, when Hansa had been eighteen and Ruby fifteen, floated through Hansa's mind. Four years later, it had changed to, *You might as well give in. Ruby gets what she wants.* Finally, when Hansa had told him about buying the ring, Jenkins's only response had been, *It's about time. Be good to her.*

Jenkins wouldn't be beside Hansa at the wedding. He wouldn't be there to tease Hansa about his anxiety or to congratulate him on finally finding the nerve to tie the knot.

There was nothing I could do! Hansa told himself.

You saved yourself by letting a monster meddle with my sister's mind. Twice.

The words weren't from Jenkins's ghost—normal people couldn't see or hear the dead that way—but they might as well have been.

"Ruby—"

In response to his saying her name, Ruby lifted her face and pressed her lips to his again. He could taste the salt of her tears.

Give her a kiss for me.

The memory of Umber's combination of threats and promises, combined with his imagination's rendering of Jenkins's horror, made him stiffen and instinctively recoil.

"I'm sorry," Ruby whispered. "I said such horrible things to you, and now here I am throwing myself at you like all should instantly be forgiven." She stood up, backing away. "I'm sorry. I'll . . . I'll go."

She turned to flee, and he caught her arm. "Don't. It isn't like that. I just . . ." She turned back to him, tears in her beautiful eyes. "I have too many awful things in my head right now."

She nodded, biting her lower lip. "Of course. And you must be exhausted. I am, too. We should both get some rest. Do you need anything before I go?"

I need you, he could have said. *Should* have said, for her benefit. "You shouldn't be alone," he managed.

"Olive said she would stay over tonight." It took Hansa a moment to place the name. Ruby had friends at the herbarium, but Hansa hadn't met many of them. "She's making a tisane to make sure I sleep. I'll see you tomorrow?"

"Breakfast?" he suggested. *Somewhere with air and sunlight, and no blood or screaming or iron doors. That's all I ask.*

Ruby nodded again. "I think the Green Jewel still serves breakfast?" she suggested. "I doubt either of us wants to cook."

He forced a smile, and saw her relax a little. "I'll see you tomorrow."

He wanted to add something sweet, or suave, or romantic, but nothing came. They said awkward goodbyes, and then Hansa was alone. He climbed into bed, but it was a long time before he fell asleep.

When he did, he tumbled into dreams of the Abyss.

The world was full of black fire. He was trying to walk between the flames, but every time he brushed against one, they seared, and drew blood, until it ran down his skin from dozens of lacerations. Still he stumbled onward, trying to flee.

He had to get out. He couldn't stay here. This wasn't his world.

"Let me help you," a voice said, as someone took his hand and pulled him through the flames, onto an endless plain, surrounded by needle-like mountains on all sides.

He turned to thank his savior, and found himself facing a creature out of nightmare, darkness made solid. Pain shot up his arm from the hand it still gripped as if with a vise of needles. He tried to scream, but the breath he drew was full of smoke, so he choked instead.

He woke coughing, shaking and sweating as if in the grip of the worst winter flu. His entire arm ached, the pain radiating upward from his tightly-clenched fist.

He had to fight to relax, to tell his body it was just a dream. Nightmares were understandable, after what he had been through.

It *was* just a dream, wasn't it?

He looked at his hand, remembering how the Abyssumancer's blade had felt when it had cut him. Could it have done something to him? Would it be stupider to ask someone, or to risk someone with the sight noticing something off about him that he *hadn't* reported?

This was the kind of quandary he would have gone to Jenkins about.

The thought hit him hard, taking his legs out from under him.

He couldn't stand to speak to other guards yet, and after his disastrous interview with Cadmia Paynes he didn't dare seek guidance from the Napthol.

He cleaned up, dressed, and then walked to the Green Jewel Inn as if in a trance.

His already dark mood was not helped when his gaze swept over the crowd in the breakfast room and he beheld a familiar figure at another table, one long leg hooked over the bottom rung of his stool as he nursed a drink and chatted with the young woman sitting next to him.

Hansa stood, prepared to challenge the half-breed before Ruby arrived, and immediately heard Umber's voice quite clearly in his mind:

Sit down. We'll talk about this in a minute.

Hansa took a step forward, with the thought, *Oh, no, we'll talk about this right now.*

Umber chuckled at something the woman next to him said, but his silent voice was cold. *This pretty girl next to me happens to be a Numenmancer. She is confident that she is well-hidden, but if the hero of Kavet approaches us right now, she is going to panic, and you and your beloved are all going to be in the middle of her undoubtedly violent response. So sit. Back. Down.*

Hansa sat, resisting the instinct to take a second look at the woman Umber had identified as a mancer. He had seen enough to know it wasn't Dioxazine, and he didn't want to put all innocent bystanders at risk by trying to see more.

He jumped as a hand touched his shoulder.

"Sorry," Ruby said. As he stood to greet her properly, her eyes widened. "Oh, darling, you look exhausted. Did you sleep at *all*?"

His shoulder blades itched as he tried to ignore the mancer and spawn on the other side of the room. "A little. Not well. How are you?"

"I . . . don't know," she admitted. "I feel numb. I tell myself Jenkins is dead and I just feel *blank*. I can't make myself believe it. I know it will hit me eventually, but until then I'm just going through the motions."

"I know how you feel." *At least you didn't wear his blood and then get arrested for his murder.* Hansa shoved the nasty thought away, and dropped his gaze to the menu so she wouldn't see it in his eyes. He was too tense, too tired, too overwhelmed, but he didn't want to take it out on her. He struggled to think of something he *could* stand to say to her. *It's my fault for not realizing what Dioxazine was years ago, and for somehow tipping her off at the door so she had time to summon that creature. I'm a coward for running. I've never felt so helpless in my life. And now I'm only sitting here because I broke the laws I swore I would fight and die if necessary to uphold.*

The silence had stretched too long while he considered and discarded ideas. She asked, "Will you have to visit his parents?"

She asked as if Jenkins's parents weren't hers, too. Hansa almost said, *That's the captain's job,* then remembered Captain Feldgrau was dead, too. "Someone from the Napthol will," he said. "They wouldn't want to see me." Ruby hadn't spoken to her parents in years, but Jenkins had kept in touch a little.

He was about to say that they should probably visit *his* parents—Jenkins had been like a second son to them, and they deserved to hear what had happened from Hansa instead of a messenger from the 126 or the Napthol—but a chuckle from the mancer behind him made the hairs down the back of his neck lift. With relief he realized she was standing up and saying farewell to Umber. She strolled out of the Green Jewel without a single glance at Hansa, and some of the tightness left his chest.

We should talk now, Umber suggested, at the same time that Ruby sighed and said, "Do you want to talk about . . . it? About . . . how it happened, I mean?"

Her wide expression and trembling lip said *she* didn't want to, but was trying to give him what he needed. Wasn't that supposed to be his job—to take care of her?

He couldn't speak aloud to Umber, but knew the spawn had previously read his thoughts, so he tried responding by clearly thinking, *Later. For now, you aren't supposed to be here.*

I was here first, Umber replied. *I'll meet you out back.*

Umber stood, and smiled at the waitress as he paid his tab. Judging by the woman's expression, the tip he left was generous.

"Hansa?" Ruby prompted.

"I'm sorry, I . . . I don't even know how to—" *Now, Quin!* "—put what happened in words. I don't think I want to," he admitted.

"Well then," Ruby said in a voice full of forced lightness and cheer. "You don't have to. But you do have to take care of yourself. I'm going to make sure you eat, then put you back to bed."

If you make me come over there, you're going to have to introduce me, Umber threatened.

"I'm sorry," Hansa said, "I need to deal with something. I'll be right back." Umber wasn't supposed to be able to come near Ruby, but Hansa didn't have much faith in the rules he had set out when demanding the second boon.

Ruby frowned, but said, "Okay. I'll order for you?"

"It won't take long," he assured her. He tried to kiss her goodbye, but she nodded and turned her face away with the excuse of looking at a menu Hansa knew she had to have memorized by now.

Trying to hide his sudden desire to strangle someone, Hansa made his way to the back door of the inn. Outside, leaning against the wall, stood Umber. Despite the frigid autumn air, he didn't even have the decency to wear a proper cloak or gloves or otherwise make any attempt to appear normal.

"What do you want?" Hansa demanded. "In case you hadn't noticed, my almost-fiancée is waiting for me."

"Oh, you're engaged again, are you?" Umber asked, without the least bit of interest in his voice. "I'm sure that's very important to you, but I couldn't care less. I need you to do something for me."

Hansa couldn't help a snicker. "No."

He turned to go back inside, and Umber stepped in the way. "I've made you into a hero, Hansa. The least you can do is play the part."

"Not for *you*," Hansa pointed out. "We made our deal. As far as I understand, that means it's over. I don't have to—"

"Fine," Umber said. "You made your demon-deal. You won the woman, and became everyone's favorite man. You are under no obligation to live up to your legend."

"Damn right."

"After all, the city was perfectly willing to lock you up and throw away the key before you were guilty."

"Do you have a *point*?" Hansa grumbled. "Or are you going to get out of the way?"

"My point is," Umber said, "maybe the girl won't blame you, when she faces the next century in slavery. But I certainly will."

Hansa sighed heavily. "What girl?"

"Oh, now you're listening?" Umber asked, quirking one eyebrow.

"Not for long, unless you get around to telling me before I decide I would rather be *inside*, with my fiancée and a nice breakfast, than *outside,* freezing, with a half-demon pervert."

Umber looked skyward for a moment, before saying, "I'll ignore the end of that sentence, and the many responses it deserves, because I don't want to see Pearl hurt."

Hansa's attention suddenly focused, all awareness of the cold fading away. "What's wrong with Pearl?"

"She ran off," Umber explained. "She has been perfectly safe inside the Cobalt Hall, but now she has ended up among very unsavory people. I need you to take her back. And to be clear, this is in no way related to our boon," Umber added. "I am asking you because you possess the traits necessary, no other reason. If you do what I say, you should be perfectly safe, but in the case that there are any repercussions, I will deal with them, as part of this simple arrangement."

"The fact that you feel the need to *say* that makes me nervous," Hansa said. But it was *Pearl.* "What do you need me to do?"

CHAPTER 14

Xaz had spent the night curled up in the back of an unheated shed. She couldn't freeze to death, but her body alternated between shivering and actually *sweating*, the result of the Abyssal power still in her body. The Abyssi—Alizarin, he called himself—came and went, a less-than-soothing warmth when he was present.

She had decided that the Abyssumancer had targeted her intentionally. She had seen the expression on his face. He hadn't been trying to get rid of evidence, and he certainly hadn't thrown that blade randomly. He had been ordered to attack her and then give himself up.

Why?

Why would an Abyssumancer—or more likely, an Abyssi—intentionally infect a Numenmancer with Abyssal power? The Others gained power through their mancers. They wouldn't casually sacrifice one.

On the other hand, if he hadn't infected her, then she wouldn't have had a bond to the Abyss. She wouldn't have been able to pull Alizarin into the human plane. Had that been the goal all along? If so, then he might have arranged for the attempted arrest, as well. Without it, she never would have been desperate enough to summon *anything*. She hadn't thought Abyssi were able to plan that well, but all she knew of the Abyssal realm came from the Numini, who disdained the Abyssi as mindless animals and therefore might underestimate them.

She had to go back to the temple. That was the only place she could get the information or assistance she needed.

The temple wasn't part of the Numen or Abyss, but it didn't exist fully on the mortal plane either. Well-rested, with proper tools and a prepared ritual space, she would have opened a rift to it on her own, but that wasn't an option at the moment. Thankfully, there were other ways. She wasn't sure if the doorways were intentionally created by the Others, or sprang up with no more deliberation than flowers after rain, but they were the only way sick or otherwise weakened mancers could get to the temple. The doorways themselves were regularly found and destroyed by Quin guards, but the temple remained safely out of reach. Even sighted guards would be destroyed by a passage through rift.

"Do you know where the nearest temple rift is?" she asked Alizarin. If she needed to scry to find it, she would need to gather tools. She didn't need anything elaborate, but given her current circumstance, she preferred to avoid any extra risks.

"Of course," he answered. "But why would you want to go there?"

"I still—" His tail wrapped around her, and she batted it away. "I still need supplies, and since you—" This time his tail chucked under her chin. "Stop that. Since you aren't Numini, I can't get them through you."

"Why do you need them?" he asked, propping himself up on one elbow to look up at her, so he was effectively spooning around her back.

"For one, so I don't get in trouble with any *more* of your kind," she pointed out.

Alizarin *hmph*ed, his tail twitching again. He hooked it around her waist, and she decided maybe it was best to just leave it there. "I can protect you from other Abyssi."

"Until you see something shiny, and run off," she said. "Your kind isn't known for long attention spans or impulse control. I also need to be able to hide us from any of the Quin guards who have the sight. That requires tools."

"Not for an Abyssumancer."

"Which would be helpful, if I were—*stop it!*" This last as he started tickling her nose. "You're the one who asked me why! Stop distracting me so I can tell you."

"You weren't saying anything interesting," Alizarin complained. "You should pet me."

"I—what? No. Alizarin, can you focus for just a moment? We need—"

"You want to," he interrupted, utterly unmoved by her pleas.

"No, I *don't*. I want to find the temple, get supplies, and then—"

"Pet the Abyssi."

"You're not a *cat*," she bit out. "I do not. Want. To pet. The Abyssi. I *want* to find the temple."

"You don't know *what* you want," Alizarin said. "Too much time among the Numini. You want to pet me."

She patted him twice on the head. "There. Okay?" His hair was incredibly soft, and seemed to reach toward her hand.

He sighed, and for a moment thought he had grown bored of the game and was ready to give up, but instead he moved in front of her. She yelped as he put a hand on her shoulder and leaned forward, overbalancing her so she toppled onto her back, and put a hand up to push him away.

He leaned down, and nuzzled at her chin, then rubbed his cheek against hers, just like an overgrown cat. Only, he wasn't a cat. He was a *demon*. A demon who, aside from the fur and the tail, was shaped like a man. The combination was unnerving in this position, no matter how pretty his fur was.

"Get off me," she said.

"Pet the Abyssi," he insisted.

"Get off me, and *then* I'll pet the Abyssi," she offered, as a compromise.

He paused to consider for a moment, and then rolled off her, propping his head on his hands as he stretched out on his back. If he had been a cat, the image would have been amusing, innocent, even adorable. Though his words had been every bit as childlike and naïve as a kitten, given his form, the posture was sensual, beautiful, and threatening.

She sat up, now regretting the deal she had just proposed, and he wrapped his tail around her waist and tugged her forward so she fell onto his chest.

"This is absurd," she mumbled. She lay against Alizarin's side—she didn't have much choice about *that,* what with his tail locked tightly around her waist—and tentatively put a hand on his shoulder, then ran her palm down his upper arm. The fur there was less than an inch long, and heartbreakingly soft. Looking closely, she could see that each individual hair was variegated, ranging from black to cobalt to emerald to aquamarine, iridescent.

Maybe a minute had passed before she realized she had snuggled against the Abyssi, and with her cheek resting on his shoulder, she was petting his chest in slow, loverlike motions. There was something hypnotic about the shine and the impossible softness of that blue-green pelt, and so even after she noticed what she was doing, at first she didn't really *care.*

Alizarin's tail twitched, tickling her spine at her lower back, and making her shudder. Of course he noticed the reaction, and did it again, with the same result.

"You have a ticklish spot," he said.

"Thanks for pointing it out," she grumbled. "For a moment I was in danger of feeling peaceful."

"You're happier now," he said.

She almost argued with him, and then she realized that she *was* feeling better . . . and she hadn't realized she was feeling badly beforehand. Her head felt clearer, and the dull ache behind her eyes was gone. It was more than just being more relaxed; touching him had settled her magic.

Power lies, she thought, remembering the warning she had been taught when she was first learning a mancer's trade. *It will woo you, and it will try to comfort you, but it lies.*

She wanted to snuggle up against the Abyssi and rub her whole body on that incredible fur, but she could resist *that* impulse, at least for the moment.

"You're right," she admitted. "I did want to pet the Abyssi. And I still do. But we need to find the temple first. We can't stay here forever."

"Why not?" he asked, with a stretch.

"Because . . ." She struggled to find reasoning that would make sense to him. Finally, she decided on, "It would be boring."

"Hm." He nodded and rolled to his feet, in a liquid motion she envied. There was strength and grace in that catlike frame—more than she could imagine, or for that matter *wanted* to imagine. His current form looked disarmingly beautiful, but she remembered what it had done to human flesh when she was almost arrested.

"How far away is the nearest temple doorway?" she asked.

"The *nearest* one, no one uses. They don't remember it's there," he said.

Xaz frowned. "Where is it?"

"In the palace," Alizarin answered.

It took her a moment to realize what he had just said. "The Quinacridone? There is a temple doorway inside the Quin central compound?"

Alizarin nodded. "Power ran in the royal line for many generations."

"Oh." She had heard rumors of sorcery in the overthrown royal house, but had assumed they were just attempts to discredit the family during the revolution.

"The next nearest doorway rift is maybe two days walking from here," Alizarin said, "but you don't need one. I can carry you there."

"*Will* you?" The Abyssi's reactions were so unpredictable to her that it hadn't occurred to her to ask him.

In response, he did just that, sweeping them out of the mortal realm and into the sphere of Other power that was the temple.

For her, entering the temple was usually like stepping into a swiftly-flowing river. The power tried to pull her away, and she needed to struggle to keep her feet. This time, it was like she had dived headfirst into the pounding surf that pounded Kavet during a storm. Normally, Abyssi and Abyssal power existed as shadows at the edge of her awareness, but the taint in her magic made her overwhelmingly aware of everything.

The temple, which she normally perceived as an icy cave filled with the scents of honey and lilac, now reeked of blood and smoke. The translucent, crystalline walls were stained and streaked with velvety-dark patches.

Worse were the Abyssi themselves. She could see them, not as solid forms but like glowing afterimages left from staring too long at the sun. They pulsed and writhed and *they could see her, too.*

"What's this?" one hissed, slithering closer to her. Its voice rang in her mind, making her head ache.

"Cold meat," another answered disdainfully. *"Reeks of Numini."*

"I've heard Numini are good to eat," the first said, *"if you can catch one."*

Xaz looked around desperately, but if Alizarin was here she couldn't find him, and the others were hanging back.

These Abyssi might just be grandstanding. The temple should be a safe place; the Others made it impossible for mancers to hurt each other there, which was the only way Numenmancers and Abyssumancers could be in the same place at the same time. But normally Abyssi couldn't see Numenmancers, or the reverse.

The few Numini she saw ducked away, ignoring her plight.

Instead, she caught the gaze of another Numenmancer, who was wrestling with a small figure who lacked the glimmer of a mancer's power.

"I thought you must be dead," the mancer said. Compared to the Others, her voice was like a whisper, barely audible. "The stir you made." The softness didn't hide the disdain and irritation in her tone. Xaz understood the emotion; every time one of them was caught, life became harder for the rest of them. "And I was left to finish your task."

Pearl. With no magic or training, the girl had to be utterly overwhelmed by the temple's power.

Bitterly, Xaz thought, *The Numini didn't waste time, did they? As soon as I was injured they cast me aside and found another for their task.*

She spun, world swimming, as one of the Abyssi touched her. She shouldn't have turned her back on it. She gathered her power to cast it aside, but the creature just laughed. The little Abyssal magic that flowed through her was just enough to get her in trouble, not enough to help her fight.

"Not yours."

The words were spoken in a deep, rumbling purr that made Xaz's bones vibrate. The power that accompanied them made the Abyssi who had harassed her seem like kittens in comparison—and, thank Numen, it was familiar.

"Alizarin," she breathed, turning with wary relief as the other Abyssi scattered.

In this place, the Abyssi's veneer of near-humanity was gone, leaving only a hair-raising sense of fangs and claws in the dark. Could she sense his power better than the others because she was bonded to him, or was he actually this much more fearsome?

"I told you, I can protect you from other Abyssi," Aliza-

rin said. *"My sire was the last lord of the Abyss. Nothing this close to the human plane is a threat to us."*

That was both comforting and terrifying.

She shook off her unease. She had things to do.

"You won't find your Numini here," the other Numenmancer informed her. "I've heard them whispering. Your Numini is in disgrace because his mancer caused such bloodshed and violence. He—"

She broke off as one of the Numini stepped forward. Given the way it loomed protectively over the other mancer, Xaz suspected it was bound to her.

"We cannot help you," it said flatly. *"You breached the boundary. You violated agreements made to us, and made agreements with the creatures of blood. You have tangled your power in the Abyssal realm, and until it is cleansed, we can make no further associations."*

"I just want to send the Abyssi *back*!" Xaz argued. "How do I do that?"

"I doubt you have that ability," the Numini said. *"Even if you did, you would probably still be unable to remove the infernal taint from your power. You must find a stronger conduit."*

How was Xaz supposed to fix *anything* if the Numini wouldn't help her? Break into the Quin dungeons to retrieve the supplies they confiscated from her home? Kill the Abyssi bound to her with her bare hands—oh, and in a way that didn't spill any blood? Neither seemed likely.

"You could ask the guard to help you," one of the weaker Abyssi who had shied away from Alizarin suggested with a syrupy tone of mock sympathy. When Alizarin turned to him, he took a step back and mur-

mured, *"I'm just trying to help your . . . what is she to you?"*

Alizarin growled. It was an elemental sound, and even the other Numenmancer seemed to hear it. She took a minute to create a bubble of protective power and tuck the unconscious Pearl inside to hold her and keep her safe, and then disappeared as she willed herself out of the temple.

"The one who calls himself Hansa. If you stay, you will see him," the other Abyssi said. *"He is working up the nerve to step through the rift at the well."*

Xaz's first response was relief—if the rift didn't destroy Hansa, the Others in the temple would. These Abyssi were held from harming mancers in this place, but would delight in the flesh of a poor Quin guard who stumbled into their sanctuary.

Unless . . .

She remembered the way Abyssal power had flowed around Hansa after he had arrested Baryte. He had been bloodied again when Xaz had summoned Alizarin, further tainted with infernal power. Could that have been enough for Baryte's Abyssi to make a connection to him once its previous mancer was dead?

Xaz didn't know for sure, but it seemed likely enough that Mars's newest hero had just become its newest mancer as well.

Either way, she didn't want to see him. She focused her thoughts and fled the temple.

She emerged from between two large boulders on the southern coast, a spot she knew well, though she hadn't used this rift in many years. Her parents' house was less than an hour's walk to the north, if one was desperate enough to cut through brackish marshland.

It was high tide, and salt spray stung her as it slapped against the rocky shore, soaking her skin and clothes. Further out to sea, she could see the islands occupied by the Osei; their wheeling winged shapes were visible in silhouette against the cobalt sky as they gyred in search of prey in the water. Their favorite prey this time of year was the blue sharks that schooled in the area, much to the ire of local fishermen.

Move! she ordered herself. She had been hypnotized by the play of light and shadow off the water, and the giant predators that hunted it. Some said the Osei were part Abyssi, a legacy of the royal house's meddling with infernal magic before the revolution and rise of the current democracy. Their tendency to eat people was one reason this isolated rift was rarely used, which meant she should get under cover.

There was a fire pit nearby, but it clearly hadn't been used in a long time. She cleared it out with rapidly-numbing fingers, then lethargically gathered driftwood and dried seaweed to burn. She wished she had an Abyssumancer's power to start a fire with her power, but had to settle for the flint and steel her younger self had hidden in a jelly jar under the rocks.

As she sat by the fire, she tested her power. Could she draw strength from the flame, like an Abyssumancer could? Could she cool it, the way she used to? She needed to know what she could still do so she could come up with a plan for what to do next.

CHAPTER 15

This is madness, Hansa thought as he stared at the well in front of him. Located at the back of a mostly-abandoned, rocky acre of scrub that had once been farmland, the well's wooden cover was rotten and half-collapsed. There was plenty of room to allow a crazy person to jump inside.

That was exactly what he had been told to do.

His breath made a white fog in front of his face as he stared into the blackness below. His fingertips trembled, but not from the cold.

No, he didn't feel *cold* at all. His heart was pounding much too fast for him to be affected by temperature.

He had told Ruby as much truth as he dared, but even though she adored Pearl as much as anyone, she hadn't understood why one of the other guards couldn't go. He couldn't tell her the assignment had come from a half-Abyssi creature instead of his captain. No matter how much Hansa wanted to cut all ties to Umber, he couldn't abandon Pearl. Not darling Pearl, who used to sit on the front steps of the Cobalt Hall for hours, and who sneaked out to deliver hot cider when he was serving that long, cold night's watch. He couldn't stand the thought of her being hurt.

He was still insane, and he knew it, to have agreed to Umber's plan.

He hadn't asked why Pearl meant so much to a half-Abyssi because he hadn't trusted him not to lie. Once Hansa got the girl, he was taking her straight back to the Cobalt Hall. He wouldn't have agreed to this plan if Umber had even implied he expected Hansa to turn Pearl over to him.

Now he was at the well.

Hansa wondered which of the many unpleasant ways he would die, if Umber was wrong, or had lied to him. Depending on how deep the well was, and whether or not it still had water, he might just break a leg, and die of infection or starvation. Or he could drown. Or freeze to death. Those options might, however, all be better than the possible ways to die if Umber was *right*, and telling the truth.

Trying to resist the instinct to hold his breath, Hansa stepped up onto the side of the well. He could not refrain from squeezing his eyes shut, as he took another step forward, his hands clenched into fists at his sides as he tried to keep himself from flailing out to try to stop his fall.

Instead of rock bottom, or cold water, he felt like he

hit a lake full of blood. Suddenly he was enveloped in warmth. His senses screamed *we'll drown!* as his eyes shot open.

Someone near him purred, *"Oh, look, fresh blood."*

"New?" someone else whistled.

"He isn't new," yet another voice replied. *"I've tasted that one before."*

Hansa struggled to keep from screaming. The voices that rippled around him had a physical quality, like hot breath on the back of his neck.

Or, suddenly, silky fur against his cheek.

"I know you," the one who had just brushed against him observed. *"You're the one Xaz stopped me from eating."*

Hansa struggled to remember all the things Umber had told him. Umber had not anticipated this *exact* situation, but he had explained to Hansa why it made perfect sense that a man who had just recently been a Quin guard would now be standing in a mancer's temple.

Then it's you who did this to me, Hansa told the Abyssi who had challenged him. The Abyssi who had slaughtered nearly a dozen Quin guards.

The world around Hansa turned green, rolling, as he realized that.

Stop that, the Abyssi snapped.

And, from somewhere else, a small whimper.

Umber had told him that technically, there was no "space" in the temple, no moving, but that everything was controlled by one's own mind. Even so, Hansa thought of himself as walking toward the small sound.

What he found, huddled at the back of the temple, was . . . almost a shadow. He couldn't quite see her, or feel her, or hear her. Umber had told him that would be the case, too.

"She isn't yours," a voice like icicles said. It was hard to hear, faint like a distant puff of wind.

"She shouldn't be here."

"That isn't your concern," the creature said. *"She was brought here. You have no claim to her. You cannot take from the temple that which you have no claim to."*

Umber had given several suggestions for dealing with the challenges Hansa was likely to face in the temple, but one had been at the top of the list, and it was the one Hansa went with now:

Run.

"I'll take you home," he said to the little girl, as he tried to wrap his thoughts around her. "Pearl?"

"Hansa?" Her voice sounded very far away, but at last, he felt her clinging back.

The hardest part is going to be getting out *of the temple,* Umber had said. *There is no physical door to open or pass through; you have to will yourself through it.*

With a demon quite possibly on his heels, one that had already nearly killed him once, Hansa found himself strangely motivated.

DOOR!

Abruptly, he was stumbling on a dew-covered mat of fallen leaves and pine needles near the defunct well, his arms wrapped around a crying child.

A moment later, the Abyssi was in front of him,

its fur glistening in the moonlight, and its tail lashing back and forth. "Quin, you and I should talk about your charade, before you go."

Hansa put his back to a tree, holding Pearl protectively as he searched for the mancer.

"Xaz is elsewhere," the Abyssi said. "As for the girl . . . I only want to talk to you. If she runs, I won't chase her."

Hansa set Pearl on her feet.

"Pearl, see the lights, way up there?" he asked, pointing the girl toward the inn that stood sentinel at the start of the path to the well. "You run toward them. Hide in the stables. There's a sweet horse there, and a kitten. *Run!* As fast as you can."

The girl took off, nearly flying, without needing another word. Umber would look for her in the stables if Hansa didn't make it out of this.

The Abyssi watched Pearl go for a moment, but then turned back to Hansa.

"So," the demon purred. "Let's start with, I recognize your taste. I've had your blood. The only thing I would recognize more easily is my own power, which is *not* the magic infecting you. A mancer wouldn't be able to tell the difference. Your story would have worked around most Abyssi. But not me. So explain yourself, before I remember I'm hungry, and decide that Xaz would probably not object to my killing a Quin guard who infiltrated the temple and stole someone from it."

Where was Umber? He had assured Hansa that he

would deal with any "consequences" of his taking Pearl from the temple. *This was a pretty serious consequence!*

"I'm not after the temple," Hansa said. He tried to edge away, and the Abyssi leaned forward, trapping Hansa between itself and a large oak trunk. "I don't care about the temple. I'm not going to *report* the temple. I learned that lesson."

The Abyssi smiled, baring twin rows of sharp teeth. "Oh, did you?" it asked. "That 'lesson' ended up making you the hero of Mars. I was worried you might have become arrogant."

"I want nothing more to do with mancers, demons, or half-breeds," Hansa avowed.

"Of course, the spawn," the Abyssi said. "The power is his. That must have been exciting for you."

Umber had lent Hansa enough power to make it through the rift and impersonate a mancer. The process had been uncomfortable to the extreme, and had involved knives and blood—and why had Hansa been surprised?

Hansa flinched as the Abyssi leaned forward, its cheek brushing against his.

"It doesn't have to involve blood," it whispered. "And, with all his magic pumping through you, he won't be able to take it back without your cooperation, so if you wish you can demand an alternative ritual."

"Why do I not feel like you're trying to help me?" Hansa asked, the words a little choked because he was straining away from the demon. Even through his cloak, vest, and shirt, his back was probably going to have a perfect map of the bark of the tree behind him later.

"Do you think I want you to *keep* that power?" the Abyssi asked.

"Mind if I cut in?"

Hansa had never been so grateful to see Umber in his life. The crossbreed stepped forward with no hesitation at all and wedged himself between Hansa and the Abyssi, facing the demon straight on. They were nearly the same height, both a couple inches taller than Hansa, and Umber didn't flinch as he looked into the glowing blue eyes.

Instead, he said, "Oh, how lovely. Blue." Leaning back against Hansa, who was frozen like a rabbit trying to evade notice by a predator, Umber reached up and caressed the demon's cheek, and then trailed his fingers through its hair. "And so soft. Dioxazine is a lucky, lucky girl."

Was Hansa going mad—a distinct possibility—or had the Abyssi just started to *purr*?

The Abyssi gave ground as Umber stepped forward a bit, now running a hand up its chest. "If the mancer ever bores you—and Numenmancers can be *so* dull—and you're looking for some fun—" He wrapped a hand around the back of the Abyssi's neck. "You are welcome to look me up."

Umber had by that point backed the Abyssi up until it was now leaning against the edge of the well; another nudge from Umber, and it obligingly leaned backward, balanced over the door to the rift. At first

Hansa thought Umber planned to push the Abyssi in, and he wondered what was going to stop it from coming back out, furious with them.

Instead, Umber kissed it.

Hansa backed away, but couldn't quite force his eyes from the two creatures, who strained toward each other, both apparently oblivious to Hansa.

Apparently oblivious . . . so *what in the name of the Abyss was he still doing there?*

After too long watching the two creatures twine tongues, he turned, and dashed toward where he had told Pearl to hide.

"Pearl?" he called, a strained whisper, as he stepped into the stables.

"Hansa!" The little girl appeared from behind a stack of barrels, and threw herself at the guard. "I got lost," she whimpered. "I got lost in there, and they wouldn't let me out . . ."

"Ssh. It's okay," he whispered. "But you've got to be a big girl now, Pearl. We can't stay here. Can you be a big girl, and hop up onto this horse with me, and I'll take you back to the Cobalt Hall?"

She nodded.

He lifted Pearl onto the horse Umber had lent him, which he had left saddled, anticipating he might need to make a quick escape. As he did so, he noted that there was now a second one, a roan stallion, in the stable. The beasts were rare enough in Kavet that he suspected the horse had to belong to Umber as well. Well, hopefully it would be there a long time, as the Abyssi and the Abyssi-spawn entertained each other.

Hansa's gorge tried to rise as that thought crossed his mind, and he failed to get a leg fully across the beast on the first try. At least his crazy, arm-waving attempt to get his balance without smacking Pearl, made Pearl giggle.

"Hold on," he warned her. "Off we go!"

As a member of the Quin guard, he was one of the few citizens of Mars who knew how to ride. Pearl on the other hand had obviously never been on a horse. She let out an exhilarated "Whee!" that made him laugh despite all else.

The second set of hoofbeats didn't register in Hansa's mind until Pearl let out a whimper, and Umber, on the roan stallion, drew up beside Hansa.

You can let the girl know I'm not going to hurt her.

Despite his better judgment, Hansa relayed the message. "It's okay, Pearl. This man helped me get you out of there."

Pearl nodded that she heard, but she didn't look up, and didn't seem to be enjoying the ride any more.

That was one of the most disgusting things I've ever seen, Hansa observed.

You've never seen some of the other *creatures of the Abyss,* Umber replied. *Where exactly do you think spawn come from?*

Another thought Hansa hadn't wanted to have.

The trick to kissing an Abyssi, Umber continued, apparently enjoying Hansa's discomfort about the subject, *is to always let him lead. Stick your tongue past all those sharp little teeth, and you will almost inevitably lose it.* Hansa squirmed; Umber chuckled. *Really, what else was I supposed to do? Abyssi are pleasure-centered. They don't have "logic," just wants. They feed, they fuck, they play. The only good way to distract them from one is to offer another. Since I wasn't about to let it eat you, I had to offer better bait.*

Dear Numen, would the visual images never *cease*? And Hansa had thought that seeing that creature rip through all his fellows had been the worst thing a man could ever see in his life. No, now he had *this* new, harrowing image in his mind.

And despite all that, he still felt obliged to say, *Thank you. For not letting it eat me.*

It would have made things complicated. Umber sighed. *Unfortunately, Dioxazine pulled her pet away before we could have too much fun. Very frustrating. Though, if you have a few hours, we could take care of your gratitude. . .*

If I join the Napthol Order, will I be able to hide from you? Hansa hadn't meant to send that thought as a question, but apparently it got across. Umber started laughing so hard, he actually had to slow his horse in order to avoid being unseated, allowing Hansa to pull ahead.

It was several minutes later when Umber caught up again. By that time, Pearl seemed to be half asleep in Hansa's arms.

She probably hasn't slept since she was taken, Umber remarked, regarding the girl fondly. *And the temple would have been exhausting.*

Why did you do this? Hansa asked, as Umber again moved alongside. *What's in it for you?*

The silence of the prime witness against you.

Liar, Hansa accused, thinking of all the other strings Umber had pulled. *Unless the Napthol Sisterhood really is that much of a problem for your magic?*

Umber snickered. *The* Cobalt Hall *is a problem. It is vested with magic. The Sisters themselves have no special powers . . . in general.* He glanced to Pearl as he said the last bit. *That one is special, in a way that means the mancers will want her. I may be half-Abyssi, but I'm also half-human. More human than Abyssi, really, since I've been raised on this plane. I know you don't think highly of me, but you should at least consider the possibility that the idea of a child being enslaved and abused might upset me.*

Hansa couldn't figure out how to respond.

After a while, Umber added, *I saved your life. I won you back your fiancée. I didn't let the Abyssi have you. You might want, at some point, to consider acknowledging that I am not, in fact, evil.*

You also pretty much assaulted me while I was in that jail cell.

Umber shrugged. *I wanted to make sure you fully considered your actions.*

So, you're saying those threats were . . . idle? Hansa asked, hopefully.

Umber chuckled. *Oh, darling, idle threats are useless. I never make them. You're a beautiful man. I meant every word I said about* that *matter.*

And that's where you lose me, Hansa said.

Oh, so saving your life—

You said yourself, you only did that to avoid my possibly becoming a mancer.

—and your reputation—

Because I forced you to.

—and saving Pearl's life . . . what, no witty comeback to that one? All of that doesn't balance out more heavily than the fact that I happen to find you lovely?

You apparently find a lot of things lovely.

Again, that damned image of Umber and the Abyssi together.

Umber shook his head. "Spoken like a Quin," he said, softly. It wasn't a jest, or a warning, or even an insult. Just a disappointed statement of fact. "We should drop the horses off at the edge of town and try to get to the Cobalt Hall before dawn. We need to pull that extra magic out of you before you get spotted by someone with the sight."

CHAPTER 16

She lay on her stomach on a mound of pillows and blankets, her knees bent and her feet swinging, as she watched the sparkle of the performer's billions of tiny bells and coins. At least, it seemed like billions, to Cadmia. They shone in the firelight, and let off a kind of music that made Cadmia tap her feet in the air.

The dancer's body rippled, swayed, undulated, in a way that Cadmia wondered if hers ever would. So far, her body was scrawny, and flat like a boy's.

But maybe, someday, she would grow up to look like her mother.

Scarlet Paynes had tried to teach her daughter some of her dance steps, but Cadmia had yet to grow into her long, awkward limbs, and she just couldn't make her body move the way she wanted to. Maybe with more time she would learn, but there never seemed to be enough time. Mother had her performances, and then hours spent with her fans and her beaus, and then a meal and then sleep so she could do it again the next day.

"It's what keeps the food on the table," Scarlet told her daughter once.

But mostly, the A'hknet dancer did not reference such hard facts of life. After all, she loved to dance. She loved the power of sensuality, and she loved the adoration she received, so why should she complain about long hours and few days off?

Cadmia fell asleep in front of the fire.

When she woke, it was just a few hours after dawn. A few others were sleeping near her, but no one she knew. She stood up and went into the kitchen, where she found some milk and an apple for breakfast.

She stepped out the door—

And into the public garden behind the Quinacridone. A woman was weeping, on her knees, with her hands pressed to the stone wall between the gardens and the inner hall.

"Are you all right?"

"I'm lost," the woman said. "I'm so lost."

"Where are you trying to find?"

The woman looked up, revealing eyes that were empty sockets. "I don't remember."

Cadmia flung herself back and tripped over something behind her. She pushed herself up, turning to see what she had tripped on.

Pearl was locked in the Quin dungeon.

"She's a monster," one of the guards said.

"Let's keep this between us, all right?" the monster in the market said. He flipped something in the air, something that

glimmered in the light: a key, which Cadmia knew went to Pearl's shackles.

"Let her go," Cadmia begged.

"She's safer here." He flipped the key at her, hard, and she flinched.

Cadmia woke with a gasp from jumbled dreams, some of her childhood, and some of her fears. She shook herself as she walked to the window, trying to make sense of the images. Her trip to the docks had probably inspired the dream of her childhood, and her anxiety about Pearl explained much of the rest, but what of the blind woman?

The Order taught its initiates to consider their dreams carefully because the Others sometimes spoke through them, but if this one had a message, it was lost to her.

Maybe it was just meant to horrify me awake, she thought, as she saw the two figures picking their way through the darkened street. One was carrying a large bundle.

Heart pounding as she imagined the worst, Cadmia drew on her robe and then dashed down the stairs, not even bothering to light a lamp. She reached the foyer, which was open to the public at all hours, just as Hansa crossed the threshold. His arms trembled and his face was flushed with the effort of carrying Pearl, but if he had difficulty entering this place he hid it well.

"She's all right," he said in response to Cadmia's

panicked expression. "Just exhausted. If I can figure out how to catch the mancer who kidnapped her I will, but in the meantime you should keep her here. I don't know why they want her or if this will make them give up."

"Thank you," Cadmia breathed. She started to reach to take Pearl, and caught sight of the other man lingering outside the doorway. Unlike Hansa, he clearly had no intention of crossing the threshold. Pitching her voice low, she asked, "Are you all right? I know I'm probably the last person you're inclined to trust right now, but if you're in trouble—"

Hansa shook his head. "Everything I told you before was true. I'm with him now only because he needed my help to rescue Pearl. After this, I'm going back to my normal life, and he's getting out of it."

Cadmia nodded, but the chill that ran down her back as she took Pearl from Hansa warned her it might not be that easy.

Cadmia wasn't strong enough to carry Pearl all the way to her bed, but the girl roused only enough to sleepily walk there and say good-night before closing her eyes as Cadmia tucked her in.

Cadmia, unfortunately, was now wide awake. A cool bath and a hot cup of coffee rubbed the grogginess from her mind, and she went to the temple, where a young woman was kneeling in the meditation area reserved for those waiting for an audience.

"Are you seeking guidance?" she asked.

When the woman looked up, Cadmia recognized

her tearstained face as that of Hansa's fiancée. They must have barely missed each other on the street.

"Yes," she said. "Please. Can we go somewhere private?"

Cadmia led them into her office. The shivering woman accepted tea, but seemed more interested in holding it in her hands than actually drinking it. Cadmia waited patiently, trying not to make assumptions about the woman's reason for being here.

"I'm such a fool," Ruby sighed.

"Why do you say that?" Cadmia had enough practice to keep her face neutral and attentive as she considered how she would react to questions about Hansa. She was almost certain now that he had been set up and had told her the truth, but she still didn't understand exactly what *had* happened or who was responsible. All her education said this puzzle couldn't fit together the way it seemed to.

If Abyssi had suddenly learned to plan, they were all in trouble.

"Hansa was a family friend almost since birth," Ruby said, staring down at the ring on her finger. Cadmia's upbringing in the Order A'hknet made her instinctively calculate its value, and decide it was either a family heirloom or evidence of months of saved wages at a guard's salary. "Our fathers work together and he and Jenkins were close to the same age. I don't even know when we started dating. At some point, Jenkins just didn't come along as often so it was just me and Hansa and everything . . ."

She trailed off. The eyes she lifted to Cadmia were sparkling with tears.

"I love him. He loves me. We're the perfect little—" She broke off, blushing.

Cadmia said it for her. She had heard the phrase a million times, usually by her mother's people. "Perfect little Quin couple?" she suggested. The phrase implied so many things. Some of the more devout used it as a compliment when they saw a couple they felt were well-matched, living well, and prepared to raise the next generation of Followers of the Quinacridone. More often, it was a jab at a couple who seemed too pure, too honest, too naïve to be true.

Ruby looked back at her tea. "I can't believe I . . ." Her voice was barely a whisper. "I'm hotheaded. I know that. My parents disowned me when I was sixteen after I tried to join the Order of A'hknet. Jenkins had an apprenticeship lined up to a ship carpenter who was willing to take him on despite his having the sight, but it would have left him financially dependent on our parents and they would have told him to cut ties to me, so he applied to join the One-Twenty-Six. And I can't help thinking . . ." When she looked back up, the tears were streaming down her face. "It's my fault he's dead. *I* killed him by being stupid and impulsive. Nearly killed Hansa, too. And Xaz! She was my *friend*. She never let me be a close friend, but I liked her."

Ruby's tears started in earnest then.

"None of this is your fault," Cadmia said, reaching out to take the tea from Ruby's trembling hand before the other woman burned herself. "You aren't responsible for the decisions other people—"

"Do you think Xaz used magic to make me like her?" Ruby interrupted. "People say mancers can do that. How can anyone trust anything if—" She broke off with a strangled sound, half curse and half sob. "Any other day, I would have gone to Jenkins if I felt this way. He would have made some stupid joke and cheered me up."

Cadmia normally had conversations like this with people crippled by guilt because they actually *had* murdered someone, which made her perhaps not the best confidant for someone struggling with Ruby's concerns. She knew the answer to Ruby's question about Dioxazine—yes, Numenmancers were capable of manipulating people that way—but Ruby was looking for comfort, not a lecture on mancers' powers.

Cadmia suggested gently, "I can stay if you prefer, but you should know that there are Brothers and Sisters here who specialize in guiding people through loss and grief. It isn't my area of expertise. Would you rather—"

"I want to talk to you," Ruby interrupted. She flinched from her own raised voice, then added more quietly, "If that's all right, I mean. They say you advise the One-Twenty-Six, and work with soldiers and even sorcerers. I know you're the one Hansa spoke to when he was arrested. They're talking about making him a captain now . . . now that it's been cleared up." She frowned as she said it.

Did Ruby doubt her beau's innocence? Had she noticed how the pieces of his arrest and exoneration didn't quite fit together? Not wanting her own bias to lead Ruby away from what she wanted to discuss, Cadmia kept her response simple. "Oh?"

"I felt so ashamed of how I acted when he was arrested, when I realized he was innocent I put on his ring. I decided on the spot, yes, this is the man I want to marry. I was going to tell him so as soon as he noticed . . ." She trailed off. Cadmia suspected that Hansa either hadn't seen or hadn't acknowledged the ring on Ruby's finger. "I went to the compound to ask what happened, after he—well, he wanted to be alone for a while," Ruby admitted. "I received dozens of condolences about Jenkins and as many congratulations about Hansa's expected promotion, just like I was him instead of me. He hadn't gone back yet, but I was Hansa's girl so . . ."

This time when Ruby paused, Cadmia thought she understood. "How do you feel about being Hansa's girl?"

Ruby sniffed. Instead of directly answering the question, she asked, "Did you know in Tamar it's considered perfectly normal for a woman to own and captain a ship? She *might* choose to marry and have a family, but she isn't expected to settle down to do it. And if she doesn't want the man around anymore, she just kicks him off the ship. They don't think of marriage the way we do."

Cadmia tried to make sense of the shift from

Ruby's grief about her brother to these seemingly less-important pre-marriage jitters. "It must have been hard to be offered condolences for Hansa's sake instead of your own."

"Hard," Ruby echoed. "But not *new.* And if I marry him, it's something I'm going to have to face the rest of my life. Dear Numen, Jenkins would be horrified to hear me talking this way. He thinks—he *thought* we should have married years ago." Cadmia could tell there was more to come, so she waited, and slowly Ruby gathered her nerve. "Hansa will be a captain in the most elite position in the country," she said. "I should be honored, but all I see is a future where I'm nothing but an extension of him. *Hansa Viridian's wife.* The only thing that scares me more is knowing it probably won't be long before I'm . . . before I'm Hansa Viridian's *widow.* I've been going through the motions because I do love him and I am proud of him, but I don't know if I can stand to give up everything and settle down in a proper Quin life as his sweetly supportive wife just to lose him. It was easier to accept he was a mancer—I could be furious and end it fast and not wait for the day someone comes to my door again to say . . . and it will be soon, because Hansa never backs down or lets someone else take a risk he feels is his responsibility."

Cadmia couldn't argue. She didn't know exactly what Pearl's rescue had entailed, but she suspected it was something few other men would have done.

"I think you need to talk to Hansa," she said. This

kind of issue wasn't her specialty, but "talk to him" was usually good advice for relationship questions. "You've both just lost someone dear to you, and faced a hard truth about someone you considered a friend. Give yourselves time to heal and support each other before you do anything drastic either way. Don't let fear drive you to any decision you're not ready for."

"You're right." Ruby sighed. "I'll talk to him. I will." She drained her tea like a shot of whiskey. "He's been so busy since he was promoted to lieutenant, and I've been so focused on finishing my master work at the herbaria, we haven't really had a serious conversation in a long time. That's all we need. To talk." She stood, gathering herself visibly. "Thank you, Sister. I'm sorry if I wasted your time."

"Time in counsel is never wasted." *At least this was a break from murderers and mancers,* Cadmia thought as she kissed Ruby on the forehead and whispered the traditional blessing, "May the Numen hold you and light your path."

She escorted Ruby out, and immediately turned her thoughts to a harder and less pleasant task: preparing for that evening's mourning service for the eleven guards who had been killed by the Abyssi. Quin monks would perform the moving-on ceremony. Her job would be comforting the living and turning thoughts and conversations away from how they had died. Lore said that souls slain by the denizens of the Abyss would dwell in the Abyss after, so it was a good thing that she was not expected to share comforting words about the next world those near-dozen would find after death.

CHAPTER 17

Hansa found the chattering of birds, mixed only with the sound of the horses' hooves, a remarkably peaceful experience, especially when compared to the events of recent days. It also felt good to see Pearl safely home.

It wasn't until they were nearly back at his apartment that it occurred to him to ask Umber, *Why did you need me for this?* Though the silent communication was not his favorite form of speech, he didn't want to risk words that could be overheard by passersby. As the sun rose, so did the people of Kavet. *You certainly didn't have any trouble handling that Abyssi.*

The denizens of the Abyss are simple-minded and easily dealt with, Umber demurred. *Even Numini are not much of a threat, since they have no interest in one of my kind. Mancers, on the other hand, are dangerous. You were safe in the temple, because it was made by mancers for people with power; they can't be held or hurt within that sphere of magic. My kind on the other hand . . . if I run afoul of an Abyssumancer, especially somewhere like the temple where my powers to defend myself are limited, I'm little more than meat.*

And Pearl? Hansa asked. *Why would the mancers want her? I didn't . . . see . . . any power on her.*

It felt strange to say that, but that was the best he could put it. With the borrowed magic from Umber, Hansa could once again see the glow to the half-Abyssi's eyes, and the veil of power wrapped around him. The Abyssi by the temple had seeped energy, which crackled like heat lightning. Pearl was just a girl. She had barely been visible amidst the magic of the temple.

You wouldn't, Umber answered as they reached Hansa's front door. Aloud, he added, "Ready?"

"Never," Hansa replied, letting them both in. He would have preferred a brief "goodbye" and maybe a firm handshake—though he could do without even that—but Umber had made it clear the power Hansa had borrowed would be visible to sighted guards and wouldn't naturally fade fast enough for him to just ignore it.

The process by which Umber had infused Hansa with enough power for him to impersonate a mancer had been terrifying and disgusting, but short and simple. Umber had greeted Hansa at Hansa's home. He had confirmed that there was no one else in the house, and then had grabbed Hansa's hand, and slit his forearm open from his wrist to his elbow.

While Hansa had been shouting obscenities, convinced the crossbreed had gone mad and was trying to kill him, Umber had matter-of-factly drawn his knife across his own palm, and then grabbed Hansa's hand again in order to let his own Abyssal blood drip into Hansa's.

Hansa couldn't remember passing out—did one ever?—but when he woke, he had been shocked again to find himself alive, not covered with blood, and unmarked where Umber had cut him. Once he had finished cursing at Umber, the half-Abyssi had said only, "There's a horse waiting for you at the stables at the edge of the city."

Hansa hoped returning the power would be less . . .

Titillating? Umber suggested.

"Have I mentioned how much I despise the fact that you can read my mind?" Hansa groused.

"You would hardly need to *mention* it, now would you?" Umber said. "Your fiancée would be pleased to realize how constantly you think of her. You don't even notice it most of the time; you're thinking about something completely different, and then suddenly it's—"

—*Ruby* . . .

"It's kind of nauseating. Oh," he added, as if in afterthought, "and, returning the power? Not nearly so easy, unless I'm willing to kill you, since just ripping the power out of you would certainly make you combust."

"You couldn't have mentioned this sooner?" Hansa sighed as he unlocked his front door.

"I could have," he said, "but then you would have wanted details, and once I gave them to you, you would have chickened out. Take off your shirt, will you?"

"Excuse me?"

"No use getting blood on it needlessly." Umber's words made Hansa freeze just inside the front door. Umber, ignoring his hesitation, slipped past Hansa and added, "Oh, and lock the door. We don't want unexpected company."

Though he followed the suggestion about the door, Hansa was still fully dressed when he followed the half-breed into the kitchen to find Umber prodding at the coals at the bottom of the hearth.

Much as Hansa didn't like the idea of listening to an Abyssi, he trusted it no less than he trusted Umber. "The Abyssi said something about other options, which didn't involve, well, bleeding. To do this."

"Nice to hear you two had a fun little chat," Umber said dryly. "Yes, there are options, if that's your preference."

"My preference is not to have to see the sharp end of that knife you wear ever again, if that's all right with you," Hansa sighed, relieved. "What is it with you people and *blood*?"

"Coin of the Abyss," Umber said vaguely. "Blood, pain, fire—"

As he imagined all the other ways this could go, Hansa added hastily, "My preference for 'no blood' does not extend into a preference for pain and fire instead."

"We'll work something out." Umber chuckled. "Fire's no good for this kind of work anyway. Fire's for destruction. Yes, I could burn away your flesh and the power would come back to me, but given our current bond, that wouldn't end well for me either. I'm building up the fire because it's cold in here," he continued. "Nothing likes the cold but the Numini and the righteous dead. Since we are neither divine nor deceased . . ." He snapped his fingers, and suddenly the coals caught, as did the new log he had added. They burned merrily, as if perfectly kindled.

Only then did Umber address the actual concern. "No blood, no fire, no pain. Do you actually expect a solution here that suits you?"

Hansa collapsed into one of the chairs in front of the fire as his hopes fell—though not too far. The demon's word had never been enough to lift them high.

"So, the Abyssi was lying. Probably just trying to make trouble," he said.

"Oh, no," Umber answered, as he moved from the fire to lounge against the counter. "Abyssi and Numini have a few things in common, one of those being that they can't lie. Not outright at least. Occasionally they will present their own misconceptions as the truth, but they cannot deliberately lie."

"So it was wrong then," Hansa said. He didn't care much about the semantics, beyond the fact that the Abyssi had not spoken any information that happened to be helpful in this circumstance.

"No," Umber replied, infuriatingly, "it was right.

There *are* ways to transfer power that don't involve blood. They would actually be safer for you. They do, however, take longer, and would require more effort on your part."

"I'm willing to put forth a little effort to avoid having you slice me open. What would I need to do?"

He realized a moment later that, with a little thought, he probably could have predicted the half-breed's response. Umber responded by leaning down over Hansa's chair, putting his hands over Hansa's to hold them in place, and kissing him.

Unlike the angry warning Umber had delivered through a kiss in the jail cell, this was soft and fluttering, as if Umber was trying to ask with his body, *Isn't this less frightening than blood and blade?* It spoke to how long and terrifying the last few days had been that, even momentarily, Hansa considered it.

As if he hadn't already betrayed Ruby—and Jenkins, and all his coworkers, and his family, and anyone else who trusted him to stay honest and on the right side of the law—enough. He didn't like the idea of letting Umber cut him again, but there was one line Hansa could still refuse to cross.

He turned his head to the side and drew a breath to say something intelligible. Instead of desisting, Umber nibbled his way down Hansa's neck with light nips, each of which made Hansa gasp. When he reached the edge of Hansa's shirt, he lifted his head again.

"As I was saying," he murmured at Hansa's ear, "the four coins of the Abyss are blood, pain, fire—and flesh. If you prefer this way, I am happy to oblige."

Speaking broke the spell. Hansa wrenched his hands out from under Umber's and pushed the other man back. "You've made your point! We'll do it the other way."

Umber pulled away with a chuckle. "I'm not quite sure *which* point I've made, but I'll leave you to tackle those thoughts on your own." He turned, and as Hansa tried to shake off the fatalistic madness that had briefly snared him, Umber began to rummage through the kitchen cabinets.

He had to clear his throat twice before he managed to ask, "What are you looking for?"

"Something stronger than cider to drink," Umber said.

"It worries me when *you* go searching for a drink."

"Almost anything I say or do worries you," Umber observed. "If it makes you feel better, it's for you, not me."

"Not better." Hansa pushed Umber out of the way, and quickly retrieved a bottle of the same kind of full-bodied red wine that could be found in almost every home in Mars. Heated with honey and spices, it was what kept most of the population from freezing during those frigid Kavet winter nights.

Umber sniffed. "That's it?"

"I don't drink much." Hansa shrugged. He resisted an impulse to try to hustle Umber along; his previous attempts to assert any control over the situation had only made matters worse.

Umber considered the bottle of wine, then filled a

coffee mug. After a little more thought, he poured a second cup, which he set in front of Hansa.

"Is this necessary?" Hansa asked. The wine was meant for mulling. It was pretty foul on its own.

Even more foul when cold, was Umber's response, as he opened a window and set the mug out on the sill before carefully closing the window again. *But you'll need it. You don't realize how hot the power you're carrying burns when you're saturated in it, but once it's gone, you'll need something to slow you down and cool you down.*

"I'll try to stop asking stupid questions if you'll get on with it," Hansa offered.

"Excellent," Umber said. "Now take off your shirt."

Hansa started to undo buttons, but despite his resolve to stop asking questions, he asked, "Would you at least warn me this time before you slit my throat or any other major arteries?"

"I need to cut your chest, right over your heart," Umber explained. "It won't be a deep cut."

Hansa wasn't naïve enough to hope that was the worst part. "And then?"

"Then I drink, to help me form a link back to my own power, so I can control how fast it flows out of you. Too fast, and you'll burn out. It may be a . . . strange . . . sensation, but it shouldn't hurt. If you relax and don't fight me, it will be over in moments."

Hansa stared at the mug of wine, considering it now.

Shaking his head, he folded his shirt and set it next to the full mug of wine. "Okay then. Let's do this before

I lose my nerve. Should I stand up or something?" He focused on the practical details, since that was less disturbing than actually concentrating on what he was doing.

"You should probably sit or lie on the sofa," Umber suggested, with a nod toward the sitting room.

Hansa sat, reminding himself there was no point to stupid questions because they not only made this take longer, there was nothing he needed to know. He didn't *need* to understand this because he never wanted to think of it again. Umber waited a few seconds, as if to see if Hansa was going to protest again, and then drew his dagger.

"You might prefer to close your eyes," Umber suggested.

Hansa did so. In his head, he started to recite an old Tamari nursery rhyme his mother used to say to him when he was a child. It was better than focusing on the knife and the half-demon leaning over him.

The sails are white, the deck is brown, the sky above is—

Ouch. There was the slice. Umber leaned across Hansa's lap, one hand on the arm of the couch to stabilize himself as he caressed Hansa's cheek then eased his head to the side.

Where was he? Tamari sailors often raised their children on ships. His grandfather had been raised that way before meeting his grandmother and settling in Kavet. If Hansa could just keep his mind in inanities like family songs and stories, he could get through this.

The sky above is blue. And there's a word we use to name

the ocean's hundred hues. Then the chorus, which always confused him as a young boy because it had words in some old Tamari language. What was it? The ocean's colors had a name, but he couldn't remember it.

When Umber started laughing, Hansa opened his eyes. "What?"

"Ayalee," Umber provided. Once again, he was far too close for comfort. "Tamari sailors call the ocean Ayalee. I don't know the song, though."

"Az Ayalee," Hansa returned, with a near-hysterical giggle, before squeezing his eyes shut again as Umber leaned down. *Keep you safe az Ayalee.*

Sailing ships. Think of ships on the water, not of the demon who was leaning against him, whose warm mouth had just touched the new cut on Hansa's chest.

Where was he? *The summer sun is hot and gold, the storm clouds cool and gray . . . red hat, gray mountains. . .*

The words of the poem scrambled in his memory as his head swam. He pushed against Umber, worried he was going to be ill. "What—"

Don't fight it, Umber said. *Relax. Remember you don't want this power.*

He could do that. Even if he was getting a little seasick.

CHAPTER 18

He lost the words of the poem and all other awareness of where he was and what he had been doing until Umber said, "Okay. Take a moment to come back to Kavet."

"Mm." Hansa opened his eyes and sat up, shaking his head to clear it. He didn't know when they had separated, but Umber was now sitting back, probably waiting for him to reorient himself for the next step. Hansa wished he could believe they were done, but the cut on his chest was still bleeding, and he had learned enough recently to know that meant the magic wasn't finished. "What next?"

There was still a residue of laughter in Umber's voice when he said, "Your turn, Hansa."

"No." He spoke without even processing the entire implications of the statement, and pushed to his feet. Gray fog encroached on the edge of his vision and the ground under his feet seemed to take a sharp tilt to the side. He ended up kneeling on the wool carpet with his head down. "How much blood did you *take*?"

"Not much. What's wrong with you is that you're leaking power." Umber stood, passed Hansa on his way to the kitchen, and returned with the mug of wine from the table. "Drink, then we'll finish this."

With the mug on the carpet in front of him, Hansa started to translate just what Umber meant when he said, "Your turn."

"You don't mean . . . I mean, you can't expect *me* to . . ."

Umber hefted Hansa with one hand on his arm, lifted his wine with the other, and deposited Hansa on the couch before putting the wine in his hand. Then he sat and began to unbutton his own shirt. "Drink your wine if you need it, and then we have to do this before you pass out."

"You couldn't have *warned* me?"

"Not unless I wanted to argue with you all night."

Given the circumstances, Hansa thought that was an unfair accusation—he had argued very little, and even tried to stop asking questions—but Umber was right that he probably would have objected more if he had been told the entire process up front.

Hansa stared at the wine for only an instant this time, then lifted it to his lips and chugged the foul stuff. Umber was out of his mind. Out of his Abyss-spawned mind. When Hansa put down the mug and looked back at the spawn, Umber's expression was tight; Hansa suspected he was trying for the sake of his Quin partner-in-madness to suppress a grin or a chortle.

"This part might take a little longer," Umber said, "but once it starts, you'll probably find yourself drifting again. I doubt you'll be aware of much."

"Thank Numen for small favors," Hansa whispered, only barely aware that the words would have earned him a censure at work.

"These particular favors come from a lower plane," Umber pointed out, before leaning back against the sofa's arm again, and lifting the knife. He cut the same spot on his chest that he had on Hansa's.

"What did I ever do to deserve this?" Hansa grumbled as he leaned forward, trying to find a way to do this disgusting thing without actually *touching* the half-Abyssi.

"As I recall," Umber answered, "you summoned me by blood and demanded a second boon. You meddled in the affairs of the Abyss." He locked an arm around Hansa's back, pulling him forward. Hansa recoiled, trying to stop himself from falling against the other man. "Now quit being such a Quin."

Ayalee, Hansa thought, as he stared at the wound on Umber's chest. The blood wasn't flowing like normal blood should; it seemed thicker. It was also darker, with an incandescent sheen.

What do you suppose the Tamari would call that *color?* Umber supplied helpfully.

Well, that ruined *that* song forever.

Shut up, Hansa snarled back. Umber put a hand on the back of his head, encouraging him. *You're enjoying this far too much.*

There are other things I'd enjoy more.

Just . . . quit talking.

Then quit stalling.

Okay. *Just get it over with,* Hansa told himself. Umber, thankfully, did not reply. He touched his lips to the blood, then had to pull back, suppressing a gag. He licked his lips instinctively and discovered that the half-demon's blood *tasted* like something you would expect from the Abyss: smoky, dark, and spiced. He still knew what it was, but maybe he could go through with this if he could pretend it was something—anything—else.

No choice, he told himself. *Just do it to get it done.*

He closed his eyes and leaned forward again, and this time closed his lips over the wound. Umber offered no encouragement this time, which was helpful, since it meant Hansa could think about anything *but* what he was doing. He could do this. Had to, really, unless he wanted to walk around looking like a mancer to anyone with the sight for the rest of his life.

He made the mistake of taking a breath, which brought with it the smell of flesh, reminding him that he was not at a tavern with a hot mug of some spicy mulled beverage, but rather pressed against another man.

Get over it, Quin, Umber snarled.

Get over it, indeed. This would have been easier if Hansa didn't suspect, given Umber's many previous flirtatious comments, that the spawn was enjoying it.

To the Abyss with it all. Hansa put a hand on Umber's shoulder in order to brace himself, and then leaned down to the blood one more time. Lips to flesh, he deliberately licked along the length of the cut, drawing fresh blood to the surface. Umber shuddered, and his fingers twined in Hansa's hair, but he didn't speak, thank Numen . . . or Abyss, whoever there was to thank.

The blood filled his mouth, and his throat swallowed, reflex he couldn't have avoided kicking in. He tried to clear his mind of exactly where he was or what he was doing, but couldn't, since he was very awkwardly bent over Umber. His neck hurt.

He could fix that.

Never lifting his lips away from the wound, he reached around Umber's back, lifting him enough to turn him. Umber let out a surprised yelp, but didn't struggle. He let Hansa move him so he was lying full-length on the couch, shoulders propped up by the sofa's end-pillow and arm-rest, with Hansa more comfortably sprawled atop him. That done, Hansa could close his eyes, and go back to what he was doing.

Vaguely, he was aware of a struggle, a *pulling* sensation, not physical but rather somewhere else.

Don't fight it, Umber said, as he had before, though this time his mental voice sounded a little dazed.

Okay. He didn't want to pay attention to that, anyway.

It was easier now. Thinking, he decided, was overrated. Unnecessary, unhelpful.

Hansa? Umber's mental voice was wobbly.

Mm?

Why hadn't he noticed before how soft Umber's skin was? It was like fine silk.

That's enough, Hansa, Umber said.

No, it wasn't.

Yes, it is. Hansa felt a strong hand, still twined in his hair, pulling his head back. He hissed in protest. *You're blood-drunk, Quin. Intoxicated, though damned if I know how.*

Hansa stopped struggling against the hands pulling him away from the wound when he saw the flesh close, sealing the blood away. It didn't matter. There were other coins of this realm, ones he had been offered earlier and refused for some silly reason he couldn't remember now.

He reached a hand under the half-Abyssi's head, and lifted him just far enough to kiss him. Lips met lips, tongues twined, but one long, deep kiss later, Umber snarled, *"Back off!"*

The blow came not physically, but in the form of raw power. It hit Hansa hard enough to knock him back, at which point Umber shoved him from the couch and sprang to his feet.

Hansa lay on the floor, dazed, suddenly aware that his heart was pounding like the hooves of a racehorse. He gasped for breath, body inexplicably heavy. He couldn't even summon the energy to lift his arm to wipe away the sweat he could feel gathering on his brow.

He wasn't sure how long he lay there before Umber

crept back, helped him sit up and lean against the couch, and placed a cold cloth across the back of his neck. He offered the mug of chilled wine, which Hansa cradled in trembling hands, sipping carefully, still steadied by Umber's arm.

"That last bit shouldn't have happened," Umber said as Hansa drank. "Abyssi, spawn and mancers can get intoxicated off blood if they aren't careful, but it shouldn't have happened to someone who has no natural tie to the Abyss."

The words reached Hansa, but they were next to meaningless. What mattered in that moment was the cold ceramic mug in his hands, and the warm arm across his back.

"I know these words mean nothing to you now," Umber continued, "but later, I hope you remember that I chose to stop you. I didn't have to."

Hansa was starting to come back to himself then, enough that his eyes finally focused. He turned to look at Umber, whose deep blue eyes swam with concern. Full lips, slightly reddened with blood, moved as the man continued to speak, but Hansa didn't hear whatever he was saying.

"Get away from me," he managed to choke out.

Umber frowned. "Well, I guess that's the gratitude I should have expected from you." He stood, lithe body uncoiling in one smooth moment, and started toward the door.

"Not what I meant." Hansa coughed. "You just—" He was *not* going to say that. Umber paused, twisting back, expression still cross. "You still look . . . feel . . .

really good." He closed his eyes after he said it, squeezing them shut as if doing so could block out the truth.

"It'll wear off," Umber said sadly. "Let me help you to bed. Sleep a few hours, and when you wake, you should be back to normal."

Hansa let Umber help him to his feet mostly because he couldn't have stood on his own. One arm looped across Umber's shoulders, he couldn't quite resist smoothing his free hand down Umber's chest. After he realized what he had done, he curled that hand into a fist, trying to control himself.

They stumbled at the doorway to the bedroom. Hansa wrapped his arms around Umber's waist and tried very hard to remind himself that he did *not* want to kiss the half-naked spawn again. Even if he smelled and felt as good as he looked.

Umber chuckled. "I guarantee, as soon as you're back to yourself, you will be cursing my name and blaming me for all of this. A good little Quin like you couldn't *possibly* be interested in anything so untoward."

The sound of the front door opening caused them both to turn.

"Didn't you lock that?" Umber asked.

Hansa nodded. "Ruby has a key."

"Ruby . . . your *fiancée*?"

Umber's expression of concern pierced Hansa's mental fog a moment too late. He heard Ruby saying, "Hansa? Are you here? I need to—"

She broke off as she stepped into the sitting room and saw them.

"Hansa? You should probably step back," Umber suggested quietly.

Ruby moved further into the room, and her eyes went to the two mugs they had used for wine, then Umber's shirt crumpled on the floor, and then back to Hansa and Umber.

"Back up," Umber said again.

Hansa took a step backward, and bumped into the opposite side of the doorway.

"Well. This explains a lot," Ruby said.

"This really isn't what it looks like," Hansa managed to say. It was perhaps the stupidest defense he could have come up with, but it was so hard to *think*.

"You know? It . . . just . . . I don't . . ." Ruby shook her head. "Never mind." She turned away.

"Ruby, wait!" He managed to step away from Umber and put a hand on Ruby's arm to try to slow her down. "Please, will you *listen* to my explanation?" He would probably tell her the truth if she was willing to hear it, but if she walked away again without even considering there might be an explanation . . .

She shook off his hand and pulled off her ring. "I think you should just keep this. It's clear neither one of us is ready to marry."

When he refused to take the ring from her, she handed it to Umber instead.

"I won't say anything to the Quinacridone," she said as she moved away.

She closed the door quietly behind herself.

Umber sighed. Hansa snapped, "Could you have

helped *less*?" Surely the spawn could have said something useful while Hansa was trying to find his tongue!

"If you recall, you forbid me from even *speaking* to her," Umber reminded him. "I can't arbitrarily violate the terms you set on the second boon just because it's convenient. Besides, there are other ways to fix this."

As soon as Umber made the offer, Hansa's irritation snuffed out. He still felt dazed, but there was one thing he felt sure about. "No."

"I agreed to help clean up any problems you got into on account of helping me rescue Pearl," Umber reminded him. "This falls in that category."

"No," Hansa said again. "This . . ." It hurt to admit it, but he couldn't avoid the truth any more. "This isn't really a new problem."

She hadn't been willing to listen to him last time either. Yes, Umber would be able to clean up this mess, manipulate Ruby once again . . . but what did it mean, if his relationship needed that?

"You're sure?" Umber asked.

"Yeah." He took the ring from Umber, and then stumbled into the bedroom. "I'm going to sleep. Then maybe I'll try to talk to her . . . explain . . . accept whatever comes of it . . ." He collapsed onto the bed. "Sleep first. Thanks," he added. "But I need to deal with this myself."

Deal with the mess he had made of his own life.

"As you wish," Umber said. "Sleep well, Quin. Good luck."

Hansa was already asleep, the star ruby ring curled in his palm.

CHAPTER 19

Xaz had been exhausted enough to drift into a deep and dreamless sleep by the fire. The rest would have been more satisfying if she hadn't woken once again snuggled against a furry blue body. Her cheek lay against his chest, and his tail was hooked securely around her waist.

They had established with their "pet the Abyssi" conversation that she *did* like being near him, and his warmth was probably the only reason she had been able to rest as well as she had, but she knew just enough about his kind to know snuggling wasn't all he was likely to be interested in.

The instant she tried to ease out of his arms, his tail and arm tightened around her and his eyes flew open. She froze, afraid to even breathe with his claws noticeably pricking the soft skin of her side.

His tail twitched, fur tickling her spine at her lower

back, just in that spot that always made her jump. Enclosed within Alizarin's arms the way she was, she couldn't go far, but ended up sneezing as fur tickled her nose. His claws probably would have shredded her skin if he hadn't retracted them just in time.

His tail moved again, eliciting the same reaction.

"Stop that," she said.

"You say that a lot," he replied.

"Because dealing with you is a lot like dealing with a three-year-old child," she snapped.

She started to pull back, but though his grip loosened a little, he didn't let her go. Instead, he asked, "Really? *Just* like that?" He stretched to emphasize his point, making her blush. She remembered the way she had stared at Cinnabar after she had been injured, and only now realized that embarrassing fixation had been a result of the Abyssal power seeping into her. Love was of the Numen, but lust came from the Abyss.

"No," she said, meaning two things: No, he wasn't like a child, and no, she didn't want to continue this line of conversation.

"No, what?" he purred.

Her instinct was to be subtle, to use euphemisms or avoid the conversation entirely, but she had to keep in mind what she was dealing with. She gathered her nerve and said bluntly, "I will *never* have sex with you. Is that clear?"

The words didn't seem to surprise or insult him. He asked almost innocently, "Why not?"

"Why . . ." She sputtered. "Because I know what you

are. And you know what I am. I'm a Numenmancer. I'm not going to have sex with a creature of the Abyss. If you were anywhere near capable of rational thought, you would have figured that out by now. Now, please let me up."

He didn't reply at all to the last words. Instead, he twitched his tail—she jumped—and said with a huff, "I'm perfectly capable of rational thought. Far better than you."

"You haven't demonstrated it," she grumbled.

Apparently he took the words as a challenge. "Point one." Xaz did her best to relax, since he obviously wasn't going to let her up until he was bored with this conversation, as he had bored of the last one. Hopefully, trying to apply *logic,* a trait traditionally associated with the divine realm, would bore him very quickly. "You like to touch me. You like to be near me. You like the way I *feel.* You like the way I *look.* Point two: Your magic is also attracted to me because we have a bond, and mine is attracted to you. You are my tie to this plane. I am your tie to the power of the Abyss. Point three: You need as much power as you can get, especially now that the Numini have disowned you."

"They haven't—"

He hushed her with a finger to her lips.

"Point four: Sex is fun. That's just a generally accepted fact. It would make the Abyssi happy, and it would make you happy.

"Final point: The four coins of the Abyss are blood, pain, fire, and flesh. Sex raises power. You don't like blood, pain, or fire, and you *do* like the look and feel of the Abyssi, and you *do* need power, and you *would* enjoy this form of raising power. Taking all these points into your oh-so-logical Numenmancer brain, tell me how you can possibly come to a different conclusion."

"You're a *demon*!" she shouted. "You have *fur*. And a *tail*. Oh, and *you eat people*!"

"You eat ducks," he said, as if that were a logical argument.

"Yes, I eat duck." Was she really having this argument? "That's because I'm not a duck. Also, I wouldn't have *sex* with a duck. Your argument sounds logical on the surface, but—"

"Until you apply human irrationality and Numini interference," he interrupted, tone haughty. "The divine realm is the only one responsible when you say no to something you obviously both want and need."

"And the Abyssal realm is the one responsible when fifty-year-old men have affairs with sixteen-year-old girls. Let me up. This argument is over."

Just when she began to fear he might refuse to accept "no," his arms loosened and he released her. "Can I have a kitten?"

"No—what?" Scrambling to her feet, it took her a moment to realize he had changed the subject. At least, she *hoped* he had changed the subject.

"I want a pet," he said.

"Why?" she asked, warily.

"To play with," he replied, brightening the instant her answer wasn't just, "No." "And I'm hungry."

"I'm not getting you a kitten to *eat*."

He deflated again. "Puppy?"

"You are a foul creature," she mumbled.

"I saved your life," he reminded her. "And I haven't eaten in days."

That made her stop. She had thought of the Abyssi she had summoned as a fiend and an annoyance, but the truth was, she *had* summoned him. If she had called one of the Numini into this plane, she would have fed it, but Numini couldn't eat flesh. It hadn't even occurred to her until then that one of the Abyssi might not be able to eat anything else.

So far, Alizarin had done exactly what she had asked of him. He had protected her and brought her somewhere safe so she could rest and recover her strength. He had helped her get warm clothing, and sustenance. He had brought her to the temple, and when the Quin guard had shown up, Alizarin had followed him in order to assess the threat he might pose. In return, Xaz had refused almost every request he had made, not just for entertainment but for *food*.

She was a *Numenmancer*. She didn't know how to treat a denizen of the Abyss. What she did know was that, even if she didn't feel guilty for abusing a creature that thus far had treated her very well—which she did—it was not a good idea to make a demon she had no magical control over unhappy.

"I'm sorry," she said. "I never expected to spend so much time with one of your kind. I know the Numini are very particular with what they can and cannot eat.

Can you tell me what works for you—beyond kittens, I mean?"

"Numini are difficult," Alizarin agreed. "Milk, honey, clear water, new fruit." He listed with a swish of his tail some of the Numini's simplest food choices when on the human plane. "Abyssi are easy. Dirt isn't food. What comes from dirt isn't food. Everything hot is food. Once it's cold it's dirt again."

"Does 'hot' include things that are warmed by fire?" she asked.

Alizarin frowned. "Fire is good, but it doesn't turn dirt into food."

"So hot means alive, or just-dead. Nothing you could buy at a butcher's or order at a restaurant."

He nodded. His expression looked pleased, but his tail was twitching in a way she had come to associate with his impatience.

"Without eating any *people*, and doing your best not to eat anyone's beloved new pet, would you be able to find yourself enough to eat?"

He nodded again, the *swish* of his tail now more lively.

"Okay then. Why don't you go . . . do that." And she would try not to think too much about it. "I'm going to go back to our room and try to get a little sleep. I'll meet you later."

"Hunt well," he bid her, before bounding off into the near-dawn without waiting for her reply.

"You, too," she sighed.

Once he was gone, the chill of the damp sea air and

winter wind settled into her bones. She built up the fire, shivering all the while and wishing fiercely that she had a way to make the flame brighter. Most of her magic responded to will and words, but her invocations did nothing here. It occurred to her that a real Abyssumancer might use blood, but her nerve failed her despite the cold.

It wasn't just Alizarin who made the idea of turning into an Abyssumancer terrifying. Though she had personal experience to know the Quins' thoughts about most mancers were more scary stories and exaggeration than truth, she suspected much of what they said about Abyssumancers was true. The Abyss was a realm of impulse and need. Dark hungers drove its denizens and infected the mancers bound to them.

That all meant she couldn't trust an Abyssumancer to help her break her bond with Alizarin. Then who? Another Numenmancer couldn't help; they wouldn't be able to see the Abyssal magic even if their Numini would let them try. Xaz needed someone with more diverse talents. Outside myths, where impossibly-powerful mancers could manipulate all four realms of existence—the Abyss, the Numen, life and death—she knew of only one creature who might have the skills she needed.

The spawn.

Spawn didn't rely on the Numini's or Abyssi's approval in order to work magic. Though they were most closely tied to the realm from which they had been born, they weren't blind to the opposite realm the way a mortal mancer was. Finally, since they were born with their power instead of having it unnaturally thrust upon them like a mancer, they learned to use it instinctively. They were supposed to be capable of incredible feats.

Xaz had never met one—or hoped to do so—because they usually utilized those incredible abilities to hide from her kind. Spawn seeped Other energy, which meant an unscrupulous mancer who could catch one could use it as an unending fount of power. She had heard of one, though, from Alizarin—he said a spawn had helped Hansa escape Quin clutches a free man. If the spawn had really granted Hansa a second boon, he would have to keep him in sight no matter what Hansa was now. If Hansa was in danger—say if a mancer with a grudge approached him—the spawn would come running.

Now that she'd had time to consider his change in status, Xaz had a word or two she wanted to exchange with the hero of Mars anyway.

CHAPTER 20

Cadmia wiped snow from her eyes, then checked her notes again. Other Sisters and Brothers of Napthol had gone by horseback to try to make the next-of-kin calls in the countryside for the deceased soldiers, but she had agreed to do the local ones. The house listed as the home address of Soldier Rosso's sister was one she remembered from her childhood as a flophouse frequented by the poorer members of the Order of A'hknet.

White flurries had started to fall a little after dawn and grown steadily heavier since, and the snow had caused an instant change in the temperament of the docks. Children bundled up in heavy winter cloaks passed through the crowd, running back and forth to deliver mugs of hot drinks and still-warm pastries from the taverns to anyone with a penny to spare. The wharf market had mostly closed down, as the women who usually sat out with their nets, ropes, and weaving moved inside so they could work without their fingers going numb. Fishermen shook their heads, packing new snow around the morning's catch even though they knew few people would come shop.

"Looks like an early winter," observed a man loitering in front of the house. She chose to ignore the bag he carried, which she had seen him hurriedly slip something into the moment he saw her violet robes.

"This might just be an early freeze," she said practically, letting him know she intended to keep the conversation casual and not harass him about whatever contraband he had just hidden. "I'm looking for Fawn Rosso. Is she around?"

The man shook his head. "Not a freeze, real winter. This snow will be here until spring. I'll bet you a week's earning."

"I never bet with a man who sounds that sure," Cadmia said. In fact, she never bet; the Napthol Order discouraged it. "Fawn isn't in any trouble. Her brother was one of the victims of—"

"Shame," the man interrupted, continuing to ignore her request. It was hard to tell if he was stalling for time, probably while someone inside cleared away evidence of illegal activity, or just giving her a hard time because she was from the Napthol Order. "I was hoping I could use that extra pay to take my daughter somewhere special."

"Sorry to disappoint her. I'm going inside."

He waited until her hand touched the doorknob to ask, "Aren't you Scarlet's girl?"

"I'm—"

"Sister!" She spun toward the frantic voice to find a young Tamari girl in sailor's garb, probably a cabin girl, slipping and sliding across the street toward her. "Sister, can you come?"

The man by the door tensed. No matter how much he wanted to harass Cadmia, he was clearly torn on whether he wanted to warn her about getting onto a Tamari ship.

"Captain saw your—" She gestured to her clothes breathlessly. "Told me to get you. It's an emergency."

Cadmia reminded herself that she wasn't a child in the Order of A'hknet anymore. Even a would-be slaver had to know that trying to kidnap a Sister of the Napthol would be more trouble than it was worth.

"Where's your ship?"

The cabin girl turned and dashed to lead the way. Cadmia followed as quickly as she could without falling, barely breaking her stride when she hit a slick patch of ice on the boarding ramp and had to grab the rail to keep from falling into the icy waters.

"She said she wanted passage wherever we were going," the captain said quickly, guiding Cadmia toward the bow of the ship. "I told her we don't carry passengers. That's when she climbed up. My first mate's been trying to talk her into coming back down, but then I saw you—that's what you people do, right?"

By the time Cadmia reached the bow of the boat, the first mate had just grabbed the woman's arm to pull her back away from the rail and stand her safely on the deck, but it didn't look like the crisis was over. The woman shoved the mate away, and though she didn't climb the rail again, she pressed her back against it.

Cadmia bit back a curse as she recognized Ruby's tear-streaked face and remembered their last conversation. She must have confronted Hansa. What had he said to her?

"Ruby, Ruby, can you hear me?" Cadmia asked, trying to get the woman to look at her.

Ruby nodded, slowly, though her eyes never quite came into focus. Her gloveless hands continued to grip the railing, her slender fingers nearly blue from the cold.

She wasn't wearing her ring.

"Did something happen?" Cadmia asked. "Did you and Hansa argue?"

Ruby shook her head. "Winsor Indathrone pardoned him," she said in a dazed voice.

"Yes, he did."

Again, Ruby shook her head. "But he—" She sniffed. "But he's guilty."

Cadmia felt a new chill, unrelated to the weather. "Can we talk somewhere private, Ruby?" she asked. She was less worried about privacy than she was about wanting to get the woman out of the freezing weather and away from the rail.

Ruby just glared. "Indathrone pardoned him. A Sister of Napthol condemned him. I saw the blood . . . and then . . . he wouldn't even make love to me," she finished in a very small voice.

Cadmia blinked, confused by the change of subject. "Excuse me?"

"He wouldn't make love to me," she said. "All the times I threw myself at him and he said no, that we needed to wait, it was so *frustrating*. He was so damn *Quin*. And I know why now. Why does it hurt more knowing that? He might be a *sorcerer*, but I can barely even think of that. But I find him with . . ." She trailed off.

"He's not sleeping with Umber," Cadmia blurted out before she could think better of it. Why hadn't she *thought*? Her only excuse was that Hansa had said he didn't intend to have anything to do with Umber after rescuing Pearl. It never occurred to her the spawn might be there when she encouraged Ruby to talk to her fiancée.

"Even you know about it?" Ruby gasped.

"I think this is a conversation for just you girls," the first mate murmured, distancing himself a little.

"I know he isn't," Cadmia asserted. "I . . . Umber and Hansa were helping me find someone. If you saw something—"

"I saw something," Ruby spat. "I saw them together. Saw even the knife."

The second change of subject made Cadmia wince. It would probably be better for everyone if Ruby just thought Hansa was attracted to men—what the Quin considered "sexually deviant." That charge could result in his losing his position in the 126, but it wouldn't get him executed. "Excuse me . . . knife?"

"Sister, tell me he's innocent," Ruby challenged. "Tell me I did not see my fiancé in the arms of another man, both wine and blood on his lips. Tell me I didn't see him nearly dead one moment, and then find him perfectly healed only hours later. Tell me Winsor Indathrone himself wasn't fooled by some mancer trick. Tell me . . . tell me that everything I believe isn't a lie."

"I—" Cadmia knew she should lie, but Ruby's words highlighted all her own doubts and fears. She saw the cost of her hesitation as Ruby's desperation hardened to peaceful resolve. "Ruby, come away from the rail."

"Sister?" Ruby said, her voice sweetly inquiring.

"Yes?"

"You . . . you and all the holy orders . . ." Ruby leaned close and continued in a whisper. "You're all full of shit."

Without warning, she shoved Cadmia, sending her sprawling. The first mate cried out, but his first instinct was to try to catch Cadmia, so he wasn't fast enough to stop Ruby as she turned, boosting herself onto the ship's rail—and over. The quiet splash was barely audible over the general bustle of the docks.

Shouts rang out and several sailors ran toward the railing.

"Merciful Khet," the first mate whispered. Despite the frigid weather, he and two others started to pull off their boots and drop heavy jackets to the deck in a frantic rush. Cadmia stared down at the dark water, but didn't see Ruby resurface.

"Lydie, get off the ship, bring back blankets, hot

rum," the captain ordered his cabin girl, who jumped to obey. "Grent, Taylor, help her."

Everyone moved as if there was a chance, but as precious seconds ticked by, Cadmia knew it was going to take more than hot rum and blankets to fix this. They would be for the valiant rescuers who were only now easing themselves into the water—carefully, because diving headfirst into the mess of lines, chains, nets, and weeds that filled the harbor was a recipe for . . .

Well, for suicide.

My fault. I knew she was hotheaded and impulsive. I knew she had just lost a lifelong best friend. I sent her to Hansa—

No! She couldn't think that way. Yes, Ruby had been upset. Cadmia had sent her to talk to the man she still loved, with whom she should have been able to share her grief and express her fears. Instead, Ruby believed she had found proof not only that her intended was disloyal, not only that he was involved with a man in conflict with all Quin dictates, and not only that he was involved with sorcery, but that somehow he had fooled everyone, including the most powerful man in Kavet.

If you thought you had been wrong about all of that, how could you possibly trust *anything* you believed to be true?

Cadmia stepped back from the rail, so the deck blocked the rescue efforts from her view. No one was paying any attention to her when she turned and ran back toward the city—toward Hansa Viridian's house.

She didn't know what Hansa had gotten involved

in, but if he had power, maybe it would be enough to save the woman who had loved him. After, Cadmia would make him talk to her and she would decide if he needed to be reported to the Quin.

If you really thought he was guilty, you wouldn't risk talking to him. What are you hoping to learn?

First she needed to see if Hansa could save Ruby. Then she could decide what to do about her own faith.

CHAPTER 21

"Hansa, wake up, or I swear to the Abyss I'll—"

The combination of the shouting and a slap brought Hansa out of his nearly comatose state.

" 'Kay, okay," he grumbled, struggling to open his eyes. "Okay. Stop hitting me."

"Hansa, you need to—"

He finally focused his gaze and discovered that the woman who had been abusing him was none other than Cadmia Paynes. "How'd you get in here?"

"The door was unlocked. Hansa, you have to get up now. Ruby's been hurt."

Hansa sat up so fast his head spun and he gagged. He hadn't felt this hung-over since a poorly conceived overnight trip with Jenkins, Ruby, and a bottle of cheap rum when they had been teenagers. "What's wrong with Ruby?"

As soon as he asked, he remembered. "Ooh . . . oh,

no." He pressed a hand to his temple as he climbed to his feet.

"I don't care if you're sleeping with the spawn or making deals with the Abyss," Cadmia said, her voice frigidly controlled, "but if this is your fault, then it's your responsibility to make it right." She threw a shirt at him, which he fumbled at, trying to remember how to put it on.

"I'm not—"

"I just said, I don't care," she snapped. "Hurry up!"

"Ruby left me," he said. "I didn't . . . I mean, there's nothing to make *right*. We're over."

"I figured that when she said she—oh, *never mind*!" Cadmia snarled. "Didn't you hear me say she's *hurt*?"

He had, but he hadn't been awake enough to think about it. This time the words reached him. "Hurt how? Is she okay?" He managed to get the shirt on. He misaligned one pair of buttons, but Cadmia didn't wait for him to fix it before she threw more clothes at him, followed by socks and boots.

"If she were okay, I wouldn't have come here!" Cadmia shouted, as he hustled to finish dressing. "Come on."

Heart pounding again now, he raced after her, pulling on his boots as he stumbled with her out the door. "Where are we going?"

"Docks," Cadmia answered. She was already nearly sprinting; he loped after her, his long legs keeping up easily despite his care not to slip on the still-falling snow.

"What happened?" he managed to gasp.

Cadmia shook her head.

When they reached the docks, a man in the garb of a sailor grabbed Cadmia's arm. "Sister, where have you—"

"Where did they bring her?"

The man dropped his gaze. "They brought healers from the Napthol, but . . ."

Hansa listened to the exchange, and felt all the warmth drain out of his body. "What happened?" he said, his voice little more than a whisper.

"Who are you?" the sailor asked.

"This is Hansa. Ruby's fiancé," Cadmia said.

The man's eyes widened. "I'm sorry," he said, words broken. "They . . . she's at the King's Ransom. We had to send for the Quinacridone to . . . to pick her up. I'm sorry," he said again.

Hansa leapt ahead. Both of them hurried after him, but he was barely aware. They couldn't mean what he knew they meant. She couldn't be *dead*. She was alive just a few hours ago. She was fine.

He fell into the door of the King's Ransom, and was instantly cussed at by a man who had been on the other side.

"Where's Ruby?" he demanded.

The man looked at him as if he were mad—which was probably how he looked. "Who?"

Cadmia had caught up. She guided him inside.

"This way," she said softly. Behind them, the sailor was giving their apologies to the person Hansa had nearly knocked over.

"You can't—"

Hansa glared at the maid who tried to keep him out of the room where Ruby lay. A single candle by the bedside provided the only light. Even in the flickering, rosy glow, reflected by an absurd glass vase full of silk flowers, Ruby's skin was icy pale, her lips white, her fingertips blue.

The sailor was speaking to Cadmia in the doorway. He probably thought his voice was soft enough that Hansa wouldn't hear, but Hansa had discovered that the world seemed to have gone very quiet. He could hear his own pulse. He could certainly hear this man's voice. "It took too long to find her in the water. The doctor is still worried about the first mate, he was so frozen by the time he brought her out. She never even woke."

Hansa gripped Ruby's hand. "What was she doing at the docks?" he managed to choke out.

"Trying to find a ship from Kavet," the sailor said.

He dropped his head. Ruby's hand was cold. Cold. Her normally bright eyes were closed, but it wasn't like people said. She didn't look like she was sleeping.

"I'm sorry," he whispered. "Ruby, I'm sorry . . ."

She was trying to get a ship, yes, but not away from Kavet: away from *him*. He had been willing to lose her, but not this way.

"I'm sorry," Cadmia said, her soft words like barbs.

"I should have told you more gently, but I thought if I got you here in time, maybe you could . . ." She trailed off, clearly deciding she had been wrong.

She wasn't wrong. There was one thing he could do.

When he had asked Umber if he could bring Jenkins back, the spawn hadn't said, *No, it's impossible to revive the dead.* He had said that, given how Abyssi kill, there probably wasn't enough of the body. He was looking at Ruby's body, which was whole and unmarred as long as he ignored the blue cast of her skin.

He reached over to the absurd vase of decorative flowers: silk lilies, in what looked like hand-blown glass. It didn't matter much; it shattered as he brought it down on the corner of the nightstand.

The sound seemed to go on and on. It took him a few seconds to realize he wasn't just hearing breaking glass, but shouting, from Cadmia and the sailor.

It didn't matter what happened to *him* after this. It was about time he accepted responsibility for the choices he had made. It wasn't his fault the Abyssi had injured him or that Umber had saved him the first time; if they had executed him then, it would have been unjust. That didn't absolve him of meddling with powers he *knew* were treacherous. He had been furious that Xaz was so close to Ruby because it was well known that, even when a mancer did nothing intentionally malevolent, the powers they worked with were dangerous to anyone around them.

He knew all that. He meddled anyway. Ruby paid the price.

He picked up one of the shards of glass. Cadmia grabbed his wrist, trying to stop him.

"Hansa, calm down," she said. "Calm down. You don't want to hurt yourself."

"I'm pretty sure he's not trying to *hurt* himself," came the sailor's voice.

"I'm doing what you wanted," Hansa said. "I'll be fine." *Fine* wasn't exactly true. He would be arrested and executed. All that was okay, though, if Ruby was alive.

Cadmia was holding both of his wrists, but that didn't matter. He heard the other man say, "Sister, maybe you should leave him alone," as he closed his hand around the glass. He just needed blood.

The glass sliced across the inside of his fingers and his palm. He whispered, "Umber, get your ass in here."

Cadmia's eyes widened.

"This was a bad idea," she whispered. The sailor clearly agreed, since he had already run out, probably on his way to get guards. It didn't matter; Umber hadn't had any trouble getting past guards in the Quin compound.

"You should probably go," Hansa told Cadmia. "You don't want to appear involved." Once again, that tight feeling in his chest made breathing and speaking difficult. Or was that panic? Or the lingering residue of last night's adventures?

"Hansa, I was wrong," Cadmia said. "I wasn't thinking clearly. *You're* not thinking clearly. A terrible thing has happened, but . . ." She shook her head, and murmured as if to herself, "They say an impulse you can't explain is caused by the Others whispering in your ears."

"I feel like I'm thinking more clearly than I have been in days," Hansa said. He had started this. He would finish it.

"I don't think you—"

Umber interrupted her, storming into the room with the words, "Hansa, what in the three planes do you think you are—" He broke off as he took in the scene. "Hansa, don't do this."

"Hansa—" Cadmia tried again, but Umber held up a hand, silencing her.

"Sister, go get a drink or something," Umber said. "Make sure we aren't bothered."

A moment later, Umber, Hansa, and Ruby were alone.

"You can bring her back," Hansa said.

Umber winced. "You absolved me of this, Hansa."

"But you *can*."

"Alone? No," Umber replied. He kept his tone even, trying to sound reasonable, but Hansa was past being reasonable. "I can heal, but she's *dead*, Hansa. Look at her. She's frozen."

"Could a necromancer bring her back?" Umber had implied that in the jail cell, too.

"Probably, but—"

"Then find one!"

"Hansa—"

"Don't argue with me! She died because of me, because of us. Because I wanted—"

"To live?" Umber suggested. "To save a young girl? Hansa, you haven't done anything wrong. You aren't responsible for her choices."

"She doesn't really *have* any choices left, does she?" Hansa demanded. "If I had had any sense at all, I would have let go of her when she first tried to leave me. Instead, I *committed* the crime she had broken the marriage off over in order to manipulate her into forgiving me. Into begging *my* forgiveness. I could have just asked you to save me from rotting in that jail, but did I stop with that? No. I let you make me into some kind of hero. Maybe that's why the Quinacridone says pride is so dangerous."

"Self-pity is dangerous, too, Quin," Umber warned. "It can make you do stupid things. Take a deep breath and remind yourself that sometimes bad things happen. We can't control everything."

"What happens to suicides?"

"What—what?" Umber asked.

"Suicides. Napthol and A'hknet both mostly say suicides . . ." His voice choked off.

"I don't know where they go," Umber said. "And even in the Order of the Napthol, individuals disagree about exactly what happens in the afterlife."

"She was *good*," Hansa insisted. "I've known her since we were little kids. She doesn't deserve to end up in the Abyss because of what I did."

"Hansa, why don't we go get something to eat and put you back to bed?" Umber said gently. "There's nothing you can do."

"You said a necromancer could help her."

"Neither of us is a necromancer," Umber pointed out.

"You could get one."

"Let's not go down that road, Hansa," Umber said. "The last thing you want is to get more mancers involved in your life."

"I've messed up my life already. I'll deal with that when I come to it. Ruby shouldn't pay for what I've done. I know you say it's not my fault, but if I'd been the person I pretended to be, then we wouldn't be in this mess because she never would have had reason to doubt me. Bring her back."

"Hansa, I can't—"

"Find a necromancer," Hansa demanded, "and make him bring her back. Convince her they saved her, convince everyone they pulled her out of the water in time. I know you can do it."

"Hansa, you don't want to do this," Umber said. Pleaded, really. "Let her go."

"I don't care what happens to me—"

"I rather care what happens to you, since my doing this would mean cementing the bond between us. Do you understand that? There are ways to work around the bond, usually. All spawn know how to do it. You make deals, tit for tat as it goes, like I agreed to help Pearl for Cadmia in exchange for her silence. I could have silenced her myself, and I would have helped Pearl in for nothing, but sometimes power does things we don't expect. Making a 'fair' deal keeps the scales even and keeps a bond from forming."

"So what do you want?" Hansa asked. "Make me a deal. I'll do it."

"You don't understand what you're saying," Umber said, speaking very clearly and slowly. "Spawn do not associate with mancers. There is nothing you could possibly offer me that would convince me to make any deal that forced me to not only seek one out, but do whatever was necessary to get one's *help*."

"I don't need to convince you."

"Which is why *I* am trying to convince *you* that *you* do not want to do this."

Hansa picked up another shard of the vase. It glistened in the candlelight.

"Blood to seal the boon, right?" he asked.

"Hansa, listen to me," Umber argued. "The third boon creates a permanent bond. *Permanent*. There is no way to break it. The symptoms of that bond vary drastically, but it is possible that you will lose all you are and become so obsessive that I'll have to lock you away."

"That's the risk I'll take, then. You know what I want."

"You don't want this," Umber sighed.

"Not really," Hansa said. "But I don't see a choice." He held up the shard of glass, examining the edge. "Do you have a preference of location?"

"Don't do this."

"I imagine the longer we wait, the more difficult it is going to be to bring her back," Hansa said. "We should get on with it."

Speaking very quietly, his gaze not leaving the shard of glass Hansa held, Umber explained, "I don't even know if I can do what you're asking of me. Even if I can find a necromancer, there is no guarantee he will agree to help, or that this will be within his power." He reached out slowly, attempting to remove the glass from Hansa's hand. When Hansa resisted, Umber held up his own knife instead. "It's my blood we need for the third boon, anyway. So listen to me: I will try to find someone who can help. I will do everything within my power to bring him back here, and you and I can attempt to find a way to convince him to do what you want." He pulled the knife blade across the flesh of his forearm, but instead of offering the wound to Hansa, he tore a strip from his shirt and awkwardly bandaged the wound. "You can still choose not to seal this boon. I ask that you wait to decide until I've done my best to discover if I'm even *capable* of fulfilling this demand. And in the meantime, I beg you to consider carefully whether, when I return, you really want to do this."

Hansa nodded, gripping Ruby's cold hand in his uninjured one.

Umber turned to go, but paused one more time in the doorway to say, "You know there's a chance that, if I go out searching for a mancer, I may stumble across the wrong kind and not make it back?" When Hansa just nodded again, Umber shook his head and hissed, "Bastard," under his breath before he stormed out.

CHAPTER 22

The falling snow meant Xaz had an excuse to keep her head down and her hood up as she walked through the thinning harbor crowds. She thought she had managed to put a veil over her power, but wasn't confident about it. Thankfully, the sight was rare and sighted guards were rarer, so she thought she would be safe as long as no one recognized her face.

When Alizarin returned from hunting and she told him her plan to find the spawn, the Abyssi didn't ask why. He was too thrilled by the idea of seeking out the spawn—who he called Umber, and who he felt would be more amicable to his advances than a Numenmancer—to ask *why*.

She had planned to go up to the city to start her search for Hansa, but the bustle at the waterfront caused her to detour. She heard Hansa's name whispered by more than one person—*Hansa's fiancée,* she thought—but that wasn't what drew her attention. The docks hummed with cold power, as if another Numenmancer had been there. Who? Even if Hansa had become a mancer, his power would come from the Abyss. How was he involved with anything involving the Numen?

You're a Numenmancer. How were you able to summon an Abyssi?

They stumbled across Umber before they found the guard. He greeted her with a dry, "Mancer. I can't say it's a pleasure to see you. Excuse me."

Xaz shivered as the spawn she had come here to find moved past her. "Wait, please," she called after him.

He turned slightly, waiting for her to continue.

Alizarin pranced toward Umber, unconcerned about the snow around his bare feet or falling on his fur, beyond a slight twitch of his ear when a snowflake dropped onto it. "Xaz has been feeling a little sexually frustrated," he announced blithely. "Think you could help?"

Xaz fought a blush as Umber lifted one sardonic brow, amused. "Sorry . . . *Xaz*, you're not my type."

This time as he tried to push past her, she caught his arm. Her grip wasn't strong, but he winced. Xaz noticed the blush of blood on the fabric of his shirt.

"You and your mancer having some difficulties?" she asked. The only time Abyssi or spawn actually *bled* was when they meant to spill power. A wound that stayed open meant something was unfinished—a dangerous state which left the creature vulnerable. Even

Xaz, who had no natural tie to the Abyss, could feel the weakness.

Umber pulled his arm out of her grip. "I would believe that the lovely Abyssi sought me out entirely for sex—and I'm flattered, Alizarin, I really am, and I would love to take you up on the offer if I weren't in the middle of something already." Alizarin purred at the praise. "But you, Mancer, want something or you wouldn't be here. Spit it out so I can say no and we can move on."

Alizarin rested his chin on Umber's shoulder, looking bored. As Xaz had suspected, he was far too interested in Umber as entertainment to consider that his knowledge might be a threat. Umber leaned back against the Abyssi, and Alizarin wrapped his arms around his waist.

Xaz said, "I need your help. Can we maybe talk somewhere more private?" This wasn't the kind of conversation she wanted to risk having overheard.

The spawn actually laughed out loud. As if struck by a sudden idea, he twisted to speak to Alizarin. "Darling, you don't happen to know where I might find a necromancer around here, do you? Ideally one powerful enough to raise the recently dead, but easily bribed."

This time it was Xaz's turn to snicker. "*You* are looking for a mancer? You really are in trouble, aren't you?"

"If you could help me," Umber continued, now completely ignoring Xaz as he addressed Alizarin, "I'll have plenty of time for more enjoyable activities when I'm done."

"If you help me first," Xaz offered, "I can cast a finding spell. I think I should be able to locate a necromancer for you."

Umber's focus returned to her. "What do you need? I don't have much time."

"Can't we go somewhere—"

Umber interrupted her with a half grunt, half snicker. He looked from her to Alizarin—who was watching the crowds hustle past them with apparent fascination—and then back to her. "You want me to strip the Abyssal taint from your magic." Alizarin either hadn't heard or didn't care, so Xaz nodded. "If the Abyssi cooperated, I might be able to, but not in this state." He held up his wounded arm. The small bloodstain had spread slightly. Whatever he had begun, he would be leaking power until it was done, or risk the magical equivalent of bleeding to death. "If you can find a necromancer—"

This time it was her turn to interrupt with a humorless laugh. "I would need tools I can't get until the Numini will talk to me again." The spawn might be powerful enough to break in to wherever the Quin kept such things, but again, it was clear he couldn't do much at that moment.

Alizarin apparently had been listening. He turned to ask, "You need a body resurrected?"

Umber nodded. "If it can be."

Alizarin brightened. "I could eat it," he suggested. "Then it *can't* be raised."

It was obviously, for the Abyssi, a reasonable idea.

Umber even responded to it as such, though he regretfully explained, "It's long cold."

Alizarin frowned. "Necromancer," he said. "They don't even go to the temples."

"I know," Umber replied. He didn't seem to mind that Alizarin's hands had drifted, so one wrapped around his waist but the other rested on top of the open wound. "How do we find one?"

"Kill something?" Xaz suggested sarcastically.

The two men looked to each other thoughtfully, apparently taking the suggestion seriously.

Seeing the contemplative looks, Xaz had to point out, "If a necromancer came running every time someone died, your corpse would already have one."

"Good point," Umber conceded.

"Abyssi are drawn to Abyssumancers. Numini are drawn to Numenmancers. The living are drawn to animamancers. Could the dead find a necromancer?" Umber asked Xaz.

"Not being a necromancer myself," she said, "I neither know the answer to that question, nor how we would expect to make a request of one of the dead even if it were true."

"Is it true," a soft voice asked from the doorway behind them, "that those devoured by the Abyss dwell in the Abyss?"

The three of them turned to see a slender woman with a strawberry-blond braid and tawny hazel eyes. Xaz's heart leapt into her throat as she recognized the violet robes of a Sister of the Napthol and she cringed in anticipation of the bloodbath that might follow.

Alizarin answered, "Yes. For a while."

The woman frowned, her eyes narrowing as she searched the area. She shouldn't be able to see the Abyssi without a mancer's power, but a Sister of the Napthol was likely observant enough to notice the way the rest of them looked toward the apparently empty air.

The Sister spoke to Umber directly. "Is it true?"

"I've heard that," he answered. He didn't seem to feel that this woman was a threat. "Do they teach you to eavesdrop at the Cobalt Hall?"

"They teach us to attend to important conversations around us," the woman said. "The Order of A'hknet taught me to eavesdrop. Am I right this is the Numenmancer they tried to arrest the day Hansa was nearly killed?"

Umber nodded. Xaz was ready to flee, but so far, this Sister didn't seem inclined to raise an alarm.

"Is the Abyssi here, too?"

Alizarin smiled proudly as Umber said, "That would be true."

"Then you have eleven souls in the Abyss. Eleven dead, to whom your demon has a blood-connection. Have *them* find your necromancer."

"Pardon me," Xaz said tightly, "but who in the name of Numen are you, and *why* are you helping us?"

Umber performed the introductions. "Xaz, this is

Cadmia Paynes of the Napthol Order, and I believe she is trying to help *me*, not *us*, because I did a favor for her recently."

"Okay . . ." Xaz said, still nervous about the stranger in their midst. The Napthol Order wasn't a large step away from the Quinacridone. "So, you're saying we send Alizarin into the Abyss." If she could do it right, that might be a good way to lose him—though she decided not to say that bit aloud. "And have him . . . what? Tell them to find us a mancer? Why would they want to help us?"

"Tell them if they find you a necromancer, you'll guide them to the Numen. That is your realm, isn't it?"

Was that possible? Xaz had never spoken to the dead and gave little thought to the afterlife. If encouraging the Abyssi to go back to his native plane willingly didn't sever his bond to her, perhaps the Numini would be pleased by her attempt to guide the souls she had bloodied back to them.

"Let's move this conversation somewhere more private," Umber suggested. "We'll go back to the King's Ransom. If we're lucky, Hansa has changed his mind."

Hansa hadn't changed his mind. He had allowed the fire to go out and opened a window to keep the body fresher, and there was snow drifting in the corners of the room. Even though Hansa had bits of ice caught in his hair and eyelashes, he looked flushed and feverish.

"Hansa, please tell me you've reconsidered," Umber said.

Hansa just shook his head. He didn't even look at Cadmia and Xaz, just stared at Ruby as if hypnotized. Grief? The effect of the open boon? Xaz didn't know enough about spawn and the Abyss to know.

"I—" Umber broke off, swaying; Alizarin caught him with a hand on each of Umber's arms, but the Abyssi's attention no longer looked solicitous. It looked hungry. Umber jerked back without a flirtatious word. "If we're going to do this, we had best do it fast. Hansa, Cadmia has an idea that we can talk to your friends in the Abyss and ask them to help us find a necromancer in exchange for Xaz helping them move on to the Numen."

A little life returned to Hansa's face. He looked around as if just noticing everyone else for the first time. "Can you do that?" he asked Xaz.

Xaz had been braced for him to react to Alizarin's presence, though she wasn't sure if she expected panic due to his near-death or fascination due to his new mancer power. Instead, Hansa's gaze skipped over the Abyssi as if he were invisible. She didn't question the fortuitous turn; they didn't have time to waste. "I think I should be able to," she said. "I've never tried anything like it." Despite her resolve not to spend time on unnecessary confrontations, recriminations, or questions, she couldn't help adding, "I never meant to hurt them, or you. I thought I was summoning a Numini. I thought . . ."

She trailed off when Hansa looked away, the grief briefly so plain on his face that she couldn't stand it. He asked Cadmia, "Why are you here?"

The question seemed to take the Sister of the Napthol aback. "I . . ." She frowned, clearly puzzled.

Once again, Xaz glimpsed the swirl of the Numen power she had seen at the docks. Ruby's body was painted with its residue, and it actively clenched around Cadmia as the Sister of the Napthol tried to consider her actions logically.

Before Xaz could examine the trace, Alizarin distracted her by reaching to Umber again. This time, the hand that brushed Umber's arm had claws that drew fine lines of blood from the spawn's skin. Umber jumped, pulled back with a hiss, and snapped, "No." He turned to Hansa. "Hansa, call this off or don't, but do it now, before I'm too weak to do anything to help and the Abyssi decides I'm nothing but meat."

Hansa's eyes had momentarily cleared as Xaz spoke to him and he questioned Cadmia's presence, but now they fogged again as he returned to his contemplation of the dead woman. "I'm not calling it off," he said.

Umber unwrapped the bandage on his arm. "Then seal this boon, and I will quite gladly drag you into the Abyss with me."

Xaz tried not to look, but her gaze was morbidly drawn back. A burst of hot power like the breath of some immense animal wafted through the room as Umber revealed a wound that was not only slowly bleeding, but had also blackened around the edges. As Hansa pulled Umber close and set his lips to the wound, that breath drew back in until the power coiled tightly around the two men and the room went cold again.

The next seconds that passed seemed unnaturally peaceful, almost romantically gentle. Xaz's gaze traveled out the open window, to the driving snow turning the world to white.

Is it warm in the Abyss? she wondered.

PART 2

"This is not what you promised me!" The Abyssi snarled and whined, his voice replete with the offensive blend of arrogant and juvenile that seemed the province of the creatures of the infernal realm.

The Numini drew back, disgusted. "Promise," *it echoed. "I would never make a promise to one of your kind. All I have done is try to clean up the mess you have created."*

The Abyssi growled. If it could have reached across the realms with its body in addition to its awareness, it would have pounced on the Numini, heedless of the death that would have immediately followed. "The blue prince," it said petulantly. "He killed my mancer. I want his."

The Numini did not need to reply in words. The blue Abyssi, Alizarin, had bonded himself to a Numenmancer. Even this low creature surely knew better than to threaten one of them *while speaking to a lord of the divine realm. The bridge of power that allowed them to speak became rimed with frost and sparked with arcs of blue electricity.*

"Then I want something else of his," the Abyssi said, compromising in the face of the Numini's wordless threat.

"I agree that Alizarin has been a . . . complication." The Numini sighed. "I understand that he often meddles with others' property. Deal with him as you see fit. I will see to the rest."

CHAPTER 23

Cadmia hadn't felt this *right* about her life in a long time. She had been feeling extraordinarily anxious for a while there, but now she couldn't remember why. The plan to help Hansa, help Ruby, and help the guards who had died was a good one, and she was glad she had been able to suggest it.

She was blind to the Abyssi itself, but she could see all too clearly when the air tore, leaving a jagged scar in reality that could only be the rift to the Abyss. Snow swirling in through the open window became steam as it struck the rapidly growing rip, which quickly became a doorway-sized hole leading to tarry darkness. A twinge of unease tried to pierce her meditative calm when she saw the portal the Abyssi had opened so they could step into its native realm in search of the slain guards.

Calm, calm, the snow around her seemed to whisper.

How much power must it take to cut a portal like that? "It probably won't stay open long," she said, when none of the others seemed inclined to step forward. "We should go."

Umber caught her arm when she moved to lead the way. "You can't really intend to go with us," the spawn said.

What a funny moment to question her. "Yes, I do," she asserted, and then put action to her claim and walked into the rift.

Like the nursery-rhyme child whose cradle tumbles when the wind blows, she plummeted into a harsh reality. She had been wrapped in a warm blanket of peace and contentment, and completely unaware how unnatural that calm was until it was ripped brutally away. There had been something . . . someone . . . with her, but they were gone now. She was achingly alone.

Not alone.

Her skin crawled as the last few minutes caught up to her, and she remembered who had come here with her. The half-Abyssi spawn. The Numenmancer. *The Abyssi.*

What have I done?

She turned, hoping futilely that the rift would still be open and she could go right back through it. Instead, her eyes found the creature she had been blind to on the mortal plane, and the sight of it made her blood run cold.

Its shape shifted, never holding a single, identifiable form, but there was no mistaking what it was: Feral.

Hungry. Vicious. Cadmia couldn't make out teeth or claws, but she knew in her gut that it *had* those things. And in the primitive, furthest-back portion of her brain, she knew that if she didn't get away . . . if she didn't run . . .

"Hold it together, Hansa," she heard Umber say. She looked past the Abyssi to find Umber with a hand on Hansa's arm, clearly trying to stop him from bolting. Both men were wreathed in a hazy indigo glow, Umber's brighter than Hansa's. "*Breathe.* He's on our side."

"Thank Numen he is," Xaz whispered. She was furthest back, as if she had come through the rift last before it disappeared. The light she emitted was gray-yellow, like the first breath of sunrise on a foggy spring morning, but so faint it seemed to disappear when Cadmia looked at her directly.

Hansa's panic gave Cadmia the strength to quash her own. She forced herself to turn away from the Abyssi. Ancient instincts screamed that doing so was deadly, but she was more than her instincts and refused to be ruled by them. Instead, she looked around, to confirm they really were in the realm whose name was synonymous with all that was cruel, avaricious, and venal.

The ground was rolling black sand littered with bones—or maybe they were shells, though unlike any found off the shores of Kavet. Many had sharp barbs. Most were deep, rusty colors instead of the bleached white or dull black that most often washed up on Kavet's shores. All hinted at creatures more fierce than a clam or a snail, like an ash-colored claw as long as Cadmia's forearm that lay, empty, inches from her feet. What kind of creature left a shell like that?

What kind of creature killed *something with a shell like that?*

The answer to that question came in the form of a chorus of low, bone-quivering growls. She looked up to see a trio of beasts that looked a little like wolves, though their low-slung front shoulders bristled with spines, their heads were flat and wedge-shaped like snakes, and their fur was the color of slick blood. Cadmia froze, her breath turning to lead in her lungs.

The Abyssi flowed in front of the mortals and advanced toward the three scarlet beasts. When it struck them, the wolflike creatures scattered and tumbled, letting out pained, yipping cries as the personified darkness wrapped around them. A whiff of scalded fur reached Cadmia's nose, and then the Abyssi moved on, leaving only a few fragments of red fur and gray bone behind.

She swallowed thickly.

Don't you dare run, she told herself as the Abyssi approached again. If it wanted to kill her, she wouldn't be able to stop it. If it was an ally, she needed to be able to look it in the . . . face? Cadmia locked her knees and forced herself to stand.

"Thank you," she managed to say. Her voice came out a tight squeak, but she was proud of herself for making it work at all.

The longer she stared into the darkness, the easier

it became. The visceral terror that had nearly overwhelmed her edged aside and she noted the colors—sparks like firefly lights, but in a thousand unnamable hues—that danced inside the shadow. They swirled and blinked, hypnotic, like the will-o-wisps whose beauty drew unwary storybook travelers to their doom.

Her voice under control at last, she asked, "Are we . . . safe now?" She hesitated on the word, because if they really were in the Abyss, they certainly were not "safe."

The creature shrugged. How something made of pure amorphous terror could *shrug,* or how it could be perfectly clear that was exactly what it had done, Cadmia wasn't sure. However, the gesture was very human, almost comical, and made her relax further.

"From the red dogs, for now," the Abyssi said. "They can't best an Abyssi."

Cadmia would have expected its voice to be a growl or a hiss, as much animal as human. Instead it bordered on musical, like something you would expect crooned to you by a would-be lover.

Xaz asked, "Can you go back to your normal form?"

"The lovely form with the blue fur, she means," Umber clarified before the Abyssi could respond. "It's easier on mortal minds."

Cadmia braced herself, every description of Abyssi she had ever read running through her mind. She knew fur, scales, tails, and claws were normal, as were poisonous barbs and razor-sharp spines and—*and what do you really know?* she chastised her thoughts. *What Order scholars have actually seen what you are now seeing now?*

The *thump* her heart gave as smoke and shadow condensed was not entirely anxiety.

Where a moment before there had been a creature from nightmare, now there was a creature who stood like a man—or, almost like a man. The Abyssi balanced on the balls of his feet. Iridescent cobalt and turquoise fur, a lashing tail, and soft, tufted ears made it impossible to mistake him for a human.

"Is this better?" he asked, tilting his head.

"Much," Xaz breathed.

The Abyssi had long, silky black hair in addition to its fur, and the quizzical gesture caused several strands to fall forward and caress one cheek. Utterly inappropriate, the part of Cadmia that had grown up in the Order of A'hknet and had been trained to put a value to everything piped up to say, *If it weren't for the fur, that face could earn a lot of money down at the wharf.* Dramatic cheekbones, full lips, heavy white lashes around wide blue eyes.

Alizarin smiled, and Cadmia felt a brief panic that he had heard her thought. Could Abyssi do that? But the expression was open, engaging, not the sly, knowing look of a man who had caught a woman staring.

"Stronger Abyssi only take on solid forms to communicate with mortals, or for play," Umber told Xaz, oblivious to Cadmia's uncomfortable moment. "His *normal* form is the one we saw a few minutes ago."

"Oh," Xaz said.

It was time to get back on task.

As soon as Cadmia could remember what that task was.

She remembered the plan she had proposed, but not *why* she had suggested it.

"We're . . . looking for the shades of the slain guards," she said hesitantly, speaking aloud to try to make sense of her own jumbled memories.

"Tell me again," Umber drawled, "*why* you felt the need to come with us?"

Cadmia opened her mouth to reply, then closed it without speaking. Why *had* she done this? She had run to Hansa thinking he and Umber might be able to heal Ruby, or possibly revive her with magic. How had that goal morphed into necromancy, resurrection, and an intended trek through the Abyss?

Hansa was also frowning. Tentatively, he admitted, "I don't entirely understand why we're here."

"Because you're a brat willing to use power you don't understand to get your way," Xaz snapped. She rolled her shoulders like someone who has slept in an uncomfortable position. "Or have you forgotten hysterically demanding that Umber save Ruby?"

Hansa paled, and stared around as if the answers might be found on this desolate stretch of shell and bone-littered beach—if you could call it that, since where the water should be there was only an endless stretch of porous rock, which undulated like frozen waves. The sand, like the stone, was black and sparkled like raven feathers. Its beauty was only marred by Cadmia's imagination telling her what creatures might come out of the dozen dark caves she could see among the stone sea.

"I . . . did," Hansa said, sounding as if he would like to deny it. "And then you came. And you." He looked first at Xaz, and then at Cadmia. In his eyes she could see the desperate need for reassurance that was ever in the eyes of a man who has done something unforgivable.

"We'll talk about it later," Umber murmured. "We have more company on the way. Alizarin, am I right that the upper-level Abyssi respect my kind's right to claim property?"

"That is correct."

"Upper-level?" Cadmia asked, before immediately adding, "Never mind. It's not a good time for questions."

Hansa let out a startled protest as Umber reached out, wrapped an arm around his waist, and pulled the guard tightly to his side. Cadmia had an instant to wonder if he would further object to being considered "property," and then Alizarin stepped up and casually looped his tail around her waist.

The Abyssi's current form was beautiful, but Cadmia had seen what Umber called its "natural" form, and she had seen what it did to the red dogs that threatened them. The only thing that kept her from screaming when she found herself suddenly clamped to Alizarin's side was long years of rigid self-control. Her chosen vocation required her to listen to the worst horrors the human race could manage, confessions from men and women who had committed atrocities most people assumed were confined to the Abyss, without flinching.

He was protecting her, so it would be stupid to argue and fight to get away.

She thought he was protecting her.

She hoped so, anyway.

Meanwhile, the creature coming toward them seemed to be Abyssi, though it wasn't like Alizarin. Its body was slender and serpentine, its skin slick, and its eyes cold and slitted. Its six limbs were thick like a lizard's, though it seemed to disregard them as it moved in long undulations of its snakelike body.

The new Abyssi paused before them and bowed to Alizarin, bending armored front legs and dropping a diamond-shaped head with long, glistening fangs in a deferential bob. Then it rose up like a snake about to strike, front legs—arms?—folded across its scaled gray torso. When it spoke, the sound was like claws on stone, a fierce etching noise that made all the hair on Cadmia's body rise.

"You bring gifts for the royal court?" it asked optimistically, its head sliding side to side as it looked at their assembled group.

Alizarin grinned, but Cadmia didn't think it was a happy expression. It showed too many sharp white teeth. "You were rude about my last gift."

The lizard-Abyssi seemed puzzled for a moment, as if he wasn't sure what Alizarin meant by "rude." Then he took a half-wriggle back, maybe a flinch. "He was my protector," the Abyssi wheedled. "You killed him while I was sleeping, and I didn't even get to eat him."

The silly notion that Abyssi were very like human beings, an idea that had been formed from Alizarin's shrugs and grins, disappeared from Cadmia's mind as she tried to parse what the lizard-Abyssi had just said. *He was my protector . . . I didn't get to eat him.*

The lizard-Abyssi took another step back and said, "Antioch has been in a rage. He says you got his mancer killed. If you give us gifts, maybe we can help you with him?"

Alizarin's grin faded and his tail lashed, releasing Cadmia. She desperately hoped he was irritated by the other Abyssi pushing the idea of gifts, and wasn't concerned enough to be considering it. Umber's question suggested that Hansa was considered his property, and she doubted Alizarin wanted to get rid of his mancer. That left Cadmia.

"He is a prince of the fourth level," the lizard-Abyssi said, Alizarin's reaction making him bolder. "You are only of the third. You will need help."

Some of the older texts in the Order of the Napthol's most restricted libraries spoke of the "levels of the Abyss." Cadmia had always thought it was euphemistic until now. If this Antioch was of a deeper level than Alizarin, he was stronger.

"He is fourth-level chattel," Alizarin answered in a grumbling voice that bordered on a growl, "and you are a lord of the high court only because I slew all the Abyssi there stronger than you. These four are *mine.*" His tail wrapped snugly around Cadmia again, emphasizing his point. "If you touch them, I will eat you. Now go away."

The lizard-Abyssi didn't stay to argue with the threat in Alizarin's voice, but turned and fled across the black dunes of sand in the direction from which it had come.

"I think I probably speak for the group," Hansa said, his throat so tight with tension that his voice came out a soft rasp, "when I say we should finish what we came here to do and then leave as quickly as possible."

"Is this Antioch likely to be a problem for you?" Umber asked.

"*Did* you kill his mancer?" Xaz sounded like she was taking that more personally than the threat to the rest of their safety.

"I didn't kill him," Alizarin huffed, responding only to Xaz. "Hansa did."

"Excuse me?" Hansa chirped.

"I'm not the one who made him throw the knife away when you arrested him," Alizarin told Hansa, sounding irritated that his role in Antioch's mancer's death was being questioned, and obviously missing the fact that the Quin guard looked terrified as he suddenly realized how many enemies he might have in this place.

The scene came clear to Cadmia.

"Baryte," she said, recalling the name of the Abyssumancer who had asked for her counsel, as well as the stink of burning flesh as he held his hand over the candle, and the abrupt horror of his death. "Antioch was his Abyssi? Is he the black Abyssi Baryte mentioned?" All the puzzle pieces tumbled over and over in her mind, trying to find a pattern that made sense. "Did *he* somehow call us here?"

"I think we should leave here *quickly,*" Hansa said. Then he winced, as if struck by a sudden pain. "As soon as we've done what we need to do."

He started to lean against Umber, flinched away, and then immediately repeated the action. Umber gave him an opaque look and shook his head, not acknowledging the touch or the comment.

Was he trying to be discreet? Cadmia hadn't thought that Hansa and Umber were lovers, but Hansa's motions had the look of a man trying to resist old habits.

Cadmia drew a deep breath, trying to find the best way to articulate the certainty that had been growing in her since they had stepped into the Abyss.

"We're looking for a shade," she said haltingly, "to help us find a necromancer back in Kavet so you can resurrect a woman whose life is so dear to you, Hansa . . . that we all left her unguarded in a public inn." Since the others didn't seem inclined to clarify why this made sense or argue with her, she continued. "We all seem to have taken extreme measures to accomplish something I'm not sure any of us would ever desire. Unless you really think Ruby would want you to do this, Hansa?"

The guard shook his head fractionally, horror and bewilderment warring in his eyes as he considered his own irrational actions.

Cadmia remembered the old warnings: *An impulse you can't explain is the Others whispering in your ears.* This time, the Others had done more than whisper, and the result was more than an impulsive walk down to the docks to visit old faces.

But were they done yet? Or were they just now starting to speak?

CHAPTER 24

The last thing Xaz wanted was to focus the others' suspicions on her, but she didn't seem to have a choice. Cadmia was too obviously right; they hadn't done this of their own free will.

"I saw Numen power all around the docks and Ruby's body," she admitted. When the others just looked at her, waiting for further explanation, she shut her eyes to block out their stares and continued. "Ruby was impulsive," she said, remembering the woman who—in another world—might have been her friend. "She had a temper. She wasn't the kind of person who would normally have run off and hurt herself, but a Numenmancer could have convinced her to jump, and then nudged Hansa and Cadmia into reacting the way they did."

"That's crazy," Cadmia objected. "Why would a Numenmancer go to that kind of trouble?"

Xaz snickered. "You two can't imagine why a mancer would think it's funny to trick you into crawling into the Abyss? It wasn't *me*," she added sharply. "If it were, I wouldn't be with you."

Cadmia's face suddenly went stone serious. She turned to Umber. "What about you? Could a Numenmancer have manipulated you? Or Alizarin?"

Umber shook his head. "Abyssi—though beautiful and powerful, Alizarin, so do not take my words badly—are not known for their forethought or careful analysis when unbridled impulse is an option. As for me, I owed Hansa a boon. That bond isn't something that can be argued with."

"How much power *would* it take to influence you?" Cadmia pushed.

Umber tensed, and Xaz sensed a defensive reply on the way. He clearly changed his mind at the last moment and said instead, "An Abyssumancer could have forced me to act, but not subtly. Even the most powerful Abyssumancer in Kavet couldn't have tricked me into stepping into the Abyss without my sensing it."

Xaz saw where Cadmia was going with her logic, but hoped there was another explanation. She would far prefer a garden-variety mancer had put them into this position.

"Why did you save Hansa's life?" Cadmia asked the spawn.

Umber ignored Hansa's squawked protest. "He had been tainted by the Abyssi who injured him. If he survived, that taint could have turned him into a mancer. I didn't want to risk it. I told him—"

"Yes, yes, you told him that," Cadmia said brusquely. "I didn't believe it then and I don't believe it now. You could have killed him. Instead you granted him a boon. *Why?*"

Umber tensed his jaw, and didn't answer.

"Could an Abyssi have done it?" Cadmia asked, looking at Alizarin. "Baryte talked about a black Abyssi. Is that Antioch?"

Alizarin considered, and said, "Abyssi come in many colors. Antioch is ashy."

"Might Baryte have described him as black?" she pressed. Alizarin gave a half shrug, half nod, as if it wasn't the description he would use but he could see why someone might. "Could he have done this? Baryte said he had a plan."

"This is a very intricate plan for an Abyssi," Umber suggested.

"Is it?" Cadmia asked Alizarin.

"For most of us," he answered. Xaz couldn't tell if he was intentionally being evasive, or was just too distracted to give the matter much thought. He was pacing a slow circle around their group, face lifted as if scenting the wind.

"I think we're looking at the wrong plane for our explanation," Xaz admitted. "Abyssi might not be able to plot, but Numini can."

The Sister of the Napthol frowned, an expression of scholarly analysis rather than confusion or concern. "I was always told the Others can manipulate humans in little ways, but can't push them into anything that violates their basic natures and values. Forgive me, Hansa, but traversing the Abyss and practicing necromancy and raising the dead is *not* something I would ever . . ." She trailed off, gulping a little, as she considered that she *had*, if ever so briefly. "And you say Ruby wouldn't have killed herself. Can the Numini force a person to do something so opposite all reason?"

Xaz wished she could just say *yes*, because honesty meant admitting how much of this blame probably fell on her shoulders. Unfortunately, whether or not her reason for coming to the Abyss made any more sense than anyone else's, she couldn't afford to sabotage her only allies here. That meant telling the truth.

"As for you, Cadmia, perhaps it's true that you allow the Numini in when you study them and pray for their guidance. They could have reached Hansa when he went to the mancers' temple to rescue Pearl." She was *not* about to tell anyone that she, too, had attempted to take the girl.

"And Ruby?" Cadmia prompted.

She had hoped she could avoid answering that one. "A few days ago, I was in a hurry and Ruby insisted on stopping me to talk. I used my power on her. It could have given the Numini a way in if they wanted to manipulate her."

She kept her eyes on Hansa as she spoke, and saw the way he gritted his teeth and his hand flexed into a fist, like he might take a swing at her. He had every right to be furious, not just for Ruby's death but for the other guards'. She hoped he could control himself long enough for them to work this out.

"But *why*?" Cadmia asked, either oblivious to the tense moment or deliberately trying to move past it. "What possible use are we to the Numini in the Abyss?"

Umber squeezed Hansa's shoulder, a simple move that made Hansa's whole body relax. His attention left Xaz completely, all hints of his justifiable rage snuffing like a candle flame.

Umber declared, "I don't personally care what the Numini want with us. I plan to accomplish our task, asinine as it is, and then get back to the human realm as soon as—" He broke off, then settled his gaze on Alizarin. "You brought us here, but you can't bring us back, can you?"

The Abyssi looked back at the spawn with amusement. After a moment he said, in tones that suggested the fact was blatantly obvious, "If Abyssi could open rifts to the human plane at will, there would be more of us there."

"Xaz?" Cadmia prompted. "You're a mancer."

"I'm a *Numenmancer*," Xaz spat, only realizing the full scope of their predicament now that Umber had pointed it out. "I have no control over the Abyss."

"We're after shades first anyway," Hansa said hollowly.

Xaz almost snapped at him, pointing out that they had bigger concerns and he needed to catch up, and then she remembered Hansa leaning forward to take blood from Umber. It didn't matter what had manipulated the two men into coming here. Hansa had sealed the third boon. The magic would drive him and

Umber to fulfill the task for which it had been raised, regardless of their wishes.

"Can we talk to the Numini?" Cadmia asked, looking at Xaz expectantly. "Ask what they want with us? If the Numini manipulated us once, they're likely to do it again," she added, when it looked like Hansa and Umber might argue. "You two are more likely to succeed if you don't unexpectedly encounter divine interference."

She had a good point—and damn her for it. Did Cadmia realize what she was asking? Yes, Cadmia had come up with the plan that sent them here, and Hansa had taken three boons of an Abyss-spawn, but every instinct Xaz possessed still told her it was nigh suicidal to allow a Sister of the Napthol and a soldier of the 126 to see her speak to the Numini.

"I'll try," she sighed, "but I can't promise they'll speak to me. They've refused recently."

"What do you need us to do to help?" Cadmia asked.

Go away. "Give me space. As much as you can."

As the others backed away, following Alizarin's directions, Xaz sat cross-legged on the debris-strewn ground and cast out her awareness.

Before her questing power reached anywhere near the Numini, it brushed across scores of Abyssi. She could feel them, including the dense gathering that must be the court. As her awareness brushed each one, she had a momentary sense of what it was doing—hunting, stalking, grooming, sleeping, playing, coupling. Abyssi "play" was brutal.

Focus, Xaz, she chided herself.

"Beings of the Numen," she whispered. In the Numen, names and words had power. Unlike Alizarin, the Numini who had given Xaz her mancer's power had never shared his name with her. *"I, Dioxazine, your chosen child, call to you. I petition you. I implore you."* A proper invocation was always threefold. Xaz had spent much of her childhood looking for synonyms for "beg" and "grovel." *"Please grant me your attention, speak to me, advise me."*

She sent up the call, supporting it with as much power as she could muster.

She waited, unmoving, trying not to listen to the distant sounds of scraping, screaming, and howling. The Numini would expect her to be a vessel ready for their regard.

An interminable time seemed to pass before the first awareness of another being trickled into her mind, along with a seeping cold that made the Abyssal wind seem balmy.

I am here.

She sighed in relief at the familiar voice. Her patron. *"I am grateful for your attention."* How those words grated on her! If one of the Numini had sent them here, it was probably him. She spoke the courtesy by rote, though, because he would disappear again if he felt she had been rude. *"May I assume you know our situation?"*

I am aware, he said. *I have a task for you.*

She had to swallow back her fury like bile rising from her gut. A task. *"You did send us here, then?"*

I was involved, he admitted. *I regret my methods had to be so crude and convoluted.* The Numini spoke about regret, but Xaz didn't think he actually felt it. *There were complications that held me from acting more directly.*

Those complications had sent her to the Abyss, and had apparently killed at least one person—more if the guards Alizarin had killed were included. She gritted her teeth, and struggled to keep her mental voice calm. *"Is it your wish that we find the guards' shades?"*

There was a long hesitation, as if the Numini wrestled with how much she needed to know. *The shades are inconsequential. If the Abyssi who slew them is willing to give them up, and you are strong enough to transport them across the veil, we will take them. They died righteously even though they died in violence. Your task is to return someone far more precious to us.*

"Who?"

Again that pause, during which she had to struggle to contain her impatience. *The Abyssi hold a sorcerer named Terre Verte imprisoned in their royal court. We need him retrieved.*

"Why?"

The chill filling her deepened. *That is most certainly not your concern.*

She didn't know much about the Abyss, but she had no desire to go closer to the gathering of Abyssi her power had allowed her to glimpse. *"Are the Abyssi the ones who caused your 'complications'?"* she asked. *"If they were able to interfere with you, how do you expect me to do better? And how will I convince the others to help me? Hansa and Umber need to fulfill the terms of the boon."*

They will help you, he informed her, *because you will tell them that Terre Verte is their only hope of fulfilling the boon. The woman's body will be cremated within the hour. A necromancer cannot revive her, but Terre Verte can. As long as they have an option that will allow them to fulfill the boon, they* must *take it.*

"That's cruel," she accused, unthinking.

I have given you your task, he declared, with a spike of chastising power that made her flinch. *It is up to you to obey, not to judge. Now return to your* Abyssi master, *and tell your companions what must be done.*

The Numini's tone was bitter and disappointed as he referred to Alizarin.

Then he was gone. She gasped and opened her eyes, shivering convulsively.

Stupid, demanding, arrogant bastard!

How she wished she could say those words to his face.

The others had withdrawn several yards, but came toward her expectantly when they saw her move.

"Anything?" Hansa asked.

Xaz cleared her throat of the fury that had tightened it. "What happens," she asked, "if you cannot fulfill the boon? The Quin will cremate the body the instant sighted guards see Numen and Abyssal power in that room. Can a necromancer still resurrect her then?"

Umber looked at her speculatively. He answered, "If it cannot be done, then once we are absolutely certain of that, the boon will be fulfilled. Speaking for myself, I have never met a necromancer, and cannot say for sure the limits of one's power without asking."

I won't tell them, Xaz decided, with a giddy blend of terror and exultation.

If the Numini could have spoken directly to the spawn and the guard, they wouldn't have bothered to go through Xaz. As long as Xaz didn't tell them about Terre Verte, they wouldn't have to go after him. They could complete their original mission—speak to the shades and try to find a necromancer—and then find a way back to the mortal realm.

"The Numini told me only that they would accept the souls of the dead guards if we have the power to bring them across," she said, hoping that even if Umber or the others realized she was lying, they would have the sense not to question her further. "If they have other plans for us, they do not deign to tell them to a mere mortal like myself." To explain her obvious irritation and how long the conversation had been, she added, "They do not like having their Numenmancer question them."

She wasn't lying to protect Hansa and Umber, but herself. She couldn't trust Alizarin to always have the presence of mind or the motivation to protect them, and without him, Umber was the only one of them with a chance of being able to navigate the Abyss and find a way back to the mortal realm successfully. If Xaz had any choice in the matter, she would do everything in her power to avoid trekking into the bowels of the Abyssal court, but if Umber went, she would need to go with him.

CHAPTER 25

What is wrong with me?

Hansa's training had been focused on how to identify and fight mancers, the mortals who *served* the Abyssi and Numini, not on the capabilities of the Others themselves—that last was knowledge reserved for the Order of the Napthol. Without Cadmia's education, Umber's Abyssi parentage, or Xaz's experience as a mancer, it was hard for him to follow the theories the others bandied about regarding what the Others could or couldn't do.

It was even harder than it might have been, because every now and then his attention would be caught by the shape of Umber's jaw or the warmth of his body and long moments would go by. Hansa would realize he had moved close to the spawn, or pressed his hand into the deep indigo glow that surrounded him and shimmered in response to his touch.

Blood-drunk, he reminded himself, remembering what Umber had called his reaction after they had rescued Pearl. He had tasted Umber's blood again just before stepping into the Abyssi, hadn't he?

Each time he noticed what he had done, he moved back, though something inside him wept to pull away from that shivering glow. It had passed last time; it would pass this time.

"There is a camp of shades outside the court, or was when I was here before," Alizarin said, sounding impatient. "We should go there."

He started walking, leaving the rest of them to scramble after him.

"Why there?" Xaz asked.

"They have walls," Alizarin answered. "And weapons. I should hunt before Antioch finds us, and you want to be somewhere safer before I leave you."

The logic seemed sound, but as Hansa tried to follow Alizarin, a feeling like ants skittering across his skin overwhelmed him. It made his muscles twitch. Before he could identify the sensation, Umber asked, "Is it possible that the shades we're seeking have found this camp?"

The Abyssi glanced over his shoulder just long enough to shrug, then said, "Shades normally appear near where they died."

Was that an answer?

Alizarin kept walking. Cadmia trotted after him, catching up and speaking excitedly. "So the Abyss really is analogous to the mortal plane?" she asked. "And there are really levels," she added. "How many?"

That was a yes, Umber supplied, for Hansa's benefit. His warmth against Hansa's side and arm across his shoulders was as much a comfort as the words, though Hansa wasn't sure which of them had initiated the contact. *They might be nearby. We can get to safety and still pursue our goal.*

As soon as the assurance had been uttered, the jittery discomfort faded.

When Hansa tried to gather his will to shrug off the spawn's touch, though, he found he lacked the motivation. This had already happened too many times for him to hope the others wouldn't notice, so what was the point?

Meanwhile, Alizarin sidled closer to Cadmia, his feet barely seeming to disturb the black sand beneath them. Hansa would have stepped back; Cadmia almost leaned toward him, as if he were a fascinating butterfly she wanted to observe. "Five," he said. "I have never been deeper than the third, but my sire was of the fifth."

"You are exceptionally excited to be in the land of the damned," Xaz remarked, speaking Hansa's thoughts in what sounded like a forcedly level tone.

Cadmia tensed, her face taking on the placid, thoughtful expression Hansa was beginning to realize was a mask. "I know I should be horrified by this entire situation, but this is a chance to learn more about the field I have spent my adult life studying. Don't you understand?"

"I understand you're the one of us who should have been arrested," Xaz grumbled.

As they moved away from the beach, skeletal structures rose from the sand to surround them. Like ancient trees fossilized in black marble, they were slick in appearance and rippled with glints of copper and rusted iron like dried blood. Luminescent pods the size of chicken eggs hung from their branches, glowing in nursery shades of pale pink, sea-foam green, and powder blue.

As they passed near one of the trees, Cadmia lifted a hand as if to touch a candy-pink orb.

Alizarin moved like smoke; faster than Hansa could blink, the Abyssi was on Cadmia's other side, his tail around her wrist yanking her back. The Sister choked out a cry, and asked, "What—"

"Watch," the Abyssi commanded. He moved Cadmia several feet further back, then reached up to bat at one of the delicate-looking pink orbs.

Hansa cringed from the shriek that followed, so he barely saw when the pod burst, spattering the surrounding area with silver ichor that steamed where it hit Alizarin's fur and ate through the back of a large conch-shaped shell resting at the base of the stone tree.

After a moment, the mercury-like substance drew together and climbed back up the stone column, higher this time, and reformed into its harmless-looking pod.

"Don't touch anything that glows," Alizarin advised. He shook himself, fluffing his fur then smoothing it back down. Hansa saw singed areas on the Abyssi's arms, face, and chest, and didn't want to imagine what would have happened to human flesh. "Except me," he added as he loped back toward Cadmia.

"Thank you," Cadmia said, her voice breathy. She lifted a hand, hesitated, then responded to the Abyssi's implied invitation by smoothing a hand down the now-patchy fur on his forearm. "Are you all right? Your poor fur."

Was Alizarin *purring*?

"It'll grow back," Xaz muttered.

"Is that from the shades' camp?" Umber asked, lifting a hand to point to a thread of lighter gray rising into the dark sky. "It looks like smoke."

Alizarin nodded, tail lashing. Hansa might not have recognized the frustrated expression if it hadn't echoed exactly how he felt every time he stepped away from Umber. If he could find a moment when the Abyssi wasn't around, Hansa would warn Cadmia that while Alizarin was being remarkably well behaved so far, it wasn't a good idea to draw an Abyssi's attention physically.

"This is as close as I should go," Alizarin said. "If they see me they will not accept you."

"Are you well enough to do this?" Umber asked Hansa. He spoke slowly, as if choosing his words with care.

Hansa pulled reluctantly away from Umber's warmth. It seemed overly optimistic to assume they would find the other guards in the first place they looked, but if they did, it would go better if they didn't see him snuggling against the Abyss-spawn man.

What am I going to say to them, anyway? he wondered. *How will I explain being here with the Abyssi and mancer responsible for their deaths?*

What if I see Ruby?

How had it not occurred to him until that moment that she, too, should be here? If shades appeared near where they died, shouldn't she have been at the beach?

Ruby, at least, wouldn't be surprised to see Umber. Hansa remembered her expression when she found them together, as if it confirmed something she had suspected for a long time.

He cleared his throat and said, "Let's go."

They walked toward the smoke, leaving the Abyssi behind.

When Alizarin said *wall,* Hansa had pictured stones. Instead, an assortment of junk—large, cracked shells, stones, and thorn-covered vines—made a neck-high barrier that spanned the empty space between the stony trees, enclosing a lopsided circle maybe a quarter acre in total. A man and a woman armed with rough, crooked spears watched them approach with serious expressions.

"Come around this way," the woman said. "There's a gate."

Hansa fought to keep his expression neutral. The shades looked like any other humans . . . if he discounted the disquieting tone of their skin and eyes. The woman who had greeted them at the gate looked like she was at the peak of a bout of flu; her skin was clammy and blotchy as if with unbroken fever, gray tinged in a way that made it impossible to tell if she had once been fair or tanned, and her brown eyes had a strange haze to them.

"I'm Yarrow, of Tamar," the woman said. "Do you know your names?"

They hadn't considered what they were going to tell any shades they met. Supposedly, the dead were sent here for a reason. Could they be trusted? Out of habit, Hansa looked at Cadmia.

"Is it normal not to?" the Sister of the Napthol asked. She sounded composed and neutral as she implied that maybe they didn't know who they were.

Yarrow nodded. "Many people don't at first. They don't know who they are, where they're from . . . how they got here. It can take weeks to sort it out, and most don't have weeks before they—well, you're lucky to have found us quickly." With the same compassionate bluntness, she asked, "Do you know where you are?"

"Yes," Cadmia answered this time.

"Weeks?" Hansa asked. He hoped Yarrow thought the panic in his voice was due to his own lost memory, because he couldn't help it. Would they have to be here that long before they had any hope of finding Jenkins and the others? *Could* they wait? Just thinking about it made something in his chest constrict. He didn't think they had that kind of time before the boon would demand they do something else, but the thought of abandoning the others was equally horrific.

Yarrow nodded and said comfortingly, "Don't worry. We'll guide you through it. In the meantime, we have a fire to keep you from the cold, and a little food we can share."

There were a half-dozen other shades in the enclosed area, most looking worse than Yarrow. A few stood near the walls, clearly acting as sentries. The others hung back, watching the new group with suspicion.

"I'm guessing you haven't been here long?" Yarrow asked. As she led them to the fire, which was flickering against the wind and belching tarry smoke, one of the other shades stood and walked away without comment.

"Not long," Umber replied. "It shows?"

Yarrow just smiled sadly. If she was an example of what a shade looked like after a time in the Abyss, it was obvious that Hansa and the others were new. "You must be hungry then. After a while the body starts to forget things like that . . ." She trailed off as if the thought had inspired another, more disturbing one. After a moment she shook herself and continued. "Early on, you still feel things like cold, hunger, and thirst, though they can't kill you."

She ducked into a patchwork, lean-to shelter and returned with a bone bowl full of what looked like some strange kind of fruit. Each was about the size of an egg, slate-gray, and protected by sharp spines. Yarrow demonstrated how to scrape the spines off on the sharp edge of the bowl before cracking the shell to eat the pulpy seeds inside.

"These quench the thirst," Yarrow said. She put the bowl down next to the fire and said, "I should check on Vim. He's one of our hunters, but was hurt today. It will give the three of you time to talk if you want."

"You *hunt* the Abyssi?" Umber asked.

Yarrow's eyes widened. "We hunt the mindless beasts who roam this level of the Abyss," she clarified. "It's dangerous but necessary. None of us could fight one of the true Abyssi."

She turned away without further word and disappeared into another of the ramshackle shelters. The other shades had drawn back, giving them privacy either from kindness or lack of interest.

"Damn," Umber whispered. "I knew finding them might be difficult, but it never occurred to me they might not be here to be found yet."

Wryly, Cadmia said, "We don't have much information from people who recall *dying*. The things I could teach the others, if only—"

She broke off, perhaps noticing that everyone was staring at her. Yes, it was her order's task to study these things, but this level of interest was as disconcerting as Hansa's incessant pull toward Umber.

Who he was too close to again.

Who cares? he thought. *Your friends aren't here to judge you.*

"'Ware!" The shout came from the far wall, and made them all jump. After years as a guard, Hansa responded to the sentry's warning instinctively. Even thoughts of Umber disappeared from his mind as he shot to his feet and put the others behind him, wishing he had a weapon.

He looked around at the shades, assuming they had plans for these situations, but instead of running to fight, those who had been armed were dropping their weapons and backing away. Hansa caught the whispered warning: "*Abyssi*."

The creature who approached the wall had a sleek, furred body, though its shape was closer to the jungle cats Hansa had seen in some Silmari art than Alizarin's mostly humanoid form. Its shaggy fur was mottled gray and black, but the eyes it lifted to them still burned a familiar, brilliant blue.

As it reached the wall its form flickered, shifting to an Abyssi's less-substantial and more terrifying natural shape as briefly as an eye-blink; a moment later it was inside the camp, solid again, and clearly focused on their group.

Umber stepped forward, pushing Hansa aside to do so. His body was rigid with tension.

"Greetings," he said, "from myself and from Alizarin. Are you seeking us?"

Supposedly, Umber had the ability to claim Hansa, and he was clearly invoking Alizarin's ownership to protect the others. Hansa noted the Abyssi's color, though, which one might easily describe as "ashy." He suspected Antioch might have no interest in respecting Abyssi rules.

"You have something of mine." Whereas Alizarin's voice had been musical, Antioch's was gravelly, scree cascading down a hillside.

"The Numenmancer belongs to Alizarin," Umber answered, his poise impressive given what he was facing. "This human belongs to me," he said, putting a warm hand on Hansa's shoulder before removing it to wave dismissively at Cadmia and add, "And this one is also Alizarin's. I'm sure you can taste his power on her."

The new Abyssi snarled, a noise that struck Hansa like a blow, driving a sharp pain between his temples. Its fur rose, as well as a crest of inky spines around its jaw and above its eyes, tipped in the brilliant green and orange stripes Hansa associated with poisonous frogs. "Alizarin owes me."

Stall, Hansa thought. Alizarin said he would be nearby hunting. He had to have anticipated a challenge like this coming. If he could sense another Abyssi so close, he would come back.

Right?

It was hard to hold to that fragile hope as Antioch stalked closer and looked past Umber's shoulder to directly meet Hansa's eyes. The light of the Abyss glowed in them like the blue heart of a pyre. "You stole my mancer," he accused.

Help came from the last place Hansa ever would have expected. Xaz said, "From what I heard, you had nearly destroyed your mancer already. Hansa wouldn't have been there if you hadn't used him so carelessly."

Another of those horrifying blinks, and the Abyssi was suddenly in front of Xaz. He lifted a hand and touched her face.

Xaz flinched, and Hansa saw beads of blood run down her cheek.

"Alizarin asked permission to give my chosen one a gift. Do you know what that gift was?"

Xaz paused an instant to think, then guessed, "The knife." Her voice was tight and strangled. "That's how he formed a bond with me."

"He *said* it would make a powerful tool," Antioch growled. "But as soon as it was time to fight, he forced my mancer to discard it."

"Alizarin didn't make Baryte throw the knife away," Cadmia said. She sounded breathy, as if it was hard to get the words out. Was she mad enough to think arguing with Antioch was a good idea, or had she, like Hansa, decided playing for time was their only way to survive this?

As Antioch flickered in front of Cadmia, he remarked, "I only need to keep one of you." The words sounded contemplative, though they were clearly a threat. He looked from her to Hansa as if trying to decide which one he wanted.

Hansa looked around, desperately hoping the shades had some kind of secret weapon they could use against the Abyssi, but they had scattered like leaves before a storm. No help from that quarter.

"Hansa belongs to me," Umber said, drawing the Abyssi's attention back to him, "and I did nothing to you. Perhaps we could discuss an arrangement?"

He's not serious, Hansa thought. *I really hope he's not serious.* He didn't think Umber was the type to sell one of them to an Abyssi if he had a choice, but he might not feel there was another option. Maybe there wasn't.

"Your human took my mancer," the Abyssi spat, "so I was going to take *him*. Baryte marked him for me.

You tried to remove the mark, but you can't own prey I already claimed."

This time, when the Abyssi looked back at Hansa, he felt the old, healed injury in his left hand flare to life again. Compared to the suffocating heat he had felt when Baryte had first cut him, this was like holding a winter-chilled hand up before a slightly-too-hot fire to warm, but understanding made him shudder.

If it hadn't been for Umber, he really could have become a mancer—not from the deep rents down his back from Alizarin, but from a tiny scratch made by an Abyssumancer's blade.

"That's why he was able to get blood-drunk," Umber said, clearly trying to pull Antioch's attention away from Hansa again. "I was able to remove Alizarin's power from him, but didn't notice your mark among the larger contamination."

Whatever Antioch might have said in return was lost. The Abyssi bounded past Umber, brushing against Hansa before shouldering Cadmia out of the way, sending her sprawling. Hansa spun, relieved to see that Antioch was heading toward another form now slipping over the gate—this one a familiar, luminescent blue.

Alizarin's humanity had faded away. As he crossed the sands, he was once again the formless terror they had seen when they first appeared in the Abyss, something Hansa flinched instinctively away from even as he breathed relief at his appearance. Knees weak, he leaned against Umber for support, listening to the rapid pounding of the spawn's anxious heart. Xaz scrambled to help Cadmia.

Antioch leapt. Alizarin met him, and they clashed as a void of darkness, claws, fangs, and hunger.

A deep rumbling came from the combatants. Hansa felt it as a grating sensation, as if his bones were moving tectonically past each other. A hiss from one of the Abyssi reached him like a sharp wind.

Come on, Umber urged, his voice in Hansa's head momentarily loud enough to get his attention. He was trying to make them all move.

Hansa's limbs felt leaden, and the others looked the same. With Xaz's help, Cadmia was pushing to her feet haltingly, her mouth set in a grim line. The Numenmancer was gray-pale except for the blood seeping down her face.

Hansa spared a look back to the two Abyssi. They were lost in a swirling miasma of indefinable violence.

"Get out!" Hansa jumped as the shade who had greeted them so graciously earlier hissed at them to leave. "Don't come back here."

"But—"

He hadn't really intended to argue, just hadn't been able to think quickly enough to process Yarrow's words. The shade snapped, "We survive here because the Abyssi have no interest in us. *Get out!*"

Stumbling, gasping, they fled the encampment.

CHAPTER 26

Xaz's only injuries were the small cuts on her face, but she felt battered. When a dog growled, it raised its hackles and tried to look big to avoid a fight. When an Abyssi growled, it wasn't posturing; it was a first attack. Power flared like a mantle, striking those within range. Just being near the two battling creatures was enough to do damage to a mortal.

They limped along, following Umber with no thought beyond *get away,* until Cadmia collapsed and gasped, "Can't."

A plume of fine black sand rose around her, looking too inviting to resist. Xaz fell next to her with little more grace.

The others didn't argue either, but sprawled nearby, alternately coughing and panting as if they had all inhaled something caustic.

Cadmia clutched a hand to her ribs, grimacing.

"How badly are you hurt?" Xaz asked, remembering Antioch striking Cadmia on his way by.

"I don't know."

"You're bleeding," Umber told her. "Your arm, your side."

The light that had grayed the sky when they first arrived had been dying since some time at the shades' camp, and even the glowing creatures on the trees seemed less numerous now. In the dim light, any blood on Cadmia's dark clothes was invisible to Xaz. Was Umber's vision better, or could he sense the blood another way?

"Let me see," Umber said.

Cadmia set her jaw as if the movement hurt, and gingerly raised her shirt. Jagged scratches ran up and down her chest and arm on the side where Antioch had brushed against her. Several were still bleeding, and the skin around them was inflamed.

Umber pulled off his own shirt and started tearing it into strips, using the pieces to apply pressure to the deepest cuts. Cadmia let out a small, pained sound at the back of her throat.

"How bad is it?" Xaz asked. She didn't like the look of the swollen flesh that surrounded the wounds. They reminded her of the brightly colored spines Antioch had lifted when angered, which in a natural creature would have warned of poison.

"The blood might attract predators," Hansa said. His words were carefully measured, as if forming them was a struggle. "We should . . ." He looked around, eyes scanning the ground, then made a waving gesture as if trying to recall the word. No, not as if searching for a word; as if swinging a sword.

"Weapons," Cadmia agreed.

Her voice choked on the end of the word and she started coughing, a fit that racked her body so severely Umber had to grip her tightly to keep her from falling face-first in the sand. By the time she had recovered, her face was flushed and covered with a sheen of sweat, but her lips were gray-blue.

Umber lifted the cloth he was using to staunch the blood, and Xaz clamped her teeth on her horror as she saw the way the skin around the wounds had started to blister and blacken.

"Can you do anything?" she asked the spawn. "You healed Hansa."

"With effort, I could close the wounds and stop the bleeding," Umber said hesitantly. "I can't remove the poison from her blood, though." Cadmia bit her lip, suppressing her first response to the obvious death sentence Umber had just declared, and the spawn added hastily, "It's an Abyssal poison. Divine power might be able to cleanse it."

They both looked at Xaz expectantly, Umber calmly and Cadmia with a desperate plea.

"Xaz?" Umber prompted. His voice was too calm, carefully managed to avoid panicking Cadmia, as if she couldn't see and undoubtedly feel the poison's rapid spread.

"I don't know if I can do anything." She was unable

to make her voice any stronger than a whisper. "I haven't had much control over my power since Alizarin bonded to me."

"Try?" Cadmia urged.

Xaz nodded sharply, and forced herself to step forward. She knelt next to the Sister of the Napthol, and touched her fingertips to a spot of unmarked skin. Cadmia jumped, reminding Xaz that her hands were usually icy. Ruby used to remark on it when Xaz accidentally touched her while passing a dish at dinner or something similar.

"Sorry," she said to Cadmia, closing her eyes and resisting the impulse to look at Hansa. "My power is cold."

It wasn't the first time Ruby had come to mind unexpectedly and it wouldn't be the last. Despite all Xaz's attempts to keep her distance, Ruby had been a friend, and Xaz was almost certainly at least partially responsible for her death. Now that the strange madness that had gripped them all had receded, Xaz didn't like the idea of trying to resurrect the woman, but if she could save Ruby's soul from the Abyss along with the dead guards, she would do it.

Finger-walking along Cadmia's skin, she found the edges of Antioch's poison and tugged at it. She envisioned her own, cool power flowing through the wounds to cleanse them like a river flooding a stagnant pool.

Instead of her magic rising in her body, an icy voice slipped into her mind. *Now you seek our aid?* it asked. *After defying us, you dare seek our assistance?*

Xaz felt a new kind of coldness wash over her, one that had nothing to do with her magic and everything to do with fury.

"Napthol is a Numini, isn't it? That means she is sworn to one of you," she murmured, her voice sub-audible, only intended for her disapproving Numini patron. *"You won't let her die."*

She has already been given to us as a tool for our plans, the Numini replied indifferently. *If those plans are not to find success, she is of no more use to us.*

Oh, those bastards. Those arrogant, manipulative—

Watch your thoughts, Mancer, the Numini hissed warningly. *Your tie to the Abyssi is making you irrational and disrespectful. We have given you a task. If you are not our servant, we have no responsibility to give you aid.*

"Is this the first time you've manipulated Antioch into helping you get your way?" she asked, this time not worrying about keeping her voice quiet enough to keep the others from overhearing. *"Or were you the one who made his mancer throw the knife at me, too?"*

If you hope to save her, you had best decide swiftly, the Numini advised.

Xaz opened her eyes, and blinked them twice to clear the rim of frost that tried to stick the lashes together. The world around her had the silver halo she knew meant the Numini were still riding her.

She said the words swiftly, bluntly. "A necromancer cannot raise Ruby unless she has a body to raise, and the Quin will have destroyed that by now." She saw Hansa and Umber both tense, their faces showing wary relief that disappeared swiftly when she continued. "There is a sorcerer who *can* raise her, though, a man named Terre Verte. The Numini want us to retrieve him from the Abyssi court."

Hansa's breath hissed in as if he, too, had been stung by the Abyssi. Umber raised his eyes skyward, took a breath, and said flatly, "You've relayed your message. Can you help Cadmia now?"

Before Xaz could turn her attention to the effort, she felt the Numini's power rush through her, not a river but a torrent. Cadmia called out wordlessly, her body spasming once as the magic struck her.

When it was done, Xaz collapsed, panting, on the black sand, which was rimed with ice in a spreading circle. She wasn't sure when Umber had moved away, but he and Hansa had judiciously stepped back from the needle-like icicles and frost heaves that grew like strange plants ringing her and Cadmia.

Umber called, "Are you two all right?"

Before Xaz could catch her breath to answer, Cadmia's dazed voice said, "I think so." As Xaz struggled to sit up, Cadmia prodded at the remnants of the wounds on her side and arm. The bleeding had stopped, though not in the neat way an Abyssumancer's wounds healed; it looked more like the injuries had been seared shut with frostbite. More importantly, though, the swelling had gone down, and Cadmia's skin had returned to a healthier shade.

As she remembered the price she had paid for that healing, Xaz looked up at Umber and said, "I'm sorry."

He gave a half shrug, his other arm around Hansa, who looked as dazed and exhausted as Xaz felt.

Briefly, Xaz indulged a fantasy in which the hero of Mars had discovered himself to be a mancer following Baryte's death. Would Antioch have been able to twist him fast enough to secure his loyalty even as he served Kavet from such a lofty role? Or would Hansa have found an excuse to resign when he realized what he was? Would he have killed himself?

"We need to rest before we can accomplish anything else," Umber said, surveying their bedraggled group. "That will give Alizarin time to come back. Or not," he admitted with a wince. "I do not think we can plan a trip into the royal court until we know if we have him on our side."

Xaz had been so focused on Cadmia, it hadn't occurred to her until that moment that Alizarin hadn't come after them. The fight had to be over by now. She looked out over the Abyss, which had now grown so dark it was hard to even see Hansa and Umber a few feet off. A breeze had sprung up as the light faded, and though it couldn't compete with a Kavet winter or come anywhere near to divine cold, Hansa and Cadmia both hunched against it.

Hansa stepped away from Umber as he asked, "Can we make a fire?"

"Do you see anything that might burn?" Umber asked in reply. "I don't know what the shades made their fire from, but all I see here is stone and sand. If we all stay close, we should be all right."

Cadmia nodded, warily looking between the two men, as if recognizing the logic in the suggestion but not entirely comfortable with it. Hansa, who Xaz would have expected to jump at the invitation to lie down with the Abyss-spawn he had been intermittently cuddling against all day, continued to make excuses.

"One of us should stand guard. I'll take first shift," Hansa volunteered. "I know I can't kill an Abyssi if one comes, but those shades talked about hunting. That means there are some creatures here a mortal is strong enough to fight."

Umber sighed, shook his head, and said, "Do whatever you want, Quin. Just don't wander off."

"Are we really helpless against the Abyssi?" Cadmia asked. "Aren't Numenmancers supposed to be able to summon lightning?"

Supposed to was the operative word. Cadmia clearly hadn't been coherent enough to realize how close she had come to dying through the Numini's stupid pride and refusal to help unless Xaz heeded their will.

She said, "Don't count on the Numini's help. They aren't that generous."

It was the closest to a direct criticism of her divine masters as she had ever dared speak aloud, but she was too tired to worry about whether they heard her and would make her pay for the words later. She led the way to a hollow where black stones and sand dunes would block the worst of the wind and reached out to smooth the sand—

Umber pulled her back an instant before a glistening, transparent tentacle no thicker than her little finger flailed upward, seized nothing, and disappeared again beneath the sand.

"What was that?" Cadmia asked hoarsely.

"I think . . ." Umber trailed off and frowned, looking around. After a moment he found a shell a little longer than his forearm, which he used to gingerly prod the black sand.

Again the tentacle came up, this time joined by several others. They slapped the shell with a meaty sound and wrapped around it, questing both directions. Just before they reached Umber's hand, he yanked on the shell, pulling the creature attached to the tentacles up like a carrot.

The little beast had a fat, bulbous body that looked like a jellyfish's, eight thick legs segmented like an insect's, and a mass of slender tentacles that groped toward Umber's hand before he threw the shell and dangling thing away. Every part of it looked watery and translucent, like something that should have been crushed by the sand in which it had hidden.

It started moving toward Umber, who pulled Xaz with him as he backed away.

Hansa stepped forward with another long, sharp-edged shell, which he used to decisively cut the creature in half.

"Be careful of sheltered places where the sand is soft and deep," Umber said. "There are small creatures in the Abyss that can devour a man or woman as surely as the larger beasts can. They just do it more slowly."

Xaz was reconsidering whether she ever again needed to sleep when she felt the approach of familiar power.

Alizarin's normal bounding stride was more subdued than usual, and as he drew close, Xaz could see scalds and tufts where his fur pulled irregularly over new injuries. It was hard to tell in the dim light, but even his colors seemed subdued, blue tinged gray instead of his normal brilliant turquoise and sapphire.

"Are you all right?" she asked, reaching toward him instinctively.

Somehow Cadmia got there first. Alizarin leaned toward her hand.

Through their magical bond, Xaz could feel the Abyssi's overwhelming fatigue, but he tossed his head dismissively as Cadmia crooned sympathetic words.

"I won," Alizarin announced. "I needed to hunt after. You did, too?" he asked, looking at the still-twitching creature. "I don't think you can eat those."

"I wasn't going to try," Hansa said.

"They taste bad," Alizarin said idly, "and their poison rots flesh, though it takes a few days to get all the way in to the heart and brain. They didn't touch you, did they?" he asked Hansa, seeming reluctant to spend time on the question.

Eyes wide, Hansa paused to look at his hands, then shook his head.

"Good," Alizarin said. "Umber wouldn't want to cut pieces off you." With no further concern, he stretched, fluffed his fur, yawned widely and announced, "It's time to sleep. You picked a good spot."

He didn't wait for Xaz to reply, but went to the hollow Xaz had considered before realizing how dangerous it was. As Alizarin paced the spot, kicking at the sand, a half-dozen creatures rose and scampered away, including a second jellyfish-beast and a strange mass Xaz might have mistaken for a brightly-colored dust bunny if it hadn't moved with deliberate speed away from the Abyssi.

We would never have made it through the night without him, she realized abruptly.

The Abyssi sprawled out on the sand, and Xaz thought for a moment he was going to leave the rest of them to find their own beds. Then he stretched, and looked up at them. Specifically, he frowned at Cadmia. "Why are you glowing like a Numini?"

"Antioch hurt me," she answered. Xaz wasn't sure if the Sister of Napthol kept the words simple in deference to the Abyssi's simple nature, or if she didn't want to dwell on her near death. "Xaz healed me."

Alizarin began to growl, then swallowed it. "Sleep here," he said, tapping the sand near him with his tail. "Nothing will try to eat you beside me."

There were two ways to interpret those words, but Cadmia clearly took them to be reassuring, because she accepted the offer. Xaz squelched an instinctive, irrational moment of jealousy as the Abyssi invited someone *else* to snuggle close. Yes, her power drew her to him, but she wasn't a slave to her power.

Besides, the cold wouldn't bother her as much as it would Cadmia.

With the magic gone and the fear of Alizarin's absence abated, the anxiety and lack of food or water during the previous day caught up to Xaz. All her muscles felt so weak she could barely stand. Cadmia lay down inches from the Abyssi, and Xaz took the spot next to her.

That left Hansa and Umber. As if on cue, the guard's sharp protest reached Xaz's ears.

"Don't *touch* me." All day long, Hansa had gone back and forth between moving close to Umber and pulling away. Xaz had resisted the urge to needle him about it only because she remembered her own reaction to Alizarin, the physical draw of Abyssal power that craved the slide of skin on skin—or fur, in that case.

"Come on, Hansa," Umber sighed.

"It's not cold enough to freeze to death," Hansa said, "and I doubt anything really dangerous will come close with Alizarin here."

Umber's reply was too soft to hear, as was Hansa's, but it must not have been flattering because Umber didn't bother to lower his voice as he grumbled, "Have I done *anything* to suggest I might be interested in assaulting you in your sleep?"

More muttering from Hansa, but this time Umber laughed. A brief, quiet conversation later, and Xaz heard the two men's quiet footsteps on the sand moving toward them. She judiciously kept her eyes closed, pretending not to notice and sparing Hansa's . . . whatever it was that was stopping him from being practical. Pride? Shame?

"Sleep, Hansa," Umber whispered, when Hansa again hesitated to lie down. The words were quiet, but they reached Xaz on a wave of power; Hansa's knees buckled and Umber caught him and lowered him gently to the ground.

"Is everything all right?" she asked. It shouldn't have taken so much energy to knock out a human unless something equally strong was fighting to keep him awake.

"Is *anything*?" Umber replied, before giving a long, drawn-out sigh and pointedly turning his back.

In the darkness, Xaz listened to the sounds of the Abyss at night: rattling, hissing noises from the stones around them as smaller creatures marked their passing; distant, baying howls too deep and undulating for dogs; and the occasional, piercing shriek as some distant creature . . . died? Was that what it was here?

Would they find out firsthand?

CHAPTER 27

It was nice to be warm. That was the thought Hansa woke up with. It was nice to be warm, and it was nice to be safe, to be in someone's arms and held gently—

The sense of peace shattered as he remembered where he was, how he got there, and who he was with. His head was on Umber's tanned arm; his own arm was around the other man's waist. And the worst part was, that was where he had wanted to be all the day before. Umber thought Hansa was worried the spawn would assault *him* if they slept next to each other. Hansa's real fear was that *he* would pounce on the spawn with less inhibition than an A'hknet monger.

For now, Umber was still asleep, black lashes making soft crescents on his honey skin. In sleep, his full lips were relaxed instead of quirked up in the half smile, half sneer to which Hansa had become accustomed. His lithe body was finely muscled, his chest lightly dusted with black hair, his—

"Fuck," Hansa breathed, squeezing his eyes shut. This was supposed to wear off.

Eyes open again, he tried to gather the willpower to sneak out of Umber's arms. He didn't want to be this close when the Abyssi-spawn woke. If Umber said anything snide—and how often did he say anything else?—Hansa was going to have to hit him.

He lifted his arm from around Umber's waist, but that was as far as he got.

The hair on Umber's chest was softer than it looked. Lower down on his stomach, it was almost fine enough to be fur, like the Abyssi's. The skin beneath was smooth and hot.

Umber's eyes shot open. They seemed to hold a thousand different colors of blue, even in the fine band left by dilated pupils. "Hansa?"

Hansa shoved at the other man, tried to push himself to his feet, and then fell, breathing as if he had just run an uphill race and lost. "Why hasn't this worn off?"

Umber rose to his knees and helped Hansa do the same, hands on his wrists the only thing that kept Hansa from reaching out again. "'This'?" Umber echoed.

Showing was easier than forming words. Umber released Hansa's wrists as Hansa pushed forward to wrap one hand around the back of the Abyssi-spawn's neck and pull him forward to kiss him. Dear Numen;

he tasted even better than he looked, and felt even better than that. Umber didn't object. He twined a hand in Hansa's hair and pressed his other hand to his lower back.

Hansa barely noticed when Umber shoved him back and his shoulders impacted the black sand beneath them. He also barely noticed the swift kick someone delivered to his shoulder, despite the fact that it was hard enough to make his fingers tingle.

Umber *did* react, slowly lifting his head and turning from Hansa to snarl at Xaz.

"Glare all you like," Xaz said. "I thought I'd warn you before Alizarin decided to make this a threesome."

The possibility of suddenly being joined by a full Abyssi was just enough to jolt Hansa back to reality and make him realize what he had been doing. He pushed Umber away, but didn't get much further than that. Umber stood. Hansa stayed on the ground, knees up with his head resting on them while he relearned how to breathe.

Cadmia asked Umber, "Is he all right?"

Umber paused, thinking too long for Hansa's taste, before he answered, "He could be much worse."

If he let go of his knees, Hansa was sure he was going to throw himself at Umber again. "What in the name of the Abyss have you done to me?" he gasped.

"*Me?*" Umber asked. "Done to *you*? This, dear Quin, is your own fault. And I find it beautifully ironic."

"If you two are . . . awake," Cadmia said, with a judicious pause that made it clear she had to consider whether or not to comment on what she had just seen, "Alizarin brought food."

Hansa pushed to his feet, shaking himself. He felt like he had taken a beating, and he was still exhausted despite having slept deeply and dreamlessly. He vaguely recalled Umber convincing him that sleeping next to each other wasn't a fate worse than death, and then . . . nothing.

Xaz had gone back to dissecting some kind of purplish fruit, and Cadmia was examining a broad, shallow shell serving as a platter for what Hansa could only assume was meat. Looking at either option made Hansa's stomach roll.

That wasn't what he wanted.

He crossed his arms, fingers bruising his own skin with the effort it took not to close the distance between himself and Umber, who had joined the others at their meal. This wasn't as bad as yesterday—it was *worse.*

I did warn you, Umber said silently.

Hansa tried to think of a way to change the subject, to focus his mind on the task at hand, but he *couldn't.*

Don't think about Umber. Think about why you're here.

He tried. He remembered what Xaz had told them about Ruby's body being burned, and the Numini's desire for some sorcerer, but he couldn't even begin to process what that meant for their next steps. All he knew was that thinking about Jenkins and Ruby and all the others *should* make him sick with grief, but when he tried to let that emotion in, it was shoved aside by the longing for Umber's skin against his.

As if desperate to start a conversation that didn't involve Hansa's relationship with Umber, Cadmia asked Alizarin, "Why are you wearing pants?"

The question was so bizarre it momentarily drew Hansa's attention. Xaz snickered.

"No one else finds this odd?" Cadmia asked defensively.

"A little, only now that you mention it," Umber said.

Hansa thought he would have noticed immediately if the Abyssi *hadn't* been wearing pants . . . maybe. He thought back to the other Abyssi they had seen in this place. He had been far too distracted by his terror and focused on details like teeth, claws, and poisonous spines to take note of Abyssal wardrobe choices.

Alizarin tilted his head in the teasing way he had. "Humans find nakedness distracting."

"I didn't realize one of your kind would worry about that," she remarked.

Hansa had already given up all his preconceptions on Abyssi. It had never been his job to know more about them than he needed to fight their Abyssumancers, so he dealt with being wrong with relative equanimity, but Cadmia was clearly more intent on understanding.

He wished he had learned more about the spawn, though. Maybe he would have known . . .

Trains crashed in his head as he considered what he *did* know about Umber's kind—specifically, as he recalled Umber's warnings when Hansa had summoned him to the jail cell.

Hansa had demanded a third boon. He had sealed it. Just before they stepped into the Abyss.

Mm-hmm, Umber said. He excused himself from the others and returned to Hansa's side.

"This . . . isn't going to go away." Hansa resisted the urge to look at Umber because he didn't trust himself if he did, but he desperately hoped the other man was about to snicker and call him an idiot. Just as long as he told him he was *wrong.*

The third boon creates a bond, Umber reminded him. *It's permanent—or at least, as permanent as your life. I've yet to find anyone who checked to see if it carried over to the afterlife.*

Much as Hansa hated having the spawn talk in his head, he preferred not to have Cadmia and Xaz overhear this particular conversation, so he responded the same way. *So what does that mean, really?*

It means . . . it means, in many ways you are lucky. Hansa snickered at the absurdity, but Umber continued undaunted. *I wasn't making idle threats before. I've seen bonds that destroy both parties. I've seen soulbonds where the submissive party weeps whenever his master's attention turns elsewhere and would starve if his master didn't force him to eat. I've seen bonds go so mad they had to be locked away. You're obviously still capable of thinking, and just as obviously not terrified of my displeasure, so all things considered, you're lucky.*

Lucky.

"Bastard," Hansa mumbled. "*Lucky?*"

"Yes, *lucky,*" Umber insisted, replying aloud in response to Hansa doing the same. "In addition to everything else I just said, you could have been flesh-bound to someone who didn't find you attractive, or wasn't attracted to men at all."

He couldn't help but notice Cadmia's startled glance his way. She immediately looked forward again, but this time Hansa was too focused on his own concerns to follow her conversation with Alizarin. Umber hooked an arm around his waist, guiding them both further away for privacy.

"*I'm* not attracted to men," Hansa snarled. "Doesn't that matter at all?"

Umber lifted a brow, as if he might have the nerve to point out that there had been moments that brought that assertion into question. Hansa remembered once more the factious teasing with Jenkins that had once caused them both to be censured, and Ruby's resigned—but unsurprised—expression as she walked out on him for the last time, saying only, *I won't tell.*

Instead, the spawn said, "Power easily and often overrides preference. You should know that from all the mancers you've arrested."

"You're *thrilled* about this, aren't you?"

"I'm not exactly weeping," Umber admitted.

"I'm not an animal," Hansa said. "I have self-control. I don't care what *power* says. I'm not—" At that point, he remembered Umber's arm around his waist. He removed it and took a step away. "I *despise* you. I will never sleep with you. Do you understand that?"

"Whatever you say."

"Son of a bitch," Hansa spat, though even the epithet lacked the strength of anger. *Talking* wasn't what he wanted in that moment, and since Umber tended to read his mind, he had to know that.

"I'm not lucky," Hansa said. "I can't think. I can be useful—I *should* be able to be useful. I'm a trained soldier. But I can't focus long enough to contribute to any kind of plan or even to . . . to . . ." He lost the thought. This would be easier if Umber had a shirt on. He had taken it off to use as bandaging for Cadmia's wounds the day before.

Hansa remembered that moment, when he knew he should have offered help, should have been standing guard, should have at least *cared* that Cadmia was clearly dying—but could only stare at the skin Umber revealed.

"You sealed the bond over twelve hours ago," Umber said, his tone conversational despite Hansa's turmoil. "The fact that you're still rational enough to notice you're impaired is remarkable. I suspect you're one of those people who has a natural potential for power. That would explain your success in the One-Twenty-Six and why Antioch found you an attractive replacement for his mancer."

Hansa hadn't thought to ask Umber about that confrontation, though he'd had plenty of questions at the time.

"Rational enough," he echoed. "I can't live like this. If we make it back to Kavet, how can I possibly function?"

"That's an 'if' I'm not certain of at all," Umber said, sounding concerned for the first time in the conversation. His gaze and tone sharpened and he said, "The four coins of the Abyss are blood, fire, pain, and flesh. Some of the bonds form in emotion or thought, which is what makes them so devastating, but a fleshbond is simple. It wants power. It will steal your reason if it needs to, but if you keep it satiated, it will leave you alone. Right now it's starving, so it's directing all your attention to the source of its desired meal."

Hansa blinked at him, trying to decipher the long string of words, half of which had been lost in a vivid, unwanted image of what Umber had looked like sprawled on Hansa's couch. He wanted to be angry, to yell and blame the spawn, but unfortunately he wasn't yet stupid enough to believe this was anyone's fault but his own. He thought he had understood the others saying his hysteria and demand for the third boon had been coerced by the Numini. Given the way their lives seemed to be going, he wouldn't be surprised if someone said the Numini had even put Rose into that jail cell to give him information about how to demand a second boon. But he had to accept responsibility for what he *could*, and that many of the decisions he made were his own. He had started on this path willingly, despite every Quin teaching and Kavet law warning him that any step toward sorcery was a slippery slope to the bottom.

He was at the bottom now.

Umber gave up waiting for a response, and rephrased in simpler terms. "The bond wants its flesh. The more you try to ignore it, the more insistent it grows. Like this."

He leaned forward; Hansa saw the movement, but had no will to pull away. Umber kissed him, almost chastely, but the brief contact was enough to derail any futile attempt at logic and make his knees weak. Umber had to catch him around the waist.

"Ruby," he protested, though he knew it was stupid even as he said it. Even if they were able to bring her back, even if their relationship hadn't been over before she killed herself, and even if she forgave him for practicing black magic to save her—doubtful—she would never accept his allying with the mancer and Abyssi responsible for her brother's death.

"I know I've screwed up," he whispered, "but I want . . . I do hope I can recover . . . something. I had accepted that Ruby and I weren't going to work out before she—hurt herself, but that doesn't mean I've given up on the kind of life I wanted. It isn't just the Quinacridone talking, saying that this, with you—" He broke off, and tried again. "Quin, Napthol, Order, mancer. It isn't a matter of 'religion' or 'morality' at this point. I want a life. I want to be able to have a family. I want . . ." Numen, he *wanted* to wrap his arms around the Abyssi-spawn and kiss the line that had formed between his brows as Hansa spoke.

"Hansa . . ." Umber looked away. "I'm not a jealous lover. I feel no possessiveness over you, beyond the need to keep you safe because you are my bond. I am going, to the best of my ability, to try not to interfere with your life."

"So, what?" Hansa asked. "You propose that I just roll over and leave your bed in the morning to go back to my wife?"

Again, that look. "No, I propose that, whatever *I* do, you are not going to have the perfect Quin life. Whether or not you were manipulated into it, the bond remains. At the very least you will need to take precautions to avoid sighted guards noticing Abyssal power on you. And as I said before, power will have its way no matter what you prefer. If you try to ignore the bond and the power gets desperate, in addition to me, you might find yourself drawn to subgroups like the spawn, maybe Abyssumancers or Abyssi outright. You can't afford to respond to a call for the One-Twenty-Six and find yourself dazzled like a schoolboy by your target."

Abyssumancers had given that as their excuse more than once when Hansa arrested them: the power *needs* this. It needs blood. It needs pain. Some of the younger ones still seemed horrified by the appalling things they had done in the name of their magic. Hansa had never understood.

He understood now.

"You're right," Umber said. "Part of what makes Abyssumancers so dangerous is that even the best-intentioned of their lot lose any moral compass when their power makes a demand. The boon has more specific needs, so it has no reason to push you to the kind of abuse a mancer may commit, but if you deny its demands, it can strip you down until you lose all reason. Maybe you would rather let yourself get to that state so you can absolve yourself of all responsibility. Personally, I hope you'll make a decision early enough that you're still capable of giving consent. As I've assured you before, I am not interested in rape."

Hansa flinched from the coarse word, the last of a series of truths he wished he could refute.

"Do you want to go back to the others now?" Umber asked, leaving the other option gently unspoken.

Hansa fought to organize his thoughts, to exercise some form of logic.

I despise you. I will never sleep with you. Those words, spoken in anger and fear and defensiveness, now gave him a barb of guilt. How many men, half-Abyssi or not, would have disregarded Hansa's countless jabs and insults and still attempted to be decent in this situation?

He couldn't find the words he needed. He believed Umber, but didn't know how to say yes. Especially *here. Now.* "I can't," he said, not answering the question Umber had asked aloud, but the other one, the implied one. "Not with Cadmia and Xaz only a few paces away and an Abyssi who might be inclined to jump in. I . . . just can't." There were so many other things wrapped up in that *can't,* but Umber nodded, accepting either the reasons he had stated aloud or the dozens of others swirling scattered in his thoughts. "If we were alone . . ." If Xaz and the others hadn't been around, the question would already have been decided.

"I can't promise privacy anytime soon." Umber didn't sound like he was pushing Hansa to change his mind, just reminding him of one of the many complications they faced.

Hansa swallowed his squeamishness. "I'm not saying no to *you*." The words heated his face, but he continued, because he hated that ugly word Umber had used and it was important to get this out in case he couldn't say it later. "I'm saying no to the *situation*. If we ever get somewhere where we're alone, or if I get to the point where I'm not able to make a decision on my own any more, you have a yes."

Umber's smile was wistful, with none of his usual cavalier derision. That was good; if he had made a smart quip in response to Hansa's struggling to give him the consent he claimed to care about, Hansa would probably have punched him.

"We should get back to the others," Umber said. Hansa tensed as the spawn reached for him, but Umber said, "Some touch is better than none. Little bits of power may tide you over until the situation changes. Being here in the Abyss helps, too; the power in the air isn't quite what your body needs, but it's close, like bread for a man who needs meat. It will fill your stomach a while."

How long was *a while*? Long enough for them to get this ridiculous boon out of the way and get back to the mortal realm? Unless his luck drastically changed course, it seemed more likely a descent into madness would find him first.

CHAPTER 28

Cadmia sighed, momentarily luxuriating in the feeling of a full belly and a comfortable spot to sit.

Once she overcame her initial hesitation, the strange food Alizarin had provided proved satisfying. The odd, spiked fruit was a deep purple, segmented inside a little like an orange, but with a flavor more akin to whiskey. She expected it to leave her parched, but the juice soothed her dry throat. The meat—which they ate raw because even Alizarin could not make a fire from bare sand and the scattered shells let off a greasy, smoky flame that made them all cough—had the soft-grained texture of high-grade tuna, and was delicious as long as she could put the image of the slimy, sharp-toothed orange-and-yellow snake it came from out of her mind.

She ate lounging against Alizarin's side the way she had once sprawled on the large throw pillows that filled her mother's parlor—except this "pillow" was warm, vibrated with energy, and was firm underneath a layer of the softest fur she had ever touched.

"You would make a good Abyssi," Alizarin declared, tapping her knee with his tail to punctuate his point.

When Cadmia had first woken tucked against the Abyssi's chest, she had frozen, caught by too many dissonant sensations: the long-missed familiarity of having a man's body next to her after a decade spent sleeping alone, the exotic feel of soft fur over hard muscle, and the trepidation that filled her as she remembered where she was and who—what—she lay against.

Before she could decide what to do, her stomach had rumbled. The sound woke Alizarin, who stretched unselfconsciously, seeming not to notice the way doing so made Cadmia's breath hitch, and asked, "Do you need food?"

That brought them to here and now.

"Thank you," she said, because the words seemed intended as praise. "Why do you say so?"

"You take pleasure in things when you have them," he said.

"She thinks too much to be an Abyssi," Xaz remarked.

Alizarin paused to consider the comment, which made Cadmia say, "Alizarin thinks a great deal, too." It was not her first attempt to get Alizarin to confirm if *all* Abyssi were so different than she had been taught, or if he was atypical for his kind. Of everyone she had come to the Abyss with, he was most open to her curiosity, but he tended to deflect direct questions about himself.

Hansa and Umber returned at that moment, though. Hansa walked with an arm around Umber's waist, but seemed unable to make eye contact with the rest of them.

Growing up with Cinnabar and other men in the Order of A'hknet who were open to male bed partners had left Cadmia jaded to such relations, but Quin were unequivocal in their opinion. Hansa would have been raised believing men were only attracted to other men out of some perverse, selfish obsession that focused their lust on others like themselves instead of "proper" partners. It wasn't easy to set a lifetime of indoctrination aside.

But sometimes it's worth it, she thought, considering the way she had once walked away from the Order of A'hknet, where education and study were generally considered a waste of time, and embraced a path of learning.

Umber joined their circle and helped himself to food enthusiastically, seeming undisturbed by its form. Hansa leaned against Umber, picking mechanically at what he was offered as if he didn't see or taste any of it.

Now that everyone was accounted for, it was time to turn their minds to what they needed to do next.

"We obviously need a new plan," Cadmia said once the men were settled.

She hated the thought of abandoning the lost guards in the Abyss, but it would be foolish to stay longer than necessary to try to save them. Assuming Antioch was the only dangerous foe they might face, or that he wouldn't return, were gambles they couldn't take. It also seemed clear that Umber and Hansa couldn't afford to pursue any path that didn't fulfill the boon.

"What exactly do we need to accomplish?" she asked. She thought she understood the gist of their need, but it seemed so silly that one way to accomplish the task was to decide it *couldn't be done.*

Hansa and Umber exchanged a heavy look, the guard looking lost and overwhelmed, and Umber contemplative. "We need to either find someone who can resurrect Ruby, or find someone with the authority to say for sure that it can't be done," Umber summarized. "According to the Numini, that means finding this Terre Verte fellow."

Cadmia's skin crawled as she imagined another mancer, a stranger, walking in and restoring Ruby to life. Despite her current alliance with Alizarin, Xaz, and Umber, it was hard to picture raising the dead without horror. She couldn't remember how she had justified it to herself during that surreal hour when she had gone to Hansa to get him to help his once-fiancée.

"And Numini can't lie?" she asked. The others nodded, and Cadmia mentally checked off another bit of information she had learned via speculation and rumor.

"Could they have misled you about this man's

powers?" she asked Xaz. "I know Others can't lie, but did they say outright *he can do this,* or did they just hint at it or tell you to tell us that?"

Xaz paused, seeming to run the conversation through her mind. "They said it outright," she decided after a minute.

"Do we have *any* leeway?" She needed to understand this situation with the bond and the boon better in order to address the problem rationally. "How is this boon enforced?"

"Fighting against the boon is . . . unpleasant." Umber's words were dry and vague, but Hansa's grimace suggested the magic's reaction was fairly immediate. "I've tried to fight a sealed boon before. It's a little like slitting a wrist then trying to row a boat."

Dramatic image.

"You have another bond?" Hansa asked.

"Priorities, Quin." Xaz's cue wasn't as sharp as usual. Cadmia could still see the tension of guilt in her face, probably as she considered her role in bringing them to this point.

"*Can* we rescue Terre Verte?" Cadmia asked, twisting to look at Alizarin as the obvious solution came to her. Surely the word of a third-level prince of the Abyss would be enough to convince Umber or Hansa this boon couldn't be fulfilled. "Without you, we have no chance of surviving the court, much less stealing someone from it. And you don't *need* to help. If you make it impossible for them, Umber and Hansa don't have to do this."

Alizarin's fur flattened and his body sagged. "Even if I refuse, the Numini will force Xaz to try."

His obvious frustration and disappointment struck her. She hadn't realized she meant to pet him until she felt his soft black hair trickling through her fingers and saw his head tilt toward the caress.

"If we're going through with this madness," Xaz said, her voice a bit too high as she considered it, "how do we go about it? Even if Alizarin is powerful enough to help us get this sorcerer away from the court, that won't help us if we're trapped in the Abyss."

Alizarin looked at Umber apologetically before he said, "An Abyssumancer would be able to open a rift."

It seemed a simpler solution in words than the others' expressions made it out to be. Umber in particular looked pained, as if he recognized the logic of Alizarin's suggestion, but still wished he hadn't made it.

"Clearly much of what I've been taught is misconception and propaganda," Cadmia said, considering the Numenmancer, Abyss-spawn, and Abyssi who were her current companions. "Are Abyssumancers as dangerous as we're told?"

"Yes," the others answered, almost in unison, voices ranging from shocked to horrified. Even Hansa joined the chorus.

Umber was the one who explained. "Mancers spend their lives fighting to balance their humanity with the demands of their power, which ultimately only wants one thing: to feed."

Cadmia looked doubtfully to Xaz, who tensed and said, "Numini don't use their mancers the way Abyssi do, so we don't lose control the same way."

The huffy reply seemed to prod Hansa out of his distracted state. He protested, "Tell that to the twenty-eight people killed in Fuscio last year when the summer temperature dropped so abruptly in the market square that they froze where they stood, or the three guards struck by lightning when we tried to apprehend the Numenmancer responsible."

Cadmia wasn't familiar with the event, but Xaz's livid expression made it clear she was. "Of course, blame the *mancer,*" she spat. "Did you even look at the scene when you arrived? Did you see the noose those twenty-eight people had thrown over the chapel's balcony rail? It was a lynch mob!"

"Enough!" Cadmia shouted, interrupting the argument before the two could come to blows. Given Hansa and Xaz had effectively tried to kill each other only a few days ago, it was amazing they had made it this long without conflict, but the topic under discussion was Abyssumancers. "We don't have time for this." The conversation had made it clear that even Xaz was biased on the subject, so Cadmia asked Umber bluntly, "If a tie to the Abyss makes one so irredeemable, why aren't you a monster?"

"I'm not a human bound magically to an Abyssi," he answered, apparently unoffended. "I *am* part Abyssi. I don't have one using me as a valuable—but ultimately disposable—source of food. *Unless,*" he continued, frustration leaking into his tone, "we find an Abyssumancer who sees me as just that."

That explained why he so clearly wished there was another way.

"Can we do this without an Abyssumancer?" Cadmia asked Alizarin.

"I do not believe so," he answered.

"Then how do we find one?"

"I normally follow the trail of corpses." Hansa set aside his half-eaten food. "Even if an Abyssumancer *can* help us, do we have a reason to expect one *will*?"

"There is an Abyssumancer named Naples attached to the high court," Alizarin said. "He will help as a favor to me."

"If we need to go to such a person," Xaz said grudgingly, "I advise that we don't mention the Numini. Even if he wants to help you, Alizarin, an Abyssumancer might be contrary enough to refuse any request that might please the Numini."

Alizarin shrugged, as if he hadn't considered that point but didn't intend to dispute it.

"No offense, Alizarin," Umber said, "but you've been accused of getting the last mancer who helped you killed. Will this Naples trust you?"

Alizarin shifted uneasily behind Cadmia. "He will help."

"Won't his Abyssi object?" Hansa asked.

"He never has before."

"Do we have *any* other ideas?" Cadmia asked one last time. No one responded, or seemed inclined to meet her eye, so she said, "Then this is our plan. Alizarin, how far are we from this Abyssumancer?"

She imagined trekking through this dangerous wilderness for days, eating the kills Alizarin brought back and engaging in battle with whatever enemies challenged them.

Alizarin rolled onto his back, thought, and said, "At your speed, not far. Less than an hour."

Cadmia did some mental geography, considered their earlier conversation about the analogous nature of the Abyss to the mortal realm, and asked incredulously, "The *Abyssal high court* is directly under the city of Mars?"

"That's . . . mighty convenient." Umber spoke with his customary suspicion.

Xaz rolled her eyes to the sky, or what would be the sky if there were anything but a sooty darkness above, and said in long-suffering tones, "The palace of the Numini is the same, or so I have been told. It isn't surprising, really. Kavet is the only country in the world with mancers. Perhaps that's because it is so close to the strongest Abyssi and Numini."

"That might explain the country," Cadmia agreed, "but what explains the capital city being exactly above—and below, I suppose—the Other courts?"

"The royal house." Hansa sounded uncharacteristically impatient. "They were accused of sorcery in the revolution, and they're the ones who first established the city of Mars. What's to say they didn't build it there intentionally?" All record of the royal house had been destroyed during the revolution, but it seemed as sound a theory as any. He moved as if to stand, then hesitated. "Are we going?"

"We're going," Umber answered, abandoning his half-eaten food and pushing to his feet.

As if noticing that the rest of them were hastily using black sand to clean their hands, Hansa said, "I don't think it's a good plan, but it's what we need to do."

Cadmia understood the need for haste, or thought she did, until she saw the way Hansa kept shifting his weight like a man whose muscles have gone to pins and needles. He was trying, and failing, to conceal the signs of his physical discomfort.

Umber was doing a better job. Cadmia might not have interpreted his stone-faced expression as anything but laconic disinterest if she didn't know the situation.

Like slitting a wrist then trying to row a boat.

She'd had enough to eat. When she stood, Xaz and Alizarin followed.

A flickering glow out of the corner of her eye drew Cadmia's attention to the butchered snake Alizarin had left a few yards off. The shining creatures that normally hung from the trees flowed over the carcass like phosphorescent slugs. Another scavenger, a trundling creature the size of Cadmia's palm with a dense shell like a turtle's, had buried its muzzle in the snake's eye. Occasionally one of the wisps slapped at it with a gleaming tendril, but though the blow let off a *hiss* of steam, it didn't seem able to penetrate the beast's shell.

"Not worth eating," Alizarin proclaimed, seeing the direction of her gaze. "Too much bone and shell, and the meat is dry."

The circle of life in the Abyss, Cadmia thought, and then they started uphill to the high court.

As they walked, the stone dunes on their left rose higher and became sharper. Dagger-sharp stones pierced the soft black sand with increasing frequency, making the footing treacherous for all but Alizarin, who avoided them with ease.

Stepping on a sharp rock wasn't the only hazard. Tiny crabs with bodies the color of fresh blood scuttled forward aggressively, snapping hooked claws if one stepped too close, and long-legged white spiders with sharp mandibles that glistened with venom perched in flat, sticky nests. Occasionally they passed old, dry bones, or newer carcasses, these latter wrapped in spider's silk or covered in the Abyss's other scavengers.

The trip *should* have taken Alizarin's promised "less than an hour," but at their careful pace it seemed to last for days. Even Cadmia didn't have the energy or attention to hold a conversation, and no one else seemed to want to try.

Alizarin often bounded ahead, impatient, and circled back. Xaz minced in the front of their group, with Cadmia next and Hansa and Umber lagging behind. They walked close to each other, touching whenever they could.

Alizarin was on one of his jaunts when they topped a rise and saw a man kneeling on the ground to butcher a . . . Cadmia had no idea what it had once been, except that it seemed to have far too many legs, each tipped with a nasty-looking barbed claw. The man was using an irregular gray blade to deftly remove each claw without touching it. He looked up without surprise as they approached, used a handful of black sand to wipe the knife clean, then sheathed the knife in a boot and stood.

Unlike the shades at the camp, whose clothes had been cobbled together from frequently-mended scraps, this man was dressed in well-fitted soft leather and fine fabric with the pulled look of raw silk. His ashy-black boots stopped just below his knees, and his forearms were protected by gauntlets of speckled gray leather. Under a tough vest of the same material, reinforced by glistening, plum-violet scales, he wore a burgundy shirt that laced at the throat. His skin was fair but had none of the ghastly pallor of the shades, and instead of being fogged and colorless his eyes were bright, coppery brown.

In case any doubt remained, the knives—the one he had just tucked in his boot and another she could see on his right thigh—made it clear what he was.

Instinctively, Cadmia looked for Alizarin, who was frustratingly out of sight. Based on her understanding of the Abyss's rules, it should have been up to Umber to speak for their group when Alizarin was absent, but the spawn had halted and seemed to have no intention of moving any closer to the stranger.

Cadmia cleared her throat. "Are you Naples, the

Abyssumancer?" She sounded more confident than she felt.

"Yes?" His gaze flicked dispassionately down her body as if to assess—and dismiss—her worth before turning to the others. Umber had taken another step backward, but Naples didn't attempt to close the awkward distance. Instead, his brows lifted as he saw Xaz. "I cannot begin to imagine the circumstances that bring a Numenmancer into the Abyss."

Xaz took a deep breath. Her voice was steady as she answered, "Alizarin, of the third-level court. He—"

Xaz didn't have a chance to finish before the Abyssumancer twisted to look behind him a heartbeat before Cadmia's eyes caught the distant, distinctive sheen of blue approaching rapidly from the direction of the court.

She tensed, wondering how Naples would respond. Alizarin had known of Naples, but she didn't know how well informed an Abyssumancer would be. Did he know about Baryte's death and Antioch's grudge? Would he be concerned about the tension between Alizarin and the high court?

Naples' expression brightened and he shouted, "Alizarin!"

Alizarin vaulted up to the mancer, who reached out confidently as if to embrace the blue Abyssi. Alizarin had implied earlier that he had a relationship with this mancer, but Cadmia hadn't imagined it to be this friendly.

When the mancer tried to lean against the Abyssi,

however, Alizarin pushed him back, saying, "You're hungry. You haven't been hunting?"

It seemed an odd question, since that was exactly what Cadmia assumed Naples had been doing before their approach. The Abyssumancer shrugged and changed the subject. "You know I always look forward to your visits, and your companions are of course welcome as well. Let's get inside where it's more comfortable. I'll send someone back for this." He gestured dismissively to the half-butchered carcass beside him. He led the way to the crest of the dune over which Alizarin had bounded with ease, then paused at the top. With a sweeping gesture before him, he said, "Welcome, all, to the high court of the Abyss."

For the first time in what felt like months, Cadmia lifted her gaze instead of cautiously watching her step.

"Oh," she whispered, as she beheld the edge of the court.

Slices of stone, like those along the beach but hundreds of times taller, formed walls with razor-edges that glistened, transparent, where they caught the light. Cadmia couldn't see over them except for the irregular obelisk-like structures that towered on the other side, some so tall they seemed to merge with the smoke-gray sky. The towers' positions appeared haphazard and they leaned crookedly, a few seeming in danger of collapse at any moment. Had they been built? Did Abyssi *build*? Or had they grown on their own, like crystals?

Outside the wall, the dark sand clumped and solidified into glass, as if the buildings had been formed through magnificent heat.

Naples led them around the wall until they found a fissure where the vertical stone had cracked, leaving a gap wide enough to allow them all to enter side by side with room to spare. There were no gates or guards, and the opening in the wall appeared to be a natural formation instead of an intentional doorway, but beyond it were signs of cultivation. An amber-colored, mosslike plant with tiny, trumpet-shaped flowers defended by fine black needles bordered the path.

The building Naples led them to—if it was a building—was blocky, with no apparent doors or windows. A sphere of cinnamon-colored light floated near the blank wall. Cadmia gave it a wide berth, remembering the wisps, but Naples seemed unconcerned as he approached. He reached up and a section of the wall dissolved like smoke caught by the wind, revealing an open doorway.

Xaz had used her power in front of Cadmia more than once, but it had been subtle and quiet. This was the first obvious *magic* Cadmia had observed since Alizarin opened the rift from Kavet. Was the shiver that passed over her skin fear, an instinctive reaction caused by a lifetime of being told mancers were dangerous, or excitement?

Alizarin took the lead, passing through the doorway and into an interior that was either as dark as the caves in which they had first appeared or hidden by magic. Cadmia started to follow, then hesitated, because the others looked like they might balk.

Naples shook his head at their wary looks. "From the outside, the doorways only respond to me, Azo, or the other true Abyssi. From the inside, they respond to anyone. If you honestly feel safer *outside,* you will be able to get out at any time."

Without waiting for them to respond, he walked inside.

Cadmia understood their reasonable fear of putting themselves at an Abyssumancer's mercy, but did they really feel safer out *here*? She followed Alizarin.

Inside, what had been a cavelike chamber had been turned into a welcoming parlor. Woven wall hangings softened the black walls and the floor was warmed by furs and leathers that had been dyed and set out as area rugs. The light was provided by orbs of flickering, ghostly flames hovering near the ceiling.

"Pardon me a moment," Naples said, as he started unlacing his bracers. "I'm a bit overdressed for company at home. Alizarin, I assume you'll want to greet Azo, then utilize the baths?"

Alizarin didn't hesitate—he loped off through one of the two doors in the opposite wall. Cadmia hoped that meant he trusted the Abyssumancer, and not that he didn't care about the rest of them.

For the first time, Naples' gaze focused on Cadmia. "The third level of the Abyss is hot, and steaming seas cover much of it. Rin hates the constant grime of this level."

"You know him well," Cadmia observed, noticing the affectionate nickname Naples used for the Abyssi.

Despite where they were, it was hard to remember he was supposedly an Abyssumancer. He appeared younger than she was, probably by almost a decade, though the poise and manners with which he presented himself made him seem older.

His wistful smile also seemed to hold too many years for his face. "It isn't hard to know an Abyssi well," he said, "as long as you don't mind blood."

CHAPTER 29

"Our other option is staying outside at the edge of the Abyssal high court," Hansa said. He couldn't help remembering the shack where he and Jenkins had found Baryte. Gore and chaos were standard for Abyssumancers' lairs. He didn't want to imagine how much worse one *here,* where the mancer had no reason to fear discovery, might be.

For a moment, he thought Umber might say staying outside was better. If he did, Hansa might agree. Then the spawn released Hansa's hand and was gone from sight, leaving Hansa hurrying after.

He emerged in a warm, brightly lit parlor. It would never be mistaken for a home in Kavet, but compared to what Hansa was expecting it was dizzying in its normalcy.

Alizarin was nowhere to be seen, and Naples was in the process of removing his armor. As Umber, Hansa, and Xaz entered, he was hanging his vest on a peg by the door. The burgundy shirt beneath clung to his skin, revealing a body muscled like a wolf's, long and lean without a hint of extra softness. When he leaned down to take the knife out of his boot, Hansa heard Umber's voice clearly in his mind: *Close your mouth, Hansa.*

Hansa jerked his gaze away just as the Abyssumancer dropped both knives onto a table next to the entryway, then turned to greet a middle-aged woman who had just entered the room. Based on her pallor and the strange, clouded color of her eyes, Hansa assumed she must be a shade.

Naples conferred with her briefly, then said, "I assume you will all want to clean up before you meet Azo, the mistress of this household. Ladies, Aurelian here will see to your needs. She is better equipped than I am to identify clothes that might fit you. You two gentlemen . . ." He paused. Uncertain?

No, politely questioning. Umber caught on first. "Umber," the spawn said. "My bond is Hansa."

"Pleasure to meet you both," Naples said. He didn't offer to shake hands. Maybe he knew neither of them would want to accept. Lightly teasing, he said, "If you're willing to follow the scary Abyssumancer upstairs, I'll show you to a guest room and find you clean clothes as well."

Once again he didn't wait for them to make up their minds, but turned and led the way.

He was young, Hansa realized, or at least appeared to be—twenty at most. The realization made Hansa's stomach turn as he considered the way he had been staring a moment ago.

As they followed Naples up a steep, winding staircase, Hansa made a point to keep his gaze anywhere but on the most obvious view. Umber had warned him that the bond might cause him to be attracted to others with Abyssal power, but he refused to let that be an excuse to be vulgar.

He kept his focus on the places where the wall was recessed to accommodate orbs like the one that had illuminated the front door. These were smaller, each about the size of an egg, and varied in brightness and hue.

"Who makes the foxfire?" Umber asked.

"I do," Naples replied. "Azo likes the colors." When the Abyssumancer mentioned the woman who apparently owned this household, his voice lifted and his expression softened. The obvious fondness he held for her, whoever she was, made Hansa strengthen his resolve to keep Naples from noticing his irrepressible fascination.

"That takes quite a bit of talent," Umber said.

Naples shrugged, then pushed open a doorway. Like the others, Hansa hadn't seen the door before it opened; he wasn't entirely convinced it had *been* there. It reminded him eerily of the way Abyssumancers were able to produce weapons from apparently nowhere, though of the two, he far preferred a door.

They stepped into another parlor, this one comfortable, but holding an anonymous quality.

"You may use these rooms as long as you're here," Naples said. "We chose this spot for the hot spring beneath it, so all the bathing rooms have hot running water. I'll find you some fresh clothes and have one of the servants drop them off before I go wash up."

Water; clean clothes. That promise was sufficient to overcome Hansa's hesitation to accept the Abyssumancer's hospitality.

It *wasn't* enough to make him forget what he had told Umber. *If we ever get somewhere where we're alone—*

At the time, that "if" had seemed impossibly far off. Now it was too close.

Past the parlor was a bedroom, and then a washroom more luxurious than any Hansa had ever seen. After some fiddling, Umber located the lever that let in a stream of hot water that started to fill the deep marble tub. While the water was running, one of Naples' servants dropped off cakes of soap, lavishly soft towels, and a pile of clothes.

Then it was just Hansa and Umber again. Umber kept his back to Hansa as he stripped and bent to check the water. Hansa suspected the spawn was specifically not looking at him, the way one would try to avoid spooking a timid animal. Watching that golden body move, Hansa felt his mouth go dry, but he couldn't make himself close the distance between them.

He had accepted his bond to Umber as a reality, but that didn't mean he was emotionally ready to embrace it—or him—fully. Knowing he was being an idiot and a coward, he backed away.

When he reached the far wall, the stone faded away, turning into an open archway. He stepped into the hall, telling himself he wouldn't go far. He just needed to be somewhere he couldn't hear water splashing, couldn't see Umber's body—so lithe and relaxed and confident—couldn't feel the bond between them pulsing, drawing him closer . . .

He squeezed his eyes closed and drew a deep breath, berating himself mentally. Umber didn't understand . . . Hansa couldn't find the words to tell him . . . this wasn't—

"Hansa? Do you need something?" He jumped, lifting his head to see Naples descending the stairs toward him.

Naples had replaced the sweat-slicked burgundy shirt with an indigo-blue one. The neck was loosely laced, revealing a chain with an amethyst pendant beneath, and the bottom had been tucked into snug black pants. His waist was cinched in a wide belt that accented his narrow hips and flat stomach.

Stop it, Hansa!

"No, I'm—" He lost track of what he was saying in the effort of not staring.

This time, Naples noticed. Their eyes met for the first time, leaving Hansa momentarily disoriented by irises too bright to be called brown. Was that a natural color, or did his power lend the flame-touched brightness to his gaze?

"Exactly how long have you and Umber been bonded?" Naples asked.

Hansa thought back, couldn't come up with an exact span of time in his apparently addled mind, and said, "A couple days."

Naples nodded thoughtfully. "It's overwhelming at first," he said. "You'll learn to manage it better over time."

Naples' position in the household and the way he spoke of the woman who owned it came abruptly clear. "You and Azo?" Hansa asked.

"For a very long time now." Naples looked up and down the stairs with a grimace. "There are more comfortable places to have this conversation. Let's step out on the balcony for a few minutes?"

This time, when he pressed a hand to the wall, it didn't mist away; there was a shimmer and shiver in the stone, perhaps as the Abyssumancer summoned the doorway he wanted instead of using one already in place.

The casual example of power made Hansa hesitate, but given he was already alone with the man, moving to a different room didn't seem any *more* stupid. The temptation to talk to someone who had been through what Hansa was now experiencing was overpowering.

A moment later they were on a balcony overlooking the dried ocean. Night had fallen, so the balcony was lit only by two subtle orbs of lavender foxfire. The bleak sky was heavy like earth, while the luminescent creatures in the dried sea made it look like a vast, starry sky. Hansa fought a sudden sense of vertigo, brought on by the seeming inversion.

Naples leaned against the railing. Hansa did the same, if only for the excuse to hold onto something—one, to fight the disorientation, and two, to fight the urge to reach out and see if Naples' hair was as soft as it looked. "Tell me about Umber?"

"I don't know him well," Hansa admitted.

"He's mortal-born?" At Hansa's confused expression, Naples rephrased the question. "He was born on the mortal plane?"

"I . . . don't know. I don't think he has been to the Abyss before," Hansa answered. Then he remembered some of the things Umber had said since they arrived. "Maybe he has. He knows a lot about it."

"Spawn inherit memories from their parents," Naples explained. "A mortal-born spawn wouldn't be able to make sense of all his Abyssi sire's memories, but they're there. He probably has some from his mother, too." He suddenly frowned, and said with a more cautious tone, "I should have asked if he's possessive before I asked you here alone."

Hansa shook his head, recalling the assurances Umber had given him. "He isn't the jealous type."

"Good. Azo will be furious if I offend a guest, especially one brought to us by Alizarin. His patronage is one of the reasons Azo and I are able to have as fine a lifestyle as we do." Hansa jumped as the Abyssumancer put a hand over his on the rail, slender fingers tapping along the back of Hansa's knuckles, which were white from gripping so tightly. "Do you realize you're leaking power?"

"I don't even know what that means." His voice

shook. With the Abyssumancer this close it was hard to draw a steady breath, but Hansa couldn't make himself step away either.

"I'm guessing an unfulfilled boon," Naples said. "Is that what brings you to the Abyss?"

Hansa nodded. "You can tell?"

"The moment I saw you. The boon . . . whispers? No, that isn't the right word. It's constantly reaching out and seeking fulfillment. No one who can feel Abyssal power could miss it."

"I'm sorry." Did that response make any sense?

"It's okay," Naples crooned, moving closer. He gently lifted Hansa's hand from the balcony rail. "You're bonded to the Abyss without any idea how to control it. You can't help sweating magic, and you can't help craving it. Luckily for you, I can help us both."

Freed of its death-grip on the rail, Hansa's hand inexorably sought the Abyssumancer. His palm on Naples' chest, he could feel the other man's heart pounding rapidly.

"Azo," Hansa said, invoking the other spawn's name in an effort to make sense of a situation that had rapidly moved beyond his control.

Naples flinched at the spawn's name, but didn't pull back. "She understands," he said.

Abyssumancer, the last of Hansa's beleaguered common sense reminded him. He recalled Umber's lesson on the four coins of the Abyss, flesh among them, and Alizarin's first words to Naples: *You're hungry. You haven't been hunting?*

Naples grabbed Hansa's belt with his free hand and pulled him forward, clearly done talking. Hansa groaned, couldn't help it, and couldn't seem to turn his head away from a kiss that made Umber's seem chaste and gentle. It was as if the last of his willpower had been exhausted when he ran away from Umber, and now his body had no intention of responding to the frantic yapping of his better judgement.

"*What—*" he managed to gasp as Naples pulled back, not going far but rather dragging Hansa with him away from the rail.

"I don't believe anyone is *that* naïve," Naples answered. He leaned back, taking them both through another doorway and into a room lit only by a single, candle-bright globe of flickering red foxfire. *Bedroom*, Hansa realized, as Naples shoved him against a post that seemed grown from the black stone floor, one of four delineating the massive, fur, and blanket-piled bed that dominated the room. "You've been staring at me since we met."

"I didn't mean—"

Once again Naples cut him off, this time with a finger across his lips that turned into a caress over his cheek, down his neck and to his chest. "Trust me," the Abyssumancer said, "I don't mind." Deft hands untied the laces holding the neck of Hansa's shirt closed, then dropped to slide under the bottom of it.

"*I* mind," Hansa managed to say.

"You can't mind much." Naples' voice was almost lost in cloth and skin as he pulled the shirt over Hansa's head and tossed it away, then started licking and nibbling his way down Hansa's chest. "You haven't asked me to stop."

There was a flaw in that logic somewhere, but Hansa couldn't put it into words as pale fingers slid down his skin and the world dissolved except for the feel of flesh on flesh.

Then it was gone. Naples reeled back; in the absence of his heat, Hansa's flesh raised in gooseflesh. He blinked eyes that didn't seem to want to work correctly in the dim light and identified Umber, who had slammed the Abyssumancer against the wall.

"Damn it," Naples growled. "He *told* me you weren't the jealous type."

"He probably also told you '*no*,'" Umber spat. "Not that I'd expect an Abyssumancer to give a damn about anyone's preference but his own."

Hansa leaned against the bedpost, trying to get his spinning mind back under his control. This was worse than the constant, gnawing craving for Umber. Getting words out was difficult, but he managed to say, "My fault. I should have . . ." He lost the thought as his eyes finally focused on the two men, both dark-haired and shirtless, Umber's broader-shouldered form pinning Naples' leaner one against the wall.

Umber glanced back when Hansa spoke, and Naples took that opportunity to shove him away.

"Hear that? He didn't—"

"Didn't fight and protest?" Umber looked like he wanted to shake the Abyssumancer again but didn't quite dare. "You know he's a fleshbond. I'm sure you can read how new the bond is, and since you're in one yourself, you know how overwhelming those first days can be. You can't even make the excuse that you're an adolescent mancer who's helpless to resist the whims of the Abyss. You're powerful enough that—"

"I'm powerful enough that, if I didn't respect your complaint, I could have stopped your heart already. Consider that," Naples growled. "I tried to confirm with him that you would not be upset. I apologize that I was mistaken."

"You don't have the faintest idea *why* I'm upset, do you?"

Naples looked Umber up and down as if the answer might be written somewhere on his body. Apparently he thought it was. He put a hand on Umber's chest and said, "Oh, I see." Umber growled and flinched away from the touch, but Naples' expression was strangely gentle as he said, "You hide your power better than he does. I had no idea how dangerously starved you are. Have you been funneling raw power into him to sustain him? *Why?* You two are flesh-bound. You should be—"

"That's a rather personal question," a soft, alto voice interrupted.

Naples broke off, face going pale as he turned toward the new speaker. All the arrogance, fury, and even attempted kindness melted from his expression, replaced by despair so clear it broke through the drug-like lust that had overwhelmed Hansa's reason.

It wasn't Umber who had stolen Naples' confidence, but a woman standing silently in the shadows at the far doorway.

Umber shook his head, muttering a curse as he pulled away from Naples. "Don't touch him. Or me. Ever again. Do I make myself clear?"

"I would never knowingly trespass on a guest's property," Naples said, the words sounding wooden as he kept his eyes locked on the other figure.

"Well," the woman said. At the single word, reverberating with irritation, Naples flinched.

"I'm sorry," Naples whispered.

"Umber, go take care of yourself and your bond," the woman said. "Take your time. When you're ready, we'll meet you downstairs to talk about your situation. I'm sure Naples will be anxious to help." Her tone was one of command, not suggestion.

"Thank you for your assistance locating my bond, Azo," Umber answered formally. Without another look to the Abyssumancer, he said, "Hansa, let's go."

On legs that felt like they might betray him any moment, Hansa followed Umber into the hall.

"I should have listened to you," he said as soon as they were alone in the stairwell. Umber had warned him that the bond might leave him especially vulnerable to Abyssumancers, but all he had heard was how his life was falling apart.

"I knew what would happen if I let you walk out of the room on your own," Umber said. "I could have stopped you. I felt it was important for you to . . . learn.

I know it sounds cruel, but I preferred to have it happen here, in relative safety, than back in Kavet."

Hansa sighed. Just the way he hadn't been able to look away from Naples would have gotten him in trouble if it had been someone in Kavet. So he also repeated himself: "I should have listened to you. I can't even blame Naples. I practically threw myself at him."

Umber grimaced. "Would you blame yourself if you had been drugged, too? You might as well have been. Naples sensed the bond's hunger and fed it. You were more vulnerable than you might have been if we'd had more privacy the last few days, but an Abyssumancer of Naples' power . . ." He reached up to stroke the wall next to the sphere of teal foxfire Hansa remembered from in front of their rooms, and the door appeared. "There was nothing you could do. When we get back to Kavet, I'll teach you how to shield yourself and hide from his kind."

"And for now?" Hansa asked. Umber had told him before that Abyssumancers were dangerous even to spawn, but Hansa hadn't believed it—or at least, hadn't believed they could be *more* dangerous to someone like Umber than they were to a soldier in the 126. Now he did.

"As long as we're here, Naples is on a short leash." He growled, rumpling still-damp hair with his fingers. "Most of the Abyssumancers you've met in the One-Twenty-Six are newly tied to the Abyss. Their Abyssi don't understand the danger or don't have the self-control to protect their mancers, so they make stupid mistakes and get caught long before they master their power. They're like kittens who can't help swatting at pretty bouncing lights. Naples . . ." He shook his head. "Mortals don't age in the Abyss, so I don't know how old he really is, but he is long past the stage of being a helpless slave to his power. Azo and the Abyssi of the court won't tolerate him unless he follows their rules."

"Don't those rules include not stealing others', um, property?" He chose and discarded a half-dozen other words before deciding on the last one, none he liked better when referring to himself and several that were worse.

"He could only abuse you because he could claim to believe—or really *did* believe—that I wouldn't mind. He probably told himself I wouldn't have let you go off on your own unless I was willing to share you." He flashed a feral grin Hansa was certain had nothing to do with joy. "Though you'll notice he was careful not to actually *ask* me."

"And he didn't need to ask me," Hansa grumbled. Both because the laws of the Abyss apparently said a human's opinions didn't count, and because Hansa lacked the ability to say no. That reminded him of something else important. "He said I was leaking power because of the unfulfilled boon. And you. He described you as starved."

Umber nodded. "I've been giving you as much power as I can risk losing to keep you coherent. Between that and the open boon, the two of us might as well put out a sign for Abyssumancers saying, *Free Meal.*" This time, his slow smile, coupled with a meaningful glance around the opulent room, looked more genuine. "Thankfully, we now have the opportunity to address one of those failings, and a plan for how to address the other. If nothing else, Azo will force Naples to help us to make up for his gaffe."

Umber reached out, and his fingers slid against Hansa's bare shoulder. Hansa tensed instinctively, fighting the flesh-craving that touch renewed, and Umber took his hand away.

"I don't want to push you," Umber said. "I know the Quin have rather unpleasant precepts about men with male lovers. As long as we're in the Abyss, I can keep doing what I've been doing, but once we're back in Kavet that won't be an option."

Hansa didn't think it was an option here, either. Naples hadn't used the word *starved* to be poetic. Now that he was paying attention, Hansa could see the way Umber's jaw and cheekbones seemed more pronounced and his tanned skin a shade paler. He hadn't seen it before because he had been trying so hard not to notice *anything* about how Umber looked. Giving away so much power had to be dangerous for him.

Either guessing or reading Hansa's thoughts, Umber admitted, "There are other sources of power here. Once you're settled, I can seek them out."

Umber was trying to give him an easy answer. The only thing easier would have been if Umber had taken Naples' approach and deftly removed all opportunity to refuse. If only Xaz hadn't stopped them that morning, when waking in Umber's arms had made it so easy to let the bond take over without thinking about it . . .

"It's not just that you're a man," Hansa managed to say, trying to express the jangling thoughts that made it so hard to step forward and take Umber in his arms when the magic wasn't overwhelming him. "I mean, yes, that's . . . awkward . . . for me, but . . . I mean . . . you know I was raised Quin. Ruby and I, we both were."

"I'm aware of that." Umber sounded puzzled. "I—" He stopped. "Quin believe in waiting for marriage. You're telling me you've never . . ." He trailed off as if the possibility was too absurd. "You're twenty-seven years old!"

"Maybe Abyss-spawn can't survive without sex, but humans can."

"They can," Umber conceded. "But why would you want to? Are you sure you ever *were* attracted to women?" He bit his lip before Hansa had to dignify the question with an answer. "Sorry. Dear Numen, Hansa, I nearly fed you to the Abyssumancer!" Hansa felt the ghost of a smile on his own face as he watched Umber try to come to grips with a fact he clearly didn't know how to handle. It was nice to see him off-balance for once, instead of Umber always being confident while Hansa fumbled.

"I don't want to pressure you," Hansa said, struggling to keep a straight face as he repeated the words Umber had recently spoken more seriously. "If you need some time to—"

"Come here, Quin." Umber grabbed his wrists and tugged him toward the bed. The grip was light enough that Hansa could have pulled away, but he followed despite his pounding heart. "I'm glad you put me off before. You deserve better than a quick tumble on the beach of the dry sea for your first time."

"Careful," Hansa said, trying to maintain a façade of humor to keep from revealing just how nervous Umber's intense gaze made him. "You're starting to sound like a Numini."

He had moved closer to Umber without even noticing. It would have been impossible not to. Now, Umber wrapped his arms around Hansa's waist.

"How can I introduce you to new and obscene acts if you've never even made love?" he purred, his tone once again sardonic, expression sultry. "Come to bed. Let me show you how it's done."

CHAPTER 30

The Abyssumancer had separated them the moment they entered the building. Xaz could only hope the hospitality was genuine, and Alizarin and Azo were enough to keep Naples in check.

Aurelian had mouthed apologies about the simple accommodations she offered Cadmia and Xaz, explaining that there was only one real guest room. She didn't say it outright, but it was clear that the guest room had been given to either the Abyssi or the Abyss-spawn, and the rest of them were lucky to have a place to stay.

Xaz didn't care if it was a space normally reserved for servants. The room was simple, but it was clean and warm. The floor was almost entirely covered by a startlingly crimson fur throw, the bed was topped by mounds of blankets, and most importantly, it wasn't likely to be invaded by the predatory beasts of the Abyss. Did anything else matter?

Well, there were the baths down the hall, which she made full use of.

The water was hot to the edge of scalding, and felt marvelous after walking through the Abyss. The heat soothed her aching muscles, and water and caked soap made quick work of sweat and grime. The fresh clothes Aurelian brought were nothing intricate—loose slacks and a shirt in the same style as everyone else in the household wore—but they were made of deliciously soft material that felt lovely against Xaz's chapped and sand-scuffed skin.

She meant only to put her sore feet up for a minute, but realized she had drifted into a doze when Aurelian announced, "Lady Azo will see you now." No matter how exhausted she had been, or how lulling the comfortable accommodations had been, she couldn't believe she had fallen asleep!

Back in the front parlor, a tray had been set out with a variety of fruit and bite-sized pieces of roasted meat. Xaz wondered if any of it had previously belonged to the multilegged creature they had seen Naples butchering, then decided that was a contemplation best avoided.

"Should we wait?" Cadmia asked, looking at the food and then around the empty room.

"I'm a Numenmancer," Xaz said. "You're human. I don't think we need to worry about falling further in their esteem."

She understood where she fell in the Abyss's hierarchy of importance. She wasn't sure if being a Numenmancer made her more valuable than Cadmia or less, but either way she suspected she ranked about as high as the jellyfish creatures Hansa had killed.

Besides, she was *hungry.* Alizarin had brought a little bit of fruit, but mostly meat, which Xaz had only eaten enough to keep from feeling like she was starving. After that, she couldn't stand it. Even this offering, which was spiced and roasted instead of raw, didn't sit well on her palate.

"I didn't expect there to be a place like this in the Abyss," Cadmia remarked as she helped herself to a small plate of food. "How would something like this be built?"

"It may have been a natural cave system Naples and Azo modified," Xaz speculated, "or the Abyssumancer may have carved it out entirely. The doorways and foxfire are clearly his work." With effort, sacrifice and ritual, Xaz thought she could create a hidden door like the ones that peppered this warren, but she would never be able to maintain one, much less the dozens she had seen here so far.

Focused on her contemplation of the magic she had seen so far, and what it implied about Naples' power, Xaz was startled when Cadmia asked, "How did you become a Numenmancer?"

Xaz bristled. She knew what the Quinacridone and the Napthol said about how her kind came into being. She stared into Cadmia's face, but saw no judgement there, only genuine curiosity.

"The Numini started speaking to me when I was a

child," she said at last. "Five or six, maybe? I don't remember when it started. They told me to keep them secret, and it was years before I connected my dreams and invisible playmates with the creatures my parents warned me about, and the tricks they taught me to do with sorcery." There was no way to describe the depth of her horror when she had finally made the connection between the wicked things they warned about at her school and the beautiful power the Numini had given her, or the extent of her hurt at the Numini's cold dismissal of her terrified, guilty questions. "When I finally understood and tried to question the Numini, they told me they had chosen me and I should be honored and grateful. Refusing them has never been an option."

Now there was disapproval in Cadmia's face—at least for a moment, before she hid it behind her professional mask—but she didn't have a chance to ask a follow-up question before a doorway opened in the far wall and Naples entered. The Abyssumancer had changed his clothes, and his dark hair was loosely tied back. He walked close to a woman who could only be Azo, the mistress of the household.

Umber was a handsome man, but unless one could see Abyssal power, there was nothing remarkable about him beyond his striking blue eyes. Azo, on the other hand, could never be mistaken for fully human. Her skin was the deep burgundy color of well-aged wine, and the hair that cascaded across her shoulders and down her back in frothy waves was plum-violet. Dressed in the same kind of loose slacks and blouse as Xaz and Cadmia, she nevertheless carried an air of lethality with her.

"The others may be delayed," she informed them, without bothering with courtesies like introductions. They already knew who she was, and clearly she already knew who they were, so what was the point? "Alizarin is hunting, and Hansa and Umber have their own needs to take care of. Perhaps you two can explain your troubles to us?"

Azo and Naples settled into one of the couches, their bodies touching at the hand, knee, hip, and shoulder. Xaz shook her head, disgusted by how slow she had been, as she realized the obvious: Azo and Naples were bonded. No wonder one of the spawn was able to keep an Abyssumancer under control.

Xaz and Cadmia exchanged a look, perhaps both wondering who would sound less stupid if they explained the idiotic logic that had brought them here. Without the explanation that the Numini had manipulated them, they had no excuse for their foolishness, but they had all agreed that the Abyssumancer was more likely to balk and refuse to help them if he knew this quest was divinely mandated.

Xaz, no stranger to blows to her pride, launched into the tale. Naples' eyes widened when he heard about Alizarin's confrontation with Antioch, and he went very still when she said Cadmia had heard about a sorcerer called Terre Verte in her studies at the Order of the Napthol, but otherwise they both listened impassively until the end.

"Alizarin said you might be able to help us," Xaz concluded, looking at the Abyssumancer, "though I'll admit, you have far more to lose by crossing the Abyssi court than we do. We hope to return to the mortal realm. I imagine that isn't an option for you."

She meant the words kindly, as an acknowledgement of his bond to Azo and the risk he would run if he chose to help them, but could see instantly that she had misjudged. Azo's face went stony. Naples froze. For a moment they both hesitated, as if in between heartbeats they existed as statues instead of living flesh.

Then Azo shoved to her feet and announced, "I need to go to the court and explain to them why we are harboring a Numenmancer in our walls. Naples, deal with them." She hesitated, met his gaze, and added flatly, "However you see fit."

She walked out without further apology.

A chill passed over Xaz that had nothing to do with divine power, and everything to do with that last, ominous command.

But Naples only sighed heavily. He closed his eyes and sank against the couch like a man whose body has been much abused and exhausted. "Alizarin has been a good friend to me," he said, his voice sounding hollow. "I would be honored to help him. And I—"

He broke off as Hansa and Umber entered, along with a breath of Abyssal power so strong Xaz instinctively looked past them for Alizarin. Naples' breath hissed in and his body tensed in reaction to the magic.

When he at last looked up again, his expression was like porcelain, crafted and emotionless.

"Naples was just about to say if he could help us," Xaz prompted, when too many seconds passed without anyone speaking again.

"We would be very grateful," Umber replied, settling on to the love seat across from Naples with Hansa beside him. Naples' controlled veneer cracked for a moment, revealing raw hunger visible in his copper eyes. Too late, Xaz reconsidered her assumption about his relationship with Azo.

He caught her looking, and as his gaze flicked to her, the spark of famine became fury—and then nothing. Cadmia couldn't help but recall the way Umber had described how hard it was for an Abyssumancer to retain his humanity in the face of his power's demands. How much effort did it take Naples to push the Abyss aside?

This time it was Cadmia who reacted to the unfocused moment, as Naples apparently lost the thread of the conversation. "Is everything all right?" she asked softly.

"Yes," Naples said, firmly, the word and tone both seeming to suggest, *No*. He shook himself like an animal exiting cold water. "I was just considering, and deciding how to begin," he explained. "I owe Umber a favor, so I would make this simple if I could, but a necromancer can't help you fulfill this bond. A necromancer could summon and control your spirit on the human plane, but you need someone with power over the Abyss in order to find her soul here and drag it back across the veil, and power over life as well in order to recreate the body."

"You're talking about a Gressumancer." Xaz had heard of mancers who could control all four planes of existence, but she gave the rumors no credence. Even when the Numini had first mentioned Terre Verte, she had assumed they referred to an especially powerful necromancer, not a mythical creature.

"What's a Gressumancer?" Cadmia asked.

"They're also known as planes-walkers," Xaz said. "They're a legend among mancers."

"Legends are based on truth," Naples said. "And based on the stories I've heard, if there's a man in the three realms who might have inspired this one, it's Terre Verte. He lived before the mancers began to be born in Kavet. The Abyssi talk about him, say he was so powerful the king of the Abyss offered him a chance to become one of them, but he refused so they imprisoned him instead."

"In the royal court," Cadmia said nervously. "Alizarin seems comfortable with his ability to manage the Abyssi of this level, but I don't know if that's an honest assessment of his abilities or an unwillingness to reveal weakness. Do you know?"

"Oh, Rin is capable of laying waste to the high court," Naples said, too casually. "He's done it before. That's how the current lord of the high court came to power." He grinned, a feral expression that showed some pride in the blue Abyssi, but more savagery than joy. "I'm powerful enough on my own to walk through the high court in relative safety, even without Azo's claim. And I have, which is how I know for certain Terre Verte is not there."

"Were the Numini wrong?" Hansa asked optimistically. "Maybe he's just a story."

Umber's voice was far, far too calm as he said, "The Abyss has five royal courts, one on each level of the Abyss." It was clear he wished he didn't need to ask Naples, "Where do the stories say Terre Verte is?"

"The fifth-level court, called the low court."

"You're mad," Hansa said. "Alizarin had to fight one fourth-level Abyssi on our way here, and it was a close call. We can't take on the entire Abyss. Xaz, I'm sorry, I know your Numini are trying to shove us into this, but as far as I'm concerned, this is impossible."

Naples yawned, seeming more relaxed instead of less now that he had revealed just how hopeless their situation was. "You didn't have an Abyssumancer with you before," he said.

"Why would you help us?" Xaz demanded. She had stumbled with her earlier question, she knew that, but she raised it again because this situation didn't make sense without the answer. "Why would you risk the wrath of the entire Abyss to drag this man out of the depths? If you just want to help Umber and Hansa, you can best do that by *refusing* to help."

Naples gave a sunny smile. "Because all things serve the divine, sweetheart," he said. "Haven't you heard?"

He knew. They hadn't mentioned the Numini, but

somehow Naples knew. Or did he know something about Terre Verte? Or was he just quoting the old adage because rescuing an innocent man from the Abyss would be considered a divine act?

She prepared to press the question with Naples further, but Umber answered for him. "He'll help because he wants this man, too. If he's as powerful as the stories say, he can break the bond. That's it, isn't it?"

As he had when Xaz had brought it up, Naples reacted to the reference to the bond as if it were a physical assault. He nodded sharply.

"If anyone can, he can," Naples said. "If you two have decided you don't want the boon Hansa foolishly demanded, maybe he can break your bond as well. I figure a man who has been imprisoned in the deepest cell in the Abyss is probably willing to make a hefty deal."

"If this man can solve all your problems, why haven't you gone after him before now?" Umber pressed.

"I didn't have a Numenmancer before," Naples explained. "The palace is an interesting vortex. Power is in flux. I can hold back the more damaging magics of the Abyss so we can survive the journey down to the low court, but that will take all my attention. I can't do it while fighting Abyssi."

The laugh that broke from Xaz's throat was startled and dry. "And you expect *me* to?" Even her Numini couldn't be arrogant enough to think she could battle the entire Abyssal court . . . right?

"A properly-trained and motivated Numenmancer

could destroy an Abyssi," Naples said, "but I'm aware you're not that well versed. I don't expect you to fight. The deeper Abyssi don't see with eyes; they see with power. A Numenmancer's power can blind them."

"And the higher Abyssi?" Umber asked. He leaned forward, one arm on the table, now listening intently. "They'll still be able to see us, won't they?"

"Through the second level, the spawn are respected and allowed to own property," Naples said. "So you could claim Hansa, Cadmia, and Dioxazine. Below that . . . on the third level, it may be assumed that we are there due to our connection to Alizarin, at least long enough for us to get through. Beyond that, Dioxazine can keep us clear."

"Even if it's remotely *possible*, it's still insane," Hansa said. "You can't really expect us to—" He broke off, breath hitching with a grunt. Umber set his teeth. Trying to refuse must have caused the magic of the boon to show its teeth.

"Maybe you should have thought of that before you demanded the third boon," Naples purred. "As it is, I don't see that you have any choice."

"You say the Abyssi offered to make Terre Verte one of them?" Xaz asked. What kind of man *was* this, that the Abyssi wanted to enthrone and the Numini wanted to liberate?

"Well, I wasn't there personally," Naples said sardonically, "but the stories say the king of the Abyss offered to make him a prince."

"Do you know anything for *certain*?" She was desperate to have some say in her own fate, and that meant she at least wanted to know why they were being sent on this impossible mission.

"I know for certain that there is a cell at the lowest level of the Abyss," Naples said. "I can scry that deep. I cannot see into the cell because it is designed to keep something or someone of great power contained, and my magic isn't strong enough to penetrate its walls. But based on everything I've heard over the years, I believe there is a man inside who can help us all."

Give up, she told herself. The Numini would get what they wanted. They always did. Her task, as it ever had been, was only to nod her head and obey.

"I'll need to consult with the Numini," Xaz said. This was what they wanted, but perhaps they didn't realize exactly where Terre Verte was, and what rescuing him would require. Naples spoke confidently, but Xaz knew her power had never been particularly strong.

"We'll take a break, then," Naples suggested. "We all need . . ." His gaze rested on Hansa and Umber for a moment with enough heat that Xaz took a deep breath, fighting not to blush. "Rest," he concluded, the word clearly standing in for what he assumed they would actually be doing. "I'll speak to Azo when she returns, and we will make further plans in the morning."

CHAPTER 31

Naples had the pretty face and earnest eyes of the best mongers in Kavet, which meant Cadmia didn't plan to trust anything he said. Thankfully, she had another expert on the Abyss to consult. If Naples knew of Terre Verte through Abyssal rumors, Alizarin probably did as well. Why hadn't he said anything?

After they separated to rest for their intended adventure, Cadmia asked the household servants if they would let Alizarin know she was looking for him when he returned. Obligingly, Alizarin came to her less than an hour later. His disquieting pallor had gone, and his aquamarine fur once again gleamed impeccably and felt like the finest silk when he brushed against her side in a catlike greeting.

Seeing him happy and well released the knot of tension that had appeared between her shoulder blades the moment Naples separated them upon arrival.

Seeing the others unharmed had helped a little, but she felt much better with the blue Abyssi near. For a minute she just leaned against him, letting his warmth soak into her before she jumped into the topic of Terre Verte.

"Naples knows about Terre Verte, and thinks he can help us get to him," she explained eventually, only reluctantly pulling away to have the conversation. "He says he's heard Abyssi talk about him?"

The words were half statement, and half question, intended not to be accusatory.

Alizarin nodded.

"You didn't say anything."

His ears and tail drooped, signs she had learned meant hurt and disappointment. "You didn't ask."

Of course. She thought about the conversation when the rest of them had discussed Terre Verte and their plans, when Alizarin had eventually suggested they come to Naples. She had asked Alizarin questions about strength and whether they could *get to* the court, and he had answered the questions she had posed aloud. It had never occurred to ask about Terre Verte because she had associated the sorcerer with the Numini.

Cadmia didn't have as much experience with Abyssi as Xaz or Umber did. Why hadn't one of them realized Alizarin probably had useful information?

Because they do *have experience with them,* she realized. *They don't expect Alizarin to be thoughtful.*

"Do you like it when I ask you questions?" Except for personal questions about his nature, he had responded cheerfully to all her inquiries, though they ranged from the nature of the five levels of the Abyss to the way he had cleverly adapted human-made pants to fit over his tail.

He smiled—a radiant, utterly honest expression that made her heart give an inappropriate lurch in her chest. "It's fun to know answers," he said.

Their conversation was interrupted by Naples stepping through the bedroom door.

He paused in the doorway, as if hesitant about his welcome. "I wanted to make sure you know I don't expect you to go with us tomorrow," he said to Alizarin, making no indication he had even noticed Cadmia's presence. "You've talked about wanting a Numenmancer for a long time, and I know the risk you've taken by bringing her to me now that you finally have one. I would never ask you to directly cross the low court."

Cadmia tensed at the implication that Alizarin was the one who had brought them here, but the Abyssi tilted his head, appearing confused. "You never told me you wanted Terre Verte," he replied. "Why would I bring you a Numenmancer I didn't know you needed?"

"You . . ." Naples frowned. "I assumed . . . You worked so hard to get a tie to the mortal realm. Why else would you bring her to the Abyss?"

Abyssi can't lie, Cadmia thought. How would Naples react when he learned the Numini had manipulated them all into coming here?

But Alizarin didn't answer that question. Instead, he said, "I'll go with you after Terre Verte."

"You—" Naples broke off, as if startled Alizarin had returned to the earlier part of the conversation. "Do you know what happened to the *last* Abyssi who meddled with this man?"

"The previous king of the low court wanted to make him one of us. Terre Verte said no, and the other Abyssi slew the king."

"That . . . seems extreme," Cadmia interjected. "Just because he said no?"

"The king murdered many Abyssi to work the magic," Alizarin answered. "Others were angry. They brought him to the crystal caves and sacrificed him where his blood would seed the crystals and make more Abyssi. It's how I was born."

"Hm. Well, if you're willing to risk it, we can talk about it—" Naples broke off. He shifted his eyes to look at Cadmia, and the warm, open expression on his face, so different from the desperate awe he wore when looking at Azo or the desperate hunger when he saw Umber and Hansa, abruptly disappeared. He finished his sentence "—later. Are you sleeping here?"

Alizarin nodded. He added, "You need to speak to Azo about your plans. She should return soon."

Naples let out a long, slow breath and nodded. "You're right." He looked around the small room apologetically and said, "If I had realized, I would have set you up in the good guest room. Alizarin, you know where to find me if you need me. Good night."

Why *hadn't* Alizarin been given the good guest

room? Had Naples expected Alizarin to sleep with the court, or somewhere out in the Abyss?

She had barely finished the thought before she realized how stupid it was. Everything Naples had said so far implied he had expected Alizarin to stay with *him*. Clearly they had a close relationship—which had involved many long conversations about Numenmancers.

"Did you bond to Xaz intentionally?" she asked.

She had assumed—and thought the others did as well—that Alizarin's bond to Xaz had been accidental, another consequence of the strange circumstances of Baryte's arrest and the Numini manipulating them. Naples apparently thought differently.

"Not Xaz specifically," Alizarin answered. "Baryte was supposed to talk to a Numenmancer for me. Antioch pushed him too hard and the Quin found him. Then he died."

"And he just *happened* to throw the knife at a Numenmancer? That didn't seem odd to you?"

Alizarin had the grace to look puzzled. He sat on the bed and leaned his head on his hand, tapping his tail on his knee as he thought. "I don't know why he did that."

"Could the Numini have made him do it?" She was willing to believe the Numini could manipulate her and Hansa that easily, but wouldn't an Abyssi or an Abyssumancer be protected from their whisperings?

Alizarin shrugged. "Maybe."

"Could Naples?"

"Probably."

"If he knew you wanted a bond to a Numenmancer and he needed a Numenmancer for his own plan, would Naples have been willing to sacrifice another Abyssumancer to achieve that end?"

"He thought I did it," Alizarin pointed out.

"He *said* so. Humans can lie." Antioch had targeted Alizarin because he considered him responsible for his mancer's death. She could understand why Naples would want to hide his own involvement.

Alizarin just shrugged.

Cadmia resolved to bring the question up again when the others were around to help her consider it, but accepted that the mystery wouldn't be solved that night. It was time for sleep.

The bed in the guest room was warmer than the Abyss and softer than stone and sand, removing all the excuses for why she had slept curled against Alizarin the night before, but he had clearly assumed she would want him to stay. She couldn't find it in her to be affronted by that; she wanted him to stay, too.

Years ago, she had turned her back on the Order of A'hknet and become a Sister of the Napthol. She had needed to reevaluate every bias and instinct she had, relearn everything from table manners to social norms, and give up vices she had never considered as such. As she climbed into bed, she realized she was on the cusp of doing something similar now.

Except this change was *madness*. The Order of the Napthol was respected. Valued. If she started to sympathize with people like Dioxazine and Umber . . . and

Alizarin . . . but she didn't even have power. People in this place treated her like what she was: a foolish human woman who had jumped in deep water without knowing how to swim.

Alizarin stretched out next to her and used his tail to tuck her snugly against his chest just as he had the previous night, but this time she found it difficult to relax. Closing her eyes to try to sleep only made it worse. Without the coarse sand and biting wind to distract her, she was hyperaware of him, of how good it felt to have his arm across her waist and feel the firm planes of muscle under the impossibly soft fur that covered his chest. Her outdoor dress and cloak had also been a thicker barrier between them than the comfortable but lightweight shirt and pants she now wore.

"Alizarin?" she asked, opening her eyes.

"Yes?" His face was startlingly close to hers.

"Please don't take this as an insult, but . . . are you a man, or an animal?"

He blinked, not offended, but confused. "I'm Abyssi."

She should have expected that patiently obvious response, because Alizarin clearly wasn't either.

"I just mean . . ." She struggled for a way to ask the question, trying not to blush, and embarrassed to consider how she had unthinkingly leaned against him the night and day before. He had never indicated that he thought anything more of it than a housecat thought of sprawling across a person's lap.

"Which one gets petted, man or animal?" Alizarin asked in his practical way.

"Animal, usually." It had been a stupid question.

"So that's fine?" he suggested, running a hand down her side. His hands felt warm, and very human, through the thin fabric.

"Animals don't usually pet back," she pointed out.

"Abyssi do."

"Do Abyssi—" That was an even *stupider* question, with an equally obvious answer.

She was having trouble asking the question because she didn't know what she wanted him to say. Drawing a deep breath, she asked herself, *Are you about to proposition an Abyssi?*

Was she?

If he said no, that he had snuggled against her for the same reason an animal might—for comfort, company, and warmth—then she would have to ask him to leave, because that was clearly not how her body was responding to his presence. It would be like lusting over a pet dog. Disgusting.

And if he said yes . . .

Alizarin had his flighty moments, but he was a thinking, rational being. He was also beautiful.

And an Abyssi.

Her last lover had been a prostitute. Some people who would consider this a step up.

Alizarin started purring again, and at this distance—none—and with so little between them, the sensation made her shiver.

"That tickles," she said, suddenly breathless.

He nuzzled at the crook of her neck, and nipped her there. She held her breath, too aware of how sharp those teeth were, but he released her without drawing a drop of blood. Then he paused, waiting.

She had the sense that he knew exactly what was going through her mind, but was giving her the authority to decide what happened next. Realizing that the Abyssi in bed with her was more considerate and patient than most of the human beasts that had frequented Scarlet's bed, that despite all she knew about the denizens of the infernal realm he cared enough about her comfort and consent that he hadn't even indicated interest until she had, made her decision easy.

She closed the scant distance between them, giving in to the desire to press her lips to the Abyssi's and tangle her fingers in his silken black hair. She was already in the Abyss. What was the worst that could happen at the end of this particular fall from grace?

No one bothered them, though Cadmia certainly felt like they slept late, satiated and wrapped in fur and blankets. They made love again after waking, and then Alizarin said, "I need to hunt and make sure the high court is clear before we go. Azo will provide breakfast for you."

"Mmm." She hadn't quite recovered her voice yet. It had been a very long time since she'd had any lover, and she had to admit that teenage Cinnabar couldn't compare. "Happy hunting."

She found her feet several minutes after he had left, bathed, dressed, and went in search of the promised breakfast before she needed to face a trip into the bowels of the Abyss. She ran into Umber along the way. For the first time since they came to the Abyss, Hansa wasn't with him.

"Is Hansa all right?"

"He offered to help prepare breakfast," Umber said. "I wanted to talk to you alone. Are you okay?"

The sincerity in his tone and expression was worrying compared to his normally cavalier, ironic attitude.

"Yes?" she answered, the word turned into a question by her confusion.

He paused, as if there was more he wanted to say, and then nodded sharply and started to go.

She caught his arm. "You can't ask a question like that and not explain yourself."

He turned reluctantly back to her. Not mincing words, he explained, "Abyssi aren't known to be kind and gentle lovers. In general, they won't heed a refusal, and mortal partners often don't survive the encounter. Given how you clearly spent your night, I wanted to make sure you were all right."

Until that moment, Cadmia hadn't thought a person could feel chills while blushing. "How did yo—"

"One of the servants mentioned that he stayed in your room," Umber explained, "and I can see his power on you now. Naples, Azo, and Dioxazine will all be able to tell."

"Oh." She wasn't ashamed of sex, but she'd never

had someone confront her so bluntly about it afterward either. "Well, I'm fine," she said. "Alizarin is . . ."

When she struggled to find the word she wanted, Umber supplied, "He's impossible. If he were as sweet and affectionate as he seems, he never would have become a prince of the third level. Either something changed him recently, or he's terrifyingly good at concealing his true nature."

Cadmia took in the words. She couldn't imagine any creature as irredeemably vicious as the Abyssi she had learned about feigning Alizarin's level of consideration. "Something changed him." She even had a good idea what. "Or some*one*. Could being bonded to a Numenmancer have done it? According to Naples, Alizarin has wanted one for a long time."

"I don't know," Umber said. "When the other Abyssi talk about him, I almost remember him. I think my sire knew him, or knew of him. Abyssi memories aren't very coherent." Cadmia had heard that spawn, like Abyssi, inherited their parents' memories, but it was unsettling to see Umber casually consult another's recollections. "One way or another, the pretty blue Abyssi we know is not the same creature he used to be. But if being bonded to a Numenmancer is what changed him, what made him want *that*?"

"Could Naples have manipulated him?" Cadmia suggested. "I gather they have a close history, and Naples is desperate to break his bond to Azo."

"No," Umber said, this time unequivocal. "Naples has been putting everything he has into this plan since he brought it up last night. He has to fight the bond to do it. When we showed up he saw his opportunity, and he's powerful enough it just might work, but I don't think he could have premeditated anything this complex." He sighed, shaking his head. "Given all the mysteries we're facing, I suppose the question of how Alizarin changed is almost moot. I'm glad for all our sakes—and especially yours—that he has. I was concerned."

"Why do you care?" she asked, curious. Before now, Umber's interest in her had been entirely as a means to an end.

As if the question made him realize he had betrayed too much genuine emotion, Umber lifted a sardonic brow. "Because, like most people born on the mortal realm, I had a mother and was rather fond of her. You do know what this kind of behavior causes, don't you?"

If the question had been asked with the same sympathetic concern as his first one, she would have tolerated it. As it was, she bristled. "My mother was the most sought-after paid companion in Kavet. I know how to count my cycle."

"Is there much call for that in the Order of the Napthol?" Umber asked, with the same casually mocking tone. "And was your mother sleeping with Abyssi?"

The habit of watching her cycle to avoid sex during her fertile period had been drilled into her from the day of her first menstruation, when her mother had sat her down to explain the possible consequences of intimacy—Scarlet being what she was, she had included "unwanted emotional entanglements" right before pregnancy—and how to avoid them. She had also taught Cadmia the herbs women could employ to further protect themselves, but those probably weren't available in the Abyss.

Cadmia was about to say something biting in return when Umber's previous words caught up to her: *I had a mother.* She knew what Umber was but had never stopped to consider where he had come from.

"Was your mother an Abyssumancer?" she asked. If so, had he seen her arrested by the Quin? Had he tried, and failed, to save her? Or had he lost her to the ever-hungry power and needed to flee his own parent?

"No." At first she didn't think he intended to say more. His gaze traveled the ceiling as if an answer was written in the slick stone. Not looking at her, he said, "Her name was Bonnie Holland."

He said the name as if she should recognize it, but it meant nothing to her. "I'm sorry. Should I know who that is?"

"Hansa would know," he said. "Speaking of my favorite Quin, let's see what he's made for our breakfast." Umber changed the subject without subtlety or apology, but Cadmia made a mental note to ask Hansa as soon as they had a private moment.

If they ever did. First they needed to travel with an incomprehensible Abyssi and a desperate Abyssumancer into the heart of the Abyss to rescue a sorcerer who had once been offered a throne in the infernal realm.

CHAPTER 32

We will be with you.

"Can't you tell me *anything* more?" Xaz pleaded with her Numini. "I am your willing servant." If having no other choices counted as willing. "I am preparing to walk into the deepest level of the Abyss for you, with allies I'm not sure I can trust. I fear only failure to achieve your desires." Also death, devouring and enslavement to Abyssi.

She thought the Numini would dismiss her again, but instead she felt his resignation like a drift of snow across her skin. *The Abyssumancer is right that our brilliance can conceal you from the creatures of the lower Abyss. We used to use it to shelter those we protected, in the world before the realms were rift. Wait to cast it until you are past the glow of fires and luminescence that light the higher levels of the Abyss. It will not help against creatures who use their eyes to hunt, and you need to save your limited strength.*

"Thank you," she breathed, grateful for the assurance.

Your bond to us will protect you, and the Abyssumancer's bond to his master will protect him, but your other human companions must not look on the lower Abyssi in their natural forms, he warned. *Cover their eyes or they will suffer madness from which even our grace cannot save them.*

Xaz shuddered, thinking of the sight of Antioch's and Alizarin's battle, and recalling that they were only from the third and fourth level. "I am grateful for your protection."

His power wrapped her, and for once she thought she felt a hint of fondness from the creature who was sending her on this likely suicide mission. *I will be with you,* he said. *Know that.* The comfort in those words was somewhat lessened when he added, *You are my chosen servant, and you are dear to me. If you fall along the way, I will bring you home.*

She emerged from her trance disoriented, coughing and sputtering, as if the Numini had exhausted any gentleness he possessed with that last statement and then needed to rid himself of her presence like a prickling burr.

The others, gathered around the table packing supplies, looked up at her expectantly.

"He says Naples is right that I should be able to hide us from the lower Abyssi," she reported. Her voice was hoarse, and there was a rime of ice gathered around her splayed fingers on the table. She cleared her throat and continued. "He also says we need to make sure to blindfold Hansa and Cadmia so they don't see the lower Abyssi and lose their minds."

Hansa froze in the middle of testing the weight of his bag, let out a breath, shook his head, and set it down with a *klunk*. "What happens if you die in the Abyss?" he asked, his voice a bit too jolly, bordering on hysterical.

"Supposedly, you stay in the Abyss," Umber said. "Some say you fall to a deeper level. Not even the Abyssi really understand."

"Well then, it's a good thing we're going to find a guy who can raise the dead out of ash."

"I'll ask Aurelian for some fabric we can use for blindfolds," Cadmia said more practically.

As she left the room, Naples came in and dropped a heavy bundle on one of the chairs—the armor he had been wearing when they first met, plus additional protection and weaponry. Xaz watched with increasing alarm as he put on the vest, high boots, bracers, and five knives—one on the outer edge of each boot, two at his waist and one strapped to his upper arm—to his outfit.

"I thought you said we *wouldn't* be fighting?" she asked, eyeing the daggers.

Naples pulled out the dagger sheathed at his upper arm, holding it up so they could all admire the fine, sinuous blade, which was glistening black and let off a reddish glow of damped power. He flipped it around deftly, showing off the fact that the weapon was all one piece, the handle made of the same material but less polished, so it was ashy, matte black. It looked as if it had been made to fit his hand.

"Anyone know what this is?" he asked.

Umber nodded. "It's made with a bone from an Abyssi," he said. "Who did you kill for it?"

"This is a souvenir from one of Alizarin's visits to the first-level court," Naples replied. "He wanted me to make a special one for him, but I needed to practice the technique before using more precious materials." Naples sheathed the blade again in one slick movement. "Did you know an Abyssi can regrow an arm in less than a week?"

He shot Xaz a look as he asked the seemingly idle question.

"You!" she gasped, grasping the meaning instantly. "You made the knife Alizarin gave to Baryte of Alizarin's own bone. *That's* how he was able to bond with me. Did you convince Baryte you were his Abyssi when you had him throw it at me?"

"No," Naples replied, "I have no idea how Rin managed that part. Has it occurred to you that your Numini doesn't seem to like you very much?"

Xaz's retort cut off and her jaw snapped shut. She couldn't make the retort she wanted because, damn it, Naples was being intentionally insulting but he was also *right*. She wouldn't put it past her Numini to prompt Baryte to throw the knife at her, then give her grief about it. Numini couldn't lie, but they had never said, *We didn't cause this.* They had only whined at her about the Abyssal taint in her power and told her she needed to fix it, which sent her to Umber, which sent her to the Abyss.

"Can we get back to Xaz's question of why you're fully armed?" Hansa asked. "And why if you need to be, we *aren't*? I can handle a weapon."

Naples shot him a condescending look. "I'm an Abyssumancer."

"So you require weaponry?"

"I require my tools."

"Blood, pain, fire, flesh," Umber murmured to Hansa, just loudly enough for Xaz to make out the words.

Hansa cringed closer to Umber and grumbled, "As long as he keeps them far, *far* away from me."

"If I end up needing your power," Naples replied, as he checked each of his daggers to make sure they were settled correctly in their sheaths, "it will be because I'm having trouble keeping the Abyss from crashing down on our heads. So I suggest you don't in that instant decide to be squeamish."

"Just how likely *is* that?" Xaz asked.

Naples glanced up just long enough to cast her an amused look. "I've never been lower than the third level of the Abyss, and I've never traveled with so many people I needed to protect. So I'm not prepared to give you odds at this time." In the middle of speaking, he turned toward the doorway, where a heartbeat later Azo appeared.

Watching the way those two responded to each

other made Xaz's skin crawl. They predicted each other's movements, moved toward each other like flowers bending toward the sun, but it was all a sham. Magic. How could two people be deeply in love yet so achingly miserable?

"You're still doing this?" Azo asked Naples. Their hushed conversation carried across the quiet room.

Naples nodded, not meeting Azo's gaze. "I'm doing it for you."

Azo winced. "You don't have to . . ." She touched his cheek.

He shut his eyes, and drew a deep breath. "You know it's the bond talking. Once this is over . . . you'll be glad. You *will* be."

"Will you?" she asked.

"Don't you think I—" He clamped his mouth around his first response, then chose another. "We'll both be." The words sounded as if they hurt him to say. They clearly hurt her to hear.

She pulled him close, and while he didn't pull away, there was an exacting care in the way he wrapped an arm around her and kissed her oh so gently.

Low enough that the words shouldn't carry to the couple across the room, Hansa asked Umber, "What kind of bond do they have?"

Xaz eavesdropped on Umber's equally quiet response, both from curiosity and self-defense. They needed Naples for this plan to work.

"Heartbond. Naples' power is what makes it affect them both, instead of just him."

Hansa didn't ask for clarification. Xaz didn't either. No one could look at the spawn and mancer in the doorway and fail to see the anguished love when they looked at each other. Given the careful dance they both performed as they kissed, it was also clear that, unlike a fleshbond, a heartbond didn't control physical attraction. That had to be awkward, given Naples' obvious preference for men and the blurred line in the Abyss between sex and power.

"Be safe," Azo whispered. "Maybe you're right about the bond, and when it is gone I will be pleased." She swallowed, an audible sound. "If *magic* is all this is, has been, then when it is gone I imagine I'll want to kill you if you ever cross my path again. So if it works, don't come back here." She choked out the words. "And . . . take care of your damned self on the way."

She spun away and walked out again.

Naples didn't look at anyone else, but devoted his attention to pulling on a cloak, tying it at the front to hide the arsenal he was wearing from any casual observer.

Umber was the one who spoke, voice gentle. "Are you going to be able to do this?"

Naples nodded sharply.

"The first thing we need to do is find our way into the court," he said. "With Alizarin, that will be easier. Xaz is bonded to him, Hansa is yours, and everyone there knows I'm—" He cut off, shaking his head. "Anyway. We move fast, following Alizarin and keeping our heads down, just long enough to get to the well. Don't speak to any of the Abyssi there. Hansa, Dioxazine, if you value your lives and your skins, *do not say a word*. They'll defer to Alizarin, and they are supposed to respect the claim of the spawn, but the royals will mess with you given any excuse. Having a mortal speak to them is an insult and thus a valid excuse."

Hansa nodded. Xaz did the same, though she was looking forward to returning to the human realm someday so she could go back to being considered a person instead of property.

Umber said, "That wasn't my concern."

Naples glared at him, eyes flashing. "Don't you think I see the way it *kills* her, when I—" He let out an inarticulate sound of frustration. "I would be loyal to her bed, if I could. I would make love to her, if I could. I know it's magic talking, but knowledge doesn't change the fact that I would do *anything* to take that look of pain from her face."

"Ever consider chastity?" Hansa suggested, before biting his tongue. "Sorry. None of my business. I mean, except for my being on the other side of . . . never mind."

Xaz had only recently come to understand the connection between sex and sustenance in the Abyss. She didn't think she would ever personally be comfortable with it, but she could predict Umber's answer.

"A chaste Abyssumancer cuts himself off from one of the four coins of power," the spawn explained. "It would be like a human trying to live on bread and water. You can do it for a while, until you get the sailors' disease and your muscles wither away from lack of meat. Azo wouldn't let him, even if he tried."

"I can do this," Naples said, concluding his answer to Umber's question, "because I do it for her." One of the servants came in and handed Naples another bag, this one smaller and made of what looked like felted fabric instead of leather. Naples held it as if it might bite, glanced inside briefly, then passed it to Dioxazine. "That's all I can offer you."

Xaz looked inside, and her breath caught. "Where did you get these?"

A sparkle of silver inside hummed with Numen power, but it was nothing compared to the long, soft plume of what had to be a Numini feather and a small vial she knew to contain Numini tears. Such powerful tools normally took weeks of ritual and pleading to acquire. It felt odd to hold them now and have no one else in the room evince any interest, but Hansa and Umber had turned back to their own tasks now and even Naples appeared only vaguely solicitous and uncomfortable.

Naples said, "One of the Numini passed through here several years ago, seeking—well, I suppose there's no harm in admitting it now. He was trying to get to Terre Verte, the witch we're after. He left those with me."

Xaz couldn't help but notice what Naples hadn't said. "What happened to him?"

She could almost see Naples considering a lie, then realizing there was nothing he could say that wouldn't raise more questions. "I don't know. I never saw him again. All I know is that the cell is still intact, and was never opened."

Xaz exclaimed, "The Numini want me to do something they *couldn't*?" The only reason she was considering this possible was that the Numini were willing to help her, but if they had already failed once, what hope did she have? She only remembered after she had spoken that they had agreed not to tell Naples about their divine orders.

"Nice of you to get around to admitting it," Naples said. "I was starting to worry you hadn't noticed the divine dancing you all around like puppets." Before Xaz could form an apology and explain why they had tried to deceive him, Naples continued. "The Numini who came here was shocked by how weak he became the moment he crossed into the Abyss, and he didn't understand Abyssi. He planned to ask one for help, because like all Numini he was idiotic enough to believe 'all things serve the divine.' After the Abyssi ate him, as I'm sure they did, the other Numini must have come up with a new plan."

"And that's when they decided to send me," Xaz said, her voice unsettlingly close to a growl.

"You, and me, and Hansa and Umber and Cadmia. If we survive this and Terre Verte can do what they say he can, we should all sit down and figure out the details," Naples said. "Because you have realized even a Numini couldn't arrange all this alone, haven't you?"

His coppery gaze settled on hers heavily, waiting.

"I . . ." She trailed off. She *hadn't* realized that. "Are you sure they couldn't?"

"Quite sure. There's no point quibbling and speculating until we've fulfilled the boon and broken the bond, but I suggest we take a hard look at all the facts before anyone returns to the mortal realm." He nodded to the bag, and the divine tools within. "In the meantime, will that help?"

Head spinning with the implications, she closed the bag. "Yes. Thank you."

Finally they were ready to go. As soon as Alizarin returned and reported the way was as clear as it was ever likely to be, Naples reiterated his instructions.

"Alizarin will lead us through the palace. Umber, you'll be a little behind him, but still at the front of our party. The rest of us walk behind, mouths shut. Except for Alizarin and Umber, we speak to no one, even if they speak to us. Try not to look at the other Abyssi, or even think about them, no matter what is said or what you see. Alizarin, are you ready?"

In response, Alizarin pushed his way through the door and back into the Abyss.

Xaz hadn't missed the slick black paths or the eerie perpetual twilight of the sky, but they seemed comfortable and homey compared to the hulking, irregular stone structure Naples identified as the palace, with its arching, cavelike maw. As they approached, she saw Naples' shoulders draw together, tensing, and couldn't help but react to his nervousness, her heart speeding.

It took less than four minutes to walk into the high, vaulted entryway of the High Palace of the Abyss, which sparkled inside like a strange geode; to pass through that first room and into an even larger hall, with doors in the walls and strange arches and pedestals of varying heights set into the floor seemingly randomly; and finally to follow Alizarin through another, smaller doorway at the far end of the room.

Four minutes, but perhaps the longest four minutes of her life.

There were creatures in the room. Abyssi, certainly, but most of them were more similar to the lizardlike lord of the high court who had first challenged them than like Alizarin. Some had several pairs of arms and legs, thick like lizards or slender and sharp like insects or spiders. They lounged on the structures about the room, occasionally seeming to sleep, but mostly looking directly at the visitors passing through.

From a distance, Xaz saw the dense-bodied lord of this court acknowledge Alizarin with a bow, never removing one front, clawed foot from the back of another of its kind it held pinned. Then, realizing she had let her attention wander, she snapped her eyes back to Alizarin. Her whole body went cold as she felt other Abyssi circling behind them, pressing close without quite touching.

Alizarin kept them moving until they once more encountered the gray-black Abyssi, Antioch.

Unlike Alizarin, Antioch had not fully recovered from the fight. His fur was shaggy, matted in places with blood that glowed indigo in the dim palace light. He had been lying against the back wall, but now he pushed himself up to growl.

Alizarin stepped forward to meet the challenge, his growl making the air rumble. Xaz had to look away as living darkness flowed around him, though doing so made her more aware of the other Abyssi, many of whom were inching closer as if drawn to the conflict. How many of them could Alizarin fight at once?

Abruptly it was over. The sudden, dead silence made Xaz return her attention to the near-fight in time to see Antioch drop back to the floor, roll onto his back and lift his chin to bare his throat. The expression in his half-closed eyes was resigned. Did he expect Alizarin to kill him?

Would Alizarin kill him? The blue Abyssi paused, his own hackles still raised, though he had returned to his solid form.

He said something to Antioch in the hissing, incomprehensible language he had spoken before, then guided their group past the other Abyssi and to the doorway at the back of the hall. There Alizarin pushed both hands against heavy double doors of shocking crimson. When Xaz glanced back, unable to stop herself, she saw that the defeated Abyssi had rolled onto his stomach to watch them go, his eyes wide with surprise.

She watched just long enough to see one of the other Abyssi pounce on him, and then Alizarin's hand was gently urging her to turn her head and look away. Behind her, she could hear a chorus of snarls and yips.

CHAPTER 33

As they passed through the doorway and Alizarin pulled it shut behind them, Cadmia realized she was shaking. She couldn't help it. Those creatures . . . They were Abyssi, like Alizarin, but they *weren't* like Alizarin. Their eyes were cold and hungry. When they watched her, she knew they stared with nothing but a predator's fascination.

Alizarin picked her up and she laid her cheek against his shoulder and waited for her heart to slow. Umber reached back and pulled Hansa to himself. Xaz and Naples looked at each other, and Naples chuckled, the sound sharp with near hysteria.

"I thought we were in trouble for a minute there," Hansa said.

"Me, too," Cadmia admitted.

"Apparently the Numini can bring even an Abyssi low," Xaz observed.

"We should keep moving, before the others tire of Antioch and consider following us," Alizarin suggested.

The room they were in was empty except for themselves. Its walls seemed to go straight up without end, without a ceiling, impossibly high; this had to be one of the towers Cadmia had seen from outside. In the center of the room was the mouth to a spiral staircase. The visible stairs were long but shallow, and made of what looked like black volcanic stone, pitted in places and in others worn so smooth she knew it would be slick and treacherous to descend.

"Are there any more Abyssal grudges we should know about before we go in there?" Hansa asked Alizarin, as they all regarded the well before them.

Alizarin shrugged, said, "I will clear the way ahead," and started down the stairs with a bounding stride.

"Alizarin is a prince of the third level," Umber said. "He wouldn't be unless he had killed or maimed enough of his kind to intimidate every Abyssi from here to there. That leaves three levels of Abyssi who may consider him an enemy."

"Don't forget he also bested Antioch," Naples remarked, as if commenting on a bit of market gossip instead of all their potential enemies. "Some will consider that a first assault against the fourth level." With a pointed look at Cadmia, he added, "It wasn't only concern for *his* well-being that made me hope he would stay behind. I can't even risk drawing power from him, because the other Abyssi will pounce if he betrays weakness. Can we *go* now?"

Hansa cleared his throat, a gesture of unease. "Just walk?" he asked.

"More or less," Naples said. "The distance and the path varies, but yes, we 'just' walk."

"Alizarin opened a rift from the mortal plane to this one," Cadmia said. "If he opens a rift from here to the low court, we wouldn't need to risk passing the second, third or fourth courts, right?"

"And the trip would end with our eyes boiling out of our skulls," Naples replied. "I need the gradual change in order to raise the power I'll need to. Even just jumping down to the third level suddenly, I don't think I could protect us quickly enough to keep us alive once we stepped through."

"But . . ." Cadmia trailed off, realizing that she wasn't raising useful objections, but simply stalling. She did not want to walk into that great maw of a staircase.

"After you, Abyssumancer," Xaz said, but this time it was obvious that her sharp tone was a cover to nervousness.

Naples shrugged. "Keep up. And watch your step. The stairs aren't made for humans. They aren't even; there are flat areas, and then there are areas where a single stair might drop six or eight feet. I don't know what happens if you fall off the edge, but my educated guess is that you won't come back."

Naples led the way, taking the stairs carefully but

not slowly. Cadmia followed, happy to take all the time in the world.

At first, the descent was awkward, uncomfortable, and nerve-wracking. At times the stairs became too small to comfortably support a foot. They all crept along sideways, and Cadmia longed for railings. At other points, the steps were unevenly wide, and of varying depths, so there was no comfortable stride.

Alizarin ran ahead most of the time, then loped back to check on them before disappearing down the stairwell again. Occasionally when he returned his fur was wet with the viscous, glowing fluid Cadmia recognized as the blood of other Abyssi. What would happen if someone below raised a challenge he could not best?

Awkward and uncomfortable became painful as the hours progressed. They reached an area where the "stairs" were so narrow and steep they couldn't truly be called stairs. They had to use the narrow ridges as foot and handholds while they scaled the way like a cliff face.

"How long *is* this staircase?" Cadmia gasped, past lungs and throat that ached from heavy breaths of the increasingly hot, dry air. She longed for a drink of water, but couldn't reach into her bag without falling.

"We can rest and eat as soon as we're back on more level ground," Naples promised. "I—gah."

Scratching. Scrambling. A whispered curse.

Thump.

"Naples?" Her voice was shrill.

"I'm okay," he said shakily. "When you reach the last handhold, get as far down as you can using your hands, then drop."

Just her *hands*? She was barely holding herself up using hands and legs both.

"Let go," Alizarin said. "I'll catch."

Squeezing her eyes shut, she released her grip on the stairs and let herself fall back. She swore when the fall was longer than she expected, but the sound was only half-complete before she landed safely in the Abyssi's arms.

"Thanks," she said, looking up. They were now on a flat area, but right in front of her was a vertical face of maybe ten feet, before the steep clifflike stairs they had been navigating. "I'm glad I didn't see that *before* I jumped," she mumbled.

Umber glanced down, scrambled a little further toward the sheer face, and then let go and landed like a cat, neatly and apparently painlessly. Hansa looked down when Umber jumped, but he seemed less enthused about the drop. He did as Naples had advised, lowering himself until he was supporting himself with his hands and there was a reasonable drop between the ground and his feet.

He landed with an "umph."

Cadmia pulled open her water bag and took a sip, swishing the water around her mouth before swallowing. The others were doing the same.

"Catch your breath," Naples advised, "and then we'll eat something before moving on. We're almost at the second level, and we don't want to stop too near any of the—"

"We're only *almost* at the *second* level?" Xaz gasped. "How many stairs can there possibly *be*?"

"How many stairs can there be, between the *five levels of the Abyss*?" Naples replied. "How many stairs did you expect to be in a well that passes between planes of existence?"

After hours of walking, Cadmia didn't have the energy to engage in the argument. Alizarin rejoined them as they pulled out rations, mostly tightly wrapped cakes of dried meat and fruit, and she sat against his side. His warmth was less soothing than usual because she could feel the way his body thrummed with pent-up energy and agitation. He put on a confident face, but he was anxious about this trip as well.

All too soon, Naples was urging them to stand again. Cadmia winced, discovering newly pulled muscles, especially in her shoulders and down her back.

"We won't stop at the second-level court, but I don't think we'll get far past it before we need to rest and cast the protection spell. I can make it almost to the third-level court on my own, but I doubt anyone without an Abyssumancer's power or Abyssi blood can stand to go that deep."

Cadmia remembered Naples describing Alizarin's home on the third level as full of steaming seas. Why had he ever wanted to come all the way up to dry, snowy Kavet?

"I'm going ahead again," Alizarin announced the

moment they prepared to move again, before disappearing into the dim well ahead of them. He had no trouble hurrying down the stairs, like a kitten bounding across hills. Was he constantly fighting other Abyssi or mindless monsters to clear their path before they arrived? Sometimes negotiating for safe passage? Or was he just unable to stand their slow, mortal's pace?

"I wish I had his energy," Xaz said.

"What are you complaining about?" Hansa asked, hefting his pack with a significant glance to the very light-looking bag Xaz was carrying, its strap angled across her chest. They had all agreed the mancers would have a difficult enough task with their magic and shouldn't be additionally burdened by supplies, but in that moment, Cadmia shared Hansa's envy.

Talk disappeared as they continued to walk, the way becoming darker and less even. When the stairs turned, twisting into the walls of a tunnel, no one bothered to complain. Naples held up a hand, summoning a pale green orb of foxfire, and in its sickly luminescence they continued into the Abyss.

CHAPTER 34

Stairs. Stairs. Cliff. Stairs. Tunnel. Stairs in a tunnel. Hansa's feet made their way across slick, half-worn stairs, many of which held pools of water that shone silvery-pink and which stuck to his boots when he stepped in them.

The only sign of their progress was the change in the air. It was thicker here, hot and oppressive. There had been a heavy scent in the caves, but Hansa had assumed it was just the dankness in there; as they exited the tunnel, the odor became foul, like marsh-water. It seemed to coat the back of his tongue and taint the taste of the water he drank to console his parched throat.

How could the air smell so damp yet still feel like sandpaper when he drew it in?

"And we have company," Umber whispered, nodding discreetly across the way before asking Naples in low tones, "Do we greet them or wait?"

"Wait and hope they won't challenge us before Alizarin comes back," Naples advised.

On the other side of the well was a hole in the wall, large but too irregular to be rightly called a doorway. Slithering out of it was a creature with the wet look of something found under a log. Its long body was lizard-like, and the color of rusty mud except for a mane of orange and black tentacles. It opened its mouth to taste the air with a flickering black tongue, in the process revealing rows of sharp teeth, including four longer ones that were curved like a viper's fangs.

With that coloring, it's probably poisonous, Hansa thought, an inane observation, since the beast wasn't the size of a rattlesnake. Given that each fang was the size of a hip dagger, a single bite from that creature would kill too quickly for poison to be a factor.

Its eyes were black pools, without visible pupils, streaked with flecks of red and orange like splattered paint. In them, Hansa could see intelligence. Abyssi.

"Hansa," Umber hissed.

Hansa jerked his gaze away, too late it seemed, since the Abyssi started slinking toward them.

"Vanadium of the second-level court greets you." The Abyssi's voice was startlingly musical in combination with its owner's slimy form, almost sweetly feminine. "You've brought me presents?" She spoke to Umber, then looked past him to the rest of them.

"They aren't for you," Umber answered.

"Surely you didn't mean to pass by my court without offering tribute?" Vanadium asked, sounding affronted. "There must be one you can spare."

"I'm afraid not."

"A loan? The pretty one, perhaps."

Hansa didn't want to know which of them she meant. Umber didn't ask. "Perhaps you should ask Alizarin when he returns. He would better understand proper, um, niceties."

Vanadium's brilliant crest collapsed when Umber invoked Alizarin's name, the color leaching from it as she drooped. "Him," she said flatly. "I knew him when he was nothing but a plaything to the previous lord of this level."

Naples spoke up. "Then you knew him when he *devoured* the previous lord of this level, too. We'll wait here if you want to talk to him about tribute."

Vanadium opened her mouth to hiss at Naples, then turned and slithered back through the gap in the wall.

"Move. Quickly," Naples advised.

They tried, but it wasn't easy. As they started down the next set of stairs, Hansa realized he was sweating, though the moisture disappeared from his skin almost as soon as it appeared. His chest ached, and his dry throat hurt so badly it was hard to swallow. Even though the stairs were reasonable for the moment, his heart pounded as if he were climbing a mountain.

Fighting just to keep moving, he couldn't judge how much time passed before Naples paused, raising a hand. He glanced back at Hansa, and then at Cadmia, who was lagging even further behind. "There's a plateau just around the bend," the Abyssumancer said. "We'll stop there to sleep."

"Thank Numen *and* Abyss," Cadmia gasped. "I feel like I have a blood-fever."

"Close enough to the truth," Naples said. "Much lower than this, your blood would start burning. All the liquid in your body would evaporate."

"Well, now I *really* look forward to tomorrow," Hansa griped as they reached the plateau and collapsed. He drank in greedy gulps, now understanding why Azo had insisted they would need so much water.

Naples took a sip and ate a couple bites of food distractedly, then sat cross-legged at the center of the plateau. He drew the knife from his upper arm in his right hand, and the one from his left boot in his left hand. Hansa recognized the black-red, wavering blade of the former. The other was simpler, made of dark metal, with a fine, slender blade and a handle made of ebony or mahogany wood.

Matter-of-factly, Naples undid the buttons down the front of his shirt, then opened his shirt-cuffs and rolled back the sleeves to just below his elbows. "Cadmia, you first."

Cadmia jumped, eyes widening. "Me first *what*?"

"I need to tie the spell to the people I'm trying to protect." He added, "It shouldn't hurt, and it will only take a moment."

She inched forward, apparently not comforted by his words. Hansa understood how she felt. He had responded much the same way whenever Umber pulled out a knife. "Do I have to be first?"

"You're the most human, and therefore you're in the most distress," Naples said. "You don't *need* to go first, but I thought you might prefer to."

Again, she looked at him skeptically.

"I'll go." Hansa didn't want the Abyssumancer touching him or cutting him, but at least he had some experience. He was starting to feel a bit jaded, in that his mind did not come up with a single scenario as he crossed the small plateau to Naples.

"Thanks," Cadmia whispered as he passed.

He shrugged, then he knelt in front of Naples. "What do you need me to do?"

"Roll up your left sleeve," Naples instructed. "To the elbow is fine."

Hansa obeyed, hoping Naples' ritual would be less dramatic than Umber's had been when he gave a similar instruction before slicing Hansa's arm open to give him the power to pretend to be a mancer.

Naples shut his eyes. Gracefully, without any hesitation or sign of discomfort, he used the Abyssi-bone knife to cut a rough triangle over his own heart.

Blood welled to the surface, but it only beaded there, seeming to thicken like tar instead of running down his skin. Power began to pool around the symbol, spreading like a thick mist which let off light the color of a particularly nasty bruise, deep cranberry-black.

"Your hand," Naples said, holding out his own as he opened his eyes, which now glowed like the Abyssi's.

Seeing that eerie light made it harder to calmly

reach out, but Hansa forced himself to do so without hesitating. Using the metal blade, Naples made three rapid, shallow cuts in the meaty part of Hansa's arm, marking a coin-sized piece of flesh. Then he touched the flat of the Abyssi-bone knife to the blood.

A wave of heat slapped Hansa, as if he had leaned toward an open flame. It passed and he shivered as both the sudden warmth and the insidious, dry heat of the Abyss abated. The sense of constant weight that had grown with each step deeper in the well lifted.

When Naples took the blade away, the wound seemed to smolder, the scar-slick surface glowing amber like hot coals.

Naples returned the knife to his own skin, this time to make a single stroke beneath the symbol he had previously carved, mingling Hansa's blood with his own.

He waved Hansa off. "Cadmia, you next."

"You'll be fine," Hansa said, squeezing Cadmia's shoulder as he passed.

Umber inspected the mark on Hansa's arm suspiciously, but seemed satisfied that it would do what it was supposed to, or at least that it wouldn't do anything *else*. He went after Cadmia, though he and the Abyssumancer watched each other with open hostility as Naples repeated the process with the spawn.

Finally it was Xaz's turn. When Naples first touched the blade to her arm, she cried out and jerked back, clapping a hand over the wound as a curse hissed between her teeth. Umber arched one brow, and Cadmia rolled her eyes, but Hansa moved closer. "Is something wrong?"

Xaz reluctantly lifted the hand she had held over the first cut Naples had made. The blood beading on her skin hissed and bubbled, letting off faint steam as white as Xaz's face had gone. Though she hadn't made a sound beyond the single cry, her jaw was set with pain.

"What happened?" Cadmia asked.

"Xaz, you're going to have to work with me here," Naples said, his tone bland and unsympathetic. "Your magic might not like mine, but my magic will keep you *alive*. You're going to have to deal with it."

She knelt in front of him again and offered her arm. Her fingers trembled, so she drew them into a tight fist.

Naples made the remaining cuts quickly. Xaz's body went rigid, but she didn't scream or pull away again. When he slicked the Abyssi-bone knife with her blood, she let out a single whimper; even Naples winced at the hissing sound made when the bone touched the Numenmancer's blood.

When Naples released her arm, the mark left behind on Xaz's skin was black like a cinder, with faint blue ripples.

Naples set his own teeth as he cut the last mark in his chest, as if joining Xaz's blood with his hurt him as much as it had her. Finally, he licked the remnants of blood from both blades before wiping them on his cloak and returning them to their sheaths. He buttoned his shirt over the symbol on his skin, which was no longer bleeding, but pulsed with dark magic.

"The further you go from me, the harder it will be to keep you within the sphere of power," Naples said, as he undid his cloak and spread it on the plateau to sleep on. "Especially while we sleep, I want to be in contact, so I'm not spending more power holding on to you all than I can actually recover resting. Hansa, you're next to me."

"Not likely," Umber replied, draping a protective—possibly possessive—arm across Hansa's shoulders.

"What do you think I might do with you an arm's reach away?" Naples snapped. "He's human, and unlike you, he won't have the instinct to defend his energies while he sleeps. That means I can draw power off him, both to help maintain the link and to strengthen it and myself while we sleep. It won't hurt either of you, and it's the only way I might have the strength to make it to the fifth level." He added the last bit when Hansa frowned, not happy about the idea of being used as living fuel.

Come to think of it, he *still* wasn't happy about it, but he realized he should have expected as much. What other use had he expected to have in this group?

They ended up in a cuddling-line like hostile kittens, with Naples in the middle, Hansa and Umber on one side of him, and Cadmia and Xaz on the other. Snuggled between Naples and Umber, Hansa found himself uncomfortable on about fifteen different levels, so he was remarkably glad when the Abyssumancer and the Abyss-spawn looked at him at the same moment and both said, "Just go to sleep."

There were good uses for magic. Falling asleep and not having to be aware of the others . . . that was a good use.

CHAPTER 35

Xaz woke sore and sweating, with a large furry body sprawled across her. Instead of waking Xaz so he could take the place next to Cadmia, Alizarin had draped himself over them. Xaz mostly had his legs, his torso crossed Cadmia, and his head rested on Naples' shoulder. The Abyssumancer had turned so his cheek rested against Alizarin's hair. On his other side, Hansa had turned his back on Naples and was nestled against Umber.

"Get off me," Xaz said, shifting to wriggle free of the Abyssi's weight. Her muscles ached from hours of walking the day before, and her shoulder and hip were needles of pain where they had been pressed against the stone.

"You're comfortable," Alizarin yawned.

Cadmia opened her eyes, shifted, and said with a wince, "Stone is not a good bed. Let me up."

Alizarin rolled off everyone, stretched to his feet, and offered a hand to help Cadmia up.

"We still on the stairs?" Hansa asked.

"Seems like," Umber answered.

He pushed himself halfway up then paused on his knees, waiting for Hansa, who said, "Still in the Abyss?"

"Unless Kavet had a sudden change of weather," Naples replied, rolling to his feet with a smoothness that made Xaz want to slap him. How did *he* manage to feel so fresh?

He slept against an Abyssi, a spawn, and a mortal. That's powerful fuel, even after the amount he must have burned protecting us.

"Sleep well?" Umber asked, as they both pushed themselves up.

"Like I took a magical hammer to the head," Hansa answered, rolling his shoulders.

They ate a brief meal, but too soon it was time to move again, this time into a place where only Naples' power would keep the deadly force of the Abyss at bay.

On second thought, maybe Xaz wouldn't begrudge Naples his rich meal.

Alizarin went ahead again; he clearly couldn't stand traveling at their slow, careful pace. The rest of them walked, climbed, jumped, skulked, even at one point crawled, in mind-numbing repetition. The rank odor of the second-level swamps fell behind them, replaced by whiffs of musk and smoke.

"Almost at the third level," Naples announced, as they descended a section of stairway that looked like a chunk of it had fallen away.

With Naples' magic suppressing the Abyss's scalding power, the air felt dead; voices and footsteps didn't carry any distance, but faded to nothing. The stairs were worn and ashy, black and white, coated in a fine dust that puffed lazily into the air with each footstep and not quite wide enough to feel entirely comfortable walking without angling one's body toward the wall. Hansa, whose shoulders were broadest, seemed most off-balance.

Looking at the wall was easier than looking out, anyway. The edge of Naples' spell was easy to recognize, because beyond it the air thickened and wavered like a heat-mirage in the fading light. It was impossible to see across the well.

Alizarin skidded up the stairs. He was still wearing his natural form when he came to a stop inches from Xaz, and she jerked back in reflex, slamming her shoulder into Cadmia. In the ensuing scuffle, Hansa let out a yelp and Umber cursed, probably as he kept his bond from tumbling off the side.

Xaz didn't spare a moment to look. Her eyes were on the Abyssi, whose monstrous form was coalescing into the more familiar furred body she knew.

He looked as if someone had splattered him with paint—if anyone had ever created a paint that shimmered in the light like the inside of an oyster shell.

Naples, who had been traveling in the middle of their pack, pushed past Cadmia and Xaz along the open edge of the stairs as if unafraid to tumble into the well. "You're hurt," he exclaimed. "How much of that is yours?"

Blood. Xaz wouldn't have realized what the sparkly, lovely but viscous goo that covered Alizarin was, but Naples better knew what it looked like when an Abyssi bled.

"Only some," Alizarin replied vaguely. "It would be best if Dioxazine casts her spell before passing the third level."

"Here?" Xaz squeaked. *"Now?"*

They had talked about waiting until after they passed the third-level court, not to mention the fact that she had expected to be on level ground, where half her concentration wasn't focused on not falling off the side.

Naples turned to her with a look she had come to know well: a mixture of irritation, contempt, and impatience.

"I just mean—" She cleared her throat, which was dry from ash. "The third-level Abyssi can *see* us, can't they? The spell is only designed to hide power, not make us invisible. If I cast it, then they see us, they will know what we're doing."

"I was unable to convince them that I have a right to claim all of you exclusively," Alizarin answered patiently. "The lord of the third level insists you join him for a feast if you want to pass his court. He did promise me I could have you all back after?" The last sentence was questioning, accompanied by a tilt of his head that betrayed a jagged tear down the side of his face, only partly concealed by his fur.

Xaz didn't want to imagine what an Abyssi feast

might include, but Naples, the crazy bastard, had the gall to look intrigued.

"Feast?" Cadmia chirped tightly from the end of the line, as if her endless curiosity was warring with the knowledge that this probably wasn't information she wanted in her head.

"Cast the damn spell, girl," Umber growled.

Was Xaz misreading his face in the dim light, or was Naples trying not to *laugh*?

Naples caught her gaze and must have seen the judgement in her expression. In explanation, he wondered aloud, "What do you think they could get Hansa and Umber to do by saying it was the only way to pass?"

"Xaz?" Hansa prompted, the panic in his voice suggesting the answer to Naples' question was, *More than any of us want to imagine.*

"I'll do the spell," she said. "How do we stop them from then *seeing* us?"

"As long as they cannot sense you, I can distract the court while you pass," Alizarin answered. His color brightened and his ears lifted again with relief.

"Will you be all right?" Cadmia asked.

Alizarin grinned, as if he were not already covered with his own and others' blood. "Abyssi do not kill each other casually," he answered, as if "all right" and "dead" were the only two possibilities. "I will find you again before you reach the fourth-level court."

He scurried back down the stairs, leaving Xaz with anxiety coating her tongue like sour milk. Could she do this?

The Numini had sent her on this mission. They had to think she could succeed. But one of them had already failed once, hadn't he? Did their influence really reach this deep into the Abyss?

She looked up and down the stairwell, wishing there were somewhere more comfortable to work, then slipped past Naples and moved as far beyond him as she could without passing into the deadly heat of the Abyss.

Their water was scarce and precious, but she knew better than to risk smearing grime on the tools she intended to use to reach for the Numini, so she used as much as she needed to wash her hands before kneeling on the narrow staircase and opening the leather pouch Naples had given her.

Inside was a tiny glass vial filled with a clear, iridescent liquid that cast a pure silver glow, and a feather as long as her forearm the color of rose gold. The objects pulsed with power. Just holding them made her heart leap into her throat, skipping merrily, as if she had just seen an old friend in a crowd.

Xaz rested the Numini's feather across her palms, and reached mentally into and through it.

I am here of your will, she said, casting the words to the Numen. An Abyssumancer could shed blood to invoke magic, but the Numen's power was best directed through words. *If that is the case, then I believe you must be listening for me.*

She pictured a sphere of soft white power around their group, acting as a veil between them and the eyes of the lower Abyssi.

"I invoke the Numen realm for protection," she said aloud. "I invoke you twice, to hide us from those who would harm us." She couldn't remember how young she had been when the Numini had taught her the power of a threefold invocation to cast and bind the magic. "I invoke you thrice, to—"

She didn't get through the final words. Power rushed through her, striking like lightning and filling the sphere she had pictured with brilliance. The shock wave began at the edges of the circle and slammed inward, so she felt it flow first over and through Cadmia, recognizing her as kindred. Umber braced against the power, but even so it sent him to his knees, hands gripping the staircase as if to battle a hurricane's wind. When it slapped Hansa, he stumbled and fell against the wall, then sprawled on the stairs with a painful *thump*.

Then it hit Naples and the Abyssumancer cried out, shuddering as the Numini's power raked over him and the carefully formed bubble of power he had cast to hold back the Abyss.

Ears ringing and vision rippling, Xaz struggled to draw breath in a world that had suddenly become all smoke and ash. Her eyes, lungs, and skin burned as Naples' magic contracted, hiding itself from the Numini like a turtle in its shell.

"Naples!" she choked out.

"*Shit,*" Naples hissed, unsteadily lifting himself onto his hands and knees.

Naples didn't give any warning; he crawled up the

stairs until he reached Hansa and set a hand to the prone guard's arm. "Sorry for the lack of foreplay," he whispered, giving Hansa a very brief kiss before pushing him back against the stairs and opening his shirt.

"What—*aack*!"

Naples straddled him and made a slash on Hansa's chest, just above his heart. Not shyly, he locked his lips over the wound. At any other moment, Xaz might have been disgusted, but she could feel Naples desperately rebuilding the power protecting them. She struggled to keep her own magic from shying away from his.

For an agonizing moment, she feared the two couldn't coexist, but at last the heat and pressure slipped away and both protective spells solidified. Xaz was able to draw a full breath again, a sensation so wonderful it was hard to imagine it hadn't dazzled her every other moment of her life.

"Breathe, you damn girl," Umber growled. Xaz looked past Hansa and Naples to find the spawn braced over Cadmia's limp form. Xaz's power had been gentler to the Sister of Napthol than it had been to anyone else, but the Abyss had not been as kind.

Umber leaned down and set his lips to Cadmia's, his breath making her chest rise and fall.

Another breath, and finally Cadmia began to cough. "What . . ." Her voice was barely a squeak, and she cut off after one word with a grimace.

"Don't try to talk yet," Umber advised. His voice was also hoarse, though not as bad. "You got a lungful of the Abyss. Naples lost the shield for a moment when Xaz's spell took effect." He glanced back to Naples to confirm; the Abyssumancer was still lying on the ground, but he let out an affirmative-sounding grunt. "You were closest to the edge, and you're most human."

Cadmia nodded, rubbing her throat.

"Get the lady some water," Naples advised.

Umber nodded, and Hansa fished out the water. Cadmia drank a few, painful sips.

"Did the spell—" Hansa broke off halfway through the question when his voice broke. He helped himself to some of the water, then went back to Naples.

"You okay?" he asked.

Naples nodded, his hair shifting in the ash. "Check on Xaz."

"I'm fine," Xaz said, as soon as the others had confirmed they were all right. Her brush with the Abyss hadn't been pleasant, but the Numini's power rushing through her had protected her from the worst of it. She was more nervous about what the Abyssi in the third-level court might have felt when her spell took effect and Naples' snapped closed and back open. "I think we should move past the court and out of the light as quickly as possible. Alizarin might not be able to distract the other Abyssi long."

"Can you stand?" Umber asked Naples, who was still stretched out on the stairs.

The Abyssumancer drew a deep breath, rolled onto his stomach, and pushed himself to hands and knees. "I think so." All evidence of the energetic grace Xaz had envied was gone as he rose agonizingly to his feet.

"Can you walk?" Hansa asked Cadmia, helping her up.

"Can *you*?" she replied, when her tug on his hand made him wobble and need to catch his balance with a hand on the wall.

"We can move slowly," Xaz allowed, seeing the way the two humans stumbled, "but we need to move."

"We're moving," Umber said. He draped his arm around Hansa's waist.

This time Xaz led the way, and the others followed. Coated in ash, throats and lungs scorched, they limped onward.

As they passed the maw of the third-level court, they walked with soft, hurried footsteps, wincing at each *crunch* of loose scree, and the tiny splashes they made as they waded a shallow, hot stream that meandered through the open arch and cascaded over the edge. By tacit agreement, no one commented on the sounds they could hear from the court: snarls, growls, and howls mixed with noises that could not be named with mortal vocabulary.

The well had never been bright, but now the limited light cast by luminescent creatures faded until they were groping their way down the stairs, feeling for the step-edges with their shuffling feet. Naples summoned an orb of foxfire, but it was a faint, yellow creation that barely revealed the way even when it hovered only inches above the ground. He had it follow the edge of the stairs, so they could at least tell when there were sudden dips, and know where the stairs ended and the endless fall of the well began.

"Fourth level ahead," Naples breathed. "I need a rest. Short."

Xaz nodded silently, but didn't dare speak aloud. The euphoria that had filled her when she had first cast the magic had faded. Keeping her spell active was like holding sand in her cupped hands. It took all her concentration to keep the grains from spilling between her fingers, and the hands that held that sand had started to ache and tremble with the effort.

"It's hard to judge time here," Cadmia said, "but it feels like it's been hours, and we have another level to go. Should we try to get some sleep while we're on a relatively flat stretch?"

"*No,*" Naples said. Xaz thought she had shaken her head, but her physical body felt far away and not entirely in her control. "Can't sleep. And do this," Naples managed to add, his voice a ragged gasp.

He stumbled, as if speaking had taken too much of his energy. Hansa caught him, and helped him steady himself until he seemed solidly on his feet again.

"Are you going to make it?" Hansa spoke quietly to Naples, but the words carried in the strange, dead air that remained inside their two protective bubbles of magic.

"Sure hope so," Naples answered.

"I . . . can I help?" Hansa asked, haltingly.

Xaz expected Umber to object on principle. When he didn't, a shiver ran down her spine. If he was willing to share his bond, he was truly worried about the limits of the Abyssumancer's power.

Naples pulled Hansa against himself and slid a hand under his shirt so he could wrap an arm around his waist, skin to skin.

The foxfire sphere brightened a little, a candle-flame briefly touched by purer air.

Onward.

They were just past the fourth-level court when Xaz felt something press against the boundary of her spell. She fought it instinctively, but a heartbeat later she recognized the power and invited it in, wrapping it carefully in her magic.

"*Ksh.*" The sharp exhalation was a reaction to the spark of recognition she felt from her Numini. With his power riding her, she couldn't help feeling his wrath and revulsion when he regarded this Abyssi.

She didn't have the mental energy to contemplate whether that was how a Numini would react to being asked to protect any Abyssal creature, or if it might be personal. All she could think clearly was, *Please! We need him, and he cannot walk safely in the lower courts any more than we can.*

The magic relaxed grudgingly, and veiled Alizarin's distinctive blue glow in its own shimmering silver, which would make him—like the rest of them—invisible to the other beasts of this low plane who saw only with power.

"Alizarin," Cadmia breathed, as she saw the blue Abyssi. "You're all right."

"Xaz's spell works," he reported. "I could not sense you until I was here. You have no scent or heartbeat from outside either."

"That's good to hear," Umber said. "Can you help Naples at all?"

Alizarin moved closer to Naples, then hesitated, twitched his tail and shook his head. Once he was standing closer to the foxfire, Xaz could see how much worse for wear the Abyssi appeared. One of his legs sported a deep enough rent that he was visibly limping.

"I won't be able to hunt until we return to the higher levels," he said. "There is not much further to go."

Not much further, he said, but it was slow going. Alizarin, who had previously seemed chaffed if asked to slow to their pace for more than a minute, walked sedately next to Cadmia. She reached up to touch him.

Hot blood, soft skin. Alizarin's thoughts, which were more sense than words, reached Xaz through their bond at the same time she saw him jerk away from Cadmia. She could feel the depth of his hunger. Abyssi were not creatures of great self-control. It was taking all his concentration to ignore the instinct to hunt the ready, nearly helpless prey that so trustingly walked beside him.

She tried to block the dark awareness from her own mind, but not before she heard an answering thought from the Numini: *She is bound to one of us, and swaddled in your power. She will not be lost if the Abyssi kills her.*

The words had the ring of a well thought-out plan rather than a just-considered declaration. Xaz had assumed Cadmia was with them for her knowledge about the Abyss and as an additional bond between their group and the Numen, but feared she had stumbled across the woman's real purpose: a sacrifice, which the Numini could justify to themselves because they had the ability to claim her after death no matter how she died.

There was nothing she could do about it, except hope she would be able to sense if Alizarin's self-control started to fray, and intercede somehow.

Meanwhile, the way grew darker, and despite Naples' spell, the air grew thick. Sounds were muffled. They had to shout in order to speak to each other, and doing so was so unnerving in this place that for most of the final descent, they did not say anything at all.

When Naples stumbled, Umber moved beside him. The movement simultaneously matter-of-fact and resentful, the Abyssi-spawn used his knife to slice across Naples' palm, and then his own. The two twined their hands together, and Naples let out a sharp gasp.

Xaz tried to sense how strong—or weak—Naples' spell had become, but as soon as she turned her attention from her own work she felt her connection to the Numen start to fray. She had to stop, close her eyes and reestablish it.

They kept walking.

Finally the stairs widened, until Naples' faint globe of foxfire could not illuminate any visible walls or ceiling. Umber was all but carrying the Abyssumancer, who had entirely stopped responding to questions. Xaz wondered exactly how they expected to carry him *up* the stairs later, or whether at any moment the Abyss would come rushing in on their little fishbowl of existence.

CHAPTER 36

There were noises in the darkness. A deep scratching, hissing ring made goose bumps rise on Hansa's skin.

Instead of shapes, he could see power. Unlike Alizarin's soft, alluring blue-violet glow, these creatures let off ripples the slick red of fresh blood, and the dark rusty color of that same blood once dried. These dark lights made visible creatures the mind could not comprehend, not and stay sane.

Close your eyes, Umber ordered. Hansa did as commanded, and Umber passed him a strip of fabric to tie across his eyes, then turned to help Cadmia. *Naples is holding back most of their power, or that glimpse would have been devastating.*

Hansa tied the blindfold into place, and then felt the pressure of Naples' arm around his waist guiding him forward while Umber led the Abyssumancer by the hand.

Blindfolding Hansa may have protected him from the ruinous sight of Abyssal power, but it made him more aware of his other senses: the heat on his skin, distant sounds of Abyssi at their gruesome play, the tangy odor of charring flesh, and an unnamable, spicy taste that settled on his tongue from the air.

They walked toward the gathered Abyssi. The noises of the court grew closer with each step, and their path started to weave irregularly as Alizarin sought the safest route. *Safest.* What an absurd word. Safest would mean turning around and leaving, if only that were possible.

A furred hand on his chest stopped him short, just before he felt movement in the air and heard something pass by. It never hesitated, and left the scent of brine and ash in its wake.

They really can't see us, he thought.

Naples' magic blocks the scent of our blood and the melody of our footsteps and beating hearts from them. Hansa bit his tongue to keep from shouting as Alizarin's mental voice slipped into his head. *Dioxazine's blocks the sight of our power and the sound of our thoughts. With no true light, I would be blind to you here as well, if I had not been allowed inside the spell.*

What would happen if they caught us? He didn't mean to ask the question, but couldn't help thinking it.

They would eat most of us, Alizarin answered. Either he was mentally more focused than he tended to be verbally, or this was a subject that had finally sobered him, because his mental voice was low and wary. *Diox-*

azine would be prey for Modigliani, lord of the Abyss, but he might share you or Cadmia with his favorites. I don't know Naples' patron, but there are not many Abyssi whose anger Modigliani would worry about, so he would probably also be taken.

Umber?

If he were alone, they might keep him for sport, Alizarin answered, *but he wouldn't survive your death.*

Hansa, Umber said, his voice cutting like a cool breeze into their conversation, *please stop asking stupid questions. Some of us don't want to know the answers.* His mental voice, Hansa thought, sounded very tired.

They were all tired. Hansa had tried, for the last half hour or so, to ignore the way the air had begun to heat as Naples' strength faded. He tried not to wonder how much of the fatigue in his legs was from descending stairs for so long without rest, and how much of it was due to Naples steadily draining power from him.

How much power could one human have, after all? With Xaz's magic hiding *their* magic, would Umber notice if Naples was taking too much? Hansa was pretty sure Naples wouldn't notice at all.

"We're almost there," Alizarin said aloud, his voice a low grumble that just barely reached their ears. Even if the mancers' magic was supposedly hiding the sounds of their passage, Alizarin clearly didn't want to test the protection by speaking up. "There are stairs here, with some debris. Climb carefully."

Hansa jumped at a low groan not far from his left ear, then realized it was a sound of protest from

Cadmia. She had been quiet since the blindfolds went on, as wary as the rest of them of drawing attention.

"Not too far," Alizarin added.

Will there be guards by the cell? Umber asked.

Unlikely. Abyssi do not make good guards, Alizarin assured them, with a touch of the old amusement in his tone. *Even Modigliani cannot convince them to attend to a closed box for long, and Terre Verte doesn't offer much amusement any more.*

Hansa consciously worked to blank his thoughts so Alizarin wouldn't answer the next question that logically crossed his mind: *What normally amuses an Abyssi?* He knew just enough not to want Alizarin to say more.

Instead, he focused all his attention on scrambling up a pile of stone and . . . other clutter. He tried to tell himself it was shells, like those littering the first level's dry sea, but when he stumbled and his groping hand closed on the curve of what could only be a skull he jerked back so abruptly he nearly brought himself, Naples, and Umber all down.

"We're here," Alizarin announced at last.

"Keep your eyes forward," Umber cautioned as he removed the blindfold.

Hansa looked around, blinking at the faint, white light cast by Dioxazine. He and Naples were standing in the open doorway to a small, not-quite-square room, short enough that Hansa could have reached up and touched the ceiling—if he had wanted to, which he really didn't, since it seemed to be writhing.

Where Xaz stood near enough to illuminate one

wall in detail, Hansa could make out sharp, needle-thin spines that rippled across the surface of the wall, pulsing, retracting and then growing again, as if they were all inside a giant, inverted sea-urchin. Umber had gone ahead into the room, though he stayed far from the walls. Cadmia lingered hesitantly behind Alizarin, who had crossed the room to a box against the far wall.

About two feet high, two feet deep, and a little longer than a man, it would have been difficult to call it anything but a coffin. The exterior sparkled, reflecting Xaz's glow from thousands of tiny crystals. What could possibly be inside but the man they had come to rescue?

Careful, Naples gasped when Hansa tried to move into the room. The Abyssumancer's eyes fluttered, half opening, and then closing again. *Doorway . . . close. Can't.*

"What?"

Umber touched Naples' face gently before saying aloud, "He opened a doorway from the stairwell to this room. Considering who's imprisoned here, opening a doorway from the inside is probably impossible, so it would be best if we didn't all cross the threshold and have this one close behind us."

Yes, Naples said.

The show of life, at least, was promising.

While they were speaking, Alizarin had crossed to the coffin. He knelt in front of it and placed his hands on the sparkling surface.

"Will the other Abyssi know when we open it?" Cadmia asked.

Alizarin shook his head. "The box is designed to hold power captive. The room is, too, in case the box is ever opened."

"It seems too easy," Cadmia said.

Easy? Naples echoed.

"Speak for yourself, Cadmia," Umber concurred.

Alizarin was still kneeling in front of the coffin, now frowning, his tail twitching.

"How do we open it?" Umber asked as time went by.

Alizarin growled in response.

Naples drew a breath, something Hansa hadn't been convinced he had done in a while. "Umber, let me down. You and Hansa stay in the doorway."

"You seem stronger," Umber observed as he set the Abyssumancer on his feet.

Naples shook his head. "This room is doing some of my work from me. Xaz's, too. It's designed to be its own bubble, to keep in what's in, and out what's out." He held up a hand and a new globe of foxfire appeared, this one deep crimson. It hung in the doorway between him and Hansa. "Come inside. That will hold for a while."

He walked toward Alizarin and the coffin, his steps heavy with fatigue, but still more than he had done independently for hours. As the Abyssi had done, he knelt in front of the box and set a hand on it.

Unlike Alizarin, Naples drew in a sharp breath, his body sparkling with power for a moment. Xaz groaned, and Cadmia caught her arm to steady her.

Hansa and Umber had a chance to exchange one

worried look before Xaz got her spell back under control.

"How do we open it?" Umber asked again as Naples examined the coffin.

"Power," Naples answered vaguely. "It's like anything in the Abyss. It wants sacrifice."

"In my experience the last few days, that usually means blood," Hansa said. "So one of us opens a vein. Again."

"Or a little more than that," Umber said ominously.

One hand still on the coffin, Naples turned, his gaze going from one person to the next in a way that made Hansa distinctly nervous, and made Alizarin start to growl again.

"Don't look at me that way, Hansa," Naples said when his attention turned that direction. "The only reason we're all *standing* at the moment is that the denizens of this level of the Abyss have built their own little sphere of the human realm. Once we go back out that doorway, I'll need you and Umber again."

"You're needed to hold back the Abyss." Cadmia's voice pierced the air clearly. "You need Hansa and Umber to help you do it. You need Dioxazine to keep you hidden." The pitch of her voice steadily increased as she continued to speak.

"Correct," Naples replied.

"How large a sacrifice are we talking about?" Umber asked.

Judging by Alizarin's low growl, and the protective tail he kept wrapped around Cadmia's waist, Hansa suspected the answer was more than a few drops.

"I am not killing someone in order to get into that box," Hansa said, though even as he said it, he felt the squeeze of the boon trying to argue with him. *The magic can threaten all it wants,* he thought desperately. *I won't do it. I'll let it kill me first.*

Naples didn't bother to argue with Hansa. He spoke to Alizarin instead. "I don't know *why* you came with us, but I know you wouldn't have done so unless you wanted this witch as much as I do. Are you going to protect her to the point of turning around now and admitting defeat?"

"*I* will," Hansa insisted, striding forward to try to get between Naples and Cadmia. That was his intention, anyway. When he tried, the muscles in his legs seemed to lock, the warning heat of the boon's power becoming a buzzing, piercing burn.

"You *can't,*" Naples spat. "Don't pretend you can. If there's a way, you'll have to find it. And even if you had it in you to turn around and leave, you can't leave without me, and I am *not* going to leave without *him.*"

"We're talking about *murder*!" Hansa shouted, flinching at the way his voice rang off the cell's walls.

"To be precise, it seems we're talking about *my* murder," Cadmia added, voice remarkably level. "And I think I'm going to have to decline."

"No, we're talking about survival," Naples retorted. "Nothing personal, Cadmia, but I did not come this far to stop here, and you're the one person in this group who is expendable. Why do you think the Numini sent you here? They must have known."

"I doubt the Numini are in favor of human sacrifice," Umber argued.

"No one's expendable, since we won't cooperate with you if you do this, and you need us, too," Hansa reasoned.

Naples drew a deep breath, and walked back toward the doorway to try to reason with the man standing there. "Look . . ." He glanced to the foxfire in the doorway, which was starting to waver, then reached up and pressed his hand to the top of the opening. He winced as the sharp spines at the top cut open his palm, but didn't pull back. As the blood dripped, it formed a lattice of strands as fine as a spider's web. "Step inside," he said, as Hansa nervously watched the growing web. "If we're going to take the time to fight, I need to make this more solid."

With all of them inside the cell, and a web of bloodred power keeping the doorway open, Naples stood in the middle of the room and looked at each of them in turn. "You were saying?"

Hansa took up the reply. "We were saying, you need us, too. You can't get to the surface without us, and we won't cooperate if you hurt her."

"You won't cooperate . . . meaning, you'll stay down here in the Abyss until your lungs burn out?" Naples asked. "Even if the boon would let you leave without doing everything within your power to fulfill it, *I* won't let you leave, and your threat not to help *me* leave is a thin bluff. Especially since, of everyone here, I am the one person who would rather die than return without this witch. So what about you? Are you willing to kill us all, including Cadmia, in your noble stand?"

"It doesn't matter what we say, since Alizarin doesn't look like he is willing to make that sacrifice," Umber pointed out. "I consider the refusal of a fully grown third-level prince of the Abyss to be suitable cause for me to declare this as something that is *impossible*. Which—"

"Which means very, very little," Naples said softly. "I didn't want to do this."

In a flash, he had drawn the blade from his right boot. Umber and Alizarin each made a move toward him, but neither was fast enough to stop him from dragging the blade across his palm. He flicked his hand in Umber's direction, and a wave of power threw the Abyssi-spawn backward until he slammed into the spines writhing on the wall. Hansa felt every muscle in his own body spasm, felt the pain as if the daggerlike blades had pierced his own back.

As he collapsed, unable to control his own muscles, he saw Alizarin finish closing the distance between himself and Naples, just in time to meet Naples' still-bleeding palm as the Abyssumancer pressed it to the Abyssi's chest.

"Step aside."

Naples' voice rang through Hansa's head, even though he was obviously speaking to Alizarin. The demon's growl deepened, becoming a vibration so low and powerful it made Hansa's bones ache as he struggled to remember how to move his arms and legs.

"Xaz . . ." Cadmia tried to appeal to the Numenmancer, but unlike Naples, Dioxazine was still blind to this world as she kept her own magic working. "Alizarin?"

"Step. ASIDE."

Slowly, tightly, tail lashing, Alizarin eased back.

"Don't make me chase you, dear," Naples said, as Cadmia inched away as far as she could without running into the walls. "Think of the man you're saving. Is one human death such a sacrifice, when the divine realm itself wants him freed? And of course, your death will save the rest of us here. Without it, we go nowhere until my power runs out, that doorway closes, and we starve to death." As if with sudden inspiration, he added, "If Terre Verte really can raise the dead, maybe he'll even take it upon himself to bring you back."

Hansa doubted Cadmia was swayed by Naples' reasoning, but there wasn't anywhere to run. Hansa had barely even managed to get an arm under himself to try to push himself up before Naples grabbed Cadmia's arms and dragged her over to the coffin.

She struggled, but Naples was stronger. The knife he had used moments ago clattered to the ground, but Hansa couldn't help but remember how many he was wearing. When Naples released Cadmia's wrists to pin her against the coffin, she hit him. Her nails drew blood from his cheek, but he barely flinched—what were pain and blood to an Abyssumancer, beyond another source of power?

CHAPTER 37

Cadmia would not calmly accept death. She didn't care what Naples said about lofty goals, possible resurrection, or the futility of resistance. As Naples levered her toward the coffin, she fought.

Hansa, Umber, and Alizarin had been neutralized with a few drops of the Abyssumancer's blood and Xaz was still lost in her trance, so it was just her, and she hadn't needed to physically fight to defend herself since leaving the Order of A'hknet. She threw everything she had into her struggle—every possible low blow, elbows and feet and fists—but Naples was stronger than his slender stature suggested. Once he had a grip on her, she couldn't break it.

The coffin's surface was scalding hot against her back, and the crystals pressed into her skin, bruising and cutting.

Yes. She could feel the power singing as it tasted her

blood and cried for more. It overwhelmed her, making even Naples' grinding grip on her wrist and throat seem distant.

Deep in that song was another melody, this one cool and soothing. She closed her eyes, trying to hear it better.

Daughter of the Napthol, it called to her. *We see your plight.*

Underneath the music was the sound of gently lapping waves. Against her closed eyelids she saw not the twitching, pulsing walls of this cell or even the black beach of the Abyss, but silver-white sands endlessly washed by crystalline waters.

She didn't question the offer, but reached mentally toward that beautiful sea and the winged form who stood beside it, offering its hand.

"Help me. Please," she whispered.

The figure who had been reaching for her turned toward another, whose voice was rimed with frost and sharp like crackling ice as it said, *How dare you risk* our *child in* your *scheme?*

I have hold of her. She will not be lost.

She felt the edge of Naples' knife at her throat, and realized the Numini's idea of "help" was different than hers. It didn't care if her blood was spilled.

I will not have her tormented this way, the second voice protested.

An icy winter draft howled through the cell. Naples hesitated, the knife moving fractionally away from Cadmia's skin.

Cadmia opened her eyes just in time to see Dioxazine turn her head toward them—and then Alizarin, freed of whatever spell the Abyssumancer had put on him, crossed the room in a flash of claws and fangs. He pounced on Naples, knocking him away. Cadmia scrambled back, but she didn't get far before the cool wind became ashen heat.

She threw her arms in front of her face and felt blood splash like a hot wave. She frantically wiped at it, only to have it almost immediately evaporate into the Abyssal air, soaked up by the cell walls and by the fine filaments of power Naples had left holding open the gate.

It had only taken a second. If Cadmia had blinked, she never would have seen it, and how she wished she had blinked, that she hadn't seen Alizarin's handsome form dissolve into the black-and-indigo blur of claws and fangs, the monster, that had rushed over Naples and left nothing behind.

Nothing but the box, which Alizarin pulled open. Dioxazine was giving off enough light now that Cadmia could make out every crystal on the coffin's lid. She could tell that the fabric wrapped around the bundle Alizarin lifted out was charcoal-gray velvet, tied by cords so black they seemed to absorb Xaz's glow and darken everything a hand's-span around themselves.

"I guess it got its blood," Umber whispered as Alizarin lifted the limp bundle into his arms.

The Abyssi glanced at Cadmia. She flinched as those

hot blue eyes settled on her. Before she could make any conscious movement, Alizarin had looked away again.

He had saved her life. She knew that. But the image locked in her mind at that moment wasn't one of a hero rescuing her, but of the creature inside, the creature that had sent a rain of hot blood down on all of them.

And a white beach somewhere oh so far away . . . had she really seen that? The image was fading, dream-like. Had the Numini been arguing?

"I hate to be the one to ask," Umber said, "but do we have another way out of here?"

Alizarin looked at the doorway, where the magic Naples had left behind was starting to tremble. He reached toward it, and the web of power clung to his skin. When he pulled his hand back, the air tore, leaving behind not a door into the next room but another rift, like the one that had taken them to the Abyss.

"Does that go back to the human plane?" Cadmia asked, heart rising with hope.

"Surface of the Abyss," Alizarin replied.

"Still so much better than here," Hansa said practically before stepping into the tear in the world. Umber followed immediately behind.

"Bring Dioxazine," Alizarin added when Cadmia started to move toward the portal. Cadmia turned back to the Numenmancer, who had returned to her trance but allowed Cadmia to guide her into the rift.

She hadn't taken the time to wonder where they would end up—in the well, in the middle of the palace, out by the dead sea, or somewhere else—and was pleasantly surprised to find herself in a familiar parlor. Nothing had changed since they had left. Even the extra supplies they hadn't been able to carry—some bundles of food, a jug of water, and extra knives Naples had considered and set aside—were still on the table.

Cadmia's relief lasted one heartbeat before Xaz let out a small sigh and collapsed. She struggled to catch the limp woman, whose body was radiating cold like a winter draft, and guided her onto one of the couches. She searched for and found a heartbeat, but didn't know anything else to do.

Meanwhile, Alizarin knelt to unwrap yards of velvet from around the man they had brought out of the lowest level of the Abyss. He was still working when Aurelian ran into the room.

"Naples," she gasped. "Where is he? Azo's fainted. I don't know what to do."

Cadmia hadn't had a chance to consider how Naples' death would affect Azo. Maybe this wasn't the refuge she had thought when they arrived.

Alizarin looked up from his prize, who hadn't moved, and asked evenly, "She's alive?"

"Yes," Aurelian breathed, barely able to form the word around her anxiety. "What—"

"Aurelian, thank you." The heavy voice from the doorway made Cadmia's stomach jerk, as if it couldn't handle another swing from anxiety to relief and back to concern. "You—you're dismissed. Prepare a meal."

"Yes, my lady." Aurelian cast one last look around

the room for Naples before hurrying to obey her mistress's command.

The silence stretched. Azo hung in the doorway, leaning on the frame as if she lacked the strength to do more. Her burgundy skin had turned a fungal gray-black with blotches of paler mauve, and her blue eyes seemed flat and lifeless as one of the shades'.

After a long, guilty moment, Hansa pushed away from Umber to offer assistance. He made it halfway across the room before he staggered, catching the arm of a couch and dropping his head and shoulders as if to fight dizziness. Umber, body trembling slightly with fatigue, caught up to his bond and urged him to sit.

Still no one had spoken. Cadmia opened her mouth to say something, but all her training—glib words and easy lies learned from the Order of A'hknet and comfort and honesty from the Order of the Napthol—abandoned her.

Azo spoke one word: "How?"

Alizarin unwound the last length of fabric, revealing a man who appeared in his early twenties. His warm brown hair wrapped him like another layer of cloth; if he were standing, it would probably fall nearly to his waist. His arms were crossed neatly across his dawn-gray leather doublet, which itself rested on top of a pristine white shirt with onyx buttons.

He looked as if he had been dressed and poised for the grave.

This task done, Alizarin finally looked at Azo to say, "It couldn't be avoided."

Azo tried to step forward but fell, one knee striking the ground as she hissed in frustration.

"Can I help you?" Cadmia managed to ask, kneeling beside her to offer a hand. Azo's response was frank, a heated look that Cadmia had seen plenty of times before—but usually from men. She didn't have a chance to limit her offer before Azo started to cough, body shuddering with the barking spasms that brought blood to her lips.

"She's too weak to feed through flesh," Umber said. "Hansa and I are too drained to give blood. Alizarin?"

"No," Azo spat when the Abyssi approached. She pulled in a pained breath, and pushed the next words out one at a time. "I'm not . . . a fool. I can smell him. His power. On you. From here. I won't—" Again her body spasmed, though whether with a suppressed gag, cough or sob, Cadmia couldn't tell.

"Can I?" Cadmia asked, this time knowing what she was offering, only unsure about whether her mortal blood was powerful enough to matter.

Umber shrugged. "If she'll accept. Heart blood's best." He made a sketching motion over his own chest, then half stood and half fell to go to Terre Verte's still form, as if unconcerned about Azo and Cadmia now. *The boon,* she reminded herself. He and Hansa had lost a lot of power in the bowels of the Abyss. They couldn't afford to neglect the boon now.

That left her alone tending to Azo, whose eyes were fixed on Cadmia in a predatory way that would have made Scarlet Paynes turn a customer away no matter how much coin he held. A look like that meant violence.

Steeling herself, Cadmia reached for one of the knives on the table, which looked like it had been made of one of the massive shells they had seen on the beach. She unlaced the neck of her shirt and shrugged the fabric off her left shoulder to expose the place below her collarbone that Umber had indicated. When it came time to set the knife to her flesh, however, she hesitated.

Azo's hand closed over hers. Her face was suddenly close enough Cadmia thought maybe she had gone back to her first response, but then the spawn's gaze dropped, the blade moved swiftly, and Azo tossed the knife aside as her lips closed over the wound.

Cadmia bit back a scream at the first sensation, blade and teeth at her flesh; she would have jerked away if Azo's arm hadn't become an iron shackle around her back. When she opened her eyes again—when had she closed them?—she saw Alizarin on his feet, tail lashing with anxiety as he watched them.

"She'll be all right," Umber said, a hand on the Abyssi's arm.

Within seconds, the pain had faded to a faint, bruised ache. "I'm okay," she said, catching her breath.

Alizarin hates the constant grime of this level.

You know him well.

The brief exchange with Naples passed through her mind unbidden, along with the memory of his blood splashing hot across her skin. Naples had been Alizarin's friend, hadn't he? Yet Alizarin had ripped through him the instant the Abyssumancer's power had been disrupted.

A deep, rumbling growl from Azo warned her to police her thoughts. She nodded to Terre Verte and asked, "Is he alive?"

"Nearly," Alizarin said.

"Nearly?" Hansa repeated. "What does that mean? Please tell me this wasn't all for nothing."

"Not dead," Alizarin clarified, unhelpfully. "But not quite alive."

"Will he wake?" Umber asked.

"I hope so." He looked at Cadmia and Azo again. "It's not magic I'm capable of making on my own, but it was supposed to be a life given to restore his life."

Cadmia didn't let herself contemplate that further yet either. "What about . . . Xaz?" she asked, hesitating in the middle as Azo's arm around her back released its death grip and moved so the spawn could pet her hair.

"She isn't injured," Alizarin said, sounding even less sure this time. "I would know if she were. I don't think it would be wise to pull her back from her trance before she is ready."

"So we just—" She grabbed Azo's free hand, which had drifted up her side and come a bit closer to a breast than Cadmia was comfortable with. Azo let out a distracted, frustrated half growl and her head lifted. Her eyes were dilated as they met Cadmia's, but the slim blue rings had regained some of their glow.

Her gaze traveled down Cadmia's face, paused at

her lips, then returned to Cadmia's eyes. "Let me know if you change your mind."

"Are you all right now?"

Azo shook her head, but said, "I can hunt now. I—" She winced, shut her eyes, took a breath. "There was no choice?"

I was the choice. Cadmia tried to come up with a better response, but could see in Azo's eyes that she had heard the thought.

"I see." Azo nodded, then stood, the move slow and unsteady. "He was willing to die to accomplish his goal." She looked at Terre Verte's still form impassively. "I hope he's worth it. I'm going to go kill something. You all should eat and rest. Your rooms are still available." She limped from the room, only pausing in the doorway to add, "Cadmia, thank you. We will speak later about how I can repay you."

"I don't know much about magic, mancers or the somewhat-dead," Hansa announced once Azo was gone, "but if there's nothing we can do about Terre Verte or Xaz right now, I second the suggestion about food and sleep."

"Naples pulled a dangerous amount of power from both of us," Umber said, wrapping an arm around Hansa's waist to walk with him toward the kitchen. "Food is a good start to getting it back. After that, I have other plans for you."

They disappeared through the door, leaving Cadmia and Alizarin alone with the two unconscious sorcerers.

"Did you want me to let him kill you?" Alizarin asked.

"No." Cadmia shook her head. "I . . . did you have to kill *him*?"

"Yes."

"To get the box open."

"Partially for that reason," Alizarin answered.

"And partially to protect me?"

He nodded. "Also because of that."

"Is there a third part?" She sounded so ungrateful. She started again, trying to explain. "I'm glad you saved me. I'm very glad not to have died down there. But I had thought that you and Naples were friends?"

Alizarin shrugged. "He said so."

"You don't agree?"

He paused, tail flicking around his body, then back out again, as if he were struggling to find the words for what he wanted to say. "Abyssi are strong or weak," he said. "We have prey or playthings or chattel, or we are those things for someone stronger."

He looked at her, as if searching for understanding. She hazarded a guess. "Abyssi don't have friends?"

He nodded.

"Because most Abyssi wouldn't understand what that means?" she asked, recalling how unlike the others of his kind Alizarin was. He nodded again. "So you killed Naples because . . . friendship isn't important to you?"

She tried to say the words without judgement, but there was a tremor in her voice she couldn't help. This was a man she had taken to bed. Had she misjudged him so critically? Did he save her and sacrifice Naples because sex was more important to an Abyssi than friendship?

Alizarin hissed in frustration, but when she flinched, his ears and tail drooped. "He *touched* me," he said, tail lashing swiftly now as he tried to make his point. "He used his power against me. I am a prince of the third level of the Abyss, but I couldn't have escaped on my own."

Cadmia rubbed her temple, trying to see the world through an Abyssi's point of view. In Alizarin's world of strong versus weak, nothing mattered but power. Alizarin was the spawn of the previous king of the Abyss. He had proudly bested Antioch, an Abyssi of the fourth level. According to Vanadium, Alizarin had been a plaything of the previous lord of the second level, before he gained the strength to best him. *Devour him* was the phrase Vanadium had used. Was that all his relationship with Naples was? When Naples showed himself to be too strong, too much of a threat, Alizarin disposed of him?

She looked at Alizarin's brilliant indigo eyes. Was she imagining the sorrow there?

She was looking at this wrong. Alizarin wasn't a typical Abyssi.

"You considered him a friend," she said, trying to make sense of the blood, "but he treated you like . . . like . . ." She struggled to find the right word from Alizarin's explanation. "Like prey, not like a friend."

Ears and tail lifted halfway, indicating she had understood him, but he wasn't sure what she thought of it. "Yes." Hesitantly. "Did I do the wrong thing?"

By Abyssi standards, he had done the only thing he could do.

By human standards . . . "You did the right thing." She remembered the moment of Naples' death with horrific detail, but something had happened just before, something her memory couldn't seem to wrap around. "If he was so strong, how did you escape Naples' spell?"

"Something interrupted Naples' power," he said. "Xaz's Numini, I think."

"I . . . oh." She frowned, trying to recall the distant conversation she had overheard. The words had already slipped from her mind, but she thought someone had been arguing?

Alizarin turned away from her to kneel next to Terre Verte again. "You should eat, too," he suggested. "And sleep."

"What will you do with him?"

"I'll bring him to a guest room. I hope he just needs some time. I will stay with him a while."

"Will you—" She broke off. Did she want him to come to her room later?

Alizarin tilted his head. "I'll be with our guest. Sleep well."

"I'll . . . try."

She enjoyed their conversations. Could she forget the part of him that was darkness incarnate—or, more difficult still, *embrace* it? Had she accepted Alizarin as her lover *despite* what he was, and if so, was that so wrong? Alizarin had sought a tie to the Numen. He clearly wanted to be more than just an Abyssi.

He had saved her life.

He had torn Naples apart, sent his blood splashing across the room, without a moment of hesitation.

And he had done so, in part, to protect her. How much of her sudden unease was because of what the Abyssi had done, and how much was because she felt uncomfortable with the fact that, given the choice, she would have chosen Naples' death instead of her own?

No matter in what form the end came.

CHAPTER 38

Umber's heartbeat was slow and even. Even when it raced, it never matched the pace of Hansa's own. The pace—Hansa knew, intellectually—of a human heart. Like the rest of him, Umber's heart was stronger, strong enough to survive levels of the Abyss that would burn a human's soul out.

After the days in the darkness, they had satisfied all their appetites in aggressive and determined fashion. Now, sprawled across Umber's chest, tangled in the last vestiges of blankets, Hansa found himself listening to the Abyssi-spawn's heartbeat and wondering what was going to happen next.

"What happens if that witch wakes and really can do what Naples thought he could?" he asked. "He breaks the bond, we return to Kavet, and . . . then what?"

"Shouldn't you be asking what happens if he doesn't

wake?" Umber rolled onto his side so Hansa fit comfortably, tucked against his body. "If Azo regains her strength and decides she is furious about Naples' death? Spawn on the human plane rarely survive the death of a bond. I don't know if the emotional attachment will have dissipated with his death, or if she is still in love with her now-dead Abyssumancer. And of course, without Naples, unless this Terre Verte can form a rift, we have no way back to the human plane at all."

"That worries me, too." Hansa had pictured it a few times, as Azo's and Naples' flustered servant had brought them all dinner. "But would I sound crazy if I said it worries me *less*?"

"Because you wouldn't be the one making choices," Umber guessed, correctly. "If the witch can break our bond, you return to normal. You get another chance at that life you wanted."

"I don't think you're evil." He blurted out the words without thinking them through. Umber chuckled. "Neither are Azo or Xaz. I have a hard time even thinking *Alizarin* is, and that's supposed to be the definition of Abyssi."

"Mmhmm." Umber trailed a hand down Hansa's back. "If—" He broke off. "Hansa, are you engaging in *pillow talk*?"

"Of course not," he replied instinctively.

Umber laughed again. "Fine, we'll call it deep and important conversation. That happens to occur on the bed. You were saying?"

Hansa briefly debated the merits of arguing the

term "pillow talk," but he didn't have much ground to argue. There hadn't been any discussion as he and Umber had limped up to this room, muscles protesting going *up* stairs now after so many days of the opposite. They had passed through the door, into the bedroom, and Hansa had moved into Umber's arms like water seeking level ground.

Part of him had wondered whether it would be for the last time, whether when he woke the witch would also be awake, and would wave his hand and turn all this into an impossibly elaborate dream.

"I was saying . . ." He valiantly struggled to remember his train of thought with Umber tickling his chest. "I was saying, mancers aren't evil, spawn aren't evil, maybe the Abyssi aren't evil and certainly the Numini aren't evil. So why is keeping all of them out of human society the central goal of the Quinacridone, and of the entire government of Kavet?"

"Oooh." Umber flopped back onto his back. "Pillow talk just turned to politics. Hansa, I don't know. I can give you theories. Humans get nervous when other people have power over them. Or, given the way Kavet's government works, one man wrote a good speech and others voted for it."

"The Quinacridone made mancers illegal. What happened before that? I mean, yes, Naples was terrifying and I'm not really sorry he's dead, but since murder and . . . other things . . . are already illegal, what happened to make them pass a law making even animamancers, healers, punishable by death? If we had never tried to arrest Xaz, I don't think she ever would have hurt anyone. So . . . yeah. What happened, before One-Twenty-Six?"

Several seconds passed as Umber drew a deep breath, and then released it in a sigh. "I don't know. I wasn't alive in those days, obviously, and given the way they're marginalized, the mancers don't keep much of an historical record. The Quinacridone probably do, since they keep accounts of just about everything, but I don't know how accurate their portrayal of that time frame would be."

Hansa frowned. It had been a little over sixty years since 126 had passed. He remembered the ancient woman of the Order of A'hknet berating him about it in the marketplace. Maybe she could answer his questions.

Then what?

"I just feel like we should . . . I don't know, *change* things."

"'Show up at the next election and speak to your fellow citizens,'" Umber said, tiredly quoting the Quinacridone mantra.

"Since sympathizing with a mancer is a crime, I don't think I would get far."

"True." Umber pulled him close again. "Maybe the deep thoughts should be saved until after our new witch wakes. He may not. If he does, he may not be able to bring us to the human plane, much less break the bond. And if he *can* break the bond, all these thoughts you're having might fade away."

"You're saying the fact that I now believe you're more than an Abyss-spawn pervert might just be the bond talking," Hansa said with a frown.

"For the record, I concur that I'm more than an Abyss-spawn pervert, but yes, it's possible the bond is affecting you, and when it is gone your opinions will change."

The possibility unsettled Hansa enough that he sat up, eliciting a groan from Umber.

"This doesn't feel like magic talking," Hansa asserted.

"When magic is involved, free will is a slippery concept. How exactly we make our decisions often isn't clear, and within that ambiguity there is a lot of room for magic to give a gentle nudge."

"I went with you to rescue Pearl," Hansa argued. "I know you put yourself at unnecessary risk to help her. You defended me against Naples, even though it made him more likely to be a problem later. You didn't let him kill Cadmia—or more importantly, Alizarin, who is a pure Abyssi, didn't let him kill Cadmia. That isn't evil, at least, it's not what I was taught evil was."

"Maybe. But just a week ago, when I tried to point that out to you, you threw it back in my face."

Hansa remembered the argument. *Spoken like a Quin,* Umber had said, after Hansa had ignored all his arguments that he might, in fact, not be evil incarnate.

"I was scared," he admitted, "and I was ignorant, and I was an asshole." He remembered a lot of the things he had said and done, not just around Umber but to others. At the very least, he had been a hypocrite; he had condemned Umber as evil while taking hold of that power with both hands and using it to try to make the world what he wanted. "A week ago, I hadn't seen a Sister of Napthol pray to the divine and have a prince of the third level of the Abyss come to her aid. I hadn't spent days walking into the deepest level of the infernal realm. I feel like I've finally started thinking for myself," he finished lamely. "Instead of believing what the Quinacridone says, just because it's easier than making my own decisions."

"Maybe," was all that Umber said in reply.

"Losing the bond could make me forget all that?" he asked.

"It probably won't make you forget," Umber said, "but you may reevaluate what has occurred and come to a different conclusion."

Hansa shook his head, even though one thing he *knew* from these last several days was that what he wanted often seemed not to come into play. "I don't *like* who I was," he said. "There are things I want, which the bond might deny me, but that doesn't mean I want to go back to being one of the Quinacridone's drones."

Umber's lips quirked, a wry smile, as he attempted to change the subject. "You just don't want to go back to abstinence. Face it, Quin. Your opinion of me would have been different if you hadn't done most of your deep thinking in bed." More seriously, he added, "I hope it isn't all the bond talking. That's a selfish wish, by the way. If it *is* all the bond, once that is broken, you'll be much happier returning to Kavet than you will be returning as you are now. But yes, I also prefer you as you are now."

"So you say," Hansa said, taking a page from Umber's book. "And how much of *that* is because of a bed?"

"Eh, you're all right," Umber returned. "You just need some practice."

"Then by all means, let's practice."

They put away unanswerable questions and stayed in bed until other needs drove them out. They bathed, ate another meal, and then looked at each other, wordlessly debating the merits of going straight back to bed.

"We should check on the others," Hansa admitted. Maybe the bond had changed him or maybe it hadn't, but one thing was definitely the same: he had been a guard, and he still had the instinct to keep track of his companions. As he thought about the group that had gone down into that cell, he found himself asking, "Is Naples really dead? I mean, I saw him killed, but what does that *mean*? An Abyssumancer, killed in a cell designed to hold in power, at the lowest level of the Abyss?"

"I don't know." Umber opened the doorway to the guest room where Xaz and Terre Verte had been moved. "I don't know how strong Naples was. I know it took an incredible amount of power to do what he did. I have no idea what he might be capable of, or what death in this place means to him."

They were speaking in hushed tones now, not because of the subject, but because of the atmosphere of the room they had just entered.

They stood in an elegantly decorated parlor. To their left, an open doorway revealed the bedroom, where the sorcerer they had brought here lay in the same funeral pose he had been in when they had first seen him. Closer, Xaz was stretched out on one of the sitting room's couches, her posture more natural but her countenance deathly still. Alizarin was kneeling next to her, his cheek resting on her wrist.

They crossed to stand beside Alizarin, and Umber asked, "How is she?"

"Cold," Alizarin replied.

Hansa touched the Numenmancer's brow, fearing the worst, and then snatched his hand back with surprise. "Not just cold—frozen," he said.

Umber reached for Xaz, as if needing to confirm. He brushed frost from her eyelids. "Should we try to warm her?"

"I don't know." Alizarin sounded strangely childlike, and the glow in his blue eyes seemed faded and lost.

"What about Terre Verte?" Hansa asked.

Alizarin shook his head again.

"How soon should we expect retaliation from the other Abyssi?" Hansa's thoughts hadn't yet moved past relief for their immediate survival and concern for the two unconscious sorcerers when Umber brought up the larger threat that still loomed over all of them.

"The high court was already angry at you for keeping a Numenmancer here. We hoped to be gone before they decided to cause trouble. Now we have no idea when we will be able to leave, and likely more enemies."

Alizarin growled, or started to but then swallowed the sound. "We have as much time as we have," he answered.

"Was the magic shielding Terre Verte's cell sufficient to keep the lower Abyssi from noticing his absence right away?" Umber pressed. "Or do they know already?"

"They might not know," Alizarin said, though Hansa didn't like the lack of confidence in his tone.

"I hate to ask," Hansa interjected, "but should we be worried about Naples' Abyssi?" Naples had been significantly more powerful than Baryte. If he understood right, that additional strength was mostly due to age, but some of it had to come from his Abyssal patron, didn't it?

Alizarin tilted his head thoughtfully. "I do not know Naples' patron. He never came to investigate my being near his mancer. He may know he is not strong enough to challenge me, so did not dare interfere."

Or he was strong enough he didn't think you were a threat, so didn't bother to object. His gaze met Umber's worried one, as the spawn clearly heard Hansa's thought and agreed.

"We have no choice but to wait, and hope Terre Verte wakes and is able to open a rift before consequences catch up to us," Umber said.

They all stood awkwardly for a few moments, staring at the corpse-still man who remained their only hope for survival like strangers gathered together by the funeral of a mutual acquaintance, unable to even share comfort.

At last Umber spoke again. "We should probably check on Azo. We may be able to do more good there."

It was a sign of how uncomfortable the quiet vigil over the two unconscious sorcerers had been that Hansa felt relieved to leave and seek the . . . would she be called a widow? Azo and Naples hadn't been married, but the bond was a stronger tie than any human ceremony declaring partnership could ever be. It seemed like there should be a word for the survivor.

Azo called them into the room when they knocked. Hansa swiftly averted his eyes when he realized she was entirely nude, combing her damp hair in front of an aggressively lit fireplace as if she had just finished a bath.

"I see you two have been enjoying yourselves," she purred. Out of the corner of his eye, Hansa saw her stretch, unabashed. "Feeling better?"

"Quite," Umber replied, sounding amused, probably by Hansa's furious blushes. *Did you expect her to be ashamed?* he asked silently.

Even if neither Hansa nor Umber was likely to react lustfully, there was still such a thing as modesty—or at least, there always had been in Hansa's previous experience. If an acquaintance from work had dropped by unexpectedly, Hansa would have at least put on pants before casually inviting him in the way Azo had done when they knocked.

Apparently undisturbed by the naked woman, Umber said, "We came to see if we can help you in any way."

Hansa was so focused on not looking at Azo—the wall hangings in this room were particularly complex and fascinating—that he let out a high-pitched yip when she touched his chin, tilting his head down to force him to look her in the eye.

"S-sorry," he stammered.

Since his own attention remained on her remarkable blue-violet eyes, he couldn't help but notice that she looked him up and down frankly before meeting his gaze again, as if inviting him to do the same. A moment later she sighed in clear disappointment.

She released him, and replied to Umber's offer. "Clearly not."

As she sauntered back to the fire, Hansa belatedly realized that her disappointment hadn't been based on what she had seen when checking him out, but that he hadn't returned the gesture. She stared into the roaring fire as she said with obviously feigned idleness, "I spent a long time with a beautiful man who would give me anything but flesh. I have no taste for that offer now." She reached out her hand as if to pet the flames before her.

"Then we will leave you to your recovery," Umber said formally. Hansa needed no urging to follow him out.

CHAPTER 39

The Numini were displeased. Xaz could feel their disappointment in the needles of ice like frozen rain falling on her skin, and taste it in the salt of the air.

We did not wish for anyone to be killed.

Dioxazine had not wished to descend to the lowest level of the Abyss and witness a brutal sacrifice of blood. She had not wished to feel the Numini reach through her in order to act, as if she were nothing more than a tool, with no will of her own.

She certainly did not wish to be here now, in this world-between-worlds, facing their condemnation.

"I'm sorry," she said by rote and habit, though frankly, she couldn't care less. It was their magic holding her here, not hers. She was so tired she would have collapsed if only they would let her.

We are not pleased.

"Then maybe you should have *done* something," Dioxazine suggested, the arrogant words escaping her.

We disrupted the Abyssumancer's power.

"Long enough for Alizarin to *eat* him," Xaz pointed out, too frustrated to be polite and obsequious. "What did you expect the Abyssi to do?' "

Do you mean to chastise us?

The world around her, a barely real plane much like a mancer's temple but built by the Numini alone, shuddered with their anger.

"No, I do not chastise you," Xaz said, trying to regain her respectful tone. "I just want to know why you are chastising *me*. I did what you wanted, didn't I? I helped bring Terre Verte out of his prison."

At the cost of a life.

"The Abyssumancer was killed when he threatened a woman sworn to the Napthol, to one of you," Xaz tried to reason.

We had plans for him.

Again, her temper ran away with her. "If you love him so much, get your witch to resurrect him. Terre Verte is supposed to be able to do things like that, isn't he?"

The Numen did not answer the question. Instead, they said, *We do not care for your tone.*

Xaz drew a deep breath, which burned her lungs with cold. "I apologize if I gave offense. I am very tired, and my words are poorly chosen."

Mortal excuses are not within our purview.

"Perhaps, but they are my limitation," Xaz sighed. "If you allowed me to rest, maybe I would be better able to understand what you want of me."

She was so cold, the way only working with the Numini could make her. She had barely even been aware of the events that had transpired after she had cast her spell; it had taken all her concentration to maintain her tenuous connection to the Numen as she descended into the Abyss. She had been pulled partially from her trance when the Numini took note of Cadmia's predicament, but even then she had not had power to act. The divine had acted through her, using her as a conduit.

What we wish, the Numini said now, *is your genuine repentance.*

"For *what?*"

You have vows to us, Numenmancer, they reminded her. *You have made agreements with our realm. And yet you scorn our will—*

This time she snapped, she knew she snapped, and she made no attempt to reign herself in. "I have lived my entire *life* by your will!" she spat. "I never asked you for favors. You chose me. You made the decision before I was even old enough to walk, though I never in my life wanted—"

Your tone, Numenmancer.

For a heartbeat she hesitated, but it was all too much. "To the Abyss with my tone! I have lived my entire life fearful of all three planes. I have been afraid to disappoint you, afraid to be harmed by the Abyssi, and terrified of coming to the attention of the Quinacridone. I have crawled into the deepest crevice of the infernal realm to do your will, and now you chastise me over something over which I had no control?"

The world around her twisted with the Numini's scandalized shock, and Xaz found herself savagely glad.

Dioxazine, you should—

"Go away and let me sleep!"

As she shouted the last, she pushed with all the power she could find. She made the words into a command, and threw it at the Numini who had held her here.

The rift the divine creatures had formed shattered.

Xaz knew she was awake and back in her body, but she couldn't feel, much less move, her limbs. She struggled to open her eyes; the lids stuck together, the eyelashes fused by ice.

She let out a moan and became aware of a warm, lightly-furred hand touching her arm, and a tongue, hot and raspy like a cat's, licking her cheek.

Finally she managed to open her eyes and croak, "Alizarin."

"I was worried," the Abyssi leaning over her said softly. "You were cold."

"Still cold," she said, on a difficult breath.

Alizarin responded by crawling on top of her and licking her cheek again. He lay down and rested his head on her shoulder.

At first he was painfully hot, and Xaz had to clamp her jaws shut to keep from telling him to go away. Then her body started to warm and remember that it was alive. The feeling returned to her fingers and toes in the form of hot pins and needles, and her chest ached as her heart drew in the icy cold blood that rushed in from her extremities when the veins opened to accept the new warmth.

At last she started shivering as violently as a woman in the midst of a seizure. Alizarin held her tightly, warming her and keeping her safe until her body lay limp, spent. Then he helped her sit up and handed her a cup of hot broth. She had no idea what was in it, only that it had obviously been sitting on the bedside in hopes of this occasion, heated only by its own power. It burned her tongue, but it thawed the knot of cold left in her belly.

"How did we get back here?" she asked when she was finally able to look around. They were obviously in one of Naples' and Azo's guest suites, though she could remember nothing of the return trip.

"I opened a rift," Alizarin replied.

"From the lowest dungeon of the lowest level of the Abyss?" she asked, skeptically. Then she remembered what had happened just before. "You absorbed Naples' power." Alizarin nodded. "How is Azo dealing with his loss?"

"She is injured, but alive," Alizarin said. "She refuses to see me."

"She won't be a problem for you, will she?" Xaz asked.

"Not in handling her, if I must," Alizarin assured her. "But I do not wish to need to."

Xaz rocked herself to her feet and leaned heavily on Alizarin as she walked toward the four-poster bed she could see through the nearby open doorway. There lay Terre Verte, the sorcerer they had saved—perhaps.

"The Numini say he may be weak for a long time, from his captivity," she said, trying to remember everything the divine others had whispered to her while she was connected to them. "They had wanted Naples to open the rift back to Kavet so Terre Verte wouldn't need to." She added, "They *wanted* a lot of things they didn't get. I told them off. You did what you did. It was the only thing you could do, and I think it was the right thing. Hopefully our guest will recover fast enough to get us home this century."

Home. She realized after she said it that technically, the human plane wasn't home to Alizarin.

"He's stirring." The man looked completely unconscious to Xaz, but she lacked an Abyssi's senses. Alizarin put a hand on Terre Verte's chest, as if to draw attention to the very slight rise and fall of his breathing. "Maybe he is responding to the power you used to send the Numini away. He didn't respond to Abyssal power, but yours is different."

Terre Verte's skin was fair and his features were delicate, masculine but finely wrought. His nails were a bit long, but there was evidence that at some point they had been well manicured. Xaz reached out to touch his hand, wondering if she would be able to sense anything about his supposed power. Before she could focus to use her magic, Hansa and Umber walked in.

"You're awake." Hansa sounded surprised but genuinely glad. "How are you feeling?"

"Fine, now," she said. She would tell them the details of her conversation with the Numini later. Right then, she wanted to know what else she had missed. "Is Cadmia all right?"

"Cadmia is fine," Umber said. "You saved her life, or the Numini did. She is with Azo at the moment."

"And how is the lady of the house?"

"Azo is . . ." He gave a wry smile. "Her full strength will not quickly return, but she is recovered enough to wish we were willing to share more than blood."

"How does she feel about our helping her after we murdered her lover?" That word "we" just slipped out. No one protested. Alizarin had shed Naples' blood, but they had all been there, and none of them would have stopped him even if they could.

"It is hard to say."

"You two lost a lot of power down there, too," Xaz said, remembering that Naples had started feeding on them when his own magic wasn't enough. "Are you all right?"

Umber raised one brow. "We have ways of raising power." Hansa blushed. "We'll be fine. Are you—"

"Is he waking up?" Hansa interrupted Umber unapologetically, drawing their attention back to Terre Verte. "I thought I saw his eyelids move."

Umber edged forward and put the back of his hand

on Terre Verte's brow. "There is more color in his cheeks, and he's warmer."

Xaz hadn't seen Terre Verte's eyes, but she felt his fingers twitch under hers. Remembering what Alizarin said about Terre Verte possibly responding to Numen power, she reached out with a tendril of magic.

Magical shields slammed up around the rousing sorcerer, knocking Xaz's breath from her lungs. Umber wrenched his hand back with a start and Alizarin drew away with an instinctive snarl.

His eyes opened, focused first on Alizarin, then half shut in a momentary flinch. Given where he had been for the past however-many years, Xaz could only imagine what Terre Verte expected when he opened his eyes and saw an Abyssi hovering over him.

He controlled himself quickly. As his expression smoothed into one Xaz could best describe as calm arrogance, a soft silver glow returned to his eyes.

"You're a Numenmancer?" Xaz asked. Naples had called Terre Verte a Gressumancer, but in that moment the only Abyssal power she sensed on the strange sorcerer was sloughing away from him, remnants of his time spent imprisoned.

"A what?" He pushed himself to his feet, leaning for a moment on the edge of the bed before he seemed capable of standing on his own.

"Do you need help?" Hansa reached forward to offer a hand. "You've been—" The cool look Terre Verte gave the guard made it perfectly clear that he knew perfectly well where and how he had been, that he didn't want to talk about it, and that he equally did not want to accept any help Hansa might give him.

Then, once again, the expression cleared. He drew a deep breath. "We're in the Abyss?" he asked.

"On the surface, in the home of one of the spawn connected to the court," Umber said.

Terre Verte looked around, then moved toward the invisible doorway as if he could see or sense it. Though obviously weak, he moved with an authoritative stride, his gaze never lingering on the elegance of the room but rather focused on some goal. When he touched the wall and it opened, he did not seem surprised.

"How did we get here?"

"We rescued you," Xaz said.

Terre Verte turned around, his gaze searching, penetrating in a way that made Xaz feel as if she were wearing far less than she was.

At last, he said, "Thank you." Another moment went by, and he asked, "And who are 'we'?"

"Myself," she answered, "and these are Alizarin, Umber, and Hansa. An Abyssumancer named Naples was with us, and Cadmia, who's a Sister of the Napthol."

She watched him as she spoke the names, wondering if he would recognize any of them, or show surprise that an Abyssi, Abyssumancer or Abyss-spawn had helped him, or . . . anything. He only looked contemplative again. "And your name?" he asked.

"Dioxazine." It was nice to be regarded as a person by someone, instead of "a Numenmancer" who was therefore less important than anyone else in the room, but she wished she knew what was going on behind that carefully controlled expression.

Despite her unease, his response was the epitome of courtesy. "Dioxazine, I am honored to make your acquaintance. I am Terre Verte. You may address me as Verte, if you like."

He said the last bit as if she should be flattered by it. "Are you the mistress of this household?"

A snorting laugh made it out of her before she could try for something more dignified. "Sorry, no."

He looked at the others, clearly dismissing Alizarin as someone—or something—that could run a household and considering Umber. Before he could ask, Umber said, "I believe Azo and Cadmia have just gone hunting."

Xaz's brows lifted. *Cadmia? Hunting? With Azo?*

Hansa of all people saw the expression and gave a half smile, half shrug.

Alizarin started toward the door as if to join Azo and Cadmia, then hesitated in front of Terre Verte, just the tip of his tail twitching with what Xaz recognized as indecision.

Terre Verte cleared his throat. "I apologize for not greeting you sooner, or thanking you for your role in my release. When I first saw you, I assumed—it doesn't matter what I assumed, suffice to say it was based on the experiences I've had with Abyssi before now. I am in your debt."

Alizarin seemed mollified by the words, but still apparently decided he would stay with the newly risen sorcerer rather than go to his lover.

"Do you think we could catch up to the ladies before their hunt?" Terre Verte asked. "I would like to introduce myself to the mistress of the household, and express my gratitude that she has opened her home to me during my convalescence."

"I would let her hunt, then choose if she wants to introduce herself," Umber advised. "She may not want to speak with you at all. She was bonded to the Abyssumancer who planned your rescue, and who was killed in the process."

If Xaz had expected to see guilt on Terre Verte's expression, she would have been disappointed. Instead, he paused thoughtfully, then asked, "Since you've used the term twice, pray tell, what is an Abyssumancer?"

He had seemed confused when Xaz asked if he was a Numenmancer, too. "How can you not know what a mancer is?" she asked.

Terre Verte simply regarded her with polite curiosity, clearly waiting for an explanation.

"A mancer is—" She stopped. How to summarize everything she was?

"I think the term *mancer* is only used in Kavet." Hansa spoke carefully. Xaz could hear him mentally editing what he was going to say, which was probably based on what he had been taught. "When we've had to speak to foreigners as part of an investigation, most of them know the word *sorcerer*. I'm not sure if they're completely interchangeable, but it's a close enough match they normally know what I'm talking about."

It hadn't occurred to Xaz that Terre Verte might not be from Kavet because his power felt so much like hers. "Are you not from Kavet?" she asked. "Did you come from somewhere sorcery isn't condemned?" It was hard to imagine such a place.

"These . . . mancers . . . aren't respected in Kavet?" It was the first time he had allowed them to see his surprise. "Why not?"

"Respected." Xaz wished it was that simple. Her gaze slid unwittingly to Hansa. "A mancer faces automatic execution if identified and caught."

Terre Verte's lips twisted with disgust. "I think I need to know a bit more about the world into which I'm being rescued." His hand played idly over the back of the couch, drumming thoughtfully. "And, if sorcery is so reviled, I believe I need to know what desperation drove you all to risk so much to bring me out. Suddenly I doubt it was done out of the kindness of all your hearts."

They each glanced to the others, clearly trying to decide where to begin.

"The Numini arranged it," Xaz said, trying not to let Terre Verte hear her anger in case he thought it was directed at him. "They—" She hesitated, not from fear of her masters, but shame as she considered what they had done. "Between multiple Abyssi and Numini fighting to do different things, it didn't work out exactly the way they wanted." The Numini had wanted her to appreciate the lengths they had gone to "for her," so they had shared some of the challenges and setbacks they had faced. Xaz grinned at Alizarin, remembering their irritation, as she added, "You were apparently *not* part of the plan." *So, after Baryte threw the knife at me, they sulked a while that their plans weren't perfectly followed before they decided to help again.* "But they did admit to arranging Ruby's death and to manipulating Hansa into taking the third boon and Naples into going after Terre Verte—um, you."

Hansa, Umber, and Alizarin were frowning and nodding, their theories confirmed, but Terre Verte rubbed at a knot at his brow and said, "Can you begin earlier?"

So they did. They described what life was like for a mancer in Kavet, and then Hansa told about his time in the 126. Umber, who had been least involved, picked up the story from Baryte's arrest to Hansa's, and then Hansa haltingly described why and how he had demanded the two boons. Xaz filled in the blanks whenever a mancer's power needed to be explained, so she was the one who described their first steps into the Abyss, and how they had made their way to the prison where Terre Verte had lain, "not quite alive," for so many years.

CHAPTER 40

Dawn in the Abyss came in the form of light creeping in from the distant hills, changing the vast, featureless sky from flat black to the paler, rusty gray that marked an Abyssal day.

"Is there a sun?" Cadmia's words masked the fact that Azo had paused again to catch her breath. The Abyss-spawn woman was clearly exhausted, but had insisted on going out. She had taken a bow with her, but Cadmia wondered if she had the strength to pull it. Cadmia hoped she hadn't been overestimating her abilities when she claimed that, aside from the Abyssi themselves, few truly dangerous beasts ventured so near the court.

Azo gestured toward the source of the light. "If you travel that way for several hours, you will reach fields of parched land that burn with forest-high flames each day. They protect the mouth of the crystal caves."

"Where Abyssi are born."

Azo nodded, and sank down to sit on a rocky outcropping with a hiss of frustration and pain.

"Are you all right?"

Azo growled. "I refuse to be this *weak*."

"My understanding is that you must be very strong to have survived what happened." Cadmia was careful to keep her words frank and avoid any hint of a patronizing tone, but she also avoided referring directly to Naples. "No one thinks less of you for—"

"*I* think less of me," Azo snapped, "and the Abyssi of the high court will think less of me. I stink like prey. I—" She broke off, and this time Cadmia wasn't sure if it was physical pain that had taken Azo's breath. Her voice was a low growl when she continued. "I survived many years without *Naples*." She said the word rapidly, like spitting out a mouthful of glass. "He would have been devoured by the beasts of the Abyss when he first fell into this realm if I hadn't—"

She broke off, coughing spasmodically. Cadmia wrapped an arm around her to keep her from tumbling off her stone perch before she recovered.

When she had, she said abruptly, "Terre Verte is awake." Cadmia looked around for the sorcerer. "Not *here*," Azo said. "I can sense him, his power."

"Do you want to go back?" Cadmia asked optimistically.

Azo gave a feral smile. "I suppose we should."

They started back across the black sand toward the royal court. They didn't have far to go, but Azo's pace was slow. On the way out, Azo had made idle conversation about the beasts of the Abyss, including which ones it took no extraordinary power to kill. This time, she said nothing, until at last Cadmia asked, "Do you want to talk about . . . anything?"

For some reason, the question made Azo laugh. "You're so tactful. Why don't you just ask: do I want to talk about the man who was not quite my lover, the man whose affection I always *knew* was nothing but magic's lie but couldn't help returning? Or do you think I should talk about the Abyssi who killed him, the one who is normally in your bed—though he wasn't last night. Did the blood frighten you away?"

"He was watching Terre Verte." She only realized how defensive the words sounded after they came to her lips.

She had slept alone for so many years, an empty bed shouldn't feel alien to her, but she had missed Alizarin the night before. She couldn't help but feel he had stayed away because he wanted to give her space to decide how she felt. She had flinched at his touch when she was overwhelmed by exhaustion and the lingering memory of Naples' blood, but the long, dark hours had made her regret the instinctive recoil.

"Even if you had no interest in the blue prince last night, there was no need for you to sleep alone."

Cadmia understood now the irritation she had seen Hansa express when Umber casually responded to his thoughts. Instead of debating whether or not Alizarin would have been jealous, Cadmia said, "If I were attracted to women, I'm sure we could have had a lovely time."

This time, Azo's laugh was full and rich, devoid of the bitterness Cadmia had heard before. "Lovely," she repeated, chuckling. "If you're ever in the mood to play, Sister, I promise to show you a time that will require better adjectives than *lovely*."

At last, Azo succeeded in making Cadmia blush. She groped mentally for a topic change, grateful now that Umber seemed to be only interested in men.

That was odd, now that Cadmia thought to compare him to Alizarin and Azo, both of whom clearly didn't care about their partner's sex.

Azo's mirth dissipated. "Umber has a lover, or had one," she said. "The Abyssi say that spawn imprint on their first lovers. How strong the imprint depends on how serious the relationship was. To be as exclusive as he is, Umber must have had someone quite special in his past. Or his present, I suppose."

Neither of them said aloud that, despite the heart-bond, apparently Azo's relationship with Naples didn't count. Given how Abyssal power worked, Cadmia wasn't surprised to learn that flesh mattered more than heart in a relationship.

If Azo heard the thought, she chose not to comment before they reached the house. Azo was hungry, so they went first to the dining room, where they found the others already gathered—including Xaz, who looked battle-worn but proud, and Terre Verte, who had taken a seat at the far end of the table.

"Oh," the spawn said, gripping the back of a chair as if a moment's surprise had been enough to nearly knock her off her feet. "I didn't know your name, but I know your face."

"I'm sorry," Terre Verte said, standing to greet their hostess. "Have we met?"

Azo drew a steadying breath and shook her head. "You have your father's eyes and jaw, quite clearly. I recognize them from my mother's memories of her husband."

Cadmia remembered Umber's explanation that spawn retained memories from their parents, but it still took her less time to understand what Azo had said than it apparently did Terre Verte. His brows lifted and eyes widened as he exclaimed, "Your mother—*my* mother?"

Xaz was the first of them to recover enough to ask, "Your mother had a child in the Abyss?"

Terre Verte cleared his throat. "I knew my parents were estranged, but I never realized quite—" Azo winced, and Terre Verte broke off, nodding as if she were saying something silently to him. More subdued, he said, "I suppose that makes sense. Please, I'm being terribly rude. You're exhausted and made to stand at your own table. Aurelian?"

The man had already taken charge of Azo's servants. As Terre Verte helped Azo into a chair at the head of the table, Aurelian jumped to pour wine and serve her a plate. Cadmia slipped into an empty chair further down, not far from Alizarin.

The space he held between them seemed cold and unnatural.

"I'm sorry," she blurted out.

"For?" Alizarin asked.

"For being a fool," she said. She needed to get these words out, and she didn't care if the others overheard. "For being overwhelmed by everything that happened and blaming it on you, even for an instant. You saved my life. I blamed you for killing your friend instead of saying thank you for choosing me and I'm sorry you *had* to choose me."

He hushed her with a finger over her lips, and his tail wrapped around her waist. "Time for breakfast now," he said. "Time for talk later."

That was fine. She leaned against him, wishing all their problems could be solved so easily.

"And this is Cadmia." Cadmia gave a guilty start as Azo said her name and she belatedly realized how rude she had been to ignore Terre Verte the way she had, but the spawn and the new sorcerer both had indulgent expressions on their faces. "She's as human as they come but might have a bit of Abyssi soul in her."

Cadmia stood, though the attempt at courtesy was marred by Alizarin's tail lingering around her waist. "Cadmia Paynes, Sister of Napthol." The title slipped out by habit, an attempt to cover her earlier informality.

"That explains it." Cadmia wasn't sure what was explained how, but Terre Verte didn't give her a chance to question him. "Pleasure to meet you, Sister Paynes.

The others have been filling me in on the rather remarkable series of events that led to this point."

"Including, apparently, the birth of your sister," Xaz said, still shaking her head incredulously. "Is that how you have your connection to the Abyss, even though you otherwise work with the Numen? Your mother?"

Terre Verte paused to consider the question. "Both my parents dabbled, my mother with the Abyss and my father with the Numen. It was common enough where I grew up."

"Dabbled," Umber muttered, apparently thinking the same thing as Cadmia. What kind of *dabbling* led one to have a child in the Abyss?

"Where exactly was that, if I may ask?" Cadmia could hear the longing in Xaz's tone.

"A very different land than yours, certainly. One without your Quinacridone strangling the populace." Terre Verte shook his head, making a sound of disgust. "All of you are welcome to accompany me when I return to it."

"I would like that very much," Xaz said instantly.

Cadmia looked away from the sorcerers as she considered, and her gaze met Hansa's. He had been quiet since they came in, and she saw on his expression the same thoughts she harbored. Kavet was her *home*. She had a life there. She didn't want to flee.

She wanted to fix it.

"It will take me some time to regain enough strength to bring any of us back to the mortal realm," Terre Verte said. He continued, speaking to Hansa and Umber as if picking up the conversation Azo and Cadmia had interrupted. "In the meantime, I will study the bond between you two and search for this Ruby you speak of, and see if I can do anything to solve either of your problems. It is the least I can do to repay your efforts to procure my release."

"We would appreciate that," Umber replied.

"Speaking of repayment," Azo said. "I, too, feel I am in your debt."

Xaz spoke first. "You have given us a safe place to stay and supported our quest to get Terre Verte even when it was clear you did not wish it yourself. You have given us enough."

Xaz didn't have the benefit of Cadmia's recent conversations with Azo. She couldn't predict the spawn's sharp, swift retort.

"Intentionally or not, you freed me from a magical entanglement I could not escape on my own. I survived the immediate sundering of the bond, but I might not have survived the days after if one of your companions had not been willing to share power, since in my madness immediately after Naples' death I would have willingly starved rather than accept Alizarin's help. Finally, almost incidentally, you have apparently freed my brother from a prison in the Abyss. I do not like unresolved debts," she concluded. "I'm sure you understand. Cadmia, what would you have of me?"

Cadmia didn't care for such things herself, but Azo's tone made it clear she was talking about more than a sense of guilt. No one had fully explained how boons and bonds worked, but Cadmia had heard enough to understand the implication.

She looked at Hansa, considering a favor she had almost asked earlier, but had held back because like Xaz she had not realized the level of obligation Azo felt.

They had come to the Abyss for many reasons. "Eleven guards from the One-Twenty-Six were killed when Dioxazine first summoned Alizarin." She kept her words as neutral as she could. None of them were the same people they had been then. "We hoped to find them here in the Abyss and help them to the Numen, but have been told it can take weeks for shades to regain their memories of who they were." She paused, remembering the pathetic encampment they had found their first day here. "Would you be willing to take them into your household? They won't be useless. They were soldiers in life. They can probably help hunt."

"Do you think Quin guards killed by an Abyssi will accept help from an Abyss-spawn?" Xaz spoke with incredulity, but also hope. The soldier's deaths had not been her intention, but that blood was still on her soul. Knowing there was still a way to help them could be a comfort.

"Some of them might not," Hansa acknowledged, "but some probably will. I think Jenkins would, and some of the others, if you tell them you know me. Then, if there's ever a way and we *can* help them move to the Numen, we'll bring them over."

"I believe I can do as you ask," Azo said. "I should be able to cast a beacon to draw them here, anyway, and I will offer them a place."

"The Numini have given permission for them to be escorted to the Numen," Xaz said, "if we can determine how to do so."

"Once they are gathered in the same place, Xaz and I should be able to create a ritual to bring them over," Terre Verte said. "Having a safe haven here will give them time to recover their memories and self-awareness so they are strong enough for the crossing."

"Thank you," Hansa breathed, relief painfully clear on his every feature. He couldn't save his friends' mortal lives, but he could keep them from wandering, lost and starving, for the next life. Cadmia smiled; she didn't have Hansa's personal attachment to these shades, but she was relieved to know they could be taken care of.

Terre Verte rubbed at his temple. It was the first sign of weakness he had given during their conversation, but it reminded Cadmia that the man had been locked in a prison until recently. "If you'll excuse me," he said, "I think I need to rest." With a wry smile, he added, "And I imagine you all have things you would like to discuss without a stranger in your midst, such as the stranger himself. Lady Azo, by your leave?"

Azo nodded, then rose. She hadn't done more than pick at her food in the few minutes they had been at the table. "I will walk up with you," she said. "My appetite is still scarce."

Terre Verte offered his arm with the casual ease of a man used to formal gestures. Azo leaned on it lightly as they exited together.

"A man used to having power," Xaz observed, the moment the doorway had closed behind the pair. "Used to having it, and having others recognize it. You would think that however long he spent down imprisoned in the Abyss would have changed that."

"Anyone have thoughts on why the Numini went to such lengths to rescue him?" Hansa asked, looking at Xaz.

"As if they would explain their intentions to me," Xaz scoffed.

Cadmia leaned forward, trying to improve her focus by moving away from Alizarin's warmth. "Does he seem familiar to anyone else?"

Hansa frowned, considering, then shook his head. "You meet more people in Kavet than most of us do."

"Particularly of the unsavory sort," Xaz added, "but he says he isn't from Kavet. Do you think he's lying?"

Cadmia shook her head. "I don't know . . . I don't think so. His face just looks familiar. I can't—you're not helping me think," she added, batting at Alizarin's tail, which kept tickling her cheek.

"We could always ask Azo," Umber suggested.

"Was anyone else surprised by that connection?" Hansa asked.

Cadmia nodded, and saw the others doing the same. "I'll try to ask her next time we're alone."

Umber lifted his brows suggestively. "Have fun."

Xaz stood with a stretch. "I'm better off than Azo and Terre Verte it seems, but I could use a nap as well. Possibly six months of hibernation."

Umber chuckled. "Alizarin, Azo's stores of meat are low. I gather Naples did much of the hunting. Would you be willing to help me replenish them? I'll be more effective with your assistance."

Alizarin turned to Cadmia as if to invite her to join them, but then his ears and tail drooped before he even spoke. Apologetically, he said, "I would like to help Azo, and we'll hunt better without mortals."

Hansa shrugged, standing and pulling away from Umber reluctantly. "I guess that means Cadmia and I are on cleanup duty. I can't say I'm disappointed to miss the hunt."

Cadmia was a little disappointed, but once the others were gone, she remembered the question she had wanted to ask Hansa ever since her earlier conversation with Umber about his mother.

The servants took the dishes from their hands as soon as they tried to gather them. While they were doing so, Cadmia asked, "Do you know who Bonnie Holland is?"

Hansa's hand clutched spasmodically on the dish he had just lifted, nearly overturning a platter of fruit before Aurelian swooped in to take it from him.

"Was," he said. "Not is. Anyone in the One-Twenty-Six does. I gather President Indathrone had objected for years to women serving as soldiers, but after Holland . . . well, he used her as an excuse to push for official limitations, though I've always felt what happened to her could just as easily have happened to a man."

"She was a guard?" Cadmia asked. That put a new and interesting spin on Umber's relationship with Hansa, especially given what she knew of spawn's inherited memories.

"A lieutenant," Hansa said. "Her company ran afoul of an Abyssumancer and his Abyssi. It's one of the stories used in training." His frown became something deeper, darker. "I guess soon they'll be telling about Company Four going to arrest a Numenmancer and facing an Abyssi. The loss of life when Lieutenant Holland went after Blakemore—that was the mancer's name—was similar. Holland was one of only two who survived. She managed to kill the mancer and send the Abyssi back, but was badly hurt in the process."

"Hurt," Cadmia echoed, trying not to let the horror she felt tell Hansa more than Umber wanted him to know, but suddenly understanding all too well the concern that had led Umber to check on her after her first night with Alizarin.

Hansa looked puzzled. "I know the doctors didn't think she would live at first," he said. "She never walked again. She chose to leave the city, and the guard paid for a home in . . . mm, I don't remember the name of the town. She died not long after. Does that answer your question?"

"I suppose," Cadmia said. "Do you know how she died?" *And how many months later?*

"She never fully recovered from her injuries," Hansa

said. The topic disturbed him, but it was also clearly history, a dark lesson he had been taught and was now reciting. "It was always implied that her death was from long-term complications of those wounds, but I heard rumors she killed herself. It was before my time."

"Shortly before you were born, I'd guess." Unless spawn aged differently than humans, a fact she had never previously considered, Umber seemed to be about Hansa's age.

Hansa nodded, confirming the timing.

"Why ask about an old soldier?"

If Umber wanted Hansa to know, he would tell him. Cadmia settled her expression into her professional mask. "The conversation where her name came up was private. I shouldn't disclose details."

"All right." He knew better than to press a Sister of the Napthol to break a confidence, no matter how curious he was.

Damn Umber. Cadmia wished she hadn't asked for more information. It had been easier to momentarily assume that, like Hansa, or like Azo's mother, Umber's mother had had an illicit, sorcery-enabled affair. The chill that settled into her bones as she considered the violent reality refused to dissipate.

When Alizarin returned, she put herself into his arms, soaking in his heat. His comforting purr and confused queries about why she was upset reminded her how different he was from the rest of his kind. How unique. And how beautiful, like all the dangerous, predatory lights in the Abyss.

CHAPTER 41

"**N**o. *No.*" Terre Verte recoiled from Hansa's touch, startling Hansa from a near-doze. Terre Verte said he would use Hansa's connection to Ruby to find her shade, but he hadn't felt a thing beyond the sorcerer's cool hands on his as they sat facing each other in Azo's dining room chairs.

His eyes opened to reveal gray irises filled with sparkling snow.

"Are you all right?" Cadmia asked. Though uninvolved in the simple ritual, she had asked to observe.

It had taken Terre Verte almost two weeks of rest and ritual before he felt strong enough to attempt this task. Had he overestimated his abilities now? Hansa said, "If you're still too weak—"

He broke off as Terre Verte closed his eyes and raked his fingers down his cheeks, leaving white trails that swiftly turned pink, then faded.

"Are you with us?" Umber asked, when Terre Verte didn't respond to Cadmia's or Hansa's words.

In one of their many late-night conversations, Umber had admitted to Hansa that he was unable to read any thoughts from Terre Verte. The man was a mystery—even more so since he evaded most questions about his past, and Azo had respected his wishes by refusing to share anything she might know.

Cadmia, unsurprisingly, had been able to get the most from the strange sorcerer, but when she pressed him about the specifics of where he had come from or how he had ended up in the Abyss, he had bluntly told her, "I am grateful to you all for bringing me out of that cell, but I am under no obligation to detail events I have every wish to put from my mind and memory. Please pass on to your companions my sincerest wish that they stop interrogating me about a life and circumstance that is saturated with blood and despair."

Cadmia had indeed passed on those words, almost two weeks ago now. After that, they had all stopped asking questions.

"I'm here," Terre Verte said hoarsely. He opened his eyes again. They had returned to their previous slate-gray. "I found your shade. I should have known where I would find her. Idiot." The last word was snarled, as if to himself.

Hansa looked around instinctively, as if Ruby might materialize in their midst.

"Where?" Umber asked.

"When an Abyssi slays a mortal, the shade falls to

the Abyss." Terre Verte's voice was barely a whisper. "The Numini slew Ruby. Of course they brought her to their realm after."

Of course. Because she had killed herself, Hansa had assumed Ruby would fall to the Abyss. Even with everything he had learned in the last few weeks about the nature of both the Numen and the Abyss, he had never paused to reconsider that assumption. Surely they couldn't be expected to drag her soul back from the Numen to—

The thought made Hansa's chest tight, his horror mingling with the magic's insistence that, yes, they would do anything they needed to or else face the consequences.

"The walls around the Numen are crystal and silver." Terre Verte continued as if in a daze, as if arguing with unspoken words. "They are too high to scale and too strong to breach."

"You can't do it?" Hansa breathed.

"It is irrelevant if I *can*." Finally Terre Verte's gaze focused. "I will not. I have seen it done. It was a horror. To pull a soul from that place—" He stood so abruptly his chair wobbled and Umber had to grab it to keep it from crashing to the floor. "*Never.* I am sorry. I cannot help you. No one can help you."

Hansa had started to stand, but gripped the back of his own chair for balance as his head spun. Their last option had just clearly declared itself impossible. A vise relaxed around his body, letting air pass in and out of his lungs and the blood rush about more freely than it had in weeks.

"I'm sorry the search was so painful for you," Umber said, his voice sounding steadier than Hansa felt, but just barely.

Terre Verte shook his head sharply, as if offended by the suggestion of weakness. "I apologize for my discomposure. It was . . . unexpected, to reach for a soul I assumed would be in the Abyss or the mortal realm, and suddenly find myself standing magically before the Numen's shining gate." He shivered, and ran his hands over his arms to settle himself. "Have I given you the information you need to resolve the boon?"

"Yes," Umber sighed.

"I could sense the bond as well while we were connected," Terre Verte reported. "I did not dare try to manipulate it, though. I am not strong enough to control the severing, and having seen how Azo was affected by the sudden loss of her Abyssumancer, I do not think it is wise to act rashly."

Light-headed from the boon's release, Hansa struggled to process what he felt at Terre Verte's words. A sense of reprieve, he decided.

Questions, decisions, put off until another day.

Part of the feeling was cowardice, not wanting to face the truth of who he might be, once the bond was removed. Even so, he was grateful for the delay.

"Not strong enough, ever," Cadmia asked, breaking in when neither Umber nor Hansa asked the obvious question, "or not strong enough for now?"

"For now." Terre Verte shuddered and rubbed his palms over his arms. "I was in that cell for—I don't know how long, actually. I'm weak, and being here in the Abyss makes the bond stronger."

"What about after we return to the human plane?"

He nodded. "I need some time to recover my strength first—a few weeks breathing mortal air—but after that I will be able to help you. I am certain of it."

Umber's breath let out in a long, slow exhalation that seemed to let a world of tension out of his body.

Hansa asked, "And when do you think we can return to the human plane?"

"Tomorrow," Terre Verte answered. "I've been working on the ritual to open a rift. It is nearly complete. I wanted to search for your shade before crossing because you all assumed she was in the Abyss, but that was the last task I needed to accomplish here."

"What about Xaz and Rin?" Cadmia asked, uncharacteristically hesitantly. She didn't quite cross her arms as she spoke, but her posture closed, as if she had started to flinch for a knife at her waist but then stopped.

Xaz hadn't discussed her desire to break her bond to the Abyssi much since their trek into the prison at the heart of the Abyss, but Hansa doubted she had forgotten it.

"That may be more difficult," Terre Verte answered. "The bond between you and Umber is solid. Concrete. The connection between Dioxazine and Alizarin is harder to understand. His power has seeped into her, and hers has seeped into him. With time and study I'm sure I can unravel it, but it may be more a slow process instead of a clean cut."

"How will it affect Alizarin?" Cadmia's voice was carefully even, as it had been when she spoke to Baryte and later Hansa in the cells under the Quin Compound. "I know Xaz has a right to her freedom, but Alizarin fought for this tie to the Numen. In my understanding, it's what allows him to reason and empathize, and makes him so different from the rest of his kind. What will happen if you break his tie to Xaz?"

"That's part of why I need to be careful." Terre Verte glanced down, looking Cadmia over assessingly. "I'm not particularly fond of the Numini, but it's not a good idea to cross them until I understand their plans, and I don't want to anger a third-level prince of the Abyss in the process. If I can free Dioxazine while allowing Alizarin to maintain a tie to the Numen, I will."

Cadmia tensed in response to the frank gaze, and didn't continue her questions, so Hansa responded instead. "The Numini put a lot of effort into freeing you from the Abyss. Why aren't you fond of them?" Beyond Terre Verte's words just now, his reaction at glimpsing the Numen had seemed one of revulsion, not awe or gratitude.

The words had been spoken before Hansa realized they probably fell in the realm of things they had all agreed not to ask.

Terre Verte's gray eyes went cold. "I did a favor for the Numini once. As Xaz may have told you, their gratitude leaves much to be desired. Freeing me from that box was the least they could do to put things right." He shook his head, and some of the life returned to his expression. "I am sorry the Numini dragged you all into their mess, but at least I can help free you from it and allow you to return to your own realm." He settled another heavy glance on Cadmia before adding, "Unless you would rather remain here. I'm sure Azo would let you stay with her for a few months, if you want."

Hansa felt like he had walked into a play while missing a page of the script. He glanced to Umber, wondering if he had been privy to a conversation Hansa had missed.

"*Do* you want to stay here?" Umber asked Cadmia. "If not, I am happy to offer any assistance you need when you return to Kavet."

Cadmia tensed, bristling like an angry cat in the face of the two solicitous gazes. It was not the look of a woman who had idly considered staying in the Abyss to, what?

Be with Alizarin? Get to know Azo? Practice her hunting?

"Thank you for your offer of support." Her words contained more grit than gratitude. "If they cast me out of the Cobalt Hall, I can go to the Order of A'hknet. I might go anyway. I'm feeling a little disenchanted with Kavet right now."

"You would be better off in the Cobalt Hall," Umber argued. "Every Abyssumancer in Kavet will want that child. Alizarin can offer some protection, as long as severing his bond to Dioxazine doesn't make him forget he cares about it, but a strong enough Abyssumancer will be a threat to him, too."

That child. The Cobalt Hall, the one place in Kavet where mancers could not go. And Alizarin could be protection if he doesn't forget he cares about . . . *it.*

"You're *pregnant?*" The words tumbled out, astonished, before he could contain them.

"I suspected, but didn't know for sure yet," Cadmia growled back. "Incidentally, boys, that's the kind of thing a woman prefers to learn for herself and share when she chooses to, *not* be told." Umber looked chastened, but if Terre Verte felt any guilt, it didn't show. Neither argued with her. "Fine. I'll stay at the Cobalt Hall—*for now.* I'll accept your help, Umber, anyone's help, to teach me what I need to know to protect myself and my child."

The Cobalt Hall would keep Cadmia and her child safer from mancers, but it was across the street from the Quin Compound and the barracks for the 126, the most likely place in Kavet to find trained men and women with the sight.

"It isn't just Abyssumancers you need to worry about," Hansa said. "You can excuse a lot of study as a Sister of the Napthol, but if someone notices an Abyssal taint on you—"

"Then I will change Kavet," Cadmia declared.

Was it Hansa's imagination, or did he see a flash of blue light in the depths of her eyes? She stared at Hansa as if waiting for him to argue. He didn't dare.

He didn't want to.

"I'll help you," he said instead.

Umber sighed heavily, an expression Hansa knew

usually came before something worldly and at least borderline patronizing.

"Both of you should wait to risk your lives to change the world until after your link to the Abyss is gone. Power—"

"Easily and often overrides preference," Hansa interrupted. The words had been indelibly etched in his brain during his first serious conversation with Umber about the boon. "I know. You think I'll change my mind. I refuse to live under the assumption that the person I am right now will die once Terre Verte is strong enough to break our bond."

In the meantime, he had come to realize how ignorant and marred the laws of Kavet and her people were. How could he serve as a guard whose one duty was to enforce those errant regulations? At the same time, how could he, who had chosen to join the 126 from a genuine desire to protect the people of Kavet, and who had been raised to believe that the democratic system was a vehicle for right, walk away from what was so obviously *wrong*?

Just don't get us killed, Umber whispered in his mind.

"I've heard of women whose personalities changed while they were pregnant," Cadmia conceded, "but I made the decision to have this child. I'm not a *victim* of the Abyss. I'm a scholar, a lover, and now soon to be a mother, and if I have to remake the world in an image of my choosing, I *will*."

That was the end of the discussion.

The next day, they returned to the well at the back of the high court.

"There is already a rift to the human plane there," Terre Verte explained when he told them his plan. "It has been mostly closed through disuse, but it will be easier to push through there than somewhere new."

Hansa found himself strangely unaffected by the prospect of having to cross the court again. Compared to the fifth-level Abyssi court, walking across the high court proved almost dull. Alizarin led the way again, with his tail around Cadmia's waist as usual.

No other Abyssi challenged them, though many cast speculative or wary glances their way. Was it Hansa's imagination, or did many of them seem to stare with more anxiety at Terre Verte than they did at Alizarin?

Once they reached the well, Terre Verte put his hands to the smooth wall, his brow tensing with concentration.

"Do you need anything?" Xaz asked. She was wearing the pack Naples had provided her with a Numenmancer's tools inside; she patted it gently as if to confirm it was secure.

The rest of them had small bags containing a few foodstuffs and extra clothing, since they didn't know exactly where they would end up or what their first steps would be once they arrived. Umber had claimed the bone blade Naples had previously wielded, saying it was too valuable a tool to be lost in the Abyss. Having seen that blade up close and personal twice already, Hansa wasn't looking forward to the next time Umber wielded it.

Cadmia wore a weapon now, as well. She had blanched when Alizarin had first presented the dagger to her—the one forged of his own bone—but he had insisted that she keep it, saying it would act as a warning to others who might try to harm her, as well as a weapon she could wield in her own defense.

"I'm fine," Terre Verte replied, his eyes closed. "It's . . ." He stopped speaking for a few seconds, and then breathed, *"Here."*

The portal he opened was not black like those Alizarin made, but glistening silver. It came into existence with a whiff of sweet, smoky aroma, like incense.

Terre Verte stepped back from the portal and gestured for them to go ahead.

Umber moved forward first, and Hansa followed. He emerged with a shiver, brushing flakes of frost from his skin as the others stepped through behind him.

"Where are we?" he asked, looking around pointlessly. The light from the portal was just enough to give the impression of clutter and perhaps walls, but no other details of the room around them.

"Somewhere dark." Cadmia sneezed, and added, "And dusty."

Terre Verte emerged from the portal last. As it closed behind him, he lifted a hand and summoned an orb of silver-white foxfire, which illuminated a vast, windowless room which had once been elegant but now showed years of disuse.

A long couch hugged one wall, which looked like it had been softly elegant long ago; now it was impossible to even tell what fabric upholstered it. Bookcases laden with texts made unreadable by time and grime filled another wall, and a round table at knee height that appeared to have been an altar dominated the center of the floor. It was draped with cloth and set with odds and ends that were hard to identify under the dust of ages, which coated every surface in the room and billowed when they moved.

Xaz started to move forward as if to examine the altar, then seemed to think better of it. She put a hand in front of her nose to keep from inhaling the musty particles that grew thicker in the air each time one of them took a step. "Is there a door?" she asked.

It was a reasonable question. The foxfire Terre Verte had summoned was bright enough to illuminate the entirety of the small room, but Hansa couldn't see any exit.

"Of course," Terre Verte said before crossing and pressing a hand to an apparently blank wall.

Hansa blinked. If he hadn't seen so many doors appear and disappear at Naples' and Azo's estate, he might have thought he hadn't seen this one previously due to the tears in his irritated eyes. Instead of an empty arch, a sturdy-looking door of slick, polished wood appeared.

"We *are* back in the human plane, right?" he asked.

"Yes," Terre Verte answered. "But this was a hidden room, not meant for the eyes of anyone who might stumble across it."

They all moved toward the doorway, anxious to get away from the stagnant air and now nearly blinding, billowing dust.

The moment they crossed the threshold, though, Hansa's breath hissed in with unwanted familiarity. Carved cherry wainscoting rose waist-high on the walls, below horse-hair lime plaster smoothed over old stone and painted soft, barely-blue gray. Like most soldiers in Kavet, Hansa had spent his share of hours re-pointing and painting those damned walls, one of the many mind-numbing tasks that could be assigned to young grunts without the authority to object or older soldiers being disciplined. Even the smell was familiar: spices of winter stews and familiar tea, ever available this time of year in the guards' mess.

All that meant they were in the last place they wanted to be.

"Shit," he hissed, anxiously looking up and down the hallway. It was a miracle no one had seen them emerge from what should have been a blank wall. "We have to get out of here."

"Where is *here*?" Cadmia asked, rubbing at her nose, probably to clear away the dust.

"We're in the Quinacridone," Hansa said. "I don't know exactly where, which means probably one of the private halls, maybe where the monks live. I recognize the—"

A figure turned the corner, one he wouldn't need to introduce.

President Winsor Indathrone was fifty-three years

old, dark-haired and shrewd-eyed. At that moment, he was wearing slacks and a shirt without vest or jacket; he was comfortably at home, which meant this hall was probably part of his personal residence. He frowned at them all, then focused his gaze on Hansa.

"Viridian? What is the meaning of this?"

Think! "We . . ." Was there *any* excuse for this? Would President Indathrone recognize Xaz? Even if he didn't, how could Hansa explain even his own presence in the president's private wing of the Quin compound?

Instead of coming up with something clever to say, he couldn't help calculating how many guards would come running the instant His Eminence opened his mouth to summon them. How many guards would, based on what Hansa had seen when they had gone to arrest Xaz, be slaughtered as Alizarin moved to protect their group.

Or, if it was true that the Quinacridone Compound was protected from the Abyss and the Numen by its own human spells, how many guards would appear to execute everyone in their party on sight.

"Hansa?" Indathrone prompted, voice colder this time, warning that it wouldn't be long before he lost patience.

He skimmed their party, his eyes never fixing on Alizarin, reminding Hansa that on the mortal plane most humans couldn't see the Abyssi at all.

Terre Verte took charge, stepping past Hansa. "Winsor Indathrone, you are the very image of your grandmother."

"My . . ." Indathrone frowned with confusion. "Who are you?"

Terre Verte extended a hand. "How rude of me not to introduce myself." Indathrone offered his own hand, as one tends to do out of habit when offered such an engrained sign of courtesy. "I am Terre Verte. And I believe you have overstayed your welcome."

The next movement was swift. Terre Verte accepted the hand Indathrone had lifted, but used it only to tug him forward before he reached up, bracing his Eminence's body with his own, and matter-of-factly broke the neck of the most powerful man in Kavet with a single, undramatic *crunch*.

"We invited that family to supper. Not to move in."

Terre Verte released him, and Indathrone's body collapsed unremarkably to the ground. Hansa stared at it, waiting for it to . . . what? Echo? The death of such a man should resonate. It should shriek in a way that made bones quiver, like when Abyssi fought. His fallen form should flicker with escaping force.

But he was only a man, and his body was only meat, so he lay there unmoving.

Terre Verte turned around, brushing dust from his elegant clothing. "Now I think I'd like to walk about my city. It has been a long time."

EPILOGUE

"I thought *you said you could control your children,*" *the black Abyssi accused, his voice an angry purr. " 'All things serve the divine,' or so you say."*

"Mortals are . . . limited," the Numini conceded. "They have unanticipated qualms, and choose to rebel at unpredictable moments."

"Thousands of years of life," the black Abyssi spat, "and that *is your belief? Mortals are unpredictable? A newborn Abyssi could tell you that a mortal will choose survival first. Faced with death, they always run."*

"Not always," the Numini minced. "Though I suppose that is a newborn Abyssi's perspective, given it is your own. Your kind sees a few centuries at most before you are destroyed by your own folly. I have seen millennia."

"You and your endless years got my mancer killed."

"You were supposed to deal with the blue Abyssi before he reached the pit."

"Antioch wasn't equal to the task."

"And the king of the Abyss couldn't send another?" the Numini scoffed. "Don't you have any power over your subjects?"

The black Abyssi did not rise to the challenge. "Abyssi do not jump to follow commands the way Numini do, especially when those commands may make an Abyssi dead. *I have no wish to be sacrificed in the crystal caves just yet."*

"They have all returned to the mortal realm now," the Numini said. "Let us wait and see what they do next. They may yet serve. If not, we both have other tools. If the worst comes to pass, these can be . . . discarded."

ABOUT THE AUTHOR

AMELIA ATWATER-RHODES started writing when she was thirteen, and has since then published seventeen young adult novels in the Den of Shadows, Kiesha'ra and Maeve'ra series. Several of her novels have been ALA Quick Picks for Young Adults, and Hawksong was *The School Library Journal* Best Book of the Year, and *Voice of Youth Advocates* Best Science Fiction, Fantasy, and Horror Selection. In 2006, Amelia decided to take a break from YA and started writing the Mancer trilogy as part of National Novel Writing Month. *Of the Abyss* is her first adult novel.